About the author

Bill Leak was born in 1956 in Adelaide, South Australia.

As one of Australia's leading satirists and most respected portrait painters, he divides his time between ridiculing his subjects mercilessly in his cartoons and caricatures, and immortalising them in oils.

His portraits are included in the collections of the State Library of NSW, Sydney, Parliament House, Canberra and the National Portrait Gallery, Canberra. He has won eight Walkley Awards (for excellence in journalism) and nineteen Stanley Awards (the awards of the Australian Cartoonists' Association), including eight Gold Stanleys for Artist of the Year.

He is the Daily Editorial Cartoonist on *The Australian* newspaper and, although he has illustrated quite a few books, he has never written one before.

heart
CANCER

BILL LEAK

ABC
Books

Published by ABC Books for the
AUSTRALIAN BROADCASTING CORPORATION
GPO Box 9994 Sydney NSW 2001

First published in August 2005

ISBN 0 7333 1631 X.

Cover design by Christabella Designs
Cover painting by David Naseby
Author photo by Andy Baker
Typeset in 11/14pt Sabon by Kirby Jones
Colour reproduction by Graphic Print, South Australia
Printed and bound by Griffin Press, South Australia

5 4 3 2 1

Acknowledgements

For their assistance, guidance and encouragement, the author wishes to thank the following people, all of whom should accept their fair share of the blame:

Arthur Downey, Barry Oakley, Carl Harrison-Ford, David Astle, Dr Ian Chung, Jeanne Ryckmans, Lo Mong Lau, Paul Le Petit and Rose Creswell.

PART I

CHAPTER 1

'You get out and wait in the car,' the old man roared.

'What for?' Frank asked.

'Just do as you're fucking well told.'

Leaving two of his five Weet-Bix uneaten, Frank shuffled outside and climbed into the old grey car. An esky covered the rust hole in the floor under the dashboard, indicating Dad had packed his provisions, so they could be gone for a while. Checking under the lid, Frank saw it was the regulation dozen, which could mean anything from a couple of hours to the rest of the day. He wondered where they'd be going, what they'd be doing, and what the hell his parents were fighting about this time.

Dad had taken Alka-Seltzer for breakfast then headed off to the garage to wash it down with a few beers. It was a sign he'd had a bigger night than usual and was likely to get a bit aggressive if Mum said anything to upset him. Obviously she had. Why had she followed him down there? She knew how to niggle the old man, knew precisely which buttons to push to make him feel worthless and incapable of responding with words. And she knew what to expect when he ran out of words, so why did she do it?

Frank could hear things smashing and tinkling, like background sound effects in a domestic drama on TV. He wished he believed in God so he could slip in a quick prayer for the stereo.

He could hear the old man ranting and bellowing from one end of the house to the other, his mother whimpering in the background. Playing the victim again as if she's the only one. If only she'd shut up her whining, maybe he'd leave her alone.

On Frank's Richter scale of parental upheavals this was about a four, and a four was nothing to worry about. Dad would lash out and belt her at six, which was a long way off yet. At seven he'd feel he had to do something, but there wasn't much point. He'd tried it once but hadn't got very far. He'd frozen dead in his tracks, so numb he hadn't even felt it when the old man finished with Mum and showed him what happens to boys who interfere.

Fuck knows what will happen if they ever score an eight, he thought.

Their next-door neighbour, Mrs Bricknell, was a nosy old bitch. Frank spotted her peering from a window, like someone watching a schoolyard brawl while cowering behind a tree. If things got too unpleasant she could draw the curtains, get all indignant, and mutter to her husband about that awful Mick Thornton. That wasn't an option available to Frank, who felt the knot in his stomach tightening as his father's voice grew louder with every barrage of abuse. His own breathing and a pounding in his ears made it hard to hear whether Mum was getting hit. No, not yet, but it was definitely a five by now so it could happen any minute.

Where was his big brother Bob when the two of them got to sevens? Sitting in the bedroom they shared, no doubt, with his hands over his ears, studying for his HSC and pretending nothing was happening. Weak prick.

'He's a good boy, that brother of yours,' Mick had said. 'Works hard. That's why he made it into a selective school. You could have too if you'd pulled your finger out.'

And where was Nina? Out of the place an hour ago. Down at the mall, shopping with her friends, as if she had the money to buy anything for Christ's sake. Probably sucking on a milkshake, Frank thought, or one of his mates' dicks. They'd tell him all about it at school on Monday. Something to look forward to.

He heard a crash. A loud one.

Please God, not the stereo. And please don't hit Mum. Just don't hit Mum.

It was Frank who had his hands to his ears now. No need. It was all over. Fifteen stone of muscle, body hair and fury compacted into a blue singlet, shorts and a pair of thongs came lurching towards the car.

'Christ Albloodymighty,' his father growled, ramming home the ignition key.

'Tell me something, Frank,' he said, as the car roared backwards

4

up the driveway, 'why do women always close their eyes when you're rooting them?'

'Dunno,' offered Frank, a sexual veteran of one rapturous encounter.

'Because they can't stand to see a man enjoying himself.'

Frank was trying to recall if Sarah Kavanagh had had her eyes open or not while he'd been on the job when he heard the familiar barking of the Cowpers' dog. It had attacked every man, beast or vehicle stupid enough to trespass on its end of the street during an eight-year reign of terror.

'I've just about had a gutful of this fucking dog,' said Mick, flinging open his door as he accelerated around the corner.

The dog's skull exploded and Frank, watching its death spasms through the rear window, felt an unexpected rush of sympathy. Making the punishment fit the crime seemed like a reasonable notion to young Frank, and if that dog deserved the death penalty for terrifying people, then its executioner deserved the same.

The rest of the trip was endured in silence. One word from Frank could be enough to set the old man off again. Glaring at the dashboard of the '52 Holden FX, Frank thought of a friend whose parents got around in a Premier with air-conditioning and a radio. It was the absence of a radio he resented most. Listening to the cricket would have provided a soothing distraction for both of them. No, too early for the cricket. The drone of race-talk on 2KY then, which would have been easy for Frank to ignore and the perfect diversion for Mick. Anything but this silence, punctuated only by the gnashing of gears, the old man's grumbled demands for cigarettes, or beers from the esky between Frank's legs, and his occasional murderous threats directed at other drivers.

'Where're we going?' Frank asked as he pulled the top off can number three.

Mick Thornton sent number two flying out the window. 'Darling fucking Point.'

All Frank knew of Darling Point was that it was where his father had been working for a couple of months, helping to construct a house which, he claimed, had five bathrooms, the smallest of which was bigger than their lounge. He had a rough idea of what to expect though. It was in the eastern suburbs, the part of Sydney where the toffs lived, people who packed off their pampered progeny to expensive private schools.

An hour later they were there. Their rustbucket was in need of a new muffler and drew a fair amount of attention as it farted its way along the tree-lined streets. Frank gazed at one Buckingham Palace after another and then, as they turned a corner, was confronted by an armada of yachts and pleasure cruisers on the shimmering water of the harbour. He wondered if the people who owned boats like these lived on them. Did they have so much money they were able to own houses as well? And if so, where did they keep the boats? In the *garage*?

Mick pulled up in the driveway of what would one day be an enormous mansion, hopped out and unlocked the gate. Frank realised his dad had not been exaggerating, for once. Five dunnies could fit easily into this place, but what was the point? Even if five people lived in it, what were the chances they'd all have to go for a shit at the same time?

He turned his gaze to the panorama its owners would soon be enjoying as they sat on their verandah drinking Crown Lager or one of those expensive imported beers. He could see straight across a bay to the Harbour Bridge and, to the left, the skeleton of scaffolding shrouding the Opera House. The shape of the construction challenged Frank's concept of what constituted a building and, while he wouldn't have been surprised to learn this one had been discovered on Mars, he found it baffling to think that Earthlings would soon be wandering about inside it, going to concerts and watching plays. By contrast, the mansion-in-progress, for all its stupefying grandiosity, was reassuringly familiar.

Mick was rewarding himself for a drive well done with another ice-cold beer. 'Come on, get over here and give a man a hand,' he said, reaching into the back of the car and tossing Frank a pair of concrete-encrusted gloves.

'What sort of job would a bloke have to be in to be able to afford a house this big?' Frank asked, picking up the gloves and giving them a good shake before inserting his fingers. He'd learned the hard way that spiders like to live in gloves like these.

'Buggered if I know, but I'll tell you one thing. A lot of honest men will work their guts out to build it and you can bet your balls the owner isn't one of them. Now get that wheelbarrow and bring it over here.'

'What are we doing?'

'We're knocking off a load of bricks and a bag of cement and this afternoon you're going to help me build a barbecue.'

As Mick was locking the gate, a silver Mercedes-Benz glided by and turned into the driveway of the last house at the end of the street. The limousine's driver walked around to open the passenger door and helped his young wife to step out. They were an Asian couple, beautifully dressed, as if they were going to a wedding or the pictures. Frank watched as they cooed and clucked and fussed over their newborn baby wrapped in pink, a lucky little girl about to spend her first night in their no doubt tastefully furnished, multi-bedroomed and bathroomed, perfectly positioned with sweeping harbour views, ideal family home.

A few minutes later the old car was back on the main road, creating noise and air pollution while impeding the flow of traffic.

CHAPTER 2

A lot of delinquents expelled from more respectable establishments found themselves very much at home in the educational dead end known as Mitchellton Boys' High in Sydney's western suburbs. Those whose behaviour proved too monstrous even for the standards of Mitchellton usually made their exit in the company of the police. Expulsions were only deemed appropriate in cases involving students whose records of criminality were less impressive than those of their academic achievements. For them, rehabilitation remained at least a possibility.

Such was the case for Thornton, F of 5A, who pulled his final stunt at Mitchellton during a science lesson in the first week of the first term of 1971. Many great scientists have suffered the scorn of their less audacious counterparts when carrying out experiments, and Thornton was no exception. His invention of the lard gun was dismissed as mere tomfoolery by the science master, Mr Schnittler, known as Adolf, when its prototype was fired off, to spectacular effect, at the back of his classroom.

With intellectual challenges in short supply, the few bright students at the school often felt compelled to create challenges of their own. It was a risky business. Any overt signs of cleverness would be punished by both the teachers and fellow students, so the safest way to proceed was to act as though you had no brains at all. On the basis of his own experience Frank assumed this had probably been the case for all the great thinkers of history and that boredom and oppression had led Newton to discover the laws of gravity and Einstein to come up with the theory of relativity. It was now time to come up with a theory of his own.

Thornton's theory was: if lard takes longer to bring to the boil than water, it stands to reason that if a test tube with a small amount of water at the bottom and a thick plug of lard forced down on top of it is placed over a Bunsen burner, something bad is bound to happen.

He proved himself right. Within seconds, the water had started to boil and the hot lard was exhibiting signs of activity.

'Hey, mudguts,' Thornton said to his target, an overweight kid by the name of James Molson.

'Whaddaya fuckin —' was all Molson managed to say before the lard made violent contact with his face, occasioning superficial burns to the cheek and nose, temporary blindness in the left eye accompanied by excruciating pain, and the spontaneous outbreak of a brawl between two of his friends and Thornton.

Molson was despatched to the sick bay. Thornton was frogmarched to the front of the room and told to wait. This was part of a routine procedure whereby the evil-doer was granted a few moments' respite to experience deep regret for what he had done and abject terror at the prospect of what was about to be done to him when Adolf returned from the staffroom with his cane. Six cuts from Adolf was no laughing matter. Those who survived them, but indulged in histrionics such as excessive wincing or the shedding of tears, were guaranteed of worse to come from their classmates who wouldn't tolerate pansies.

Adolf had perfected the deadly four-plus-two combination. The first four strokes were delivered to the tips of the fingers with such force that blood blisters erupted under the fingernails. The final two required a subtle realignment of the torturer's position, so the strokes hit their target in a line starting at the tip of the smallest finger and ending on the bony, protruding base of the thumb. The devastation was such that recipients would forgo masturbation for one night and, in extreme cases, two. Adolf was widely regarded as a 'two-nighter', and today he was in sparkling form.

But on the sixth stroke Frank grabbed the cane as it landed on his hand, wrested it from Adolf's control, and said, 'Your turn now, sir.'

'Give me that cane, Thornton. Come on, son, give it to me now.'

'I intend to, sir,' Frank replied. 'Just put out your hand. I'm going to give you six.'

'Give me that cane, Thornton!'

'I'll give you the cane, sir, by Christ I will. But you'll have to hold out your hand.'

The teacher made a lunge for the weapon. Frank whisked it aside, like a matador evading the bull with a flourish of his cape. When the snorting beast regained his composure, faced his tormentor and made ready for the next charge, Frank switched from matador to picador, taunting his quarry with thrust after thrust.

Encouraged by a cheering crowd, Frank abandoned bullfighting and took up fencing, menacing his opponent with swipes and jabs until panic drove Adolf out of the room and down the corridor. Frank gave chase, swishing the blade to within inches of the teacher's backside, to the delight of the spectators who roared along a few steps behind.

As Schnittler careered towards the top of the stairwell, the door of an office opened and the headmaster emerged, bringing proceedings to an abrupt halt.

'Get in here, Thornton,' he bellowed. 'I've just about had a gutful of you.'

Having arrived as a reject from notorious Mitchellton, the new boy at Huntingdale High School was aware his reputation had probably preceded him and had no doubt the toughest kids in the school would be relishing the prospect of demonstrating just how unwelcome he was. As he strode about the quadrangle waiting for the first blow to fall, he speculated how many it would take to overpower him. That there would be a first blow was inevitabile. His only concern was that it would be struck by him.

'The trick, son,' Mick Thornton had told Frank on the morning of his first day at his alma mater, 'is to get 'em down and keep 'em down. To get 'em down you have to make sure you get in first, and to keep 'em down you have to kick the shit out of 'em. If you let 'em get up, you're fucked.'

Never had a father imparted such valuable words of advice, and never had a son been so grateful on so many occasions as Frank Thornton was during his four years of incarceration at Mitchellton.

He looked at his watch. Five minutes to go before his first class. To his surprise, the only thing to have struck him so far was not a fist but the presence of girls — in large numbers and bewildering varieties. Until now, girls had been something Frank encountered only outside school hours. It made him regret he hadn't managed to get himself expelled a few years earlier.

Frank looked at his timetable and saw that he was due in a first-level English class under the tutelage of Miss Mariani in room 5/2 in Block D. But he had no idea who Miss Mariani was, or how to find her.

'Can I help you? You look like you're lost,' said the loveliest of three girls walking nearby.

Frank was better prepared to come up with an appropriate response to a gang of school bullies than he was to these few friendly words spoken by a beautiful girl. Incapable of speaking this new language, he simply proffered his timetable for the girls to inspect.

'You've got to go to the second floor of D block. You know where that is?'

Frank shook his head.

'It's the maths and English block. We're going there too, so come with us. I'm Linda, by the way. And this is Natasha and this is Megan.'

'Hi,' Frank managed.

'And what's your name?' Linda went on, as if unaware there was a good chance he wouldn't remember the information required.

'Frank.' It was coming back to him now. 'Frank Thornton.'

'Hi, Frank,' they said in unison.

It sounded like music to him. Maybe they're the school choir or something, he thought.

They walked through some doors and Linda issued directions with the authority of a traffic cop. 'Up the stairs, down the hallway, third door on your right. Okay?'

'Yeah, okay. Thanks.'

'See you round,' one of them said, as all three waved and disappeared.

Frank climbed the stairs thinking, Christ, I hope so.

He fell in love for the fourth time in as many minutes when Miss Mariani opened the door of room 5/2. Teachers, he thought, are not supposed to look like this.

Frank would go on to spend many months analysing the various components of Miss Mariani's beauty during the hours in class and conjuring up images of it in his bedroom at night. With practice, he was able to do this by starting at her feet and working upwards. Eyes tightly closed and hands above the sheets until further notice, he'd concentrate on her slender ankles and shapely calves first, then inch his way over her knees, pausing there for a minute or two before allowing himself to dwell on precisely the length of her thighs he was permitted to observe in real life before the sight was terminated by the hem of her miniskirt. From then on his imagination had to work a little harder to satisfactorily provide the details of what lay beneath, but it was a task he was prepared to persist with. After he'd clambered over the mountains of her breasts he was back on more familiar territory, his hands were now free to move, and he had no trouble recalling her long neck or seeing her full lips coming towards his own ... her dark brown eyes closing behind those long lashes ... her cropped black hair now matted with sweat as she howled and convulsed with orgasm after orgasm. When she could take it no more, considerate Frank would allow himself to come too, Miss Mariani would evaporate into the darkness, and back to the ankles he'd go again.

Here, seeing her for the first time, all Frank knew was that if he was going to be able to concentrate on Shakespeare and Jane Austen this year, Miss Mariani would have to start wearing a bag over her head and invest in a pair of overalls.

'You must be Frank,' she said. 'I'm Miss Mariani. Everybody, this is Frank Thornton. Now, Frank, find a seat so we can start. You can sit there, next to Roy.'

Frank walked towards his classmate, whose dark brown beard was in astonishingly rude health. He wondered if some genetic deficiency was retarding his evolution into manhood. His shaving routine, carried out on irregular intervals, involved removing bum fluff from his chin and the clear-felling of the odd pimple or two. Or perhaps this Roy was so stupid he'd repeated each year of school several times and was looking forward to matriculation coinciding with his thirtieth birthday. His shoulder-length hair, the beard, aquiline nose and heavily hooded eyes made him look like Jesus Christ, adding weight to Frank's suspicion that he hadn't been expelled but executed, and was now waking up in heaven.

Roy's other-worldly gaze and the way he was nibbling on his biro suggested he was deep in thought — and anything but stupid. As he took his seat beside him, Frank was hazarding guesses. The meaning of life? The origin of the universe? Things he'd put to rights when he became prime minister?

12

'Jesus Christ,' murmured Jesus Christ, pointing with his biro, 'that Debbie Harrison's got great tits.'

Two seats further up, in the row to their right, sat a girl wearing a shirt so thin it failed to obscure her light-blue bra.

'Blue bra?'

'That's the one. There are thirty-two tits in this room and hers are the best, although the teacher's come close. Anyway,' said Roy, turning to face Frank and offering a hand, 'Roy Humber.'

'Frank Thornton,' Frank replied, as impressed by Roy's urbane manner as he was by his expertise in the field of comparative anatomy.

'Just quietly,' Roy said quietly, 'you're the bloke who got the arse from Mitchellton, aren't you?'

'That's me.'

'Well done,' said Roy, adding a light slap on the back for emphasis. 'We've all heard the story. You're a fucking champion.'

Frank smiled. He wasn't the caveman of Mitchellton in his new school; he was a champion. No, better still, he was a fucking champion. What's more, he'd made his first new friend, there were thirty-two tits in the room, and the teacher's were up there with the best of them. He'd died and gone to heaven, all right.

'You see that skinny bloke over there with the ponytail? Well, he's a fucking champion too. I'll introduce you to him at recess. He got the arse from St Michael's last year.' Roy moved closer to Frank and added in a whisper, 'But he got the arse in more ways than one, if you know what I mean.'

If I do know what you mean, thought Frank, and I think I do, then Ponytail over there is bloody lucky he didn't go to Mitchellton.

Frank settled back in his seat and colluded with an all-knowing chuckle. We're men of the world here at Huntingdale, he thought. Men of the fucking world. We don't have a problem with sharing the room with thirty-two tits, so why should we worry if two of the twenty-eight balls also in attendance are the pride and joy of a practising poofter?

It wasn't as if he didn't harbour secret perversions of his own. His passion for classical music and jazz was something he'd kept hidden from the troglodytes of Mitchellton. Art, too, was a problem. Frank had never fully recovered from his childhood experience of standing for the first time in front of paintings — real ones — when his parents took him to the 'Big Art Gallery' in Melbourne and left him there for a couple of hours on his own.

He'd spent the first five years of his life in Melbourne and, apart from his enduring allegiance to the Swans football team the memory of that art gallery trip was his only souvenir. He'd been delving into books about artists and perving on reproductions of their paintings ever since. Who knows? he thought. I might even be allowed to indulge these shameful obsessions at Huntingdale.

'So what's his name?' Frank asked when his first double period with Miss Mariani was terminated too soon by the sound of the bell. Another hour wouldn't have hurt, he thought, after checking his timetable and confirming his next rendezvous with her wasn't until after lunch the following day. It seemed an unreasonably long time to wait for something as important as an English lesson.

'Who?' said Roy.

'The bloke with the ponytail.'

'Neil Puesner. Everyone calls him Puss.'

'And he doesn't mind?'

'Mind what?'

'Being called Puss.'

'That's the least of his worries. Hey, Puss!'

The approaching Puss, silhouetted against the backdrop of the classroom windows, reminded Frank of the spindly figures in Giacometti's sculptures, or a praying mantis in school uniform and a wig. Puss stuck out. At seventeen years and six foot two inches, he had already attained as much height as he ever would and seemed to dwarf Roy, who, while almost as tall, carried a lot more weight and dwarfed everyone else. Frank, who had often been grateful for his height advantage over most of his peers at Mitchellton, felt Lilliputian in his present company — the runt of a litter of three.

'Puss, this is Frank Thornton.'

'G'day, Frank,' said Puss, extending a hand apparently fashioned from pipe cleaners. Frank worried they might be mangled if he gripped them too hard.

'I'm in a bit of a rush,' said Puss, as his tendrils enveloped Frank's fingers with a force that threatened to break them all. 'You want to come with me? I've got to duck into the art room.'

'I'll grab something from the canteen,' said Roy. 'You guys want anything?'

14

Puss and Frank placed orders for a sausage roll and a pie, and Roy agreed to meet them in the art room.

'What are you going in there for?' asked Frank, who had never spent recess time indoors and wondered if, by doing so, he was about to be in breach of the rules. It would have been a caning offence at Mitchellton.

'I'm doing some paintings,' Puss explained, 'and I've just discovered oils. Trouble is, oils stay wet. If some bastard's done some finger painting on one of them I'll break his fucking neck.'

Puss was not conforming to Frank's idea of the homosexual stereotype and it was about to get worse.

'You think this Joe Frazier can beat Muhammad Ali?' he asked.

Ali hadn't fought for nearly five years after having been barred from boxing for refusing to be conscripted to serve in Vietnam in 1966. In the meantime, Joe Frazier had become the most feared heavyweight boxer in the world.

'Ali's a bit out of practice,' Frank said, 'and Frazier's defended his title four times.'

'Don't underestimate Ali, mate,' Puss sneered as he opened a door, 'the "Fight of the Century" will be all over in two rounds and Frazier will be flat on his arse.'

The walls of the art room were covered with drawings and paintings of various degrees of ineptitude, all displaying a recklessness and confidence that excited Frank. He felt inspired to get one of his own onto the wall as soon as possible, regardless of how awful it might turn out to be.

'These are mine,' said Puss, gesturing towards a group of four paintings leaning against the back wall. 'It's the wet one on the right I was worried about. Looks as though no one's touched it, thank Christ.'

All four featured groups of gaunt figures in what appeared to be outback landscapes. Depictions of rock formations had been attempted and a lot of paint had ended up as either bright blue or dark, cloudy skies.

'Drysdale,' said Frank.

'What?' said Puss, with the guilty look of a man who'd been caught in the act.

'Russell Drysdale. They remind me of his paintings.'

Puss answered this with a furious silence.

'Nothing wrong with that,' Frank offered.

'No, no, nothing wrong with that. I just wasn't expecting you to make the connection. No one here's ever heard of Drysdale.'

'I'm interested in paintings. I go to the gallery in the Domain sometimes and have a look around.'

'I went a couple of weeks ago while I was tripping. It was fantastic. You ought to try it some time. Do it together if you like.'

Acid! Frank had seen the obligatory Department of Education anti-drug films and remembered a solemn American voice warning him about LSD: *Some people have been taken on a psychedelic journey from which they've never returned.* It sounded like a good idea, especially if you were one of the lucky ones who didn't come back.

'Mate,' he enthused, 'I'm in.'

The aromatic fanfare of hot pies and sausage rolls heralded the arrival of Roy.

'Whaddaya reckon?' he asked Frank as he handed out the delicacies. 'He's good, isn't he?'

'Yeah, he sure is,' said Frank, taking his first tentative bite, testing for heat and structural deficiencies before going in hard. You could never be too careful with pies.

'Show him some of your drawings, Puss,' said Roy. 'Wait till you see these.'

Puss opened his school bag, pulled out a folder and cast a furtive glance around the room.

'Christ Alfuckingmighty!' A naked Miss Mariani disported herself on a desk with a bearded satyr that had a familiar aquiline nose.

'I should be so lucky,' said the satyr.

'I've got some beauties here,' said Puss. 'You've met the headmaster, but have you met Mrs Chadwick yet?'

Frank was confronted with an image of Mr Ogilvy's bald, bespectacled head coming up for air from his arduous task between the massive thighs of a squirming, giggling woman who made Rubens' whoppers look anorexic.

'Unbelievable,' said Frank, picking up one obscenity after another.

'Keep your voice down,' Puss said. 'I don't want these getting out, if you know what I mean.'

'Fair enough,' said Frank, 'they could get you into the shit all right.'

'They did at my last school.'

'What happened?'

'Well, I started doing drawings like these. Teachers with students, teachers doing all sorts of stuff with other teachers, you know the sort of thing.'

'Yairs,' said Frank Thornton, newly anointed man of the world. Mindful that St Michael's was an all-boys Catholic school staffed entirely by men of the cloth, he wasn't sure he knew 'the sort of thing' at all.

'This dickhead prefect pinched some of them and took them home to his parents, and they took them along to a P&C meeting. Demanded the headmaster do something. So he did. He expelled me the next day.'

'What a cunt,' said Frank.

'No, he wasn't. He didn't want to kick me out — he was forced into it. I felt a bit sorry for him really.'

The concept of feeling sorry for a headmaster was new to Frank. Too perplexed to speak, he waited for Puss to go on. After a reflective pause he did.

'I'd always rather fancied him, to tell you the truth. And, as it turned out, he rather fancied me too. Poor old dear.'

Frank's sister, Nina, had always had a room of her own, while he and Bob had to share — Bob on the top bunk, him below.

Nina, now twenty-one, had moved out a year ago after her status had progressed from girlfriend to wife to mother, all in the space of six months, which had given Frank and Bob the luxury of rooms to themselves. As if that arrangement hadn't been good enough, nineteen-year-old Bob decided soon after to move to rat-infested squalor within walking distance of the University of New South Wales, from where he intended to emerge one day as a teacher. The upshot of all this sibling migration was that Frank now had the place to himself every afternoon when he came home from school.

His mother, Molly, farewelled her irascible charges at a Greenwich nursing home at five, took the train from St Leonards and would appear at six-thirty. Mick, a brickie's labourer, started work early and knocked off at four. Some residual sense of familial obligation and the need to eat usually combined to drive him out of the pub between seven and eight.

This meant, on arriving home, Frank could do as he pleased. What pleased him after his first day at his new school was to make a couple of Vegemite sandwiches and drink what was left of a carton of milk from the fridge. He washed this down with a cupful of OP rum from a bottle he kept hidden in a shoebox under his bed, and this pleased him too. He loved the way it quickened his pulse and the clean, burning sensation it left in his throat. What pleased him next was to look through his record collection and christen the new album he'd stolen on the weekend.

ESP by Miles Davis. Miles on trumpet, Wayne Shorter on tenor, Herbie Hancock on piano, Ron Carter on bass and — the one who interested him most — Tony Williams on drums. According to the sleeve notes, Tony Williams had been seventeen — his age! — when this recording was made in 1965.

He put it on the turntable, turned the volume up and lay down in his favourite position, between the speakers, on the floor.

He'd read about the lives of men who made music like this. They did it hard. Nightmare lives, some of them. And what came out of it? This! How much pain and anger did they have to have in them? How did they bottle it up and turn it all into something so bloody sublime?

Life can be good, he thought; not only good, great. Really fucking great! But for it to be that fucking great maybe you have to be living in New York City, impoverished, heroin-addicted — and black.

CHAPTER 3

'Don't freak out, Frank.'

It was Puss's voice. He knew that. What he couldn't understand was, why was it echoing? And why wasn't Puss speaking with just one voice, but dozens? A whole choir of Pusses, slightly out of synch with the movement of his mouth. And why was his mouth now a hole in his cardboard-cutout face, through which Frank had a clear view of the Harbour Bridge?

'What's happened to your eyes?'

'Nothing's happened to my eyes, Frank. You okay?'

'Puss, something's happened to your eyes. I can see straight through them. I can see the Harbour Bridge. They're just holes, man, so is your mouth. I can see the bridge through that hole too.'

'Here, Frank, touch my eyes.'

With a gentle brush of his hand, Frank wiped the top of Puss's head clean off. He now had an uninterrupted view of the bridge. No — bridges. Lots of bridges. Lots and lots and lots of very big bridges, proliferating, some cavorting like dancers. The least you should be able to expect of a bridge, Frank thought, is that it stays still.

'Shit, Puss, I'm sorry.'

'Sorry for what, Frank?'

'Didn't mean to wipe the top of your head off like that.'

A million Pusses laughed at once. A moment ago the Puss voices were miles away, now they were close, all around him. Deafening — and slowing down too. Like a record being played at the wrong speed and getting slower and slower and louder and louder and …

'Try to stand up, Frank,' said the booming Puss voices at the rate of one word per minute. 'Here, I'll help you.'

The hand Puss extended was made of some translucent material, through which veins and all internal workings were clearly visible, and each finger was eight feet long. Frank looked at his own hands to make sure the same thing hadn't happened to him. They seemed in order, but given his arms were now so long he could reach out and touch one of those harbour bridges, it was a bit hard to tell.

'Fuck, Puss,' said a voice originating somewhere inside him, in similar, minute-long words. 'What's happening?'

'You're okay, Frank,' sang the demon choir, six octaves below middle C. 'You're just tripping, that's all.'

A sensation of movement through space confused him. I'm walking, he thought. It seemed strange for someone half a mile tall to be able to walk. Even stranger, from this height, to be able to see every blade of grass struggling to avoid his giant steps. There were brightly coloured little animals running around in the grass too. It was a jungle down there, full of these tiny, scurrying creatures. How come he'd never seen them before?

'Coltrane,' he heard the voice coming from inside himself say. '*Giant Steps*. Coltrane.'

'Just keep walking, Frank. You're peaking. You'll be okay soon.'

'I'm okay now, for fuck's sake. Man, am I okay.'

'Ha ha ha,' sang the celestial Puss choir, trumpeting like angels wafting about in the iridescent sky above the Botanic Gardens, the noise rebounding off the neon trees. Or maybe it was that fluorescent kookaburra over there doing all the laughing. It couldn't be Puss — Puss was made of gas. Or maybe light. Yeah, light — Puss was made of light. Getting brighter now. Too bright. Look at the kookaburra instead. Christ, where's the kookaburra gone? And the bridges? Only one bridge left — and it was made of neon too. Maybe the ferry monsters had eaten the other bridges. Of course! The ferry monsters had eaten those bridges for sure.

'You ready to go to the gallery, Frank?' said the Puss voice. Only one this time. Frank turned to look at him. He wasn't made of light or gas any more. Someone had lit a big candle inside him and he was glowing. This struck Frank as perfectly normal — everything else was glowing too. People passing by on the footpath were glowing beautifully, leaving trails of light as they glided along. He touched the sky. It was a vast canvas of blue light-dust he could draw on by wiping it with his fingers, like condensation on the windscreen of a car. He drew a wavy squiggle, watched it slowly disappear before drawing another one. Different colour this time. Good squiggle too. Prettier than the first one.

'Yeah, I'm ready,' he said. 'I want to see the cows.'

'What cows?'

'Elioth Gruner's cows. You know the ones. In the gallery.'

'Come on then, we'll start there. At the cows.'

Two seventeen-year-old boys climbed the steps to the Art Gallery of New South Wales. They looked like nice enough kids. Both a bit scruffy perhaps, in faded jeans and T-shirts. Tall, athletic-looking fellows. On closer inspection, the one with the ponytail didn't look athletic so much as emaciated. They disappeared into the gallery, walked through the foyer, turned right and stood in front of Elioth Gruner's painting *Spring Frost*. For a minute or so they appeared spellbound. The shorter of the two turned to the beanpole and whispered urgently into his ear. They took one more look at the painting, turned and ran from the gallery, racing down Art Gallery Road towards Mrs Macquarie's Chair, screaming as they passed bewildered onlookers, none of whom could see the herd of purple monsters stampeding after them, the concrete shattering under their cloven hooves or the streams of light they left in the wake of their mighty horns.

It was a close call, but the cow monsters had given up the chase by the time the boys reached the water's edge. They collapsed, exhausted and laughing, on the grass verge and stayed there for the next few hours, gazing in wonder at the kaleidoscopic water of the harbour; seagulls turning into pterodactyls, swooping and plunging into effervescent explosions like bombs hitting stained-glass windows; the melting landscape, transforming and reconfiguring itself in myriad different ways. When, finally, the sun went brown, they gathered themselves up and headed for the bus stop in a magical glow of golden twilight.

The flyscreen door at the Thorntons' house revealed itself as quite a complex structure when subjected to close scrutiny by a teenager in the waning phase of an LSD trip. Frank spent several minutes marvelling at the intricate patterns mutating in its wire lacework, opened it and plunged into the darkness within.

A small patch of white light smouldering on the kitchen table drew his attention. As he approached, the light dimmed and went out.

Flicking on the overhead light, he was surprised to find himself in recognisable surroundings. There was everything, stolid as ever. The laminex pattern on the kitchen table was its usual uninteresting self and, where a minute or so before a flat square of neon had glowed, there was now a scrap of notepaper. The message read:

> Frank,
>   Dad and I have gone to the club. Cross your fingers and we'll win the jackpot! Bit of dinner in the fridge. Heat it up.
>   Love, Mum.

Like the man who, after holidaying in exotic surroundings, comes back to find his home has grown smaller and shabbier during his absence, Frank, on his return to reality, was disappointed by its immutability. The exhilaration he'd experienced that day had found its antithesis here. Miracles weren't about to happen in this moth-eaten place. There were no multi-coloured creatures darting about amongst the worn-out pile and stains of the carpet.

He became aware of physical discomfort too — he was shivering, grinding his teeth, his clothes soaked with cold sweat. He headed to the bathroom. Standing under the shower, he could feel every drop of water as it bounced off his skin, each frayed nerve burning in response to a thousand tiny assaults.

So that was it, eh? The thing they all talked about: acid. That was the stuff Bob Dylan got from his Mr Tambourine Man, the shit that shot John Lennon up with Lucy in the Sky with Diamonds.

Ah, the water felt good now — his skin absorbing it like a sponge. He stayed under the shower until the hot ran out, dried himself quickly, wrapped the towel around his waist, made a detour via the fridge for some milk, turned on the telly and fell onto the couch.

The TV blurred and droned as he reflected on his foray into the psychedelic world of hallucination. He found he could recall the unreal experiences he'd had that day as easily as any real ones he'd had before, but the memory of it made him shudder. He wanted to obliterate it, pretend it had never happened. Being transported into another dimension where things could happen over which he had no control was the scariest experience he'd had in his life. And now the phone was ringing.

'Frank, it's me, Puss. How are you feeling?'

'I'm okay now ...'

'That was pretty good shit, eh?'

'It was pretty fucking wild, all right.'

'Listen, this girl, Jude, is having a party tonight. She's a friend of Linda's. She might have the hots for you, Frank.'

'You're kidding.'

'No, believe me, I'm not. A mate of mine's borrowed his oldies' car. We can come by and pick you up in about twenty minutes. That okay?'

'That's great.'

'Cool. And by the way, I've got some more acid if you'd like some.'

'Mate, I'm in!'

Frank ran into his bedroom and started rummaging through piles of clothes on the floor, looking for a clean shirt.

After eight months at Huntingdale High School, Thornton, F of 5A had developed the swagger of a celluloid Chicago mobster and a line of patter to go with it. Acting on the assumption that those he was trying to impress probably hadn't read the authors he was plagiarising, he managed to intimidate and charm via paraphrasings of Wilde, De Sade and Voltaire — to name a few — with the tough, laconic style of Kerouac articulated in a working-class Australian accent peppered with expletives and enhanced with borrowings from his father's endless lexicon of catch phrases and obscenities.

While those around him were growing hairier by the day, waging war on the home front to establish their right to look like Robert Plant or Jimmy Page, Frank was cultivating his black hair along Chet Baker lines; but only to collar rather than shoulder or arse length. When catching a glimpse of himself in dark windows or bathroom mirrors, from a certain angle and under favourable lighting, he occasionally recognised the young James Dean and wished he was allowed to smoke at school, or at least be permitted an unlit ciggie hanging permanently from his lips to complete the picture.

Rumours were spreading about Thornton, F and his two inseparable friends, Humber, R, and Puesner, N. Puesner — or Puss, as they called him — was an unabashed pervert; a poofter who didn't even have the decency to pretend otherwise. Humber was a known smartarse, who not only studied foreign languages but spoke them and had been caught reading books in them as well. He also big-noted himself by flaunting his knowledge of astrophysics and esoteric science so as to cause embarrassment to his teachers. As for Thornton — well, the boy was a bad influence, simple as that. He'd been expelled from Mitchellton and you didn't get expelled from that hellhole for good behaviour. Everyone knew his father was a drunk and a no-hoper whose fibro house stood out even amongst those other slums down near the railway station in Mitchellton. The kid was an arty-farty two-bob lair, but a tough cookie just the same. You wouldn't let your daughter go out with him. Word had it he was going through the girls in the school like a packet of salts and had his eye on a couple of the teachers too. The three of them were fast company: the naughty boys of Huntingdale High, who had taken the marijuana and smoked the LSD.

Someone would have to teach them a lesson sooner or later.

While they had plenty of admirers among their fellow students, some loathed them and would have liked nothing better than to give all three the hiding they deserved. And they would have too, if only Humber wasn't such a big bloke and they weren't scared shitless of Thornton.

But Turner, W of 6C wasn't scared of any of them, and he had a claim to fame.

Two weeks ago he'd gatecrashed a party and been urged by the hired bouncer to leave. His response, which resulted in the bouncer being rushed to hospital, had failed to impress the birthday girl, who called the police and regretted she'd done a deal with her parents that saw them agreeing to stay away until three.

For his own part, Wally Turner was deeply dissatisfied with the outcome. Why had the stupid bouncer picked on him just because he'd turned up pissed? If he was going to throw anyone out, why hadn't he started with those druggies, Thornton, Humber and their big, skinny poofter mate with the ponytail?

Frank, Roy and Puss had developed the habit of spending their lunch hours in the art room. This gave Puss the chance to paint in front of a captive audience, enabled Roy to expound on whatever lofty ideas he was preoccupied with that day, and Frank the opportunity to gain an insight into the artistic process while being intellectually stimulated. His own attempts to add something to the collection of paintings on the art room walls had proved so sloppy, inept and disappointing that he'd decided his strengths lay in the appreciation of art, rather than its execution. He made himself useful by learning to toast cheese sandwiches in the enamelling kiln, which, at seven hundred degrees, could do them to a turn in four-point-three seconds. They were reduced to small flecks of black ash if left in there any longer, which meant Frank's responsibility was a demanding one, requiring a level of precision unattainable on days like today, when he'd dropped acid before going to school and had seen a double period of English with Miss Mariani go by in a nanosecond and a sneeze take half an hour.

'Oh fuck!' roared Roy, watching dense smoke billowing from the kiln as Frank opened it. 'You've done it again! That's both of my sandwiches gone, both of Puss's, and now we've only got yours left and your mum always uses that shithouse cheddar. Let me do it.'

Frank relinquished his post and busied himself gazing through the window, watching the trees at the far end of the playground marching slowly back and forth in dignified procession.

'Well, look who's here,' he heard a satanic voice declare. 'Little fucking Picasso himself.'

Frank turned to see Wally Turner transform into a gigantic ogre with bright blue skin and flame-red hair.

'So what are we painting today, poof-boy?'

The ogre trudged up to Puss and shoved him aside, hoping for a response that would give him an excuse for a bit of lunchtime poofter-bashing.

'Get 'em down and keep 'em down, Puss,' Frank heard his dad's voice say, echoing inside his head. 'To get 'em down, you've gotta get in first ...'

Frank could see Puss's dad hadn't taught him the same lesson. If anyone was going to get in first, it would be this Wally Turner bloke from 6C.

'Fuck off,' Frank heard his own voice say.

'What did you say, cunt?'

The ogre was now trudging towards him in slow motion.

Frank saw his own arms reach out and pick up *Untitled #1*, a bold attempt at abstract plaster sculpture by a student who had seen a Brancusi and was clever with his hands. He watched the ogre's giant blue fist whistle past his own right ear as he moved carefully out of its way, and then stared amazed as *Untitled #1* exploded into a million glowing snowflakes around the staggering ogre's head.

'... And to keep 'em down you've gotta kick the shit out of 'em,' Dad was saying as he laid the boot into the monster, which was changing colour and making animal noises on the floor.

'Fuck, Frank, you're going to kill him,' he heard Roy's voice say. Where was Roy? The voice sounded like it was coming from another room. No, here he is — great big Roy, coming down out of the sky at me, landing on me — look out, Roy, we're both floating down onto the floor where the ogre's lying — careful, Roy, we're landing on the monster and here we are amongst his teeth and purple blood and all the snowflakes.

Mick Thornton came home at about seven-thirty, took his dinner from the oven and joined Frank and his wife at the table. Nobody said anything. Molly Thornton had nearly finished her meal; Frank's was going cold.

After a mouthful or two, Mick broke the silence. 'We're all a bit bloody quiet here tonight, aren't we?'

Frank's mum darting looks at Frank; Frank shoving his peas around the plate with a fork; his dad looking at both of them in turn. It was getting pretty tense, Frank thought, not quite down from the acid yet, but getting there.

'You in trouble at school or something?'

'I think so, man.'

'Don't fucking call me "man"!'

'Language, Mick —'

'Whaddaya mean, you "think so"? Are you in trouble or what?'

'Apparently I got expelled.'

'Whaddaya mean "apparently"? Have you been into those fucking drugs again?'

'Mick! Language!'

His father was standing over him now.

'Well, have you?'

'Yeah. Must have —'

Val and Bruce Bricknell had heard the goings-on in the Thornton household before. They didn't think much of that young Frank, but by Christ he took some beatings from that father of his. This time it was beyond a joke. This time they'd have to call the police.

CHAPTER 4

'All Johnny Rotten has to do is spew up during an interview in Denmark and he's page one news in bloody Australia,' Neville lamented, tossing his *Daily Mirror* aside. 'Johnny-Come-Fucking-Lately they should call him.'

Thanks to Neville's passionate belief that punk rock had originated in the bar he managed, and had thrived thanks to his heroic support for bands like Radio Birdman and The Saints, the international success of the Sex Pistols struck a raw nerve. Radio Birdman may have been developing a following amongst Sydney's Hell's Angels and running low on venues, but they could still get a gig at The Pharmacy. Neville wouldn't complain as he mopped up the blood and assessed the damage after every show. It was the price someone had to pay for musical integrity — a commodity Neville regarded as far more valuable than a bit of negative publicity for the pub.

'Look at this,' said Frank, pointing to a story on page five. 'A bloke's been killed in a hit-and-run and they've referred to him as "Ulf Heckel, 44, unemployed of no fixed address".'

'So what?'

'Well, it doesn't tell you much about the poor bastard, does it? There was a great German painter called Erich Heckel. This guy might have been his son or something.'

'So what?'

'Think about it. A few years ago I could have been killed in an accident and I would have gone down in the papers as "Frank Thornton, 19, offal shoveller of Meatworks Dormitory D, Broome, WA". A year or so after that I could have fallen off a boat and I would have been "Frank Thornton, 20, shitkicker on a prawn trawler in the middle of the ocean".'

'What were you doing on a prawn trawler?'

'Everything. The rest of the crew were bludgers and the captain was a junkie. Good bloke, though. Name's Harvey. Spoke to him on the phone just the other night and he said he's been off the gear for six months now.'

'Sounds a bit more like hard work than what you're doing here,' said Neville. 'Bit more interesting too. If you get piss-bowled by a bus when you knock off work tonight you'll just be Frank Thornton, 23, bartender of fucking Petersham or wherever it is you live. Anyway, put the paper down and get down in the cellar. This keg's nearly run out.'

Frank looked at his watch. Ten minutes before his shift started at six. The bar was already crowded with the Friday evening business crowd. Later, about eight, it would be jam-packed with punk-rock fans and junkies, who'd frighten this mob out.

'Fair enough,' said Frank. 'Who's playing tonight?'

'The Bleeding Farts.'

'Oh Christ,' said Frank, putting the paper down and heading for the cellar.

It was going to be a big night. The Bleeding Hearts were a punk band with a cult following, every member of which would turn up when they played at the Farmer's Arms on Oxford Street. Like the band, it had been many years since anyone had referred to the Darlinghurst hotel by its original name, and now even the posters advertised it as The Pharmacy. The new name couldn't have been more appropriate. It was a place where a multi-million-dollar trade in alcohol raged on one side of the bar — where Frank earned his money — while an equally lucrative drugs trade took place on the other — where he drank and did his shopping.

Down in the cellar, Frank smoked a joint. He was ready for anything when he surfaced through the manhole and commenced work behind the bar. Well, almost anything.

It had been more than five years since he'd seen Miss Mariani and, if possible, she was even more beautiful now, standing in front of him and ordering a couple of beers, than she'd been when he'd fantasised about her during his time at Huntingdale High School.

'Two dollars forty, thanks,' he said, placing the drinks in front of her, maintaining his composure.

She handed him a fiver and smiled as he came back with the change.

'Hey, you're Frank, aren't you?'

'That's me. And you're Miss Mariani. Nice to see you again.'

'You can call me Sophia now.'

'It's a (pause) beautiful name. I'm surprised you remember me. I wasn't at the school for very long.'

'You made quite an impression while you were there.'

As Frank tried to decide what she'd meant by this remark he became aware of another customer, large and wearing army fatigues, leaning in front of Sophia and commandeering her two beers.

'Here,' said Frank, 'wait your turn, mate.'

'I'm not waiting for my turn, I'm waiting for you to shut up. Come on, Sophie, there's a table over there.'

For the next two hours Frank was back in English class, only this time it was worse. In those days, Miss Mariani's life outside the school had been a matter of intense speculation: maybe she had a boyfriend; maybe a de facto; maybe even a kid or two; or maybe — just maybe — she was single and liked teenage boys with bum fluff and pimples. Now, whether she was married to him or not, she was getting about with some oaf in military uniform which made it seem unlikely she'd fancy a no-longer-pimply former student with spiky hair and a dragon tattooed on his arm.

Then again, she did turn to him occasionally and smile when GI Joe wasn't paying attention. And she did come back to the bar, lean across it and give him a peck on the cheek when she said goodbye.

Frank, who thought he'd been ready for anything, was definitely not ready for this.

'It was nice to see you again (pause) Sophia. Really nice.'

'Good to see you too, Frank. See you again soon, I hope.'

'Come on, Soph,' called GI Joe.

Frank, following her with his eyes, tried not to look elated — and failed — when she turned and waved before disappearing through the door.

What is she doing with him? Frank thought. Big brainless boofhead.

'Testing, testing,' came a loud voice over the PA. 'Testing, one, two, three.'

There was the sound of guitars tuning up and the clientele was changing over. Chains hung from safety pins puncturing the clothes and faces of the crowd pushing its way to the bar. The Farts would be rasping away any minute now, making music which, in Frank's opinion, stank to high heaven. He opened the manhole and climbed down the stairs to the cellar where he smoked another joint. He was going to need it.

Wow, that Miss Mariani! he thought. That Sophia! I smoke to forget.

It didn't work, of course. Frank had Sophia on the brain and under his skin. And there she remained until, three weeks later, she appeared once again at the bar of The Pharmacy.

This time it was different. This time it was a Monday, the quietest night of the week. This time, Frank dared to think, there was a chance — however slight — she'd come to see him, because this time she was alone.

For ten minutes they exchanged platitudes in moments between the demands of customers. Sophia showed no inclination to move from her stool at the bar. Good sign, thought Frank.

At five to seven Neville emerged from the cellar and threw him a wink.

Frank soon convinced himself she had turned up with the sole intention of seeing him. Why else would she make an arrangement to meet soldier boy at a restaurant in Paddington at eight and pop in here, of all places, an hour before? Why else would she be discussing details of her personal life with him, even intimating there were problems between her and her husband — a 'difficult' man whose name, Frank learned, was Regimental Sergeant Major Kevin Parker?

'So what do you call him — Reg?'

This brought a wry smile, an endearing rush of colour to her cheeks and a change of subject.

'So what have you been doing since you left Huntingdale, Frank? Did you go to another school, finish your HSC?'

'I'd sort of run out of schools by that stage. I took off.'

'What do you mean, "took off"?'

'Went hitchhiking. Finished up going all around Australia. Did a lot of different jobs. Read a lot,' he added. Miss Mariani was the English teacher, after all.

'You like this work?'

'It's okay.'

'Hmm.'

Sophia took a sip of her drink. Seeing her eyelashes as she dipped her head, Frank remembered how long they were and wondered what the eyes hiding behind them might be expressing right now. Boredom? Disappointment? Miss Mariani might have been hoping for a more impressive CV from a clever former student. When her eyes revealed themselves again, they didn't show either; rather a mixture of pity and concern.

'You know, Frank, I thought it was terribly sad — all that drama, you being expelled. I'll tell you the truth: I thought you were one of the brightest kids I'd ever had in a class. I enjoyed — if you'll forgive the expression — having you.'

Now it was Frank's turn to lower his eyes. This time he wondered what he was hiding from her. Embarrassment? Acute. Shame? Profound.

'Your essays were always so clever and funny. I thought I might have been helping to foster someone with a career in writing. "He was one of my students. I taught him all he knew" — that sort of thing.' She laughed. And her hand reached out and stroked his forearm.

What state are you in when you're more than acutely embarrassed? Or one step further along from profoundly ashamed? Grateful? In love?

'I was really shocked by what you did,' she went on, reverting to her teacher's role, 'because I didn't think you were the violent type.'

He hadn't thought he was either. Though there was ample evidence to suggest they were both mistaken: a blue head, purple blood, lots of teeth and a million glowing snowflakes in a sealed plastic bag. Exhibit A, your Honour.

'I'm sorry for what I did to that guy. I thought he was going to hurt Puss.'

'He would have, don't worry. He was a creep. And he's since gone on to bigger and better things. He got five years for rape and assault.'

Frank wasn't surprised. But he wanted to know about Sophia Mariani, not Wally Turner.

'Still teaching at Huntingdale?'

'I left two years after you did. Went back to uni: I'm doing my master's degree and working part-time as a tutor, teaching HSC English to spoilt eastern suburbs brats whose parents don't think they're getting value for money from their posh private schools.'

They both laughed. On common ground now, Frank sensed the naughty boy of Huntingdale was in cahoots with the naughty teacher. Then he caught her looking at her watch and feared he was wrong.

And yet ... Why would she have leaned across the bar to kiss him before she left? And why would she have told him 'Reg' would be heading off the following Saturday morning for a two-week training camp in Townsville and arrange to meet him for dinner that night?

Five more sleeps. It seemed an unreasonably long time to wait for something as important as an English lesson, let alone a private tutorial.

The two most romantic and exhilarating weeks of Frank's life followed when, with her military husband away, Sophia enlisted Frank on his own tour of beauty.

Eager to create a good impression on his first mission, the young recruit didn't flinch when, after having climaxed five times to his one, his commanding officer breathlessly declared him a Five-Star General and demanded he do it again. Remembering a lesson he'd learned well at school, he headed straight for her ankles and worked his way up. By the time he'd clambered over the mountains of her breasts, she'd found he was able to continue to issue fierce small-arms fire until, with her cropped black hair now matted with sweat, she howled and convulsed with orgasm after orgasm. Considerate Frank indulged himself by firing off another mortar of his own, then, when Sophia collapsed onto the mattress with exhaustion, back to the ankles he went again, thinking, you can't get too much of a good thing in a fortnight.

His fantasy-turned-reality ended a few hours earlier than expected, thanks to Regimental Sergeant Major Kevin Parker's decision to take the last seat available on the early plane home. Frank shouldn't have been surprised: according to certain intimate details Sophia had divulged to her new lover, evacuating prematurely was entirely consistent with her husband's nature. This time he came too soon for both of them.

Sophia had decided not to meet Frank the night before her husband was due home. It was asking for trouble. Kevin's plane was due to touch down at 0900 hours. The trip from Richmond airbase would take about forty-five minutes. They'd have to play it safe. She'd wash the sheets the afternoon before and eliminate all traces of Frank's presence. It wouldn't look good if they were in the machine when Kevin came through the door.

Frank agreed. They'd be able to meet again soon enough. Kevin was forever going away on his training camps, bivouacs or jamborees, or whatever they were called.

They kissed that morning at breakfast, and held each other for so long they both became embarrassed. Frank turned, opened the door and left. Sophia went back to the kitchen table and cried. Frank walked from her flat in Elizabeth Bay to the station at Kings Cross, thinking that, if he kept his sunglasses on, nobody would see he was weeping like a baby. He found himself hoping war might break out between Australia and somewhere else — anywhere else — as long as it enabled someone to do the right thing and shoot a Regimental Sergeant Major.

Later that night, Neville nudged him in the ribs at eleven-thirty when he saw Sophia walk in. 'You can piss off early,' he said. 'I'll finish up here.'

'Maybe we should go to my place,' Frank suggested, as his old VW started after the third attempt. 'Or book into a hotel.'

'No, it'll be okay. He won't be home till ten. We'll set the alarm for seven. And I'll change the sheets when you leave. There's nothing to worry about.'

She was right. They'd have been mad to miss out on this last night together. They laughed, kissed, and drove dangerously.

At 4 am, Sophia switched off the light and turned onto her side. Frank, lying behind her, snuggled up to his favourite place for sleeping —where his cheek could rest against the back of her neck.

How do I feel? he asked himself. Exhausted? Yes. Tired? No. And what's this other thing? Is it happiness ... or its opposite? He was so close to this woman. Maybe he was experiencing the thing they referred to as intimacy; this bit — after the wild sex — lying here, listening to her breathe. He could feel her breathing too, through the gentle movements of her tummy under his hand.

There was something else he could feel; after several minutes, he reckoned he knew what it was.

'I love you, Sophia,' he whispered.

He'd never said 'I love you' to anyone before and no one had ever said it to him. He wanted to hear her say those three words. He lay there, listening for them, wondering what would happen next. Maybe he shouldn't have said it. Maybe there was a script for this, their final scene, and that line wasn't in it. Maybe there were rules for this sort of thing and he'd broken one. Or maybe she didn't love him and to say she did would be telling a lie.

She said nothing, just cried softly. He pressed his cheek harder into the back of her neck and held her tightly as they both pretended to fall asleep.

Sophia was no longer pretending, but Frank was wide awake when he heard the front door open and saw a light go on in the kitchen at half past five.

He clamped his hand over her mouth and jolted her awake. Sophia, panic-stricken, gestured towards the balcony door and lunged at Frank's clothes. No time to worry about them now; Sophia could shove them under the bed. All he needed were his keys. There they were, on the bedside table. He swept them up and, a second later, was standing naked and shivering on the balcony. So far so good.

The sliding door had cooperated by opening noiselessly. So what if it was still wide open? It wouldn't look suspicious; she often slept with it open. There was silence inside. Through the curtains, Frank could see the light was still on in the kitchen. Good. The big bloke hadn't gone into the bedroom yet, so Sophia would have had plenty of time to get his clothes under the bed. She should be doing an Oscar-winning job of playing Sleeping Beauty now. But what the hell was he going to do?

There was a downpipe a couple of feet from the balcony, as if a prescient builder had foreseen tonight's emergency and placed it there deliberately. Frank stuffed the keys into his mouth, climbed onto the railing and reached for the plumbing. He found it surprisingly easy to gain purchase with his toes in the gaps between the bricks. And, for the first time in living memory, he found the old VW easy to start, although he had to repress a scream when his freezing flesh made contact with the even colder car seat.

It could have been a lot worse, he decided, as he drove naked through the almost-deserted streets of the Cross, but it had been a close-run thing. What if they'd both been asleep when His Lordship had arrived? It didn't bear thinking about. And what if Sophia had agreed to stay at his place instead, and her husband had come home to an empty house? That didn't bear thinking about either. As long as she'd managed to get his clothes under the bed, everything would be all right. Then again, what if he noticed the bed was warm on his side? Sophia would have thought of that, surely, and positioned herself accordingly. What if he could smell him? What if there were wet patches on the sheets?

Jesus Christ. Calm down, Frank, calm down. You're nearly home. You're nearly home and fucking hosed. Calm down!

Sunday nights were quiet at The Pharmacy. Drug dealers and their clients accounted for most of the customers. They'd come and go but didn't drink much. Frank's shift was four to twelve and he usually spent most of the time reading the paper.

Not tonight, however. Tonight he spent his time spilling beer, fumbling change, dropping glasses and waiting for the phone to ring. She had to ring. She had to tell him she was okay. Maybe she'd walk through the door carrying his clothes in a plastic bag, and they'd have a clandestine giggle together and talk in hushed tones about their miraculous escape.

Eight o'clock. Why didn't she ring?

Nine o'clock. Still no phone call.

A group of nurses, all regulars, made their way to their usual table in the corner by the window. One of them, Grace, came to the bar, ordered four drinks and asked Frank to put them on a tray.

'Hey,' she said as he was preparing two vodka, lime and sodas, a schooner of New and a Coke, 'you know that friend of yours who's been coming in here a lot lately — that pretty woman with the short black hair?'

'You mean Sophia?'

'Yeah, Sophia Parker. She came into emergency this afternoon. Had an accident.'

'What sort of accident?'

'Fell down some stairs or something. She looked pretty fucked up. You should give her a call. I'll give you the ward number.'

Frank stared blankly as she wrote the number on a beer coaster.

'Thanks, Grace,' he managed and took it from her with a trembling hand.

'Hey, Neville,' he said, 'I feel a bit crook. Have to go to the toilet. Back in a few minutes.'

In the cubicle, Frank fell to his knees and disgorged an impressive amount of vomit for a man who hadn't eaten a thing all day. When the convulsions subsided, he rose to his feet on shaky legs. He heard the door of the gents open and shut. Somebody coming in for a piss. He wiped his mouth with toilet paper, threw it into the toilet and flushed again.

When Frank opened the door, Kevin was waiting.

Frank heard his father's words again: 'The trick, son, is to get 'em down and keep 'em down. To get 'em down you've got to get in first and to keep 'em down, you have to kick the shit out of 'em.'

Kevin's dad, it seemed, had taught his son the same thing.

'If you let 'em get up, you're fucked.'

Frank wasn't getting up.

Frank was fucked.

CHAPTER 5

'You look fucked,' said Mick. 'What happened to you this time?'

His father always found it annoying when Frank landed in hospital. It was drinking time wasted — standing around in waiting rooms while someone patched him up, having to go outside for a smoke. Not to mention the bills.

It was hard for Frank to talk at all, let alone come up with a complex series of lies and omissions. He tried, through gritted teeth and a jaw locked shut with pins and wires, but it came out as a sort of sustained buzz.

'I can't understand a word you're saying. Can you write it down?'

The neck brace restricted Frank's movements and made it impossible for him to see his hands, but he sensed they were in pretty bad shape.

He tried moving his fingers. There they were! Poking out of plaster casts but all present and correct. That was one good thing. Ten good things, in fact.

'They tell me a bloke gave you a hiding.'

'Yes,' Frank buzzed.

'Who was he?'

'Big bloke.'

'For Christ's sake, Frank, speak up. Nurse!'

Nurse Caldicott, who had been on duty when Frank arrived and had heard the story, responded. The bandages around Frank's head were about ten deep over both ears, rendering him almost deaf. He could see Nurse Caldicott and his dad were deep in conversation but what they were saying was anybody's guess.

'Is that true, Frank?' Mick asked.

'What?' he buzzed.

'The bloke who belted you. Nobody knows who he was and you don't know him either.'

Frank grunted.

'He wouldn't happen to be some bloke who found out you'd been rooting his wife, by any chance?'

There was no doubt about the old man: his brains might have been shot but his instincts were in good working order. Frank said nothing but made the mistake of closing his eyes; a gesture Mick interpreted as a yes.

'Well, you got off fucking lightly.'

Mick thanked the nurse, put on his coat and left.

'Thanks for coming, Dad,' Frank attempted.

Instead of projecting outwards from his mouth, the words went backwards, escaping through one of the cracks in his head to be absorbed by the pillow. It was always like that when he tried to talk to his father. The old bastard had never listened to a word he'd said.

Frank wished he could talk to the bastard in the next bed. Surely the hospital had some rules regarding what radio programs patients could listen to and at what volume. A commercial talkback station with relentless advertisements and the occasional top-forty song had been his neighbour's choice and now Frank was stuck with it too. However many bandages they'd wrapped around his head, it wasn't enough.

The tubes going up into his broken nose hadn't eliminated his sense of smell either. His bed was the closest to the toilet and the industrial-strength hospital disinfectant the nurses used only made the stench worse. Its chemical pungency encouraged rather than diluted the odours, transforming them into something so virulent Frank was sure his hair would be standing on end if the bandages weren't holding it down.

Oh well, he thought, I'll get my own back when it's my turn.

Panic struck an hour later when he realised it was. The nurse had told him to press a little button if an emergency arose. He had a vague recollection of a little switch on the end of an electrical cord. Where would a sensible nurse have put it? Somewhere in reach of his fingers, surely.

Everything seemed to hurt but he didn't care. He'd gladly break another rib or an arm as long as he could find that buzzer. If he could lift his head, he might be able to have a look around. Through excruciating effort he managed to raise it about an inch from the pillow before the neck brace stopped him.

He tried working the fingers of both hands but they weren't registering contact with anything promising.

Both his arms were in plaster, but thanks to a new-found ability to swivel his eyeballs further than he'd thought possible, he could see the right one was only encased up to the elbow. It was his best hope. He tried to move it in a swinging action, and passed out as an express train of agony shot up from his shoulder, rattled his remaining teeth, ran over his brain and ended its short but spectacular journey by colliding at full speed with the back of his skull.

'Oh, Christ!' he heard when he came to a few second later. There were buzzers going off all over the place now.

'Nurse! This bloke in the next bed's shit himself.'

For a couple of days Frank was grateful for the anonymity afforded by his bandages and plaster. His black eyes and swollen lips also helped.

He was even more grateful when Grace — the nurse who'd assisted the ambulancemen when they carried him out of The Pharmacy — agreed with his whispered suggestion that large doses of morphine could be just the ticket in his particular case, and took it upon herself to administer his medication tenderly and often.

What about his friend, Mrs Parker? Grace was only able to report she'd been sent home an hour or so before he'd arrived on Sunday night. Badly bruised ribs and a few stitches in a gash on her face. Nothing serious.

Nothing personal either, thought Frank, when told that, no, she hadn't phoned the hospital to ask after him.

And what of the bloke who'd bashed him at The Pharmacy? Did anyone know who he was? Grace and her friends hadn't noticed him and weren't able to help the police, who were there when the ambulance arrived. Nobody else had seen the man come and go, Neville didn't have a clue and, no, Frank assured her, he'd never seen the bloke before in his life.

'Don't worry, I'll look after you, babe,' Grace said, closing the curtains and administering the morphine. 'Have you up and about in no time.'

Grace, he thought, of all people. Oh well, salvation came in many forms, so it was said, and Providence could have provided it in far less agreeable ones.

It was a form he'd studied closely from behind the bar and, thanks to Grace's preference for skimpy tops and hotpants made from amputated jeans, was one he knew well. About five foot four, eight stone, with large, firm breasts — both strangers to a bra — and crowned with a pretty, round face.

She had short, spiky hair, the true colour of which was difficult to determine. He'd seen it at both ends of the spectrum but right now it was jet black beneath her comical nurse's cap. Her collection of little earrings, usually arrayed in neat displays along the edge of each ear, were absent at work, but he could see the line of tiny punctures that accommodated them.

On the third day, Frank's mum came to visit. She sat awkwardly on the green vinyl chair, fidgeting, fretting and dabbing at her cheeks with a soggy handkerchief between coughs. You'd think Nurse Thornton had never seen the inside of a hospital in her life.

'Nasty cough you've got there, Mum,' Frank said. She was supposed to be comforting him, wasn't she? Not the other way round.

'The state of you, dear!'

'Just a few broken bones and bruises. Good as gold in a couple of weeks.'

'I hope you've learned your lesson this time.'

'What lesson's that, Mum?'

'Well, if as Dad said, you're going to go having an affair with another man's wife ...'

'Make sure he's a little bloke?' Frank finished.

Molly shook her head. Frank could read her thoughts: what a hopeless case, so much like his father. One working in a pub, the other living in one; one being sent to hospital, the other sending people there.

'I've brought you some chocolates and a bit of fruit,' she said, placing a plastic bag on the bedside table.

'Ask the nurse to stick them in the blender for me. Otherwise I won't be able to get them up through the straw.'

'Should have thought of that,' she said and sighed. 'You've got to laugh.'

'I'd love to, Mum, but it hurts too much.'

Sighing again, Molly rose to her feet, lingered for a few moments to caress her son's forehead, then set off for the hospital canteen. She returned ten minutes later with a more practical chocolate milkshake.

Roy, who visited Frank the next day, was doing it hard. After topping his final year at university in Honours Mathematics, he had discovered that his credentials were of little use when it came to finding a job. With classified ads for mathematical geniuses few and far between, Roy was resigning himself to a life in academe, where he could help others to become as highly qualified and unemployable as he was. This held a certain appeal for his perverse sense of humour, which found its outlet through comments made at inappropriate moments and practical jokes. Having heard some details of Frank's condition, Roy had selected his gifts carefully.

'There you go, mate,' he said, handing him the packet of chewing gum first. 'And that's not all!'

'Oh, Roy, you shouldn't have,' buzzed Frank, grimly controlling the urge to laugh as Roy showered him with two all-day suckers, a bag of chocolate-coated almonds, a new toothbrush, a couple of pornographic magazines and a tube of personal lubricant.

'Close the curtains, Roy.'

Roy did as instructed and drew the chair close to Frank's side. He had to concede Frank was in a bad way. Best not put him through any further agony by making him laugh. It was hard enough for the poor bastard just to talk.

'I have to say, Frank, you do look pretty fucked up. Do you know who did this to you?'

'Of course I do. But I don't want you doing anything about it, okay?'

'Okay. But tell me what happened.'

Frank gave a brief account of his brief affair with Sophia Mariani and his even briefer encounter with Reg in the toilet at The Pharmacy.

'I could find this bloke if you want me to, Frank. Play a little trick on him. You know the sort of thing.'

What Roy regarded as little tricks were considered serious offences by those who didn't think they were funny.

'Thanks, Roy, but no. He squared things up. The bloke's a fucking soldier — I'm lucky he didn't shoot me. And if you knew who it was I was rooting, you'd be surprised he didn't.'

'Someone I know?'

'Do you remember Miss Mariani?'

Roy stared hard at Frank as his emotions switched from compassion to jealousy. 'You bastard,' he said when the change was complete. 'You lucky, rotten bastard. If it had been me and he had shot me, I'd have died a happy man.'

Frank dearly wanted to gloat. But gloating could have led to chuckling and he wasn't prepared to take the risk. 'Just quietly,' he said instead, 'you're not dying, are you?'

'What do you mean?'

'You know — killing yourself. You look more fucked up than I do.'

'Is there a mirror around here, Frank?'

'You know what I mean.'

'You're the patient in here, not the doctor. And don't worry about me — I'm fine.'

Roy rose from the chair, pulled back the curtains and wished Frank a speedy recovery. On his way down the corridor, he stuffed his jacket pocket with a bag of syringes he spotted lying on a tray in an empty room.

The next day, Frank was sitting propped up on pillows reading a Patrick O'Brian seafaring novel and developing a fondness for narcotics to rival Roy's. He kept dozing off from time to time and waking up with forlorn but insistent erections. He wondered when might be an appropriate time to ask Grace to attend to one of them. All in a day's work for her, surely, he thought, and nodded off again.

Frank was calling to Captain Jack Aubrey from his vantage point in the crow's nest of the *Leopard*. Only he could see the *Waakzaamheid* ghosting nearer under skysails. The seventy-four must have picked up the first whisper of air, and when it brought her within gunshot she opened up with a series of rippling broadsides. The lookout crashed through the sails and landed heavily on the deck.

When he awoke, his plaster-encased fingers were trying to get a grip on the mast. The blanket had slipped to the floor, leaving the mast exposed, and Grace was discreetly drawing the curtains around his bed.

Now's as good a time as ever, he thought.

'Got a bit of a problem here, Grace.'

'You certainly have,' said Grace. 'It's the morph, Frank. That's what's causing it.'

'Don't think it's got anything to do with the morph, Grace.'

'Morph blocks you up. Heroin does the same, you know that. You haven't had a shit for nearly four days. Roll over.'

'Christ Almighty,' he pleaded, 'you're not going to …'

'Have to, babe. Don't worry, I'll help you get to the loo in time.'

'Couldn't you get one of the other nurses to do it? One of the old boilers?'

'All in a day's work, love,' she said and gently helped him to roll over onto his stomach, as determined to ignore his menacing appendage as it was hellbent on demanding her attention.

Frank had never had a litre of warm soapy water syphoned into his rectum before and was unprepared for its cataclysmic effects.

'Try and hold onto it, Frank,' Grace advised as she extracted the tube and started packing away the implement of torture.

'You've got to be joking.'

Six broken ribs, a fractured skull, missing teeth, broken arms and a jaw held together with wire failed to hinder Frank's progress as he lunged for the toilet. He would have made it too, if the door hadn't been locked.

'Jesus Christ,' said the bloke in the bed next to Frank's after the worst of it had been cleaned up and the orderlies were swabbing the deck with several gallons of disinfectant. 'What are you trying to do — kill a man?'

Grace came back to check on her patient. Her genial manner and indifference to the stench made Frank wonder if she was the best professional in the business or had been born without a sense of smell.

'You okay now, darl?' she asked. 'Can I do anything for you?'

'Actually, yes,' he said, gesturing towards his despised neighbour. 'While you're on the job, how about ramming this bloke's radio up his arse.'

'How would you like a few more broken ribs?' the neighbour offered.

'How would you like to get fucked,' Frank replied.

'Now, now,' said Grace, drawing a curtain between the warring parties and propping Frank up on his pillows again.

'You couldn't give me another hit of morph, could you, Grace?'

He tried for the same pitiable expression he'd seen on the faces of Bangladeshi children in advertisements for World Vision.

'One more, Frank, but that's it. Roll over.'

The morphine obliterated pain and embarrassment as it surged through his veins, leaving bliss and oblivion in its wake.

No doubt about that Grace, he thought, she knows some pretty unusual ways to get rid of an erection.

CHAPTER 6

When Frank woke he found himself disoriented in a world of half-light, silence and euphoria. For the second time in his life, he thought he'd died and gone to heaven.

A quick look round told him he was wrong again. The half-light was due to the phenomenon known as sunset and because no one had turned on the lights. The silence was thanks to his neighbour having turned off his radio. And the euphoria? Well, if morphine didn't make you feel good, you wouldn't take it, would you?

Frank took advantage of the painless freedom of movement he knew he'd enjoy until the drug wore off, turned his head to the left and took a good hard look at his obnoxious neighbour, now sleeping. Big bastard — sixteen stone, easy. Greasy shoulder-length hair the colour of dark chocolate. A few stray tendrils like the tails of sewer rats flopped over his forehead, partially covering an eye and coming to rest on a bloated, pockmarked cheek. His pudgy nose looked like a boxer's — the kind that had been hit so many times it would feel like a lump of gristle. Perhaps he'd decided to compensate for his lack of nose by cultivating the Zapata moustache that extended either side of his mouth and cascaded off the first of his chins to a length of about one and a half inches. It was so thick above his lip it obscured his mouth completely, posing the question as to how food could possibly penetrate it. Clearly, tons of it had.

Frank speculated about what could have happened to him. His shoulders, chest and back were criss-crossed with bandages and his neck was encased in a brace with metal buttresses. It made Frank's rubber brace seem genial by comparison. His broken arms were crossed in a pious gesture and his legs, both in plaster, were hoisted aloft by cables attached to plaster-encased feet the size of soccer balls. At the ends of the cables, massive steel weights dangled.

Bikie, Frank thought. Probably came off some Harley-Davidson at about a hundred miles an hour, which wasn't quite fast enough.

'You've got a couple of visitors, Frank.'

It was Grace. She gestured towards the door and there was Puss, peering into the room like a child taking a tentative peek into a cave where a dragon might be lurking.

He'd brought with him a short young man with an expensive haircut, neat trousers and a Hawaiian shirt, who strode into the ward and busied himself inspecting the hospital furnishings and equipment.

Encouraged by a wave and some reassuring noises from Grace, Puss followed.

'Jesus Christ, Frank, there's more plaster on you than there was on that sculpture you smashed over Wally Turner's head.'

'Steady on, Puss,' said Frank, 'don't make me laugh. Six broken ribs in there, mate.'

While Puss extracted the details of Frank's encounter with his assailant, his tiny friend made a close examination of the bed Frank was lying on.

'He king-hit me when I walked out of the dunny. Don't remember much after that.'

'Who was he?'

'Fucked if I know.'

'Don't bullshit me, Frank. You're not talking to your mother now. Besides, Roy told me: he was the husband of the delectable Miss Mariani.'

'Delectable?' said Frank, puzzled. 'I didn't think she was quite your type.'

'Frank, when we were at school I used to pray for that woman to straighten me out.'

Puss's mystery friend joined them and took command of the green vinyl chair, but only after examining it first.

'Frank,' said Puss, 'this is Shorty Bannister.'

'That's a great shirt, Shorty,' said Frank. 'Could you turn it down a bit?'

'Greg,' said Shorty.

'Shorty runs an advertising agency,' said Puss. 'It's going really well — gangbusters, in fact. Isn't it, Shorty?'

Greg nodded.

A man of few words, thought Frank. One so far.

'Shorty's been giving me a bit of freelance work. Storyboards, layouts — you know the sort of thing.'

Frank, who had never heard of storyboards or layouts and wasn't sure what freelance meant, nodded and said, 'Of course'.

'Oh good,' said Greg, suddenly coming to life, 'in that case you might be able to give me a bit of help. I'm preparing a pitch for a company that sells medical equipment. Everything from dentist's chairs and hospital beds to life-support systems. The account's worth a fortune. If you had to sell that sort of stuff to doctors, what angle would you take?'

'Patient comfort,' said Frank. 'Convince the doctors that the bed I was trying to flog was more comfortable than any of the others. I'd be telling them that all the gear I had on offer was designed with the comfort of the patient in mind.'

'Wouldn't you be emphasising the health advantages first?'

'People in hospitals are either going to get better or they're going to die — let's face it. All the doctors want is for them not to be ringing their buzzers all day because their backs or their arses are sore. The nurses in this place spend half their time running around adjusting pillows and cranking back supports to stop pricks like this bloke in the bed next to mine from whingeing all day.'

'Why don't you get fucked,' said the prick in the bed, who had woken up.

'That's what your doctors are looking for — anything that keeps bastards like this bloke quiet.'

Shorty was impressed.

'I've brought some books for you, Frank,' Puss said.

Mordecai Richler, Henry Miller, Anthony Burgess. All his favourites. Dear old Puss.

'You should see the things Roy gave me,' said Frank. 'Have a look in the top drawer, but don't touch anything. I don't want your fingerprints on it. When I get out of here I'm going to have him charged with attempted murder.'

Puss and Shorty burst into laughter. Frank sensed he was in danger of doing the same.

'Cut it out,' he pleaded. 'If I laugh you'll have my ribs popping like champagne corks.'

'I like the way you use the language,' said Shorty, delving into his briefcase and handing Frank some typed sheets. 'See what you can do with this.'

'What is it?' said Frank.

'It's called a brief,' said Puss. 'Maybe you could come up with an angle or two for an ad campaign. You could bullshit under wet cement with a mouthful of marbles. What do you reckon, Shorty?'

Shorty needed no further convincing. He'd already heard Frank do it with a mouthful of wire and broken teeth.

No need to rush into things, thought Frank, who didn't want excessive stress delaying his recovery. He decided to prioritise his commitments to maximise efficiency.

Desolation Island had to be finished first. After that it would be a toss-up between the Burgess and the Miller. He'd save Richler's *The Apprenticeship of Duddy Kravitz*, even though several friends had told him it was hilarious. He calculated his ribs would be ready for the onslaught in about a fortnight.

The work for Puss would have to come last. He had to read this 'brief' and jot down a few ideas. It *was* brief, so couldn't be too hard, but it was also work and could wait until he was good and ready.

Relations between Frank and his neighbour had started at the level of loathing and deteriorated from there. The effort of turning their respective heads was equally uncomfortable for both, so they contented themselves with abusive exchanges seemingly directed at those in the beds on the opposite side of the ward.

His name was Mr Ken Bottomley, but his regular visitor — referred to as Face — addressed him formally as Bottler and, occasionally, Botts. Face's Bandidos jacket confirmed the two were bikies, more concerned with the well-being of Bottler's Harley-Davidson than with Bottler himself.

'How is she, Face?' Bottler would ask.

'She's gonna be okay, Botts mate,' Face would reply, thus relieving his friend's anxiety and allowing the conversation to move on to more frivolous matters such as gang-bangs, rapes and assaults.

Frank could hear every word. The bandages over his ears had been removed, revealing a complex network of stitches on the shaved back of his head, now glazed with a high-gloss varnish to keep the

47

embroidery dry in the unlikely event he'd enjoy the luxury of a shower in the coming weeks.

While Bottler and Face plotted revenge and mayhem, Frank battled through Antarctic storms, survived countless gory adventures and eventually swashbuckled his way to the final sentence of *Desolation Island*.

The decision as to what to read next saw Burgess's *Enderby* win by a margin of ten inches over Miller's *Rosy Crucifixion*, which was precisely that much further away.

The first word was one he'd never seen written before: 'PFFFRRRUMMMP' — a linguistic invention intended to approximate the noise of a loud fart.

'Hey, Bottler,' Frank gritted through his clenched jaw. 'I didn't know you knew Anthony Burgess.'

'I don't.'

'Well, he's quoted you right here in his book,' said Frank, attempting a rendition of a farting noise by flapping his lips. 'It's something I heard you say last night.'

'Fuck off,' said Bottler.

A week later, Frank was persevering with Miller's *Rosy Crucifixion*, despite the unavoidable erections that popped up every few pages.

At about midnight, when the other patients were snoring in atonal chorus, Grace, noticing that Frank's reading light was on, asked if he felt like a cuppa.

'That'd be lovely, Grace,' he said.

She returned a few minutes later, drew the curtains around his bed, placed the mugs of tea on the chest of drawers and, finally, did the right thing.

'I'm on night duty tomorrow, too,' she whispered, dexterously wiping several billion potential baby Franks from her chin and his belly with an absorbent paper towel. 'Better get rid of the evidence.'

The next morning, Frank found himself imbued with a new sense of purpose.

The brief from Puss's friend, Shorty, consisted of three photocopied pages of poorly worded praise for Suk-it-up Tidy-Wipes, a household necessity vastly more efficient than a host of similar products on the market. Thanks to the ingenuity of the researchers in the laboratories of the Modicare group of companies,

Suk-it-up Tidy-Wipes represented nothing less than a technological revolution.

Frank started jotting down notes as ideas — or 'concepts' as he'd now have to call them — came into his head. He considered the handwriting. Not bad for a man with plaster casts covering most of his hands. He made several sketches that seemed adequate for their purpose.

If that's a day's work in advertising then maybe it's the job for me, he thought, then turned over a fresh page, wrote down Puss's phone number and buzzed for the nurse.

'Nurse, would you do me a favour and ring this friend of mine? His name's Neil. Could you ask him if he could come and see me today? I've got some work to show him.'

'Of course, Frank,' she said.

'And, Nurse Caldicott — if you could ask him to bring a black texta pen? I'll need it to finish the work I'm doing. Tell him to make sure it's the biggest, thickest one he can get.'

Nurse Caldicott was back within minutes. 'Your friend said he'd be over around six. Is there anything else I can get for you?'

Frank still had a day to kill. 'Copy of today's paper would be good, if you've got one.'

By mid-afternoon, Frank was as up to date on current affairs as he felt he needed to be. Having read the comics, he found himself staring at the nonsensical clues of the cryptic crossword. He knew Puss devoted himself daily to the solving of these impenetrable puzzles. Perhaps it was time to give it a go.

He looked down the list of meaningless phrases, truncated sentences and unanswerable questions and stopped when he came to: No noose is good noose (7,6).

What the hell could that mean?

The answer seemed obvious enough: the bloke compiling the clues didn't know how to spell 'news'. Then again, he probably could, given the nature of his occupation.

Frank gave him the benefit of the doubt and reread the clue several times, finding the pun as amusing as it was perplexing. What was this bloke getting at? Whatever it was, at least he had a sense of humour. Gallows humour in his case, Frank thought, and chuckled.

Then, with the closest thing to a howl of delight a man with his jaw wired up could muster, Frank inscribed 'GALLOWS HUMOUR' in the blank spaces for fifteen across. He'd completed almost half the puzzle when Puss arrived at six-thirty.

Soon Puss was helping with the rest of the clues, each one a revelation. Frank learned that some words contained other words, words appeared between words, some words became new words when you read them backwards, and that homophones, acrostics and spoonerisms were just a few of the weapons in the crossword compiler's armoury. But the thing that excited him most was the discovery of the anagram. How could he have attained the age of twenty-three without being aware of such wonders?

'Stifle is the only word that's an anagram of itself,' said Puss, causing Frank to stare blankly for a few moments. He then mentally rearranged the letters in 'itself', composed them into 'stifle', and shouted 'Brilliant!' in his triumph.

'Good. Now, about this —'

'I've got a horn,' Frank said, 'slap-bang in the middle of my name and I'd never even realised it. Look — "front horn tank" — that's an anagram of my name! Tank Front Horn — that's me! Let's work out some anagrams of Neil Puesner. Let's see ... you've got a penis in there, Puss. And a nurse!'

'Not now, Frank. I really wanted to know if you've thought about the ad.'

'I've done it. A campaign idea, a slogan — the lot.'

Frank made his pitch. Puss was amused but not persuaded.

'It'll cause a bloody outrage, Frank.'

'Isn't that the whole idea?'

'I'm not sure Shorty's quite ready for this. We'll see what he thinks,' Puss said and packed Frank's notes into his briefcase.

'Penile nurse!' Frank announced. 'It's an anagram of Neil Puesner!'

'Very good, Frank,' said Puss, waving from the door, 'you're catching on.'

'God, you go on with a lot of crap,' said Bottler after Puss had left the room.

'Fuck off,' Frank said and fell to musing about the anagrammatical possibilities of 'Ken Bottomley'.

He reached for his notepad, started scrambling letters.

'Hey, Bottle Monkey,' he said.

'You talkin' to me?' said Bottler.

'Yeah,' said Frank. 'Get fucked, Bottle Monkey.'

He'd had a busy day: read the paper; developed an advertising strategy that would launch his new career; sold the concept to Puss; discovered a new addiction in cryptic crossword solving; and fallen in love with anagrams. And the night was but young! He found himself humming 'Amazing Grace', even though he'd always hated the song.

A week later, after the otolangologist had removed the wires and pins from his jaw, Frank was mortified to wake up from the anaesthetic and find it felt as riveted as ever. The news that his diet would continue in liquid form for another fortnight wasn't welcome either, but being told he could leave the hospital the next day certainly was.

It would be a lonely night. Grace wasn't on duty and, while his maxillomandibular fixation may have been removed, the one he'd developed for Grace had not.

Mordecai Richler came to the rescue, making pleasant work of the hours Frank had to kill before everyone else in the ward was asleep.

Bottler was always the first to go. By ten-thirty, he could hear him snoring in his familiar flamboyant fashion. Frank had analysed the Bottomley Nasal Orchestra's work and was in awe of his vocal range. Most nights, Bottler spent the first half hour or so tuning his various instruments. When satisfied all were prepared, he'd let the whole band rip at once in a fanfare that made the *1812 Overture* sound like 'Baa-Baa Black Sheep'.

At midnight, even the newcomer to the ward — an arrival from yesterday who had come off second-best in a confrontation with a bus — had succumbed to whatever miracle drug they were pumping through him and had stopped moaning at last. It was the moment Frank had been waiting for.

There, where Puss had left it in the drawer next to his bed, was the big black texta pen. With the sure hand of a signwriter, he inscribed the word 'cunt' across the soles of Bottler's plastered feet in enormous capitals, went for a pee and, on returning, admired his handiwork for a minute before climbing back into bed, switching off the reading light and doing his best not to think about Grace. Those casts on his arms and hands were there for another couple of weeks, and that still wasn't a job he could attempt alone.

Three pile-ups were reported on Parramatta Road during the peak-hour period on the morning after the billboards went up. There was a bad one in Balmain, and up in Palm Beach someone had driven off the road and straight into a newsagency.

'The clown responsible for this should be put in jail!' said an indignant caller to the king of Sydney talkback radio. There were few defenders of this latest advertising outrage, and they were rapidly cut off. The talkback king was in full moralising mode and nothing was going to stop him.

Frank's desk, in a corner near a window overlooking Miller Street, North Sydney, was covered with the morning's three major newspapers. Each featured front-page photographs of his billboards, accompanied by articles about standards of public decency and where it would all end.

'Looks like you got the trifecta, Frank,' said Shorty. 'All three papers, front page.'

All over Sydney, motorists, commuters and passers-by were being affronted by billboards featuring three images of a beautiful dark-tanned girl with untidy blonde hair. Each photo showed the girl from the top of her head down to her belly button. She wore a tiny pink bikini top, made for a woman with breasts about half the size, and held in her right hand a recently licked ice-cream cone, which poked impertinently into the bottom left-hand corner of each shot. In the left of the three images, several dollops of ice-cream appeared around the girl's mouth and dripped from her chin. The little creamy patches had a translucent quality. The middle photo showed the girl wiping her mouth and chin with a deft swipe of a paper towel, and the one on the right showed her with chin and mouth as clean as a whistle. To the right of this arresting triptych was a deep-etched picture of a cylindrical container of Suk-it-up Tidy-Wipes and the slogan: 'Get rid of the evidence!'

'Wait till they see the ones we've done for the telly,' said Frank.

The next day, after three weeks in the advertising business and one week back on solids, Frank received a phone call at four in the afternoon from Harry Parkinson, whose agency enjoyed a reputation as Australia's number one.

'Frank Thornton?'

'That's me.'

'Harry Parkinson here. We want you to come and work with us.'

'It'll cost you.'

'What'll it cost? You tell me.'

Hmm, thought Frank. I was getting ten grand a year at The Pharmacy, I'm on twenty-six here …

'You'll get me for seventy-five.'

'Can you start on Monday?'

'What time?'

'Would nine-thirty suit?'

'That's a bit early, isn't it?'

'Make it ten-thirty.'

Frank was up and running.

CHAPTER 7

A skinny kid from Queensland knocked out Basher Blackwell towards the end of the second round. Neither Frank nor Puss could believe it had happened. They'd paid good money for the tickets and Frank had put two hundred and fifty dollars on Basher to win.

The first preliminary fight had been so pathetic Frank and Puss had vacated their seats in preference to playing the pokies in the room next door. They kept an eye on the succeeding two bouts via the TV screen, making sure to return to their seats in time to see Basher enter the ring. They'd lost about fifty dollars each by the time he did and were glad to get out of there.

The first round was a non-event: both boxers sizing each other up and working out their strategies. A second or two before the bell, Basher let fly with a combination of lefts and rights that definitely won him the round. It gave the impertinent little Queensland bastard something to think about and Puss and Frank a reason to relax.

'He'll kill him,' Frank said.

Puss agreed. 'We'll be back playing the pokies after the next round,' he said, 'and you'll have another two fifty to play with.'

The bell sounded and the little terrier from Queensland commenced proceedings with a new attitude and a series of sharp left jabs that shocked Frank and Puss with their power and timing almost as much as they shocked Basher.

'Come on, Basher — hit him,' Puss urged.

'He'll be right, he'll be right,' Frank insisted, rising to his feet. 'Oh fuck!'

Back in the pokies room, the pair were too appalled at what they'd seen to speak. They drank their beers in silence and communicated through sullen gestures, nodding towards the bar for refills and pointing towards the cashier for more rolls of coins. There was an understanding between them that when the machine had swallowed all but the cab fare home it was time to leave. When the moment arrived, they rose and headed for the door.

'Still can't fucking believe it,' Puss mumbled.

'One hell of an uppercut,' said Frank.

It was raining. Pissing down. Their mutual emotional desolation was expressed by Puss as he wailed, 'Where do all the cabs go in the fucking rain?'

Frank sat in the bar of The Rocks Push, trying to describe the tragic spectacle of Basher Blackwell's last fight to Roy Humber. It wasn't easy. There was a trad-jazz band in full swing, playing the sort of music Roy enjoyed most and which, in Frank's opinion, was precisely what gave jazz a bad name.

Roy, who liked to bet on the horses but had no interest in other sports, least of all boxing, suggested to Frank he should either shut the fuck up and listen or piss off.

Frank was making up his mind when he noticed a large man wearing a beanie, a black overcoat and dark glasses take a seat at the other end of the bar.

'That's him!' he hissed, tugging Roy's sleeve.

'Who?'

'Arthur Blackwell! That's him!'

'Arthur who?'

Frank left finger-clicking Roy alone and, trying to look as casual as possible, ordered a beer while standing next to Arthur 'Basher' Blackwell. Two nights ago he'd watched Arthur's knees turning to jelly after the combination of lefts and rights that had knocked him out. Now Frank realised something similar was happening to his own.

Two months earlier, Arthur Blackwell had written off his beloved Ford Mustang when he veered off Barrenjoey Road in Palm Beach and ploughed into a newsagency after seeing Frank's advertisement for Suk-it-up Tidy-Wipes.

He was an artist and illustrator in the Dickensian dungeon also known as the art department of the *Sun* newspaper, where, after five or so years, he was becoming tired of airbrushing pimples off celebrities' faces and deep-etching photographs of politicians. His three years of training at Sydney's Julian Ashton Art School and subsequent two years spent wearing out pencils, charcoal sticks and brushes at the Slade School in London were starting to seem like a waste of time.

Arthur knew his boxing career was over. There were plenty of up-and-coming young fighters whose form he'd been studying closely, knowing full well it was only a matter of time before one of them battered the bejesus out of him, to everyone's surprise except his own, and that bloke had materialised in Marrickville two nights before.

Arthur removed his shades, though it wasn't easy to tell the difference. His eyes were black and swollen, the left also boasting a gash that divided the eyebrow into upper and lower halves, sewn together with all the delicacy one might expect of a farmer stitching a hessian bag.

Frank raised a comparatively pristine right eyebrow at the sight of Basher Blackwell replacing his shades with a pair of half-moon reading glasses of the type one would expect to find on the end of a professorial, rather than a pugilistic nose. His left brow went up even further when Arthur pulled a copy of *Goya: Man Among Kings* from another pocket, sipped his beer through swollen lips, and started reading.

Frank had two heroes and here he was, standing at a bar next to one who was reading a book about the other.

He noted that Arthur was starting on a chapter dealing with the subject of Goya's Black Paintings. Frank planned to make a pilgrimage — one of these days — to the Prado Museum in Madrid to see those very paintings, reproductions of which had been known to have an effect on his knees not unlike the one he was feeling now.

Arthur seemed to sense he wasn't the only one reading his book. He flashed a glare in Frank's direction that moved the wobbliness from Frank's knees to his bowels. Something had to give, and it would have to come from either his mouth or his arse.

'Frank Thornton's the name,' he blurted, thrusting out his hand, 'I'm a big fan of yours. I was there on Tuesday night. Couldn't believe it when that little prick knocked you out. Had two hundred and fifty on you too.'

'In that case I suppose I owe you a beer.'

'No, no, that's not what I mean. I thought you were way out in front up until that stage. I didn't think the other bloke had a chance.'

56

'Someone out there was punching shit out of me, Frank, and I don't think it was the referee. Come on, let me buy you a beer.'

'Thanks, Basher.'

'Call me Arthur. What'll you have?'

Frank's bowels stopped troubling him as he found himself conversing easily with Arthur, who seemed to know even more than he did — and he considered himself something of an authority — about Goya.

'He was the greatest, wasn't he, Arthur?' Frank gushed.

'He was a great man. Great men make great art. Pissants paint pictures.'

It seemed to Frank that Arthur had very strong opinions about art for a man who made his living by punching other blokes' heads in.

'Do you paint yourself?' he asked.

'I do a bit. When I can find the time.'

'When you're not training?'

'There's no dough in boxing for me any more. I work for a newspaper. Touching up people in photographs — not in the ring.'

'Good money?'

'Shithouse money. It's a job, though. Leaves me a bit of time to paint.'

'Ever thought of working in advertising?'

'No.'

'In that case, I might be able to help.'

Frank wrote his phone number on a beer coaster. 'Give us a call in the morning.'

'What sort of work do you do?' Arthur asked.

'Copywriter. Always on the lookout for someone who can draw. Plenty of work if you like the idea of doing storyboards and illustrations. I come up with ideas for ads. Actually my first one is still my best. Remember the Suk-it-up kitchen towel campaign?'

'Oh right,' said Arthur. 'You're the cunt who cost me my car.'

CHAPTER 8

Frank hated Christmas.

'Christ' was a word regularly heard in the Thornton household. 'Fuck' was too, Frank thought, but you didn't have to meet once a year to celebrate the anniversary of its introduction into the vernacular.

His disdain for the industry he'd worked in for several years now intensified as Christmas drew near. Atheist though he was, it seemed to Frank that Baby Jesus wasn't being invited to his own birthday party these days. Profit revivals were what Christmas was all about; the prophet's arrival had nothing to do with it. Coca-Cola advertising had invented Santa Claus, and it was as hard to draw a connection between him and the birth of Christ as it was to work out how an annual bonanza for chocolate manufacturers related to his death.

He looked again at the design for the staff Christmas card he'd been asked to create. It featured a fluorescent baby, glowing away in a manger in Chernobyl. The three men in Frank's nativity were wise enough to be wearing radiation-proof overalls, all were clearly shocked by what they saw, and a speech bubble had one of them exclaiming, 'Jesus Christ Almighty!'

Yep, it looked good, all right. Frank chuckled quietly and decided it was time to show it to Harry Parkinson.

Parkinson's response showed that not only did he possess sensibilities but they were capable of being offended. 'Jesus Christ Almighty,' he roared. 'I should have known better than to leave the job to you.'

Frank's design was replaced and he left for his Christmas break under a cloud as poisonous as the one that had caused havoc across Europe earlier in the year.

It was being widely claimed that Chernobyl had changed the world forever. Frank's own world had changed so dramatically he often wondered if Chernobyl was to blame. At thirty, Frank was a confirmed bachelor and determined to remain one; yet, less than a month after the catastrophe, his girlfriend Natalie had moved in with him and, seven months later, here they were planning Christmas together with their relationship still intact. So intact that Frank was taking the risk of going accompanied to the annual barbecue at the family home for the first time.

If Natalie's parents hadn't been on their dream holiday on the *Fairstar*, Christmas this year would have been spent in Avoca, ninety minutes drive north of Sydney, where her parents' cottage sat amongst gum trees, parrots and possums, within walking distance of the beach. During the time they'd been living together, Frank and Natalie had visited the place twice. Her parents seemed to like Frank. They'd made him feel part of a family Frank likened to the Brady Bunch in jokes that disguised jealousy with contempt.

The day's activities would have included a swim and sandcastle building with Natalie's nephew, Adrian, who, at two, was as ambitious when undertaking such projects as he was inept at seeing them through. His six-year-old sister, Phoebe, was too grown-up for sandcastles. She could read stories to glamorous Aunty Natalie now — not the other way round — and thought the world of funny Uncle Frank.

Instead they were spending Christmas Day with Frank's family. Natalie couldn't understand why Frank was so on edge about it, coming up with alternative suggestions every other day, manufacturing excuses not to go that varied from the improbable to the downright rude.

'Honestly, the way you go on,' she said, 'you sound like you're ashamed of them.'

'Not ashamed of them,' Frank said. 'It's just that, for the first time ever, I could be spending Christmas Day with my girlfriend's family instead.'

'Your girlfriend's family is not an option so let's just enjoy ourselves, shall we?'

The day got off to a bad start.

They'd spent Christmas Eve partying hard with friends. So Santa, on seeing them both sprawled on their bed and Frank still fully clothed, left hangovers as presents and went straight back up the chimney.

Natalie woke to the sound of Frank retching in the bathroom, leaving her with no choice but to head for the kitchen and do her retching at the sink.

'How can you even look at a beer after a night like that?' she said some time later, blowing on her camomile tea and sipping with caution.

'Hair of the dog,' Frank said. 'Works wonders.'

And it did, but it always took more than one. After three, Frank was revitalised to the point where he felt capable of affecting the cheerfulness expected of lovers on Christmas Day. He ambled off to the bedroom where he'd hidden Natalie's French perfume and sexy lingerie in a drawer.

When he returned she was still seated at the kitchen table, but now she had a present in front of her too, which she insisted he open first.

Its shape and weight told him it was a book and filled him with confidence. Frank had difficulty choosing presents. It was a risky undertaking and a bad choice could leave you feeling embarrassed. If you were too extravagant you ran the risk of making the other person's present seem trifling; a situation even worse when reversed. A book seemed just right, he thought, as he ripped open the wrapping paper.

He feigned happiness at discovering it was *Cities of the Red Night* by William S. Burroughs, a paperback copy of which sat somewhere on his shelves. He'd read it, twice, three years before. This one, a hardback edition, was an improvement, but a letdown just the same.

He opened the card, hoping the message would give him an opportunity to show some real enthusiasm. It said: 'For my darling Frank, merry Christmas, with all my love, Natalie.'

Oh well, he thought as he kissed and thanked her, at least my present is going to come up trumps.

'Have a look inside,' Natalie whispered.

There on the title page was a handwritten message: 'For Frank Thornton, in hope he is still alive, William S. Burroughs.'

He stared, blinked, and stared again. When he turned his stare to Natalie's eyes, his own were filled with tears. It was a wonderful gift, the most precious object he had ever owned, and he didn't know what to say.

Natalie, a photographic model, had recently been on an assignment in Los Angeles.

'On the flight, I sat next to a journalist named Jack Ames,' she said. 'He told me he was going to Kansas to interview Burroughs for a feature article in a magazine. I know how much you like him so I asked the guy if he could get him to sign a book for you.'

Frank had never seen expensive French perfume and lingerie look as cheap as Natalie's did when she unwrapped them and responded with delight. His present for her now seemed thoughtless and banal. Undies and splash-on for a model. Like giving a screwdriver to a carpenter.

He fondled his book, opened it, took another look at the inscription, and felt unworthy.

'Two peas in a pod, you are,' was what Molly would say to her two little boys, ruffling identical haircuts that served to make the pair look more like identical twins than brothers separated in age by two years. But Bob and Frank were separated by more than just age. They resided in the same house but they lived in different worlds and those two worlds were constantly at war. They didn't know it of course, but they were fighting for the love of their father. Mick didn't have much love in him, and the little there was wasn't enough to go around. Bob got a little, Frank got none.

'Only a mother could pick you apart,' was another one of her well-worn phrases. This one would often get an airing over the dinner table. Across the laminex, slopping peas and gravy, Bob and Frank would scowl at each other. They could pick each other apart, all right; they could tear each other apart. They would grow apart eventually and, even when their ages were still in single figures, both knew the process was already under way.

The process had been complete for many years before the day Frank took Natalie home for Christmas dinner. She did an involuntary double-take when Frank introduced her to his brother, Bob. He rarely mentioned Bob, yet his brother looked like a quieter version of him: the shorter, abridged issue, with the X-rated chapters left out. A mother could pick them apart but a stranger would have to look twice.

Familial similarities were less discernible in their sister, Nina. Natalie fell to wondering how these three siblings could have resulted from three collisions occurring in the same uterus between three sperm cells originating in the same pair of balls. Frank and Bob? Well, obviously. But Nina? Natalie had a habit of assessing people by making mental notes of how their appearance could be improved. A weight-reducing diet would be her first recommendation in this case. It would take three months and a loss of twelve kilos to trim Nina's body down to the shape it probably was about ten years ago, and that would have been a very attractive one indeed. A dash of deep burgundy would get rid of the mousy hair and there was certainly nothing wrong with her eyes that a bit of mascara wouldn't fix. Nothing wrong with her cheekbones either, or her mouth — arguably her number one asset. Get those teeth capped and Nina could be doing advertisements for toothpaste. There were the makings of a very pretty woman in this sister of Frank's, but it took a well-trained eye like Natalie's to see her.

No cosmetic treatments, not even surgery and liposuction, would ever transform her husband, Red, into anything aesthetically appealing but surely plucking a few hundred hairs out with a pair of tweezers to create two eyebrows out of one wouldn't be too much to ask.

Nina and Red's children — Matthew, eleven, and Amanda, eight — were so beautiful that Natalie immediately assumed Nina had been married before, or undergone IVF. Then again, if someone said that handsome, fine-boned, dark-eyed and black-haired Matthew was Serbian, you'd probably believe it. And Amanda, despite her fair complexion and carbon copies of her mother's eyes, *did* have her father's curls and could also pass for southern European, so maybe they were Red's kids after all. Poor Nina.

As for Bob's wife Melissa, what did it matter if she was presentable but plain in Natalie's eyes? It was clear that in Bob's eyes she was the most beautiful woman on earth, had provided him with the world's most adorable children — Angus, four, and Jasmine, one — and it was how they saw each other that counted.

By the time Frank and Natalie got there at three, the junior members of the Thornton clan were bored with most of their presents and had broken the rest. For them, Frank's arrival was more like witnessing the second coming of Christ than commemorating his first with cakes and cordial. Flash Uncle Frank could always be relied upon to provide lavish surprises and this year he had a whole carful.

But each show of generosity towards his nephews and nieces constituted an unconscious act of cruelty towards their parents, whose offerings were instantly forgotten when superseded by Frank's.

The gifts he'd bought for the adults were gratefully but resentfully received, as each despondent recipient smiled while reciprocating with novelties and ashtrays.

'Old money-bags, eh?' Mick sneered, opening his box of a dozen bottles of Johnnie Walker Black Label whisky. He passed Frank one bottle of Red Label in return.

Natalie noticed the dark looks that passed between Nina and Molly, aware this exchange of gifts had upset them both.

'They're not real pearls, are they, Frank?' gasped Molly, weeping when Frank confirmed that they were. She was as overwhelmed by her son's generosity as she was aware of the impossibility of ever being able to wear them without appearing ostentatious amongst her friends.

'You can't please all the people all the time,' Frank grumbled to Natalie as they headed to his car to fetch the microwave for Nina.

Nina was overjoyed when she opened the box. She'd been badgering Red to buy her one for years.

''nother beer, Frank?'

'Thanks, Red.'

'Nice-looking tart,' Red said as he groped in the ice-filled sink in the laundry. 'She on the game?'

He was a big bloke, Red. He worked hard and it showed. At first glance you'd dismiss him as overweight, but on closer inspection you'd notice his arms and upper body were hard as rock beneath that sweaty T-shirt and carpet of black hair.

Frank chose to ignore the remark, happy to see Natalie heading towards them, bringing with her the chance to relieve the tension by formally introducing his brother-in-law.

'Red?' she asked.

'Redenko,' Frank explained. 'Red's Yugoslavian.'

'Serbian.'

'Sorry, General,' said Frank, steering Natalie away. 'My mistake.'

'Is he a military man?' Natalie asked Frank, once out of hearing range.

'"General" is a private joke — short for general anaesthetic. Bloke's a crushing bore, especially when he's pissed and starts on all that tribal stuff. If you want to really give him the shits, try calling him Croatian.'

With Matthew's radio-controlled dune buggy crashing into everyone's legs and stirring up the dust, Mick yelling at him to take the bloody thing out onto the street, and Angus in trouble for tearing the dress off Jasmine's doll, Mum's announcement that she was going inside to prepare the salads gave Frank a welcome escape. He winked at Natalie and nodded in the direction of the house.

Nina wasn't affronted by Natalie's good looks or the simple elegance of her short cotton dress. The two of them drifted into the lounge with glasses of cask Riesling and settled for a while on the couch where Nina spoke openly to Natalie about her irresponsible but loveable brother. Her reassuring, almost congratulatory, manner unsettled Natalie, who hadn't been aware she was engaged in the process of civilising a primitive man or doing a commendable job of persevering with a difficult work in progress.

In the kitchen with his mum, Frank had the chance to give her a cuddle at last.

'You're not sick, are you, Mum?' he asked.

'Just a bit of a cough, that's all.'

'Have you seen a doctor?'

'I will if these pains in the shoulder get any worse.'

Dear Molly — a nurse who was as obstinate as any of her elderly patients when being urged by her to see the doctor.

'I'm okay, Frank,' she said. 'How about you?'

'Good as gold,' he replied, taking a beer from the fridge. 'What do you think of Natalie?'

'I haven't had a chance to talk to her much yet but she seems nice. Very pretty girl. Where does she come from?'

'Born in Sydney. Parents live up the Central Coast. Her mum's Spanish. Got her looks from her which was bloody lucky. Her dad's got a head like a beaten favourite. But she's not just a pretty face, Mum, she's bright too and she's always so kind to me. That's why I love her, I guess. She's just so ... kind.'

'And are you kind to her, Frank?'

Natalie was at a loss to understand why Frank had been apprehensive about introducing her to his family. She watched as he talked and joked with his sister and his mother while pricking the sausages and slicing the ham. The solidity of their mutual affection was as enduring as the tarnished laminex on the table, as dependable as the ugly chrome and vinyl chairs. Maybe this was what he didn't want her to see: the closeness he shared with these two women. It proved he was capable of intimacy, so why couldn't he be intimate with her?

'More pricks in these sausages than there are in advertising,' Frank announced. 'Better get out and get the barbie started.'

'I can't get over how alike they are,' Natalie mused as she watched Frank join his brother in the backyard.

'I'm afraid so,' said Molly. 'As they say, dear, "like father, like son".'

Natalie looked confused.

'I think Natalie was talking about Frank and Bob,' Nina explained.

'Oh, yes, Bob and Frank do look alike, don't they?' Molly said, realising her mistake. 'But that's where the similarities end. Frank's more like his father.'

'But don't let that worry you, Natalie — Dad has his good points too,' Nina added with a sympathetic laugh.

Molly grinned grimly and changed the subject to the whereabouts of the canned beetroot and that *blessed* mayonnaise.

The barbecue dominating the backyard was an impressive brick structure destined to outlive the fibro house. The time had come for the men to get the fire going. Frank and Red started the process, but it was ultimately accomplished by Bob, who told them to get out of the bloody road.

Frank and Mick were working on the whisky. As Bob blew onto the fire to encourage the flames, Frank held his father back, 'Don't you blow on it, Dad, or it'll go up like a bloody bomb.'

The joke appealed to Mick and Red, but didn't amuse Bob, who feared it might be true.

Natalie warmed to Frank's brother as he went about his business while the other men quaffed drinks, offered advice from the sidelines and complained about the smoke getting in their eyes. It was also Bob who assumed control of the tongs, making sure the sausages didn't get burnt and the chops and steaks were done to a turn. She observed the way he prepared meals for Melissa and Angus before taking some leftovers for himself — all that remained after everyone else had tucked in.

There wasn't enough of Molly's Christmas pudding to go round, so some of the adults had to content themselves with cake. All in all, though, it wasn't a bad feed. Everyone except Natalie had achieved bloatedness by the time it was finished and Matthew and Amanda felt satisfactorily sick.

'We'd better be getting off,' said Bob. 'Time to get these babies home to bed.'

'Christ, it's not even eight o'clock,' said Mick, glaring at his son.

'Come on, Angus, there we go,' said Bob, lifting his son onto his hip while Melissa wrapped Jasmine in a cotton blanket. 'It was a pleasure to meet you, Natalie.'

'A pleasure to meet you too, Bob, Melissa. Goodnight, Angus,' she said. The boy proved too shy to accept kisses from strangers. Jasmine, on the other hand, gurgled appreciatively.

'She's getting a bit clucky, that sheila of yours,' said Mick, prodding Frank with his elbow.

Frank dismissed the remark with a shrug.

'If you're not up to it, Frank, I'll do the job for you,' Red said.

'Fuck off,' said Frank. 'Jesus, Dad, we've knocked over my Christmas present already. Better get started on one of yours.'

Two hours later, Natalie started hinting to Frank that she thought it was time they left. The effects of the night before were taking their toll and she was finding it hard to keep awake.

'Make Nat a cup of coffee, will you, Mum?' said Frank. 'She's nodding off over there.'

'I think she's tired, dear,' Molly said.

'Just do as you're fucking well told,' Mick snarled.

Molly scurried towards the kitchen and Frank fixed his father with bleary eyes. 'I hate it when you talk to Mum like that.'

'Yeah, well, if you talk to your father like that you'll get a smack in the head from Santa.'

Red grinned. This Christmas suddenly had the potential to become something more memorable, but the momentum was spoiled by Natalie who drew Frank away and whispered something to him.

'Drink your bloody coffee and lighten up.' Frank responded.

'That's an awful cough, Molly,' Natalie said, settling back into conversation with the other women.

Nina, too, was concerned and insisted her mother visit a doctor. But her words were drowned out by Frank and Mick's raucous response to Red's suggestion that Aussie Rules was a game for fucking poofters.

Another argument broke out soon after when Nina told Red it was time to go home and Red told her to piss off.

'Come on, love,' she said. 'The kids are both asleep in front of the telly and I think Mum should be getting to bed.'

Natalie, watching from the kitchen as Red growled and swore at Nina, wondered why neither Frank nor Mick felt compelled to intervene.

She took matters into her own hands, thanked Molly for a lovely night, grabbed Frank by the elbow and told him they were going home whether he liked it or not.

'Ah, all right,' said Frank. 'Night, Dad. Night, Red.'

'See you, Frank,' slurred Mick. 'Nice to meet you, sweetheart. Happy Christmas.'

Inside the house, Natalie gathered their bags and Nina and Molly escorted them both to the door.

'Night, Nene,' said Frank, bestowing kisses, not noticing the tears. 'Night, Mum.'

Frank slumped in the passenger's seat, as animated as a sack of rice. Natalie fastened his safety belt around him. She'd spent the day with two quite different men. She loved the one she'd watched conversing with his mother and sister in the kitchen, but she didn't love this one at all. She expected to hear him start snoring any minute, but instead she heard chuckling.

'What's funny?' she said.

'My dad,' he slurred, 'such a funny old bastard.'

'About as funny as cot death,' Natalie added, just loud enough for Frank to hear.

'What?'

'You heard.'

'Don't you talk about my old man like that, you fucking snob,' he roared.

'And don't you talk to me like that, you fucking pig!' she roared back, slamming on the brakes. 'Get out! Get out of my car and walk home for all I care. And when you get there, don't be surprised if I'm gone. I don't love you any more, Frank, and I know you don't love me.'

'What are you talking about?' Frank said. It was starting to rain and cabs were pretty thin on the ground in Mitchellton at the best of times, let alone Christmas Day.

'You don't love me because you don't love yourself. Frank, you don't love anybody!'

'Crap.'

'Get out!' she screamed. 'GET OUT!'

'Fuck's sake,' he grumbled, deciding it was better to do as she said than listen to more of the same all the way home.

Natalie hit the accelerator with such force the car's tyres screamed as she drove off.

'Bitch,' Frank muttered, standing in the deserted street in the drizzling rain. 'Anyway, who do you think you are?' he shouted, as if Natalie might still hear him. 'That's my fucking car!'

Now where the fuck was he? He'd grown up here half his life and hadn't a clue. Parramatta Road was up there somewhere, a couple of blocks away. He might have a chance of picking up a cab there. Christ, where's my fucking wallet? Oh shit …

He could have found his way back to the family home and crashed on the couch but he opted for a bench in a nearby park instead. It was raining but it wasn't cold. Quite pleasant actually. Anyway, even if he didn't respect himself, he'd know where he was in the morning.

PART II

CHAPTER 9

The blood ran from a gash above the drunk's left eyebrow, down the lines in his cheeks and ended in a shapeless billabong on his filthy singlet. No longer crimson, it had dried in the sun to a network of stagnant black stains. He'd been rolled in the early hours of the morning and now, at two o'clock on this hot Sunday afternoon, was a crumpled obstacle on the harbourside footpath that wound around the Botanic Gardens.

Frank, his sister, Nina, and her teenage daughter, Mandy, meandered around him along with the rest of the crowd.

'You can't go back to him, Nene. I won't let you.'

'It's not up to you to decide, Frank. I know you've never liked Red but he does have his good points.'

'Name one.'

'Oh, please, don't give me this "I told you so" crap. Let's just wait and see.'

It wasn't the first time Nina had been forced to evacuate the Morrow family home. On previous occasions she'd sought refuge at Bob and Melissa's place, usually for periods of two or three days, but that was when their son Matthew was alive and Red was more predictable. These days you never knew what to expect, and this time Nina hadn't seen it coming.

Redenko Morosevic was a volatile man, proud of his heritage and his stubbornness — a quality he preferred to think of as defiance. But he'd tired of having to articulate his name, syllable by syllable, to every ignorant Australian he met and, on turning twenty, had changed it by deed poll to Red Morrow. He regarded this as his one humiliating admission of defeat, and two decades later still felt phantom pains from the amputation.

It wasn't the only pain Red Morrow felt but it was the only one he knew the cause of. He wasn't about to admit defeat again, no matter how much he lost — on the races, the poker machines, or in any other way. The loss of his son, for example, didn't represent a failure on his part. As a responsible father, he'd warned Matthew about the dangers of drugs, and if a seventeen-year-old kid was stupid enough to inject heroin into his arm there was every chance he'd get what he deserved. If anyone was to blame, it was the dealer who'd cut the stuff with lime and, as a responsible father, Red would wring the bastard's neck if he found out who he was.

Nor was he prepared to admit defeat over the recent loss of his wife and daughter. They'd come back soon if they knew what was good for them and Nene could expect another hiding when they did because, on second thoughts, she was one more pain Red could identify: a pain in the arse.

Sick of Red's beatings, Nina needed to get away for a while — and needed more protection than her brother Bob could provide. If Red made up his mind to drag his woman back to the family cave by her hair, knowing he'd have Bob to contend with first wouldn't be a deterrent. And with Bob's own cave only a few streets away, he wouldn't have far to drag her.

So Nina gave Frank a call. Red had never visited Frank's inner-city apartment and would find himself a barbarian at a very high-security gate if he did. Furthermore, if Frank was intimidated by Red, he'd certainly never let it show. Nina was surprised when busy, stressed Frank unhesitatingly agreed; even more so when he turned up a couple of hours later to take them back to his fortress in his car. Now she was finding that staying at his place was like having a holiday in a luxury hotel, despite Frank's heavy drinking and the chaos that went with it. There was so much rubbish and so many bottles all over the place that Nina found it hard to believe Frank employed a cleaner who turned up once a week, but still, she wasn't in any hurry to leave.

Standing now with Frank near Mrs Macquarie's Chair, Nina followed his finger as he pointed towards an imposing home in Darling Point and told her that was the place Dad had taken him to steal the bricks that became their barbecue.

Mandy, seventeen, the age at which her brother had died, wasn't sure which imposing house they were referring to and couldn't have cared less. It was too hot to be walking around gazing at the harbour like tourists with nothing better to do. Why couldn't they have stayed with Uncle Bob? They'd been stuck in the inner city for three weeks now and it was the second time her friends had been to a party they'd told her about a day after the event. Some holiday!

'Head back now, shall we?' said Frank.

Mandy shrugged, concealing relief with a show of indifference. She knew why Uncle Frank wanted to head for home. Home was where the fridge was and he hadn't had a drink for two hours.

They were forced to make a wider detour around the drunk they'd passed half an hour before. Two ambulancemen were lifting him onto a stretcher.

'Might as well take him straight to Mission House,' Frank heard one of them say.

Frank and Nina slowed down in deference to Mandy's curiosity. They were looking towards the Opera House when she emerged from the small crowd of onlookers and said, 'Mum, it's Grandpa.'

Mission House was a three-storey sandstone building two blocks south of Sydney's Finger Wharf on Woolloomooloo Bay. It had started its life as a home for sailors, so its transition in the 1950s into a home for drunks was less disruptive for many of those who called it home than might otherwise have been the case. On the upper floor were hospital-like rooms for those who needed special care, usually after bashings, and occasionally those who had been set on fire by passers-by making sinister use of the drunks' metho for their own entertainment.

The rest of the place was a dull arrangement of dormitories. Below them, in the basement, was the 'proclaimed place', PP, where drunks could seek refuge when there was nowhere else to go. Most found the risks involved in sleeping on the street or in a park preferable to the PP's stench of vomit, piss and shit.

By the time Frank, Nina and Mandy arrived at Mission House, following the directions given them by the ambulance driver, the area was packed with tourists and, as Frank grumbled, was 'a bastard of a place to find a parking spot'. These were the first words uttered during the short trip from Art Gallery Road to Woolloomooloo.

'You'll get one here somewhere,' Nina muttered distractedly.

'I'll keep looking,' said Frank. 'You go in, Nene. I'll go for a walk with Mandy and meet you back here in an hour or so.'

'Don't you want to talk to your own father?' Nina cried, glaring at her brother through tear-filled eyes.

'No, you talk to him, Nene, he likes talking to you. Be back in an hour.'

Nina slammed the door of Frank's new BMW.

'Fuck's sake,' he hissed as he steered the car back into the traffic and resumed his search for a parking spot. He found one two blocks away, opposite the Tilbury Hotel.

'Already walked a marathon today,' he said to Mandy as they stepped out of the car. 'Pity you're not eighteen yet, eh? Could have popped into the beer garden for a drink instead.'

'I've been to plenty of pubs and have never been asked to show ID yet,' Mandy replied indignantly, thrusting her precocious breasts forward and providing two good reasons for Frank to believe her.

'In that case, I'll have a beer. What do you feel like?'

'One of those super-expensive cocktails with an umbrella on the top,' said the woman of the world, feeling like she was on holiday at last.

'My, Mick, you have been in the wars,' said a sturdy woman, who introduced herself to Nina as Nurse Pawlowska. 'That'll teach you to go wandering off on a Saturday night, won't it?'

Nina slumped into a chair and watched with the detached curiosity and intense interest of a movie-goer as the cast of two played out a mundane but touching scene. Kathy Bates would make a good Nurse Pawlowska, she thought, with her easy blend of sternness and compassion. Mick could only be played by Chips Rafferty, but Chips in his heyday would have had to lose a lot of weight to play the role with conviction.

Suddenly, from right of stage, three new actors entered the scene, descending the stairs. Two were coppers, the other a small man with a lined face who shook hands sombrely with the policemen and ushered them out the door.

Who's this? Nina thought. James Cagney? Same wiry frame, same hardness about the lips, same gangster's demeanour, only older; nearly bald, and toughened by life in a way that made Cagney's glamorous hard men look soft.

She watched as he opened and looked into her father's eyes, checked his pulse, the dryness of his skin. Nina heard him instruct the nurse to get some water into him and give him a shot of thiamine. He then spoke some soothing words to her father and walked out of the screen directly towards her.

'Jack Hayes,' he said, extending his hand. 'I'm your old man's doctor.'

Nina rose to greet him. 'Oh, thank you, Dr Hayes,' she heard her own, breaking voice say. 'I'm so grateful you took time to come in and care for my father.'

'To be honest,' he said with a smile, 'I didn't come in to see Mick. I don't usually work here on Sundays, but there's been a death in the family.'

'Oh, I see …'

Jack Hayes wrote his number down on a scrap of paper and assured Nina she could call him any time and visit her father as often as she wanted.

'It'd do him the world of good if you popped in from time to time. Pleasure to meet you, Nina,' he added, before leaving the set from the door on the left. Nina followed, after a failed attempt to elicit some words from her father, and a word of thanks to Nurse Pawlowska for her help.

Outside, the heat hit her like a blast from a furnace. She looked at her watch. Frank had said he'd meet her again in an hour and the procedure had only lasted forty-five minutes. It took her half an hour to find her brother and her daughter chatting happily in the beer garden of the Tilbury Hotel.

'When was the last time you spoke to him, Frank?' she asked as she snapped her seatbelt on, glaring ahead through tear-stained eyes and dark sunglasses.

'Mum's funeral.'

Mum's funeral, she thought, recalling it with a shudder. Dad and Frank drowning their collective sorrows and the whole fiasco ending with Frank and Red engaged in a brawl over Matthew's death. How could Frank have accused Red of being to blame? And what a time and place to choose! Thank God for Bob, who'd intervened and settled things down — only to have Frank tell him to get fucked, mind you.

Nina knew Frank had been shattered by Mum's death but he'd never said anything about it. Even when she rang to talk about it, he just said he was lonely and didn't have a home to go to any more. Rubbish! He had a beautiful home — far better than the family shack in Mitchellton.

'That was years ago.'

'Never mind that,' Frank snapped. 'I've talked to him often enough. Fuck him! He's never talked to me in his life.'

Nina said nothing. It was as impossible to talk to her brother about their father as it was to talk to their father about him. Two peas in a pod, they were.

CHAPTER 10

'What's this?'

Frank had found a faded photograph amongst a pile of charcoal drawings in a neglected corner of Arthur's studio. Against a backdrop of sparkling ocean, a muscular young man in bathers was smiling at the camera while leaning proudly against the bonnet of a yellow American car.

'Hold it up. Can't see it from here,' said Arthur, from behind a large canvas on an easel. He was naked to the waist and his face, upper body and arms were smeared with almost as much paint as the picture he was working on. His feet, too, were bare and covered in splashes of colour. In between was a heavily encrusted abstract on linen that had started life as a pair of dungarees.

'It's you, isn't it?'

'Yeah, that's me,' said Arthur, squinting at the image from the other side of the room. 'And that's the car I wrote off when I saw that ad of yours.'

'No wonder you had the shits with me.'

''66 Mustang. Best car I ever owned.'

Frank thought about Arthur's new convertible parked outside the studio and had his doubts. He placed the photo to one side and resumed his explorations.

Poking around in Arthur's studio was like carrying out an archaeological dig in a dust storm. Every time you made a significant find it had disappeared under a fresh stratum of finished and unfinished canvases, drawings and paint rags by the time you returned.

Frank had been engaged in this Sisyphean cycle for many years, ever since their first chance meeting in a pub in The Rocks. On many occasions during that time he had insisted on rescuing some valuable relic by buying it and having it framed. Negotiating a price was never an easy matter, however, due to an irreconcilable conflict between Frank's determination to pay a respectable sum and Arthur's refusal to accept money from his friends. So the average price for a Blackwell masterpiece was a few beers; an above-average piece comprised a few beers and several bottles of wine; and an expensive work included a pie with sauce or some fish and chips.

'I don't need to sell them, Frank,' Arthur would argue whenever his friend raised the subject of mounting an exhibition. 'That's why I do the commercial work. Why would a man want to get involved with the art scene if he didn't have to?'

Frank sympathised with his view of the local art industry but couldn't understand why, with so many paintings cluttering up his studio, Arthur never felt the slightest inclination to show them to anyone. Convinced of Arthur's greatness, Frank felt the burden of duty weighing on his shoulders: he owed it to humanity to make this man known. In a world overrun by second-rate artists, it was absurd that a first-rate one should be depriving the starving of nourishment.

Besides, one of the books Frank had started but never finished was his carefully researched biography of the great Arthur Blackwell, the only master of modern painting no one had ever heard of.

'You give me the shits,' said Frank, falling onto one of Arthur's paint-covered couches and throwing his notebook on the floor.

'Look,' said Arthur, changing the Sonny Rollins CD Frank was sick and tired of hearing and replacing it with another one by Sonny Rollins, 'every wanker showing paintings in Sydney says they're doing their work just for themselves, but they do their work for anybody but themselves. That's why they need galleries to sell the stuff so they can earn a living. I earn my living by doing illustrations and storyboards, and what I do here I do for myself. If anybody wants to see them they can come around and knock on the fucking door.'

It was an argument Frank had heard many times. This time he decided to surprise Arthur by coming from another angle.

'If you won't do it for yourself, what about doing it for me?'

'What the fuck has it got to do with you?'

'The book I'm writing about you. Nobody's going to buy the thing if they've never heard of you.'

'Don't be silly, Frank — as if you'll ever finish it. You've never finished anything in your life!'

Arthur had a point. We all have our crosses to bear and laziness was one of Frank's. He totted up a mental list of the literary infants snoozing away in his computer crèche: his biography of Arthur; the life story of the saxophone player Mark Simmonds; and many more. Some remained foetuses from neglect; some grew occasionally in fits and starts; others attained puberty and even adolescence, but none ever reached adulthood or found their way to a publisher.

Nevertheless, Arthur's jibe cut him to the quick.

'Let's line up an exhibition. I'll drum up the publicity and you'll be up and running. Your storyboard days will be over. And then I will finish the bloody thing. I've already written enough about you to make *War and Peace* look like a nursery rhyme. All I've got to do is edit it, get some photos taken and it's ready to go.'

'Oh, for fuck's sake, Frank. I'll finish cleaning up this bloody mess and we'll go to the pub.'

The bloody mess Arthur was referring to was a new landscape Frank considered one of his best. He watched helplessly as Arthur wiped vast areas of it from the canvas with an enormous palette knife and yet another fine painting disappeared without trace.

Arthur Blackwell didn't match the genteel stereotype of the artist at work. He looked more like the boxer of old as he pitted his still-athletic, paint-spattered body against his canvas, sparring it into submission. It was like watching Muhammad Ali putting the finishing touches on Sonny Liston.

Although few in number, Arthur's portraits were, in Frank's opinion, some of his best work. The first one he'd seen — a self-portrait, naked to the waist, daubed on in great dollops and smudges of purples, greys and browns — reminded Frank of the work of the German artist Lovis Corinth. On Frank's insistence, Arthur had turned his hand occasionally to portraiture, but only of friends. He steadfastly refused Frank's advice to bung one in the Archibald Prize or turn a dollar out of a commission or two.

'I don't want anyone else calling the shots,' was Arthur's explanation. And that was that.

When he got round to painting his portrait of Frank, he refused to allow his subject to see the work in progress.

'Surely to Christ I can have a look at it, Arthur,' Frank pleaded, after some twenty sittings. 'A man's got a right to know what you're doing to him behind that canvas. I'm getting pretty tired of looking at the back of it.'

'You can have a look tomorrow,' said Arthur. 'I'll finish it in the morning. Pop in for a few beers after work.'

The next day, Frank arrived with beer and expectations at around seven o'clock. The door to the studio was open, Arthur was nowhere to be seen, and Frank was confronted by a terrifying doppelganger staring at him from the other side of the room.

The artist appeared from behind a vast canvas and approached his subject quietly, as prepared for abuse as he was for praise. When he received neither he realised Frank was in a state of shock and fetched a six-pack of medicine from the fridge, identical to the one dangling like a pendulum at the bottom of Frank's left arm. A dense fog of silence descended in the studio and there was nothing they could do but sit on the couch and open bottle after bottle while they waited for it to clear.

As the tonic began to take effect, Frank started to come to terms with Arthur's brutal summation of his appearance, adjusted himself to his radically reduced sense of self-esteem, and recovered from this uppercut to the jaw of his vanity from a man who knew how to land a punch.

There was no doubting the strength of the portrait. Every square inch of it was alive with splashes and drips of paint, bashed on in a way that seemed reckless or accidental. Contemplating Arthur's clumsy-looking mitts, Frank felt too spiritually inadequate even to speculate as to whether another guiding hand had directed them to create such perfect order out of so many chaotic ingredients.

'It's a great painting, Arthur, I'll give you that,' said Frank at last. 'It's just a pity it's of me.'

Later that night the painting belonged to Frank. It proved to be one of his most expensive acquisitions: Arthur was as sozzled as ten men when they finally parted company and not one of them was a cheap drunk.

The portrait — freshly framed — moved in with Frank and took over the lounge room. The man in the painting was the man Frank had spent his whole life trying not to become, and every day he experienced a little moment of horror at the realisation he was turning into him, whether he liked it or not.

'You can't love me because you don't love yourself,' Natalie had cried at the climax of their final fight. At the time he'd dismissed it as absurd, but he couldn't dismiss from his memory. He didn't understand the statement, but it echoed in his mind every time he confronted this painting he loved of a man he despised.

CHAPTER 11

Arthur preferred to paint landscapes and often went bush for weeks at a time. When he came back, he'd secrete his latest hoard of half-finished canvases in his cluttered studio and commence transforming them into something that bore so little resemblance to whatever it was he'd seen out there that Frank found it hard to understand why he embarked on the safaris in the first place.

The most recent trip had seen him taking notes in painterly shorthand at Lake Mungo. A day after he returned, Frank popped into his studio after work to see the results. After looking at a few of them, it looked as though Arthur may as well have spent the time on the moon.

'I suppose it would be too much to ask,' he said, 'that in a roomful of landscapes, a man might find a fucking tree or a sky or a cow?'

Arthur was wiping himself down with turps and preparing to change into something presentable enough to have a chance of measuring up to the famously relaxed dress requirements of the Bellevue Hotel.

'I'll whack a carcass or Ned Kelly into one of them if you like,' he quipped, 'if it'll help you sell your book.'

The task Frank had set himself for the night was too daunting to undertake without assistance. On the way to Arthur's studio he'd called for back-up, and dear old Puss hadn't let him down.

'I'll see you in the Bellevue,' he said, 'but for Christ's sake, Frank, try not to keep me waiting there too long.'

Puss had turned into a homebody, preferring a lifestyle along conventional married lines. His de facto of eight years, William ('not Billy or Willy, please'), was twelve years his senior and functioned comfortably in his dual roles as stabilising influence and spouse.

When asked about his occupation, William would sigh noisily, roll his eyes and claim he'd never worked a day in his life. Family money was in plentiful supply, along with an inherited house in fashionable Paddington, the maintenance of which seemed to occupy whatever time was left to him after his daily round of shopping, reading the newspapers in restaurants and coffee shops, and preparing gourmet meals for hard-working Puss when he arrived home in the evening.

Truth to tell, Puss was about as hard-working as Frank. Having become acclimatised in his early twenties to being ridiculously overpaid for his work as a finished artist in advertising, he accepted his title literally and saw no reason to strive for higher things. Puss was no Arthur Blackwell. Where Arthur's illustrations were major masterpieces of a minor genre, Puss's were pedestrian. While Arthur committed his energy to a quest for immortality through painting, Puss — having miraculously escaped AIDS in spite of years spent in gay bars, bathhouses or worse — was content in the knowledge that, through not dying, whatever desire for immortality that lurked within him had been sated.

These days, he was rarely seen in pubs. They bored him. He cut a solitary figure at a table in a corner of the Bellevue, absorbed in a book, oblivious to the noise around him.

Puss closed his book and pushed it aside when Arthur and Frank arrived, making room for what would accumulate to a large number of beers. Then, it was hoped, Arthur could be moved on to spirits. As long as he stayed with the beer, both Puss and Frank knew there was little point in attempting to persuade him to mount an exhibition of his work. It would only be after progressing to whisky or tequila that he'd be susceptible to suggestions. Even then, their chances of success were marginal.

'What's that you're reading?' Frank asked.

'A very good novel by a young Australian author I know. It's called *Gang-Gang*.'

'*Gang Bang*?' said Frank. 'Sounds interesting.'

Such high-minded discussions about literature tended to exclude Arthur. In deference to his sensibilities, Puss and Frank moved on with a few in-depth exchanges.

Frank: So, Puss, how's work?

Puss: Good as gold. And you?

Frank: More of the same.

Puss: How about you, Arthur? Getting much painting done?

Arthur: A bit.

Silence.

'My shout,' said Arthur.

'Not looking too good, is it?' Frank said, with Arthur away at the bar.

'No,' said weary Puss. 'William's got plans for renovating the kitchen, but I don't think Arthur's very interested in that sort of thing.'

'I'll get him onto the footy. Big game coming up this weekend.'

Arthur returned, placed the beers on the table and, quite unexpectedly, took it upon himself to get on with the job.

'We don't see you in the pub much these days, Puss. I get the feeling Frank wants to talk me into having an exhibition of my paintings and he's asked you to give him a hand. Am I right?'

'You're not wrong.'

'Well, what do you reckon?'

'Great idea.'

'Right. You blokes know all the galleries. Where should I have it?'

'Vacant Space Fine Art in Woollahra is very good —'

'From what I've heard, I don't think Vacant Space would be quite Arthur's speed,' Frank interrupted. 'How about giving Barry O'Connor a call?'

'I'm not calling anybody. You call him. I've heard he's a bit of a prick.'

'They're all pricks. O'Connor's just the prick with the biggest space, and you're going to need it.'

'Barry O'Connor it is then.'

Another awkward silence followed. The big man knew it took a while for someone who'd been knocked out to recover and there were two of them on the canvas.

Frank regained consciousness first. 'My shout,' he said. 'Same again?'

'Not for me, thanks,' said Puss.

He knew what to expect if he stayed for a drink or two with Arthur and Frank. Having done so in the past and very nearly died, it wasn't something he wanted to go through again. Booze had never held much attraction for Puss. While his brain was still struggling to recover from being bombarded with hallucinogens in the seventies and the shock of his decision to cut off its amphetamine supply in the mid-eighties, his liver had escaped relatively unharmed.

'William's made dinner. Congratulations, Arthur. It's about time you brought your work out of the closet.'

Returning from the bar with two new ones, Frank decided it was probably best to drop the subject of the exhibition. He didn't want to put the venture at risk by giving Arthur the opportunity to change his mind. Bringing up family was also inadvisable in Arthur's case. A brief and ill-fated marriage had left him with a burden of debt and guilt, and a son he loved but didn't know.

Family's out, the exhibition's out and work's been covered, Frank thought, placing the beers on the table and resuming his seat. Talk of art, especially the art of Goya, was an inexhaustible subject, however, with no potential for disagreement, and Frank had fresh material.

'Bought a new book on Goya the other day. Best reproductions I've ever seen.'

'Another waste of money. It's getting hard to talk to you about Goya, Frank, because you've never actually seen his paintings and you don't know what you're missing. If you want to see how the blood soaks into the canvas in *The Third of May* you have to get close enough to watch it happening. If you'd spent half as much on airfares as you have on books, you'd have been able to visit the Prado a dozen times by now. Then we could talk.'

'I'll do it one day. I've got a job, remember. It's a matter of finding the time.'

'Bullshit. It's your job that stops you from going there but not because you never get a holiday.'

'What do you mean by that?'

'Come on, Frank, you work in advertising — selling dunny rolls and lipstick. That's why you dabble in the deep stuff by dipping into it in books. It keeps it at a safe distance.'

'That's not fair.'

'Yes, it is. I think you keep putting it off because you do know what you're missing.'

Arthur could be a real bastard sometimes, Frank thought. Conversing with him gave you some idea of what it must have been like to fight him. Words, like his famous left jab, came out of him from nowhere, and if he strung a few together they could knock you to the floor. So much for Goya. What was left? The footy? No, the Swans were having a bad season, they'd have a tough time against Essendon on Saturday, and neither of them wanted to talk about that. Sex, on the other hand ...

'So, Arthur,' he said, 'getting any?'

'Got a drought on. Couldn't pull a root in a garden. You?'

'Mustn't grumble.'

Arthur took this to mean Frank's love life was in its usual chaotic state and he was right.

The law of averages had come down hard on Frank. Every woman he'd been involved with had told him he was incapable of maintaining a relationship, and they couldn't all be wrong. It wasn't as if he hadn't tried. He'd managed to stay with Natalie for fourteen months, three weeks and two days, remaining faithful to her the entire time — except, of course, for the odd occasion when one or the other of them had been away on business.

For a while he thought he'd found the love of his life, but she decided otherwise. Natalie had an annoying predilection for analysing his every action and utterance. She mined his insecurities, discovered an inability to commit and an incapacity to love, then went on to nag him about his heavy drinking. It made no sense to Frank, who countered by rattling off a list of his good points: he was generous, charming, well-read and funny. She didn't disagree but considered the nuggets he'd cited as fool's gold.

Then there was that awful Christmas and that was the end of that.

One thing Frank did acknowledge was his inability to organise his love affairs in chronological order, which was the reason they tended to overlap, ending in tears and melodrama. And you didn't have to be Sigmund Freud to work that out.

His recent affair with Hannah had been a case in point.

Hannah, a PR executive for a chain of clothing stores whose advertising account was handled by Parkinson's, had seen all the warning signs in Frank but chose to ignore them. For over a year she saw to it that any business between her company and its advertising people was handled by her and Frank Thornton, and usually in more convivial environments than conference rooms.

Somewhere under Frank's layers of bravado and offhandedness there lurked a caring man, she thought. Hidden in his hairy chest was a heart of gold. Nobody else saw it, but there was a broken little boy inside Frank Thornton and she was going to reach out to him and hold him in her arms.

After one of their lunches, during which Hannah had drunk a bit too much and kissed him goodbye, Frank started to think about her. *She's a bloody good sort, that Hannah Raymond, and I think she's got the hots for me; always rather fancied her, now I come to think of it.*

The next time they met, Frank suggested dinner instead of lunch and Hannah eagerly agreed. She responded more or less as he'd hoped she would when he surprised her with a bunch of roses and it was pretty clear from then on there wouldn't be too much work-related subject matter in their conversation that night. It only took a couple of bottles of champagne to confirm she had the hots for him and Frank wasn't one to look a gift horse in the mouth.

A couple of months later Hannah called around unexpectedly, found him in bed with some silicon-implanted tart he'd picked up in the pub and Jesus — talk about tears and melodrama!

'How old are you now, Frank?' Arthur asked. 'Forty-four, forty-six?'

'Forty-fucking-one, thank you very much.'

'Maybe it's time you slowed up a bit. Every time I see you you're with a different sheila. That last one I met, what was her name? Anna or something?'

'Hannah.'

'I liked her. She still on the scene?'

'Afraid not. Mad as a cut snake. I'd only been seeing her for a couple of months and the pressure was on. Started dropping hints — wanted to get married, have kids, the lot.'

'All sheilas want to get married at some stage and have kids. It's in their blood. They get to a certain age and sex gets to be serious business for them. It doesn't necessarily make her mad as a cut snake, mate.'

'It wouldn't if she wanted to get married and have kids with some other bloke. I'm telling you, Arthur, she wanted to do that with me!'

'Fair enough. Maybe she was mad.'

'Thanks a lot,' Frank grunted.

'Then again, she could've been in love, I s'pose.'

'Oh, here we go. What's this? Dr Basher Blackwell's Lonely Fucking Hearts Club. You going to give me a lecture on love now, are you?'

Like all good boxers, Arthur knew how to bob and weave. Frank's hardest punch had missed him completely.

'Women are like eggs,' Arthur said. 'You crack their shells when you get into them and mix your white up with their yolk. Next day you walk away and, because your shell hasn't been cracked, you think nothing's happened. But that might not be the case. Something might have happened to her. It's quite possible for a woman to fall in love, even with a cunt like you, see?'

Frank shifted uneasily. He was a scary bloke, Arthur, especially when he was leaning forward in his chair and staring you in the face. You wouldn't want to be in a small room with him and the door closed. He was behaving like the bad cop playing the good cop, but he could switch roles any minute and Frank didn't like the line of questioning. He sipped his beer and noticed he was getting close to the bottom of the glass. Arthur would stop when it was empty — give him a breather, at least. He took another sip.

'Did she love you, Frank?' Arthur asked.

'How would I know?'

'Maybe she fucking told you and you were too stupid to believe it.'

'Maybe. Jesus, Arthur.' Frank drained the last mouthful, replaced the empty glass on the table and nodded in the direction of the bar.

'Has she been in touch?'

'She's rung a couple of times. She's probably out with some new bloke as we speak.'

'Maybe, maybe not. Just because you go out and root someone else the moment she's out the door doesn't mean she does the same. Might be sitting around at home missing you.'

'Oh, don't give me the shits. Your shout.'

Arthur came back with the usual two beers, augmented by a couple of double scotches. It was a good sign in Frank's view. He felt like a long session tonight.

'You're a funny bloke, Frank,' said Arthur, at it again. 'You can't go on getting pissed and snorting coke for the rest of your life. You'll meet your match one of these days. Most men would give their eye teeth to marry a girl like that Anna.'

'Hannah.'

'I said 'annah.'

Avuncular expressions didn't suit Arthur. He was wearing one now and it was starting to get on Frank's nerves.

'Anyway, you're not one to talk,' he said. 'I haven't noticed you making a dash for the altar lately.'

'It's different in my case. My ex-wife always said I wasn't really married to her, I was married to my work. She even said she felt jealous of it in the way most women feel if they find out their bloke's having a bit on the side.'

'Fucking ridiculous.'

'No, it's not. I realise now she was right. I was married to my work. Still am.'

'Suppose that explains a lot,' said Frank, grinning.

'Yes,' said Arthur, not grinning. 'It probably explains why I don't like the idea of putting my paintings on display — letting other people perve at them or touch them. Or buy them and take them away.'

'Oh, I see,' said Frank. 'I thought you meant it was why you can't help fucking them all the time.'

Arthur had a big, booming laugh at one end of his emotional keyboard, his fists at the other, and very few notes in between.

'Your shout, you stupid bastard,' he said, letting rip with a few cadences from the laughing end.

CHAPTER 12

They say that inside every fat man there's a thin one wanting to get out. If there was a thin man inside Barry O'Connor, he'd long since given up trying. Barry was a fat man who wanted to be fatter; an ugly man who explored new ways of making himself uglier. For a year or so, it was with muttonchop whiskers the size of T-bone steaks. When they disappeared he cultivated a thin Daliesque moustache that twirled at both ends while a Ho Chi Min beard did likewise on his chin. What was left of his hair erupted into a ponytail at the top of his collar and wispy sideburns cascaded in little curls down the side of his face. His head looked like a fly-fisherman's hat, offending the eye from every angle.

By the time Barry met Arthur Blackwell he'd given up on hair altogether. He shaved his entire cranium once a month, which left it as smooth as a billiard ball for the first few hours, until nature started taking its course. A month later, when it looked like a bulbous pink cactus, out would come the shaving gear and the whole repulsive process would begin again.

His dress operated along similar evolutionary lines. The muttonchop period of '95 coincided with a year during which he was seen only in suits in various shades of blue: powder blue, cerulean, cobalt. The progression reached its nadir with a particularly incandescent hue, seemingly illuminated by some mysterious power source in one of the pockets. Worn with lurid shirts and wide ties, the intended effect was to shock, and shock it did. There were people who suspected O'Connor was a work in progress, turning a dollar by modelling the haute couture abominations of some pervert of the fashion scene.

Frank wasn't expecting escorting Barry O'Connor to Arthur's

studio to be a challenging undertaking. He realised how wrong he was the moment he opened the cab door from within to see O'Connor's purple-clad arse coming at him slowly, blocking out all light like an eclipse. Frank's instinct for self-preservation propelled him out of the opposite door as Barry's bulk found its way inside and finally came to rest.

When the English Egyptologist Howard Carter entered the tomb of Tutankhamen in 1922, he had an expression on his face which was unique in human history until, in 1997, it appeared again on Barry O'Connor's when he entered Arthur Blackwell's studio in Surry Hills.

It took a big man to make Arthur Blackwell look small, but next to Barry O'Connor he looked minute. Nevertheless, he had gone to considerable lengths to create a favourable impression on his prospective new art dealer. Frank had never seen Arthur in a suit before, even though he'd baulked at a collar and tie and was wearing a white T-shirt underneath.

After fifteen minutes, O'Connor had seen enough. And, by the look of things, so had Arthur.

'Fucking great. Just fucking great,' said Barry. 'What about a show in, say, March? We'll put it on to coincide with the Archibald. Give the bastards a run for their money.'

'March is all right, I s'pose,' Arthur mumbled, gazing in every direction except Barry's.

'We'll have to talk about commission, how many paintings we're going to show, how many drawings, how we're going to select —'

'Talk to Frank about all of that. He's the boss. Thanks for coming.'

Frank guided Barry towards the door and away from Arthur, who'd turned his back and was heading towards the fridge.

Arthur handed Frank a beer when he returned from easing Barry into another cab. Frank twisted the lid off angrily and dropped it onto the floor. They each sipped in silence, waiting for the other to drop his guard.

'I should never have let you talk me into this,' said Arthur.

'What the hell are you on about?'

'I wouldn't trust that bastard as far as I could kick him. And let's face it, Plugger Lockett couldn't kick him more than a couple of inches.'

Frank drained his beer, placed the empty bottle on a table and shook his head. Then he turned abruptly and strode to the door.

'Well, we're off to a flying fucking start, aren't we?' he roared, before slamming it and storming away.

Alone at last, Arthur ripped off his suit and kicked it across the floor. He lurched about the studio, going from painting to painting, examining them like a nurse checking her patients were okay. It felt as though that fat oaf had raped every painting he'd touched.

Arthur picked up his empty beer bottle and hurled it at the wall, where it exploded into a million satisfying shards. Then he did the same thing with Frank's.

'Fuck,' he screamed. 'Fuck fuck fuck!'

Some women take pregnancy in their stride; others have a more difficult time. But no woman was ever so badly affected during her nine months as Arthur Blackwell was during the six it took to put together this exhibition.

Some of Arthur's births were more painful than others and the gestation periods varied wildly. The quality of the offspring varied wildly too — ranging from the sublimely beautiful to the hideously ugly — but his enthusiasm for producing them never waned.

It was a gruelling cycle, made tolerable for Arthur and his friends only by its predictability. When Arthur was working on a painting he was on top of the world. You could meet him in the pub or go out for dinner with complete confidence. But if he'd just finished one, he'd lapse into post-natal depression. So you'd make a point of avoiding him for a few days, and things returned to normal.

When he found himself in the family way with a whole exhibition, it was a different matter altogether. He was, Frank thought, a human preparing to give birth to a whale: an ordeal neither was likely to survive. With Frank, in effect, as its sire, Arthur resented the entire process and expressed it through tantrums. The prospects for them remaining together as a couple weren't promising.

Frank suffered Arthur's indignities with uncharacteristic forbearance, never once retaliating. Although sorely tempted, he knew what Arthur could do with his fists besides paint.

The relationship between Arthur and his art dealer had been a case of hate at first sight. It was left to Frank to act as go-between. First he'd argue with Arthur about which paintings should be exhibited.

Then he'd arrange to have the ones they'd agreed upon taken to the gallery. There O'Connor would fly into a rage, insisting he'd seen others he preferred during his one and only visit to Arthur's studio, and send most of them back. Arthur would fly into a rage of his own on seeing them return, and the whole cycle would begin again.

In defiance of all prognostications, the whale emerged intact on the due date — a Friday — at the Barry O'Connor Gallery, Paddington, between the hours of 6 and 8 pm.

Arthur had gone into labour that morning and immediately sought medical assistance at the bar of the Berkeley in Redfern. Beer did nothing to help ease the contractions, so he opted for an epidural of scotch after lunch and didn't set a limit on the dosage. By the time Frank found him there at five, he was feeling no pain, no desire to cooperate and no sense of responsibility whatsoever.

'You'd better have a few glasses of water, mate,' Frank said, 'or a coffee or two. We've got to get you changed and to the gallery in less than an hour.'

'Why do I have to be there?' Arthur slurred. 'The pictures are there, aren't they? They don't need me now.'

'I've been on the blower to every arts journo in Sydney. They'll all want a word with you. The place is going to be packed to the rafters and the show looks great. Surely to Christ you want to see it!'

'I've seen them all before. I painted the things. I'm not fucking going and that's that.'

A police officer confronted by a man in a highly emotional and dangerous state has to suppress the desire to reach instantly for the truncheon. The enlightened officer knows that the civilised way to restore order is to maintain a calm attitude, find the right words and impart them in a forceful but caring way. To his credit, Frank opted for this approach.

'Well, Arthur, you can go and get fucked.'

Frank pushed his way through the crowded main salon, which housed twenty-six large canvases; through the smaller one, where thirty framed drawings hung; past the doorway to the other large room, which was full of portraits and figurative paintings; and barged his way straight into the gents. He needed a Valium — maybe two — to calm down. He needed to regain his composure, play the part of the urbane charmer and establish the reputation of the mysterious genius responsible for creating this spectacular display, even though he'd left the ungrateful pig pissed at the Berkeley and never wanted to see him again.

Fuck the Valium, Frank thought, as he racked up a long line of cocaine. He snorted it so hard he could have sworn he felt it collide with his brain and shatter it in one almighty explosion of delight. Ah, that's better.

Frank made his way to the table where the drinks were being served and defied establishment protocol by downing two glasses of paint-stripper cask red on the spot before striding away with a third.

The first face he recognised was Roy's, stuck between hunched shoulders and negotiating a course through the crowd toward him, glass held aloft in an unsuccessful attempt to prevent its contents spilling onto the fashion statements he was buffeting in the process.

'Where's Arthur?' he asked.

'Fuck Arthur,' said Frank. Several haircuts swivelled in response. 'Where do you think he is?'

'The Berkeley?'

'All fucking day.'

'You're Frank Thornton, I believe,' said a mouth surrounded by a neatly trimmed goatee. 'Victor Hollings, *Sydney Morning Herald*. Barry tells me you helped organise the show. Is Mr Blackwell here yet?'

'I'm afraid Mr Blackwell won't be attending tonight.'

A notebook appeared from the breast pocket of a plain black jacket and a thin white hand started scribbling with an expensive gold fountain pen.

'Pity. I was hoping to meet him. Bit of a mystery man, isn't he?'

'Actually, he's a very shy man. Bit of a recluse. Doesn't like crowds.'

The pen was flashing away, inscribing indecipherable dots and dashes.

'Just the same, it's surprising he wouldn't come to the opening of his first show.'

'Not really. Arthur's one of those artists who likes the works to speak for themselves. I tried to talk him into coming but he insisted it was inappropriate.'

A woman who could also write shorthand was jotting down his every utterance and staring at him from behind red-framed glasses shaped like wings. Frank noted she had matching lipstick, and it had taken quite a lot of it to cover her sensuous lips. Come on now, he thought, keep your mind on the job.

'Why "inappropriate"?' said yet another voice, coming out of a closely shaved head with horn-rimmed glasses too thick to see through from the outside. The stout body it surmounted was clad entirely in black. A hand poking out of one of its sleeves thrust a microphone with the ABC logo on its side in Frank's face.

'Mr Blackwell,' Frank chanted in his best radio voice, 'was determined this exhibition should not be regarded as an exercise in self-aggrandisement. He wanted his paintings and drawings to be the focus of attention, not him.'

'The work is so muscular and aggressive,' said the goatee. 'Not what you'd expect from a timid type.'

'He's anything but when he's alone in his studio. Rather like the quiet man who turns into the life of the party, but only when surrounded by friends or family.'

They all seemed to like that line, beavering away at their notepads. You're going great guns, Frank, lay it on thick.

'You'll all be familiar with the story about Bonnard when a retrospective of his work was mounted in the Met in New York. He turned up before the doors opened and the crowd had to wait outside while he fussed about, adding little touches to one canvas after another. Well, Arthur Blackwell's a similar perfectionist. I had to physically restrain him from doing the same thing this afternoon. The only way to distract him was to get him started on a new painting. He's probably working on it right now.'

'Good,' said the lipstick. 'Let's have a look at the work of this perfectionist.'

'Well done, Frank,' whispered Roy. 'You could bullshit for Australia.'

'I'm glad that's over,' said Frank. 'Let's get back to that drinks table.'

'I'll join you shortly,' said Roy, making a beeline for the red glasses and matching lipstick.

At the drinks table Frank found himself standing next to Puss, who introduced him to a beautiful woman with black shoulder-length hair whose name, if Frank had heard correctly, was Shin-Shin.

'Sorry?' he said.

'Xin-Xin,' Puss repeated, 'Xin-Xin Leroq. It's spelt with an "X". Two of them, actually.'

'In that case, chin-chin,' said Frank, tapping his wine glass against hers.

It took a lot to embarrass Frank, and even more for him to embarrass himself, but he was acutely aware he'd managed it this time. Xin-Xin's unaffected smile indicated she'd taken his gauche comment on the chin-chin, but he knew it was time to be careful.

Xin-Xin Leroq, he mused. It was the sort of name that women as beautiful as this one seemed to be given as a matter of course. You could hardly be born with a name like Xin-Xin Leroq — or Zsa-Zsa Gabor — and grow into something looking like Mother Teresa.

'Xin-Xin's an author. Her latest novel's brilliant. I was reading it that time we met Arthur at the Bellevue,' said Puss, coming to the rescue.

Frank dimly recalled a book with a racy title. *Gang Bang*? He looked Xin-Xin up and down, grappling with the possibility she might be an expert on that sort of thing. Highly unlikely given that her exposed arms didn't feature tattoos and her features hadn't been got at by some silversmith with a rivet gun. He was glad he was turned out in a suit for once. She wouldn't notice the silly-looking dragon snaking its way down his arm as it had done for the last twenty years.

'I vaguely remember,' he ventured. 'What was it called again?'

'*Gang-Gang*,' said Puss.

That's right! He'd read a review of it recently, too. What was it about? The outback? Or was he getting it confused with another bestseller by another author about the time she'd spent in Paris, all alienated and out of her cultural depth?

'Of course,' said well-read Frank. 'I read a review that said it's selling like hot croissants in Paris. Did you actually write it there?'

'I've never been to Paris.'

'Sorry. Must be getting it confused with another book.'

'Yes, you are,' said Xin-Xin.

Frank felt she'd let him off lightly, judging by her look. If she'd been as up herself as most authors were reputed to be, that would have been the end of it. Better tread carefully, Frank. She's given you a second chance but don't count on a third.

'Let's grab another drink and have a look at the portraits, shall we?' Puss suggested.

As they made their progress from the landscape to the figurative, it became necessary to detour around an enormous roadblock clad in a yellow suit with head freshly shaved. Barry O'Connor was deliriously happy and, noting the red dots proliferating from one sold picture to another, Frank realised why.

He nodded in Frank's direction and flashed him a conspiratorial grin. Frank felt his anger towards Arthur cooling and his loathing of O'Connor overheating. He might have the shits with Arthur, but he knew whose side he was on.

Frank was concentrating on catching glimpses of the back of Xin-Xin's neck when he felt the icy stare of a malevolent presence. There on the other side of the room was his portrait, proclaiming all the things about himself he didn't want Xin-Xin to know. Something had to be done.

He'd read about something called 'personal space' and suspected he might be violating hers by taking the liberty of touching her lightly on the shoulder and steering her towards Puss's portrait. But the risk paid off and the three of them came to a reverent halt in front of it.

'It's good, isn't it?' he murmured to Xin-Xin. An innocuous question, far preferable to what he might have felt compelled to blurt out if they'd been standing in front of his.

'Very good,' she said. 'I feel I've hardly known Neil until now.'

Christ Almighty, Frank thought, under no circumstances can I allow her to drift over there and get a good look at the one of me.

'I like the way it's painted too,' Xin-Xin continued. 'It all looks as if it happened — how can I put it? — by accident.'

This was unbearable. Not only was Frank already obsessed with this woman's appearance, but he agreed with the things she said. He was always impressed by people whose ideas about painting were intelligent, thoughtful and right, which was invariably the case when they concurred with his own.

'It's just so alive, too. The paint doesn't seem to have had a chance to get overworked. Looks like something has just danced across the canvas and left the painting behind.'

Frank not only agreed with her this time, he was glad he had a notebook in his pocket. He'd jot that down and slip it into his biography of Arthur.

'Reminds me of another painter's work,' said Frank, testing her out. 'German bloke. What was his name again?'

Careful, Xin-Xin, he thought, if you say Lovis Corinth I'm going to marry you.

'Corinth?' she asked. 'Lovis Corinth. Great painter.'

Frank felt a sensation in his knees he hadn't experienced since that night at The Rocks Push when he'd first stood next to Arthur. Coincidentally, he was standing next to Arthur this time too.

'G'day, mate,' Arthur said, touching him on the elbow. Frank was so shocked that he gave a little jump.

'If it isn't the man himself. Arthur, I'd like you to meet Xin-Xin.'

'G'day, Jing-Jing,' Arthur managed. 'G'day, Puss. Have a word with you, Frank? Just for a minute.'

'Listen, mate,' he said, blasting fumes into Frank's face so toxic they felt as if they were taking off a layer of skin, 'I just heard what O'Connor was saying to those pricks over there.'

Oh Christ, here we go.

'Arthur, please, could we step outside for a breath of fresh air? The show's a big hit. Don't stuff it up now.'

He took Arthur by the elbow, coaxing him towards the door. Arthur withdrew his arm and stayed put.

'Okay, what did he say?'

'I heard him saying I'm just a commercial artist who does a bit of painting on the side.'

'I don't think you heard him right. He's been singing your praises all night.'

'I heard what he said and I'm going to job him.'

'Don't be silly, Arthur. He's pissed, you're pissed. Let it wait till the morning. Anyway,' Frank went on, desperately trying to make light of something that was looking darker by the minute, 'if you punch O'Connor in the guts you'll be into him up to your elbow before he notices something's happening.'

'In that case I'll punch him in the fucking head.'

This time Frank didn't try touching Arthur's arm to steer him out of the place; he lunged at him and tried to throw him over his shoulder like a fireman rescuing a hysteric from a burning building. Arthur shoved him away and started out in O'Connor's direction.

The crowd surrounding O'Connor suddenly parted, leaving him to enjoy the celebrated artist's company alone.

'Commercial artist am I?' Arthur roared. 'Commercial fucking artist, eh? I wasn't until I let you get your hands on my paintings. If anyone's commercial around here, O'Connor, it's you.'

For a second, the only sounds in the gallery were those of scribbling pens. Then the colossal amount of bile in Barry O'Connor's belly, accumulated over the past six months, spewed forth.

'You ignorant fucking bastard,' he bellowed. 'Who the hell do you think you are, talking to me like that?'

'I'm the bloke who did all these paintings, that's who I am! And I'll tell you who you are — you're the cunt who stole them from me. Now come on — outside!'

'I'm not going outside, you are. Get out of my fucking gallery before I get the coppers to come and throw you out.'

What followed was brutal but brief. One tremendous punch from Arthur and it was goodnight Barry.

Frank ran at Arthur from the side, crash-tackling him to the floor before he could go on with it. 'Get 'em down and keep 'em down,' Mick Thornton had said. Arthur subscribed to this approach too.

'Fucking idiot,' Frank growled into Arthur's ear as he held him pinned to the floor. While anything but calm, Arthur didn't put up too much of a struggle as Frank shoved him towards the door and out into the street.

With Arthur slumped in the back of a cab and on his way home, Frank again found himself the centre of attention.

'Well, yes, Mr Blackwell can be a bit volatile at times.'

'Is it true he works as a commercial artist?' the goatee asked. Frank didn't like the stress he put on the adjective.

Steady, steady. One fight's enough for one evening.

'Arthur has been doing advertising work on a freelance basis for many years. He does it so he can paint pictures like the ones you see here tonight.'

'Is it true he used to be a professional boxer?' said the shaved head with the horn-rimmed glasses.

Frank had had enough. So what if Arthur had been a boxer? He could paint, couldn't he? Ten minutes ago these jumped-up twerps were drooling over his paintings. Now it was as though they didn't exist. Forget about a review — now we've got a story!

'Did you see the punch he laid on that fat bastard over there on the floor?' Frank asked.

'Indeed I did,' said the shaved head.

'Well, what do you think, you idiot?'

It was Roy's turn to play the conciliator's role.

'Come on, Frank,' he said. 'Let's step outside, get a bit of fresh air.'

CHAPTER 13

'You can never find a cab when you need one,' Roy grumbled.

The invitation had said 6–8 pm but everyone who had ever been to an opening at Barry O'Connor's knew such instructions were meaningless. It was only the serious collectors who arrived on time. The rest turned up because they considered themselves more see-worthy than any boring pictures, and turned up late, when heads were ready to be turned, the photographers from the social pages here hard at work and the party was in full swing. The busiest hours of an O'Connor opening night were after 8 pm, not before.

Tonight's had probably been the first to ever finish on time. Frank could see O'Connor's assistant, Andreas, ushering out the last few stragglers, eager to close the door on them and one of the less illustrious events in the gallery's history.

Oh well, thought Frank, he'll be able to soothe O'Connor's bruises by applying a poultice made of receipts.

'Here's one,' said Roy, whistling. When the cab pulled up, Frank insisted it take three other passengers who, Roy argued, had not been waiting as long as they had.

'Wait another minute or two,' said Frank. 'Puss hasn't come out yet. Might want to come with us.'

'Well, where the hell is he? I'm hungry. And I could do with a drink.'

'Ah,' said Frank, 'here he is.'

'Right,' said Roy. 'Now I see why you wanted Puss to come along.'

Frank had almost resigned himself to the idea Xin-Xin would not be joining them for dinner. It was a safe bet she now thought of him as an oaf. Even he had to concede that, although his intention had been noble, his behaviour could hardly be construed as dignified. He'd had his three strikes and was out.

But you never know, you never know.

'Oh God, he's a vile creature, isn't he?' Frank heard Xin-Xin say to Puss as they walked towards him and Roy. He hoped she wasn't referring to Arthur.

'He certainly is,' said Puss, 'and it's not the first time he's been belted at one of his opening nights. Mind you, I doubt anyone's ever done such a job of it as Arthur. He's a bit of an expert in that department.'

Xin-Xin shuddered at the recollection. Seeing someone knocked senseless was something you watched between your fingers during the nasty bits in a film. It wasn't the sort of thing you expected at an exhibition opening.

'Xin-Xin Leroq,' said Puss, 'Roy Humber.'

'Nice to meet you, Roy,' she said.

'I've booked a table at a restaurant around the corner,' said Puss. 'Would you two like to join us?'

There is a God, thought Frank.

'Love to,' he said.

Roy's fondness for practical jokes and offensive remarks had by now matured into full-blown idiosyncrasy. Observing Xin-Xin's demeanour, Frank was sure that while he may have come close, he hadn't disgraced himself completely in her lovely eyes. His biggest fear was that Roy might do it for him.

'What about you, Roy?' asked Puss. 'Are you in?'

'I could eat a dead baby with cholera,' Roy announced.

'I'm not sure they have that on the menu,' said Xin-Xin. 'They've got suckling pig, though, and it's just as good.'

Frank recalled Arthur saying something about the possibility of him meeting his match one of these days. Roy, it seemed, had met his.

And maybe — just maybe — so had he.

By the time they reached the restaurant, Frank was badly in need of a drink.

Suave, linen-suited William was waiting for them and had secured a table well positioned next to a window. Typically, he'd insisted on a spot in the non-smoking area; atypically, Frank couldn't be bothered to kick up a fuss.

Things got off to a promising start. Without the need for any manipulations on his part, he found himself seated next to Xin-Xin.

'Yes, I will have a drop,' he said as William offered a handsome bottle of Spanish red, enticingly presented in a net of metallic thread that conjured a sexy image of a gold-mesh stocking on a black girl's leg.

He took note of Xin-Xin's eagerness to sample some of it herself and, as they examined the menus, also noted she refilled her glass before he did. Another point in her favour. Frank liked a woman who didn't mind a drink.

Xin-Xin ordered the suckling pig, as did Frank. When it arrived he marvelled at the well-mannered efficiency with which she demolished it. He liked a woman who enjoyed a good feed. Come to think of it, there wasn't much about this woman he didn't like.

'He what?' Frank heard an incredulous William ask Puss. A conversation had clearly been under way for some time but Frank's ruminations on gold-mesh stockings and Xin-Xin's appetites had rendered him momentarily deaf.

'He decked him,' said Puss. 'One punch. Bloody good one, though. Out like a light.'

William was appalled.

'You couldn't exactly say O'Connor didn't deserve it,' said Frank.

Xin-Xin turned towards him on hearing this. Frank felt he was being inspected.

'Not that I condone violence, of course.'

It was time to change the subject.

'So,' he said, 'how did you two meet?'

'Xin-Xin's parents run a company. Shorty and I do their advertising,' said Puss.

'You could say Lenny Matthews brought us together,' said Xin-Xin, a comment that amused Puss as much as it confused Frank.

'Lenny Matthews?'

'The main character in my book,' Xin-Xin explained. 'Neil recognised himself in Lenny.'

'So he's a poof, is he?' Roy was at it again.

'Actually, he's an Aborigine,' she said dryly, 'a closet Aborigine. He goes through hell deciding whether he should tell his parents.'

Everyone laughed. If it was a battle of wits Roy was after, she'd fired off another warning shot.

'I think I might duck outside for a ciggie on that note,' said Frank.

'I'll join you,' said Xin-Xin.

Frank couldn't believe his luck. If there was one thing he couldn't stand it was people who crusaded against smoking. Especially women. How many times had he been with a woman who'd started parroting the health warnings on the packets when he'd lit a harmless post-coital ciggie? He was getting to the stage where he was looking for something about Xin-Xin to dislike — and fantasising at the same time about them both lighting up after sex.

'I'm sorry about Roy,' he said, watching the play of the lighter's flame as it enhanced little details of her face. She had a mole just above her left eyebrow. It had missed her cheek by an inch or two but still qualified as a beauty spot. 'Not everyone understands his sense of humour.'

'Well, I do,' she said, 'and Neil does. He's just trying to cause a bit of mischief. You can tell he's not really homophobic.'

'Oh, but he is,' Frank warned, 'he's afraid to go home. And if you met his wife, you'd know why.'

She smiled at him and he smiled back.

'Better go back inside then,' she said.

'One more ciggie?'

'Oh, all right.'

Phew! he thought. Better ask a couple of curly ones. Mightn't have much time left.

'Look, Xin-Xin,' he began, 'could we meet again some time? Maybe go to dinner or something?'

'That could be a bit difficult.'

'Sorry. Shouldn't have said that.'

'No, no. I'm flattered. It's just that I'm, well …'

'Married?'

'Not quite, but almost, if you know what I mean.'

'Of course,' he said. 'Better go back and join the non-smokers.'

He opened the door for her, felt her body brush against his as she walked past and thought: a lesser man would burst into tears around about now.

The party began to break up. William and Puss put on jackets, Xin-Xin picked up her bag. Frank excused himself and headed for the gents. On the way he picked up the tab and put it on his credit card, which he then put to further use in the toilet. He deserved another line of cocaine for the hell he'd gone through helping Arthur mount an exhibition that had culminated in utter disaster. Not to mention finding — and losing — the woman of his dreams on the same night.

He felt like slamming his fist through the toilet door, but instead walked out stoically, determined to show magnanimity in defeat.

'Let's bat on a bit,' said Roy. 'We'll go to AD's.'

After Dark, or AD's as it was known to its insomniac habitués, was a wine bar in Kings Cross where you could always get a drink and hear jazz.

'Sure,' said Frank. 'Anyone else care to join us?'

He knew William and Puss would say no, but was clinging to a hope Xin-Xin might say yes.

'Better not, thanks,' she said, 'much as I'd like to. Best music in Sydney. And I love jazz.'

Christ Almighty, thought Frank. She even likes jazz! There was nothing he didn't like about this woman. Well, one thing, but he hadn't met him. And he didn't want to.

'Can't talk you into it?'

'No, thanks. I don't usually drink this much and I'm not looking forward to the morning, I can tell you.'

And that was it. Frank was grateful for the little peck on the cheek she gave him as they said goodbye, but Puss, William and even Roy got one of those too.

'Right,' said Roy as they put on their jackets, Frank picked up his shoulder bag and they made for the door, 'this is the plan: we're going down to AD's, where we're going to get shitfaced, and after that we'll put a few bob on The Favourite on the way home.'

The Favourite wasn't called The Favourite for nothing. The girls who worked there were beautiful, and sexy as hell.

'That's what I like about you, Roy,' said Frank. 'You're a real ideas man.'

CHAPTER 14

Why, why, had he given a set of keys to Harriet?

All he'd wanted was a one-night stand, so how had it come to this? One one-night stand had led to another, each more torrid than its predecessor. At the time, Frank concluded that if he hadn't found love with Harriet, at least he'd found romance. And he couldn't get enough of it.

It wasn't the first time Frank had become infatuated with a woman he didn't know and then spent weeks, or even months, screwing before going to the trouble of finding out who she was. For nearly two months he'd shared his bed with a stranger named Harriet and was having the time of his life. Until she moved in. Now, three weeks later, they'd become acquainted and he'd realised he was involved in a relationship with someone he had nothing in common with and didn't like.

He wasn't sure what it was about her that irritated him most. Sometimes it was her smell: unpleasant, even after a bath, and capable of reasserting itself within minutes of being drenched in perfume. Then again it could be the make-up, caked on and left there all night so in the mornings it was all over the pillow. The smeared mascara made her eyes look like two abandoned coal mines. Even her Penthouse-centrefold body was starting to get on his nerves.

It could be any number of things, he thought, but right now it's her voice.

It was like a power drill — harsh and relentless. And pounding straight through his ear holes. Never mind that what it said was drivel; it was the tone he couldn't stand, especially on mornings like this when he'd woken up with a force five, and everything hurt, up to and including his hair.

Frank had fallen into a habit of categorising the morning-after effects of drinking on a scale of nought to ten. A force ten constituted a hangover and was a condition suffered only by novices. Frank had had his fair share of forcetens but, after years of training, had whittled his handicap down to the point where his average day teed off with a force three. This involved a 'thick head' as distinct from a 'throbbing headache', a symptom that kicked in at force five. Anything above a force seven was a cause for concern and couldn't be treated at home. Two or three beers needed to be administered immediately, preferably while still in the prone position. Following this, cocaine provided the surge of energy necessary to attain the vertical and get the legs moving in the direction of the pub, where a range of options were on hand to combat whatever combination had caused the damage in the first place. Bloody Marys were Frank's usual remedy but experimentation had shown they couldn't be relied upon in all cases.

Another symptom that manifested itself at force five was nausea, but this was rarely a problem for Frank. Roy had once told him that the little tube that runs out of the stomach is on the left and that's why the trick is to lie down on your right side when you go to bed pissed, and stay there. Frank had cultivated right-side lying down ever since and was sure that little nugget of medical knowledge had saved him from going the way of Jimi Hendrix and Mama Cass. He dreaded the thought of one day waking up on his back with a force nine. If that ever happened, God help him.

A few paracetamols would ease today's force five, once Harriet shut up, and it should disappear completely after a coffee and a heart-starter. The hard part was piecing together the events of the previous evening in case something important had happened. What he needed was a reference point, and to locate it all he needed was a bit of peace and quiet.

What was she banging on about? The words dissolved into each other in a continuous Black-and-Decker drone. Come to think of it, what was she doing here at all? Wasn't she supposed to be spending the weekend at her mother's place?

'I thought you were staying at your mum's.'

'I wanted to surprise you so I came home.'

Frank felt a small abdominal convulsion. He'd only given her a set of keys three weeks ago and she was already referring to his place as home. Oh, Harriet, you harridan, what are you doing in my fucking house?

'Sorry about that,' he said. 'Got a bit pissed with Roy.'

It was coming back to him: Arthur's exhibition opening; Arthur turning up legless and belting O'Connor; going for dinner somewhere and winding up at AD's.

'Fuck you. Arsehole.'

From the most wonderful man on earth to arsehole in three weeks. They were getting acquainted, all right.

The good news was he could hear her stomping into the bathroom. He didn't know what she did in there but it always took about an hour. It was the window of opportunity he needed. He thought again. Better this time. Must be a brain cell or two surviving up there somewhere.

Oh my God! That woman — friend of Puss's! Xin-Xin Something-or-Other. The one who wrote that book about Paris. Or was it the outback? *Gang-Gang* — that was it.

Snippets of their conversation were coming back.

Talked at the gallery. Knew quite a lot about painting. Knew about Lovis Corinth — pretty impressive. Standing in front of Arthur's painting of Puss ... that's when everything went pear-shaped. Arthur clocked O'Connor and I had to send him home in a taxi. Then what happened? Went with her to some Spanish restaurant.

God, she was beautiful. Went outside with her for a smoke and we talked. But what did she say?

Frank recalled lighting a cigarette for her and watching the glow on her face; tried to conjure up that face now, wanting her there in front of him.

Straight black hair, Asian features, beautiful eyes. What was it about her lips? Why can't I see them? Why can't I see her, for God's sake. All he was getting was an identikit picture.

Think!

I asked to see her again and I think she told me she was married. Then she left and I didn't even get her number. Then? Down to AD's with Roy, red wine and beer and tequila and a shitload of coke and how the hell did I get home and what does it matter? She didn't give me her number, she's married, and that's that.

'I've had it with you, Frank,' said Harriet, when she eventually emerged. 'I've been thinking things over in the shower.'

108

'You gave yourself plenty of time.'

'And I found this,' she added and threw his credit card at him, wrapped in a crumpled receipt.

Frank inspected the document. He didn't usually pay for drinks at AD's with a credit card but there was always a first time. Maybe the ATM hadn't been working.

The docket read 'Angie's Body Repairs and Lube Service' and came to six hundred and eighty dollars. That's right! He'd stopped off at The Favourite on the way home with Roy. Bit steep though — six hundred and eighty dollars.

'You don't have a fucking car, Frank,' Harriet said.

'Must have popped in there for a haircut.'

'Fucking arsehole. You come home shitfaced one more time and I'm out of here.'

Frank reached for the phone.

'Roy?' he said. 'I'll see you at the Bellevue in half an hour.'

There was a short pause.

'All right, the Aurora then. I've got a force five and a thirst you could photograph.'

Nina had walked into the door again. It happened quite a lot but, gee, she'd hit it hard this time.

It was time to ring Frank. He wouldn't mind — he knew she wouldn't ask unless it was absolutely necessary.

The last time they'd stayed with him Mandy was seventeen. She was twenty now. Frank had driven all the way to Mitchellton to pick them up and take them to his nice flat in the inner city. He'd let them stay there for a month.

In the end, it was Nina's decision to give Red another chance, despite Frank's protestations. Red wasn't a bad guy, she'd insisted, but Frank was right: he had a temper on him. Especially when he'd been on one of his benders and hadn't come home for a couple of days. Worse than Dad.

Today he was off at the races with Tony. He could come home as good as gold and the three of them might have a pleasant weekend together; see a game of League, go to the pictures after dinner. But it was better to be on the safe side. You could never be too sure with Red. So she rang Frank.

'What's up, Nene?' Frank said. 'Has that bastard Red belted you again?'

'Not really, Frank. He just lost his temper, that's all.'

'Look, Nene, did he belt you or not?'

'He got a bit rough, nothing serious.'

'Christ. Has he hurt Mandy?'

'Mandy wasn't home when it happened. He's at the races with Tony and you know what the two of them are like once they get together. Especially if they lose a few bob.'

'Look, I'm just going out myself. If he doesn't come home early, give me a ring on the mobile, get into a cab with Mandy and get over to my place. I'll make sure I'm there to let you in.'

'Thanks, Frank. Are you sure that's okay?'

'Of course it's okay, Nene. Doesn't matter what time it is — just give me a call if you need me. Give my love to Mandy.'

'Thanks a lot, Frank. Bye.'

It was then Frank realised his phone was another casualty of the night before.

CHAPTER 15

Why, why, had the world of men narrowed itself to this one?

Phillip was all health food, vitamin pills and freshly squeezed oranges. If you are what you eat, it wasn't surprising he'd metamorphosed over the years into something more vegetable than animal.

Xin-Xin could hear him pottering in the kitchen. That meant he'd been for his daily jog and come home with the weekend papers. Now he'd be tucking into his bowl of Bircher muesli with nuts, grains, dried fruit and the acidophilus yoghurt that comprised one of the two kinds of culture Phillip was interested in. The other was ancient history — the culture of the past. It seemed to Xin-Xin that things only became exciting for her professor-in-residence after they'd been buried for a millennium or two.

Her recollection of the evening before was a bit sketchy but she remembered the exhibition Neil had taken her to had turned into a fiasco when the artist, Arthur Something-or-Other, had a punch-up with that repulsive Barry O'Connor. And Neil had introduced her to his friend Frank Thornton. God, he'd looked embarrassed when he got her book mixed up with the one by Mira Michieu about Paris.

She remembered going to Cervantes, ordering the suckling pig, and sitting next to him. What was so attractive about the man? Good-looking, in a rough-around-the-edges way. Tall, rangy, bony sort of a bloke. The type, she suspected, that seemed to live forever in defiance of a diet where the three main food groups were drugs, booze and nicotine. Mid-forties or thereabouts. Hair that had once been black but was well on the way to grey. She liked that — it gave him away. A rough diamond. And rough diamonds are a girl's best friend.

Come on, that's nonsense and you know it. That man would be trouble. Nice hands, though, and a surprisingly gentle smile. Not stupid, either.

She could hear Phillip in the bathroom now, grunting, getting all that roughage out of his system. What was wrong with the man?

Not much as far as her parents were concerned. They had their reservations, Xin-Xin was sure of that, but no one would ever be quite good enough for their brilliant baby girl. Perhaps this one's almost good enough, she thought, recalling how damned nosy they'd been lately, with Mum forever asking if Phillip had finally 'popped the question'. It was her business, not theirs, and thank God he never had. It would have been easy enough to tell them she'd said no but impossible to explain why: Phillip wasn't quite bad enough for their brilliant baby girl.

Lenny Matthews had been her great love when she first moved in with Phillip. She'd watched that beautiful Aboriginal boy suffer as she created his life, nurtured him as he almost bloomed against the odds, and despaired when he failed. Xin-Xin had held him to her breast, crying, as he'd died dead drunk on page 273, and she was still mourning his loss. They had a lot in common, she and Lenny. They'd been through it all together and understood each other's pain.

And now a saxophone player, who didn't have a name yet, was coming into her life, catching her on the rebound and offering salvation. Man, did she have plans for him: *crazy mixed-up music baby, crazy mixed-up love.* The fictitious men in her life were those she dreamed of when she lay in bed with Phillip; they were the ones who needed her because she alone could understand their anguish. But there were no demons in the man she could hear flushing the toilet; no damage had been done to him that only her love could repair.

She thought about the day ahead, bored already by the mundaneness of all it held in store. The morning would be tolerable once the hangover wore off. Phillip would disappear into his study and emerge about lunchtime, expecting her to have something ready and waiting. There was a chance he'd ask why she'd arrived home late last night, but it wasn't his way. Their relationship was built on trust and Phillip always checked himself if he felt inclined to pry.

Anyway, she thought, I only went to an exhibition and had dinner with some friends. No need to mention Frank Thornton.

Phillip would talk about the dinner party they were hosting that night, but leaving its success in her hands and dependent on her choice of menu. He knew she loved to cook and wouldn't have it any other way. Besides, he liked an afternoon nap on Saturdays, especially if the evening looked like being late. He was a sensitive new-age guy who, like his insensitive old-age father whose chauvinistic attitudes he despised, knew just how to get his way.

'I've made some coffee, darling,' he called, 'and I've got the papers.'

'I'll be out in a minute,' she said, surprised at how gravelly her voice sounded. All that red wine.

We'll make that twenty minutes, darling, she thought, as her fingers groped in the bedside table for the paracetamol. That's about how long it takes for these little life-savers to start kicking in.

An hour later Xin-Xin was standing in the kitchen, holding the now-cold coffee. She poured it down the sink and prepared another pot. The black silk kimono, a dragon embroidered on the back, slid against her skin. She enjoyed catching glimpses of herself in the hallway mirror whenever she wore it, liked returning the surprised expression of a very attractive young woman, thinking as she turned away: that was me.

She spread the newspaper on the coffee table and turned to the arts pages. A few rainforests had been sacrificed for the greater glory of the Archibald Portrait Prize, which had opened a week before. But she could find no mention of last night's exhibition. She turned back to page one and a headline caught her eye: FRACAS AT GALLERY OPENING.

Two paragraphs informed readers that a scuffle had broken out at a fashionable Paddington art gallery, leaving the proprietor in need of medical and legal advice. Terror-stricken art lovers had to run for their lives when the artist, ex-Golden Gloves light heavyweight boxing champion and occasional painter Arthur Blackwell, rampaged through the crowd, threatening all and sundry. His manager, Frank Horton, was quoted as saying, 'Arthur can be a bit volatile at times' (continued page 4).

'Can't even get his name right,' Xin-Xin muttered as she turned to page 4 where she found two more paragraphs of nonsense in which the paintings themselves finally rated a mention: 'Our art critic, Victor Hollings, reports: "Mr Blackwell would have been better advised to maintain his fiercely protected obscurity than to burst onto the scene with this mishmash of clichés. One portrait, that of friend and fellow commercial illustrator, Neil Puesner, embodies the shortcomings of Blackwell's oeuvre. What Blackwell may consider an example of bravura technique and earthy realism is, in fact, no more than a caricature of the type that, had it been submitted for the Archibald, might have been vulgar enough to have taken out the Packers' Prize."'

'Pompous prat,' Xin-Xin muttered.

She shoved the paper away and marched into the bedroom to get changed. Her regular burning desire to tackle the cryptic crossword had been extinguished by the cold water Hollings had poured on Frank Thornton's friend's exhibition.

Xin-Xin usually enjoyed the shopping but wasn't in the mood for it today. Still, it had to be done.

As she picked her way through the fruit and veg she found herself thinking it was about time Phillip took a turn at the shopping. Prince bloody Phillip, locked away in his study all day or curled up on the couch. Who does he think he is?

Her local butcher was the most expensive in Sydney and had everything, including what she'd decided to cook — suckling pig. Xin-Xin was a woman who could prepare a gastronomic masterpiece with little apparent effort, through a technique known only to those who could afford to shop in the same food stores.

Even Phillip, who had seen this trick performed for the past three years, felt moved to express his admiration when he saw what she'd put on the table for their lunch.

He was topping a slice of Tasmanian brie with sun-dried tomatoes and pickled capsicum when Xin-Xin's mobile phone rang.

She saw the number on the screen and answered quickly.

'It's Michael. Is this a bad time to be calling? I've got to speak to you.'

'Oh, hi, Mum. No, it's okay, we're just having lunch.'

'He's there, isn't he? Obviously. I'm free this afternoon and I was wondering if you —'

'It'll have to wait till tomorrow. We're having some people over tonight and I'll be busy for the rest of the afternoon. I'm doing suckling pig.'

Phillip put down his slice of crusty Italian bread and stared at Xin-Xin.

'All right, Mum. I'll come over tomorrow at about two.'

'Okay, darling,' said Michael. 'Sorry I rang you at such a bad —'

'Bye, Mum.'

'Darling, we have to talk,' said Phillip, after a pause.

Had she said something to give the game away? Maybe the phone was turned up too loud.

'I love you and trust you, and you trust me, right?'

Bring it on, Prince Phillip, Xin-Xin thought as she nodded in agreement. If we have to have it out, we might as well do it now.

'Darling, if you'd just told me. We could have discussed it, talked it over.'

'I just didn't feel that I could.' Tears welled in her eyes, unexpected. The truth was, she felt ashamed. Phillip, for all his faults, hadn't deserved this.

'It's not just me I'm thinking about, it's Leon too.'

'What's Leon got to do with it?'

'Well, Leon's Jewish for goodness sake!'

'So?'

'So he's not going to be able to eat suckling pig, is he?' Phillip shouted. 'You know I don't like pork because it gives me indigestion, but Leon?'

Suddenly the tears had gone.

'I'll go back to the shops and get some seafood.'

'Oh, would you, darling? I'll go if you like.'

'No. I'll go right now.'

As Xin-Xin drove to the shops she made up her mind that when she saw Michael the next day it would be for the last time. She didn't want to jeopardise her relationship with Phillip by having a sordid affair with the likes of Michael Halliday. There were better ways of jeopardising it than that.

She spotted a parking space near the butcher's, pulled up, and wondered if Frank Thornton had found the copy of her book she'd dropped into his bag last night.

CHAPTER 16

'Shit,' said Frank as he stood at the bar with Roy waiting for heart-starters. 'I left my bag somewhere last night — probably at The Favourite.'

'Anything important in it?'

'The usual — diary, toothbrush, Valium, party biscuits and a gram of marching powder.'

'Maybe you left it at AD's. Give Daryl a call later on and see if it's there.'

'I can't.'

'Why not?'

'Because my phone's in the bag too. If the bag's there, Daryl will look after it. But for Christ's sake, remind me to swing by The Favourite at some stage to check. I'll have to make sure I've got the mobile with me tonight.'

'Why? You never use it.'

'Nina rang just after I talked to you. Red's been knocking her about again. I told her if she needs to get away from the bastard she should call me and come over to stay at my place.'

'Fair enough. You should keep your mobile in your pocket, you know. You're forever losing that bloody bag.'

Frank hated phones. Stationary ones were bad enough but mobiles were insufferable. Always interrupting. He'd put off buying one for years, and when he'd finally succumbed had managed to lose three in as many months. The one he had now — his fifth — was better than the others, thanks to a volume control on the ring tone. Roy, who'd chosen it for him, had programmed it to ring discreetly enough to be inaudible when stashed away in the little zipped-up pocket inside his bag from where it rarely emerged. Aside from a soft ring tone, Frank required three things of his mobile: that it be out of sight, out of mind and out of range.

'Be a good night down there tonight,' said Frank, 'Rick Manning's band is playing.'

'I thought you said it would be a good night.'

'Your taste's in your arse and your arse is somewhere back in the 1940s. You're missing out on sixty years of music.'

'Sixty years of self-indulgent crap.'

'What's it to be, gentlemen, two schooners of the usual?' asked the barman.

'Does half a cat bleed?' said Roy.

Frank pulled the newspaper from under his arm as they sat down.

'Did you see what that prick Hollings had to say?'

'We'd better give Arthur a ring,' said Roy. 'He'll need a bit of cheering up.'

'You know Arthur — we won't see him for a few days. I, for one, won't be missing him. Once he'd decided to stay away, he should have stayed away. Everything would have been fine.'

'Come on, Frank, it was a dream come true for Arthur. Most of the paintings were sold by the time he turned up and he got his chance to belt O'Connor afterwards. Icing on the cake.'

'Have to admit, it was lovely to watch. Wasn't the highlight of the evening though.'

'What was her name again?'

'Xin-Xin. Xin-Xin Leroq. She's a writer. Just brought out her second novel. Puss tells me it's terrific.'

'I was watching you through the window when you went outside for a smoke. I could tell you were trying to put in a bit of spadework. Did you get her number?'

'Afraid not. I think she's married.'

'You can't win 'em all, Frank. By the way, how's Harriet?'

'Don't ask. Found the receipt from The Favourite. I turn up pissed one more time, she's leaving.'

'In that case, we'd better get started. My shout.'

The opening round saw Frank and Roy go beer for beer at the Aurora front bar for a couple of hours. According to Roy, the regular ingestion of food — or 'the lumpy bits', as he called it — was essential to the maintenance of life. On his insistence they adjourned to the restaurant area where they swallowed some down with the aid of a couple of bottles of wine.

Thus fortified, they proceeded to the Bellevue in Paddington. There the contest continued, to a backdrop of football and races on the tellies and the roar of fellow champions battling it out in bacchanalia of their own. Many a poorly trained contender suffered near fatal blows to the liver, and just as many walked out bankrupt as a result of ill-advised investments on horses and in poker machines.

Both Roy and Frank lasted the distance and, as usual, their final destination was AD's. At ten o'clock, they hailed a cab to take them there.

'Christ, your phone,' said Roy.

'Oh, that's right. We'll have to stop off at The Favourite to see if I left it there.'

They pulled up a few minutes later in front of an innocent-looking terrace house. A small sign by the front door advised visitors that all the major credit cards were acceptable within.

'This'll only take a sec,' said Frank. He stepped out of the taxi and bounded up the steps.

Roy watched as Frank was welcomed by the madam. The two of them stepped inside and closed the door. A minute or two later Frank came back, empty-handed.

'No luck?' asked Roy.

'My bag wasn't there,' Frank said, 'but something else was. Harry Parkinson's daughter.'

'Bullshit.'

'It was her, all right.'

'Did she see you?'

'No, thank Christ.'

Frank's boss Harry Parkinson was taciturn, brusque and, to everyone's surprise, especially that of the woman to whom he'd been married for thirty years, queer. He was hated and feared by his staff but none of them wanted to work anywhere else. Harry's was a resilient company that had outlived and crushed innumerable rivals.

Harry Parkinson had his first shave at around the same time he'd come bursting out of the sexual closet, unearthing a face which had never developed a chin and which none of his employees recognised. He was fat, sweated a lot inside his crumpled linen suits, and was always in soft focus somewhere inside the dense clouds of smoke emanating from his pipe. He was a big spender, although he was yet to find a retail outlet selling generosity at a reasonable price. You couldn't buy a gift for Harry because he was the man who had everything, including a twenty-one-year-old daughter who was working at The Favourite.

'Better ring up beforehand the next time we go,' said Roy.

'Could be a bit embarrassing.'

'Is she a good sort?'

'Rather be in her than the Boy Scouts,' said Frank as the cab dropped them off at AD's.

Rick Manning was a virtuoso saxophonist whose improvisations were pure pleasure for those who understood the language of jazz and pure torment for those who didn't. Tonight the former were outnumbered by the latter, who were shouting to make themselves heard above the noise of the band. The band was playing louder than usual in order to be heard above them, and the resulting cacophony was deafening.

'Thanks a lot, mate,' shouted Frank as Daryl handed him his scuffed leather shoulder bag.

'No worries, Frank. I helped myself to my commission,' said Daryl. His idiot grin left Frank in no doubt that forgetting his bag had cost him one of his vitamin Es. At least.

'Fair enough,' he said, hoping Daryl hadn't helped himself to the charlie too. Daryl had a nose like a vacuum cleaner, a fact confirmed a few minutes later when Frank investigated the contents of his bag in a cubicle in the gents. He chopped up a decent-sized line for himself on the lid of the cistern and decided Daryl had let him off lightly.

He stuffed the gear back into his bag and did a quick check to make sure his diary and phone were still there ... and found himself pulling out a brand-new copy of *Gang-Gang*, 'a novel by Xin-Xin Leroq'. She'd taken the trouble to sign and date it on the title page, which was touching, but what interested Frank most was the bookmark she'd inserted. It was her card, complete with phone number and email address.

Access! Where would we be without email? thought the greatest Luddite in advertising as he visualised his forefingers clattering out a courtship on the keyboard come Monday.

'That charlie must have been good,' said Roy. 'You've got a grin on you like a split watermelon.'

'Bugger the charlie,' said Frank. 'Look what was in my bag.'

'You rotten bastard,' said Roy, shaking his head as he inspected the cover of Xin-Xin's book. 'You lucky, rotten bastard.'

Frank loved the tenor saxophone and, for his money, nobody in Sydney played it better than Rick Manning. He also loved trios, regarding them as bands pared down to their essentials. He settled back, shut out the noise of the unappreciative majority, and let the music go to work on him. The lines of Manning's melodies were ribbons floating on a cloud of rhythm and harmony. This, he thought, is as good as it gets. Listening to jazz, fondling Xin-Xin's book and thinking the two of them might meet again had lifted his mood to a plateau from where he could see a magnificent view of the future.

Roy was more interested in the form guide. If the music was made of ribbons on clouds, they were floating well above his head.

'Can I have a line of your charlie?' he asked.

'Go for your life,' said Frank.

According to the critics quoted on the back, Xin-Xin's book was going to be well worth a read. 'An astonishing achievement,' gushed one. 'One of the year's best,' rhapsodised another.

I'll make my own literary judgments, thank you very much, Frank thought, and was about to start reading when Roy came back in a state.

'Julie's here,' he said. 'What should I do?'

'Has she seen you?'

'I don't think so. I'll piss off back to the Aurora. I don't like this music anyway. You coming?'

'I'll leave after the next set and meet you there. Where have you been if she asks me?'

'Think of something. I'll see you later.'

Frank went back to Xin-Xin's book, hoping Roy's wife wouldn't spot him or, if she did, that she'd see he was alone and leave him alone. Frank had no time for Julie and believed the feeling was mutual. His aversion to Julie had been established the moment he met her and saw she had no lips. He'd always regarded lips as a basic requirement for loveliness: acceptable in all shapes and sizes, as long as they were there, framing the hole with the teeth in it. Their absence spoke volumes to Frank, signifying a tight-arsed wowser with a mean streak and no fun whatsoever. How Roy had ever been attracted to her was beyond him.

Insightful Roy had once suggested that Frank was wrong to think Julie hated him. Over a beer at the Bellevue, Roy explained he got that impression because she was jealous of him. The pair of them did spend an awful lot of time together and maybe — just maybe — Julie felt left out.

Frank, for whom jealousy and its consequences had been defined by a regrettable incident in the toilet of The Pharmacy, had scratched his head, adopted a reflective pose and said, 'Roy, that would have to be the silliest thing you've ever said in your life.'

He hadn't actually seen Julie yet but he knew she was lurking around somewhere and it made him feel uneasy.

He made a careful study of Xin-Xin's signature (a good, strong, confident hand indicative of a healthy sex drive and excellent taste in blokes) and turned to the potted biography.

Xin-Xin Leroq graduated from Sydney University with an Honours degree in English literature in 1993. In 1994 she left Australia to do a Master's degree at Columbia University, New York, which she completed in 1996. Her first novel, *Lost Sheep*, won the Fleetwood Award for the most outstanding book by a first-time Australian novelist, 1997. Ms Leroq lives and works in Sydney, Australia. *Gang-Gang* is her second novel.'

Rick Manning announced the band was taking a break. For the first time ever, it was welcome news to their biggest fan. Frank needed to concentrate if he was to savour every word and, hopefully, read between the lines. He turned to the first page.

The grey birds jabbed their rough red heads at the few seeds remaining in a worn-out gum tree. Lenny listened to their mutterings, recognising familiar phrases, catching occasional new ones. They ignored him as they pecked and gossiped, just like the elders when he'd done something wrong.'

'Hello, Frank,' said Julie Humber. 'What can I get you to drink?'
'Oh. Hi, Jules. I'll have another one of these, thanks.'

Frank felt like a worn-out gum tree being jabbed by the beak of a gang-gang cockatoo as Julie pecked at the bark of his cheek. Gloomily he followed her progress towards the bar. The coke had worn off and he could swear that the part of his face where she'd kissed him had sobered up.

She passed him his drink and sat down. 'Enjoying the band?'

'The last set was fantastic.'

'I got their new CD the other day. It's brilliant. Mind you, it's not the sort of thing I can listen to when Roy's around,' she said, and threw in a wink for good measure. 'Have you seen him today?'

'No,' Frank said.

'Neither have I. Oh — here they are!' She stood up and waved to two attractive females who steered their way towards them as she organised more chairs. 'Lola, Susie, I'd like you to meet Frank. Frank's a mate of Roy's, but don't let that put you off.'

Both of them giggling and taking off their jackets; Frank jumping out of his chair and shaking their hands. A minute later he was at the bar ordering four more drinks.

CHAPTER 17

By eleven o'clock, Nina was finding it hard to concentrate on the video of *Thelma and Louise*, even though Mandy seemed to be enjoying it. Red still wasn't home by the time the movie finished. Perhaps he'd had a big win and he and Tony were batting on for a while. It was nothing to worry about. As long as they didn't bat on too long.

Nina went to bed at one and lay awake for an hour before deciding it might be best to call Frank and take him up on his offer.

Frank's phone was in its usual place in his bag and his bag was in its usual place somewhere under a table at AD's. Frank may not be responding to phone calls but he was very busy responding to messages of an altogether different kind — and starting to transmit a few of his own. Urgent ones they were, too. And Lola was picking them up loud and clear from between her legs, also under a table at AD's.

Nina left a message, turned the telly off and threw a blanket over Mandy who had fallen asleep on the couch. She poured herself a glass from the bottle of red she'd opened earlier that evening and sat in an armchair, waiting for the phone to ring.

Half an hour later she called again.

'Come on, Frank,' she whispered as she held the phone to her ear with her shoulder and drained the last of the bottle into her glass. 'Answer your fucking phone!'

Frank groped on the floor for his bag and reached inside. In the darkness under the table, his fingers did a quick search. Ah, there it is! he thought.

He crumpled the small plastic bag of cocaine tightly into his fist, excused himself and headed for the toilet.

It took Nina a moment to realise where she was when she woke. She'd fallen asleep in an awkward position and had pins and needles in her right arm. She looked at the clock, saw it was 3 am, grabbed the phone and tried to call Frank again.

He must be home by now, she thought. She tried him there but he didn't answer.

'Wake up, Mandy,' she said, shaking her and turning on the light in the lounge. 'Come on, love, wake up.'

'What are you doing?'

'We've got to pack a few things and get out. We're going over to Frank's place.'

'Why?'

'Because Frank said we could go and stay with him if Dad didn't come home and I got frightened. Well, I'm frightened. So come on, let's go.'

Mandy hadn't been around last time Red came home drunk, but she's seen her mother's face afterwards and knew what it meant when she said she'd walked into the door. She jumped up quickly and got busy.

Their bags were packed and Nina had called for a cab when Red Morrow came through the front door. 'What the fuck is going on here?' he said.

The Morrows' neighbours, Bruce and Joy McKell, were heavy sleepers. It took a lot to wake them up. They'd heard the goings-on next door dozens of times before but this was beyond a joke.

'Call the police, love, for Christ's sake, call the police,' said Joy.

Bruce had had a gutful. He wasn't about to stand idly by and let this sort of thing go on. The coppers could take too long.

'You call the coppers, darl, and I'll go over there and see what I can do.'

'Oh for God's sake, Bruce! There's no need for you to get involved. Just call the police. Bruce! Bruce!'

But Bruce was already out the door.

While Joy McKell was giving a policewoman her neighbours' names and address she heard more screaming and the booming voice of Red Morrow telling her husband to fuck off or he'd get it next. She was trying to explain to the policewoman it was a genuine emergency when Bruce ran back into the house screaming at her to tell the coppers to get over here now and call a bloody ambulance for Christ's sake.

'Tell them to get over here now, Joy, the bloke is going to kill them both.'

'Who are the good sorts?' Daryl asked through his pill-induced grin.

'Dunno. Friends of Julie's, I think.'

'Things are looking up a bit, aren't they, mate?'

'Yeah, ta,' said Frank, heading back to Julie and the two good sorts.

Lola and Susie turned out to be colleagues of Julie's, who turned out to be a PR manager with a recording company called Amplitude, which happened to specialise in jazz. All this was news to Frank. It was one of those things Roy had probably told him while he was pissed, in which case he needn't have bothered. He was pissed now too, so it wasn't a detail his memory would retain for long, but it was of significance now.

'What's the book, Frank?' Julie asked.

'It's called *Gang-Gang*. I'm told it's pretty good.'

'It is. I've read it,' Lola chimed in.

Lola was tall, dark-skinned and vivacious and Frank was tipping she'd be from Chile or Brazil. Latin America, definitely. That being the case, she probably liked a line or two of charlie. And another two or three of those double scotches wouldn't do her any harm.

For a man who'd been drinking since ten o'clock in the morning, Frank's adroitness in manoeuvring himself to a position next to Lola was nothing short of remarkable. It was done with such skill nobody noticed he'd moved at all. Within minutes, the two were engaged in whispered conversation, necessitating contact close enough for Frank to get a good whiff of her neck. He was no connoisseur when it came to perfume but smell was extremely important, and Lola smelt very promising indeed.

'Man,' said Lola, squeezing his thigh for emphasis, 'these guys are hot.'

'My word,' he murmured.

Lola. It rolled off the tongue. He found himself thinking about the words of that old pop song and remembered that the Lola in question had turned out to be a transsexual. He checked her chin for an emerging five o'clock shadow, just in case. Smooth as a baby's bottom.

She was saying something about Rick Manning sounding like Jerry Bergonzi, and he was agreeing, even though he'd always thought of him more as the Joe Henderson type. He listened carefully the next time he played a solo and realised she was right.

'See?' she said.

She knew her jazz, no doubt about that.

He started planning the CD selection for later on. A bad choice could bugger things entirely. Latin-style music was out for a start. She'd know more about that than he did.

The band was between sets and Frank rose to buy another round.

'Sit down, Frank,' said Julie, 'it's my shout. What's everybody having?'

Frank was of the old school that required men to foot the bill no matter what. He wasn't rich but he should have been, and that wasn't the only reason. It had occurred to him that he'd drunk at least a waterfront mansion over the years, and a holiday cottage or two had found their way up his nose. He comforted himself when such thoughts arose by thinking that, while he mightn't have managed to save his fortune, at least he'd spent it wisely.

And here was Julie insisting on another shout — tight-lipped, tight-arsed Julie. He acquiesced and, after approving of Lola's choice of another double scotch, decided he'd better stick to beer. The aim of the exercise was to make sure Lola ended up drunker than him and it wasn't as if he hadn't had a head start.

One song later and Lola was at the bar. When she came back she had the same again plus a round of tequilas. Frank was able to relax now, knowing the preparatory work had been done. He was under starter's orders, steady in the saddle and looking forward to the ride.

When the band finished their final number to rapturous applause from those few who had stayed till the end it was almost four o'clock. The transfer of the charlie from Frank's bag into Lola's purse had been dexterously handled and Lola was straight off to the toilet. Not quite as straight as might have been the case without four double scotches and two tequilas under her belt, but she was upright and Frank was impressed. He liked a woman who could drink at his pace without turning into a gibbering idiot, and then move on to the cocaine. And there were the ecstasies too — he'd forgotten about those. It was nice to know they were there because you never know, you just never know.

He was in luck. When Lola returned from the ladies with a sniffle she'd contracted in there, she confided she'd had an E a couple of hours ago and was in just the mood for a top-up.

The tablets were kicking in nicely as the four of them emerged into the fresh air.

'Who wants to bat on?' asked Julie.

Lola and Frank had abandoned any pretence of decorum and were disporting themselves in a way that was probably illegal in a public place.

'You two obviously do but I doubt if you want us to come and watch.'

In the cab it flashed into Frank's mind that he'd made some arrangement to meet Roy. Oh fuck him, he thought, and went back to groping this gorgeous, voracious, black-haired, dark-skinned, late-twenties, doped-up-and-ready-to-go Latino love doll.

The fare came to fifteen bucks. Frank tossed the driver thirty and told him to keep the change, thinking the poor bastard would probably lose a fare or two in the time it would take him to pull up somewhere and have one off the wrist.

They stumbled up the stairs and resumed groping in the lift. By the time they made it to the door of Frank's apartment, Lola's legs were wrapped firmly around his, leaving Frank solely responsible for keeping them both vertical. He fumbled for the keys with one hand and clung to her thigh with the other.

As soon as they crossed the threshold their clothes started coming off, nudity being achieved somewhere in the vicinity of the kitchen. Frank consolidated a solid grip on her behind, hoisting her aloft again so that, while not yet having made the beast with two backs, they were a beast with two legs.

And a very top-heavy beast it was that proceeded down the hallway, hastily and eagerly, all the way to the bedroom where it crashed — panting and slavering — on top of the bed, and Harriet.

CHAPTER 18

Eddie Longman, an art director with Parkinson's, had just returned from a pleasant brunch with his wife and their teenage daughter when he received a phone call from Frank Thornton.

'Still on for the footy, Frank?'

Frank had forgotten all about the footy.

'The game starts at two,' said Eddie.

'Ask you a favour? Can you come and pick me up? Just spent the night in the Surry Hills cells and I don't have any dough for a cab.'

'Oh shit, Frank,' said Eddie, laughing. 'What have you been up to this time?'

'Tell you when I see you. I'm leaving the cop shop now and I'll see you on the corner of Riley Street and Oxford.'

Thirty minutes later Eddie was beside Frank and beside himself with laughter in the bar of the Olympic Hotel, across the road from the football stadium.

'Why didn't you take her somewhere else?' he managed.

'I was well away by that stage.'

'And the shiner?'

Frank ran a finger over his right eye, which was pretty swollen but didn't hurt much. The lumps on the back of his head were worse.

'Harriet belted me with the bedside lamp. Got me on the back of the head too.'

'And who called the coppers?'

'Probably the old bloke who lives downstairs. What shits me is that I'm the one who ended up in the cells. The coppers should have lumbered both of the bitches for grievous bodily harm.'

'What did they do you for?'

'They let me off with a warning, but it's lucky I left my bag at AD's again. I would have ended up on a drug charge.'

'You've gotta laugh.'

They were still laughing when Roy walked in.

'What's the joke?'

'Wait till you hear what Frankie-boy got up to last night. Christ, it was funny.'

'It had fucking well better be,' said Roy. 'He left me waiting at the Aurora all night and I dropped four hundred on the pokies.'

Frank loved the Swans. They had evolved in South Melbourne before moving to Sydney, just as he had. His grandfather had told him they were originally called the 'Bloods' but had changed their name after drafting a pack of West Australians in the 1930s. The old name appealed to Frank. He found it infinitely preferable to the Swans which he considered more appropriate for a team of ballet dancers.

There were some traditionalists in South Melbourne who still insisted on using the old name, but in Sydney, Frank was the only one — an eccentric anachronism amongst the crowd, fighting a losing battle for a long-lost cause. Eddie and Roy, Swans supporters to the core, thought he was mad.

'They're the Bloods, you ignorant bastards,' Frank snarled as the three of them groped their way towards their seats, juggling beers, spilling them, and making enemies.

'Careful, mate,' grumbled a fellow Swans supporter.

'Sorry, mate,' said Frank.

'Watch what you're fuckin' doin',' snapped a Brisbane Lions supporter.

'Why don't you get fucked,' Frank suggested.

Out of a crowd of forty thousand people he suspected he was the only one who'd spent the previous night in the lock-up, where he'd slept maybe an hour or so, and that his was probably the only head with a force seven raging inside and a black eye on the outside, plus a clutch of lumps like a relief map of the Himalayas. By the time they were seated he was beyond irritable. Seeing all the Swans flags and placards did nothing to improve his mood. They were the Bloods and that was that.

'Go you mighty Swans!' roared Eddie as the umpire bounced the ball and the battle commenced.

'Go you Bloods!' bawled Frank. His voice echoed so agonisingly inside his head he decided that was enough direct involvement from him today. He took the first sip of one of his beers and pulled a pie out of his pocket. He didn't want to see his team beaten today. He'd rather go home and be beaten by Harriet again than see his beloved Bloods lose to this despicable Brisbane side. A win, on the other hand, would be a deeply satisfying experience — something he needed badly.

Another of life's most uplifting experiences was taking money out of Harry Parkinson's tightly gripped wallet, and there was a good chance Frank would enjoy that the next day. The idiot, who knew nothing about football but hailed from Brisbane, had backed the Lions to win in a two hundred dollar bet with Frank at two-to-one.

The indomitable Tony Lockett, the Bloods' star full forward, booted the first goal of the game.

Frank felt better already.

'Plugger Lockett,' Roy intoned as they resumed their seats and the roar of the crowd subsided. 'If that man had tits on his back I'd marry him.'

By the time the siren sounded at the end of the final quarter, the local team had shown how brutally Sydney can repel invaders from the north. Frank, Roy and Eddie were as exhausted and proud as if they'd played the game and kicked the six winning goals themselves. They headed straight to the Cricketers Arms for refreshment and a post-match analysis.

By midnight they'd refreshed themselves to the point of post-match paralysis and didn't have the strength to complain when the barman said, 'Last drinks, gentlemen, please.'

Frank made an unsuccessful attempt to hail a police car he'd mistaken for a cab. This revived memories of the night before and, as he slumped in a taxi, the prospect of what might be in store when he arrived home filled him with such foreboding he considered checking in at a hotel instead. He'd seen the dark side of Harriet and was in no condition to go through it all again. But a man has to do what a man has to do.

He gritted his teeth and hoped for the best as he opened the door, switched on the light and gazed at the carnage confronting him.

The first thing he focused on was the television. A tomato sauce bottle had penetrated the screen with such force it appeared some victim from a snuff movie had tried to make good his escape by leaping out of it, only to bleed to death on the floor.

How she'd managed to destroy the furniture was anybody's guess, but Harriet had gone about the business with great attention to detail. Crockery and glassware formed a carpet of shards to which various appliances, the computer, bookshelves and countless other objects he no longer recognised had been added in a series of apparently cathartic explosions. Harriet had clearly done this sort of thing before. It didn't look like the work of an amateur.

Frank felt an intense wave of relief. For all her faults, Harriet had been as good as her word. Okay, her manner of exit was a bit melodramatic, but it could only mean one thing: she was out of the door and out of his life.

The things he cared about most — the paintings and framed drawings — seemed to have escaped unscathed. The glass in most of the frames had been smashed but the drawings inside had survived.

Christ! The Goya etchings!

He ran into the hallway and found all three untouched.

Fuck! The phone!

Smashed to pieces. That reminded him: Nina had said she'd give him a call if that mongrel husband of hers went out on the piss and cut up rough. Maybe she'd tried to call him on the mobile. Shit! He'd left the bag at AD's again with the mobile in it.

As he dropped — uneventfully this time — onto his dishevelled bed, Frank thought of one of his dad's old phrases: as happy as a canful of worms on their way home from a fishing trip. That's how I feel, he thought. That telly was fucked anyway.

He'd been meaning to buy a new one for years.

CHAPTER 19

How long was it since they'd had sex? Xin-Xin couldn't remember.

Showed how memorable it was. In a couple of months Phillip would be thirty-six. According to the literature, men reached their sexual peak at eighteen. Xin-Xin wondered what the average half-life of a man was, because this one wouldn't move the needle on a Geiger counter now. Women, apparently, peaked at about thirty-two, which meant she could expect hers in another three years. At this rate it would come and go without Phillip noticing. Maybe he had what the women's magazines referred to as 'erectile dysfunctional problems'. She might have to get him onto the Viagra. Grind up a couple and slip them into his Lapsang Souchong.

She could hear him clunking crockery and cutlery into the dishwasher. Was he exacerbating her headache on purpose? A change of tone indicated he'd turned his attention to the saucepans. How long would this go on? She couldn't remember how many pots and pans she'd used to prepare last night's meal but she knew the conversation had started in ancient Rome and, by the time their guests departed around two, still hadn't made it to the modern world.

She groped for the paracetamol. He's driving me to drink, she thought, squeezing his pillow around her head to block out the noise.

Now he'd decided to add a soundtrack — that vile Toni Childs CD — and intensify the torture by singing along in his tenor-to-alto warble.

Crash! Something hit the tiles, probably the wok. Percussion now! When the garlic took effect, she'd no doubt be treated to a trombone solo. I suppose he'll expect me to applaud ...

'Phone, darling,' Phillip suddenly whispered round the corner of the pillow. 'It's Lawrence.'

'Xini, sorry to ring so early,' her brother said. She glanced at the clock and saw it was almost eleven. 'You busy?'

'Why?'

'Thought you might like to pop over, that's all.'

Phillip was lingering.

'I'm going to see Mum at two,' she said, remembering her rendezvous with Michael.

'Come over now and I'll make some brunch.'

Xin-Xin weighed up her options. Phillip had told her he'd be busy all day, marking essays. The last thing she felt like right now was muesli with him and muzak with Toni Childs. The second-last was making another mercy dash for her stupid brother. She knew what he was after and was sick and tired of him. And his slut of a girlfriend. The second-last narrowly won.

'That's sweet of you, Lawrence,' she said. 'I'll just check that it's okay with Phillip.'

Phillip responded with a well-if-you-have-to look and a roll of the eyes. Xin-Xin told Lawrence she'd be there in half an hour.

'Could you make me a cup of coffee, darling — good and strong?' she said to Phillip, and headed for the seclusion of the shower.

'So what time will you be home?' Phillip asked as Xin-Xin sipped her coffee and dragged on a frowned-upon cigarette. It was her second for the morning and she knew he was counting.

'About six. Is that okay?'

'Fine. I'll make you some dinner for a change.'

Mum and Dad had meant well when they'd bought apartments for their children five minutes' drive from each other and the family home. At around the fourth minute of her drive to Lawrence's place, Xin-Xin thought how much happier she'd have been if they'd found something for Lawrence further away. On the moon, perhaps.

Using her key, she let herself in. The lift glided upwards to the penthouse. It gave onto a marble entrance hall, on the other side of which the door to her brother's apartment was open. The smell of freshly made coffee and a couple of croissants on the table were evidence that Lawrence had made an effort. Xin-Xin usually found it touching when her brother made efforts, but this time he needn't have bothered.

'I'll be with you in a sec,' he called from the bathroom.

She poured herself a coffee, lit a cigarette and looked out over the harbour. You could see all the way to Manly. It was a better view than hers. Wasted on Lawrence.

He gave her a peck on the cheek, poured himself a coffee and sat down.

'Croissant?'

'Not hungry, thanks.'

When asked, Lawrence would say he was six foot tall. He was usually wearing boots with two-inch Cuban heels at the time, so, technically, he was telling the truth. If asked about his build, he would describe himself as lean. He was, in fact, scrawny, with the raffish look of a seventies punk-rock star, suggestive of late nights, a hedonistic lifestyle and malnutrition. His high cheekbones, full lips and craggy features were considered sexy by rebellious young girls and ghoulish by their mothers. His hair, when freshly gelled and fully erect, poked upwards to a height of about three inches and made his head look like a black toilet brush on top of a very long handle. The similarity was reinforced by his preference for tight jeans and long-sleeved T-shirts, most of which were a few sizes too small, sweaty and in need of a wash.

'Where's her ladyship?'

'Still asleep.'

'Is she ever awake?'

Lawrence ignored the question. No point trying to talk up Evie's qualities to Xin-Xin. He couldn't think of any that would impress her. Within minutes of their meeting, Xin-Xin had relegated Evie to the art-school-reject, would-be-model, bimbo category. Evie, in turn, had written Xin-Xin off as the up-herself, pseudo-intellectual sister. A year later, neither had seen any reason to modify her first impression.

Today, things were going according to an established routine for the Leroq siblings. Phase one consisted of a brief bout of platitudes. Phase two would commence with Xin-Xin making some innocuous enquiry about her brother's professional life, to which he would reply with a sequence of lies. He had to make them good ones in order to achieve a desirable outcome in phase three.

This would start with Xin-Xin taking from her bag a notebook in which she kept a record of how much money she had loaned him in her role as buffer zone between Lawrence and the parental family fortune. At the moment he was in her debt to the tune of nearly forty thousand dollars and it had been a long time since he'd threatened her with repayment.

The procedure would conclude with Xin-Xin handing Lawrence money, in the form of a cheque or in cash. The amount varied according to her mood, her patience and how convincingly he'd told his fibs.

Lawrence suspected her mood today was anything but generous, the patience factor wasn't working in his favour and she hadn't believed a word he'd said. He didn't fancy his chances of snipping her for much more than a grand.

Although the Lord had never made Lawrence truly thankful for what he was about to receive, He'd blessed him with an ability to ensure he got it in large amounts. While he'd shown no artistic ability whatsoever during his two years at art school, Lawrence had mastered the language of art-speak which stood him in good stead for what then became his career. He'd honed his skills to the point where he was later able to invest a dog turd cast in bronze with such significance that its proud new owner felt convinced her bubble-wrapped *objet d'art* was a thing of beauty and an investment forever.

Using bullshit to sell dogshit had become a way of life for Lawrence since he'd dropped out of art school. His father had come to the rescue in his hour of want, buying him a funky warehouse, along with an obligation-free gift of half a million dollars to be spent on carefully selected, fashionable stock — of the challenging, cutting-edge variety of course. Benny Leroq's commercial intuition had shown itself to be infallible when it came to oriental antiques and he didn't doubt that the boy had inherited a similar gift in the more lucrative realm of non-commercial art.

His belief in Lawrence's abilities was vindicated on the opening night of Vacant Space Fine Art, Woollahra.

A signwriter had shown Lawrence a collection of freeway signs emblazoned with meticulously rendered obscenities where one would normally expect placenames or direction indicators. Lawrence chose the most scandalous example and featured it on the opening night invitation along with a photo of the artist himself. The discerning eye of critic Victor Hollings had recognised the profundity behind the profanity, the sensitivity and genius lurking behind the contemptuous sneer on the handsome face of this rough tradesman, and wrote a review as glowing as the signs themselves.

Lawrence sold them all within an hour and took orders for more. The former blue-collar worker posed for photographs and insisted he was only prepared to answer questions related to technique. Those with aesthetic enquiries should direct them to Mr Leroq. Lawrence was up and running.

Now in its thirteenth year, the business continued to give the impression of prosperity. Xin-Xin alone knew that Lawrence was broke. For a man with such extensive means, his inability ever to make them meet was, at first, a source of amazement and, these days, a source of annoyance. She knew he drank too much and lived lavishly, spending every dollar as it arrived. She sighed every time she saw yet another photo in the social pages of her brother with some glamorous airhead hanging off his skinny arm, and lately she wondered how frequently she'd been duped by the stories he'd told in phase two.

'Xini, I've got a big show coming up. Hector Mitchell. It's already got so much publicity. We can't miss.'

'The guy who does the street signs?'

'That's the one.'

'Forget it,' she said. 'The next time you need money, ask Dad.'

'But Xini, what about our arrangement? You know I can't ask Dad.'

Xin-Xin collected her things and made for the door.

'You'll have to, Lawrence. I can't keep lending you money forever. And I hope the show goes well, because I want you to start paying me back.'

Lawrence was affecting a pout.

'It's for your own good, darling.'

She gave him a goodbye kiss; a gesture of affection and pity for a man with the doleful demeanour of a dog about to roll over and beg.

He would have, too, if he'd thought it would have done any good.

Neither David nor Igor Oistrackh could improve Xin-Xin's mood as they negotiated their way through the exultant first movement of Bach's Double Violin Concerto in D Minor. And if they couldn't, nobody could. Not even the BMW helped. She used to love cocooning herself in the sports car's leather-clad sanctuary, listening to CDs of Johann Sebastian or Miles. Six months later and it was just a car like any other. Got her from A to B, but what about the other twenty-four letters?

She stabbed at the accelerator, stabbed at the ashtray, tried to take a stab at identifying her feelings. Depressed? No. Fed-up, frustrated, angry? All three.

She looked at her watch. Not even twelve-thirty. She was supposed to be meeting Michael at two. What the hell. She might as well turn up early and get it over with.

Ellen, the lead character in Xin-Xin's first novel, had fallen for Max Hessler QC, the perfect arsehole. Overendowed with good looks and rat cunning, he was the kind of man who breezed through life without a moment of self-doubt. And why shouldn't he? Studying law had taught him the difference between right and wrong: wrong was illegal and could land you in jail; right was permissible and, if you couldn't get arrested for it, why not do it? Xin-Xin remembered the sadistic pleasure she'd derived from his creation, embellishing his every characteristic like a cartoonist unable to resist adding just that extra inch to a politician's nose. She recalled her feeling of superiority and pity for Ellen as she let him have his way with her naive heroine, just as he'd had with the other women he boasted about to his learned friends in the plush bar near his Phillip Street chambers. The hardest part had been inventing ways to convince the reader that Ellen — a highly intelligent young woman not unlike herself — could possibly have been attracted to him.

For three months, Xin-Xin been having an affair with Michael Halliday QC, who fitted Max Hessler's description down to the last detail. As a highly intelligent young woman, she now found it difficult to understand how she could ever have been attracted to him. If God is writing my life, she thought, He's got a sick sense of humour. Well, He's had His fun with me. They both have: God, and the man who thinks he is.

The gates to Michael's private Fantasyland were open. His Range Rover, glinting in the driveway, occupied centre stage. Pink pebbles crunched and grated under her feet as she made her way to the front door. She rang the doorbell. When there was no answer, she walked around the back to see if he was by the pool, working on his tan. Not there either. His yacht was absent from its mooring at the end of the private jetty, the connecting link between the verdant playground of his garden and the turquoise one of his harbour. Or, as it suddenly appeared to Xin-Xin, a rat's tail tapering into the water from the backside of his backyard.

He'd said two and two it would be. You didn't tamper with the entertainment schedule of a man like Halliday QC: 10:30 am, boating on the harbour; 2:00 pm, Xin-Xin in the bedroom.

She returned to her car and poked about in the glove box for a piece of paper and a pen.

Michael, arrived early — 12:45. Sorry I missed you — would have preferred to see you so I could have spoken to you face to face. Easier this way, though. Better too — you like to have things 'in writing'. I don't want to see you again and I don't want you to call. I know you've never condescended to read either of my books. Do me a favour and read my first novel. There's a character in it you might recognise. But don't bother suing for defamation — I didn't meet you till after the book had been published. It's called Lost Sheep. *Available in all good bookstores.*

Baa,
Xin-Xin

She folded the letter and slid it under the front door.

The sight of the harbour ambushed her as she turned her car down the winding hill towards Rose Bay. She'd been so busy making significant decisions and taking stands she hadn't noticed it was the most perfect of autumn days. It was a good opportunity to pull up, take a quiet walk, gather her thoughts and consider what to do next.

She became aware of the concerto. The third movement — her favourite — had begun. Amazing how the first and second movements could have been playing all that time and she hadn't heard a single note. The music and the view colluded, fixing her to her seat and erasing everything she felt had been conspiring against her. She forgot about the financial quagmire her relationship with her brother had become; the travesty that had been her senseless affair with Michael; the emptiness and loneliness she felt when Phillip wouldn't leave her alone. She sat, still and calm, right up until the last sumptuous cadence, then let the final chord drift into silence.

She clicked the CD player off and stepped out into the real world. The wind was a bit cold. She abandoned her plan of going for a walk, opting instead for a coffee and a snack. There was a newsagency on the next corner. She could pick up a paper and settle down with the cryptic crossword. The afternoon wasn't panning out too badly after all.

'I'll have the baked cheesecake, thanks,' she said, handing back the dessert menu.

'Cream or ice-cream?'

'Both. And a long black.'

How Xin-Xin retained her sixteen-year-old figure at twenty-nine was a mystery to everyone who had seen her eat.

'We did a deal,' her mother, speaking on behalf of the other billion or two Asian women on the planet, had once explained to her daughter. 'We got the choice between peripheral vision or eternal youth.'

She whipped through the crossword in a trice, except for one lousy clue that threatened to take up more time than the rest put together. And it wasn't as if she didn't have plenty of letters already in place.

You, Eve? (6,6).

'Second person,' she finally wrote, put a tick under the puzzle and lit up a ciggie to go with the coffee.

As she flicked through the paper, she glanced again at the rubbish Victor Hollings had written about Arthur Blackwell. The man went into raptures at the sight of Hector Mitchell's street signs then dismissed Frank Thornton's friend with a paragraph of pretentious prose.

Frank Thornton, she mused. Wonder if he's reading my book.

She paid the bill, put the newspaper in her bag, picked up her jacket and made for the bathroom.

At the washbasin she paused to look at her reflection and felt that momentary rush of terror she'd experienced often as a child, failing to recognise the person looking back at her. It was a third person she was staring at. Familiar, yes — she saw her often enough — but a stranger just the same.

Back in the car, she didn't feel up to Bach. She rifled through various CDs in the glove box and found *Grace Under Pressure* by John Scofield.

Just the thing, she thought. I'll be needing some of that by the time I get home.

It might have been autumn but it was spring-cleaning time and she wanted it all over and done by tonight. She was tidying up the mess in the rooms of her emotional household: two down, one to go. The job wouldn't be finished until she'd taken the Ajax to Phillip.

Never put off till tomorrow what you can put off till the day after — that had been her policy when dealing with Phillip. Well, today was the day after and it had to be done. Her hands felt cold and sweaty on the steering wheel. Why did they always do that when she was feeling lonely, frightened and lost?

Xin-Xin unlocked the door of her home and glanced over her shoulder before slipping inside. An onlooker would have thought her a burglar using a stolen key. She felt like one as she slipped her sneakers off and padded towards the kitchen. Ten past four. Poor Phillip. He wouldn't be expecting her for another two hours and still had all those papers to mark. He worked hard, you had to give him that. And he was loving too; loving, honest and reliable. Only a very spoilt woman could ask for more.

She felt increasingly wretched with every minute. Standing in the kitchen, she wondered why she'd gone in there. A cup of coffee ... that's right. She took the percolator from the stove and was making for the sink when she became aware of a noise.

She opened the study door a fraction; quickly closed it after the facts had been established. She'd never seen the girl before, probably one of his students. What did it matter? She'd had a glimpse of two awkward people caught in the act but her brain had taken a snapshot of it; one of those photos that could draw you back to look at it — again and again — for the rest of your life.

She went to the bedroom and slammed the door, lay down and closed her eyes. Saw the photo again, a few more details this time. One thing was obvious. Phillip had his problems, but erectile dysfunction wasn't one of them.

She could hear their voices now. Were they whispering? Whimpering? Or was it an angry exchange? She didn't want to know. She wrapped his pillow around her ears, muffling the noise: the footsteps in the hallway ... the front door closing ... the voice at the door, too scared to open it and come in.

'Xin-Xin,' the voice said. 'Xin-Xin ...'

She was giving him the silent treatment. He always thought she did it on purpose. It had never occurred to him that she mightn't have a clue what to say.

Another plaintive call, another pathetic knock on the door.

She knew what to say now. 'Fuck off,' she roared, and he did as he was told.

This time she didn't attempt to suffocate the noises with the pillow: doors opening and closing; footsteps going this way and that; a cupboard door squeaking open. What was he doing? Getting a suitcase, perhaps. Ah yes — he was in the laundry now. Getting some clothes for the next few days. Now the bathroom — go on, get your crap out of the bathroom — fucking toothbrush, fucking shaving gear, fucking sleazy two-timing fucking ...

Xin-Xin heard the front door close, the sound of his Civic starting up. She stared at the ceiling. The tears were like lemon juice, burning her eyes. Squeezing them only made it worse.

Fucking bastard! Cruel, duplicitous bastard. How could he do this? How could anyone do this?

To me ...

CHAPTER 20

Frank had a natural flair for work avoidance. A gift from God, he called it, which had enabled him to become successful and grossly overpaid for doing virtually nothing in the field of advertising. Incredibly, after nearly twenty years in the game, he sometimes found himself wondering if there might be easier ways of earning even more money.

Probably not, he thought, as he unlocked the door to his office and saw the layouts for the Mollycoddle range of baby-care products on his desk. The dynamic young company's future success depended on Frank's unique ability to come up with world-beating slogans, and they needed one by Friday.

Over the years he'd learned that high-profile jobs like the Mollycoddle account should not be rushed into. Creative minds work best under pressure and it's best to let the pressure build up. It was a task he would apply himself to on Friday morning and not a second before.

Right now it was Monday and Frank had more pressing matters to deal with.

First, his force four demanded immediate attention. Thanks to Harriet's assault and its souvenir contusions, this one was a cut above the average — maybe even a five — and the home remedies hadn't done the trick. He made a quick inspection of the fridge: one lousy beer. It wasn't doing anyone any good just sitting in there so he drank it, but it still wasn't doing anyone any good.

He checked in the bottom drawer where he kept a spare gram or two of cocaine for emergencies. Empty. Eddie, whose office was on the floor above his own, was his best hope.

'Dianne, do you know where the man himself is?' he enquired of Eddie's secretary after finding the office locked.

'He's on a shoot and won't be back till after lunch.'

No beer and no cocaine. If Frank had been in a unionised workplace he would have organised a strike on the spot. But in the laissez-faire environment of advertising, the individual had to rely on his own initiative. Within seconds he was on the phone.

Dave Peters, or Mister Whippy as he was known, was a hard worker. Most of his business was conducted at night and he hated being prevailed upon for emergency deliveries during the day, especially in the mornings.

But Frank was a good customer and didn't mind paying a bit extra so, yes, he could meet him an hour later at the coffee shop three doors down the road and, yes, he could do two grams.

Frank checked his wallet for cash: twenty dollars. Hardly sufficient for two grams of the health food of a nation.

Under normal circumstances he would have proceeded to the accounts department and asked for a cash advance, but a recently installed manager had been paying close attention to Frank's file over the past few weeks. The unctuous little prick had even gone so far as to ask the odd question or two and Frank didn't fancy the idea of further interrogation so early in the week. The nearest ATM was two blocks away and always had a long queue on Monday mornings.

He rang Sandra, the creative department secretary. She couldn't type and had bugger all else to do. A walk down to the ATM would do her the world of good. Frank wrote down his PIN and told her to make it five hundred.

Having earned a rest, he stretched out on his couch and opened the sports section, where he was delighted to find a photograph of Plugger taking a high mark that made the front page worthy of framing.

Frank threw the paper to the floor, leapt to his desk and banged out an urgent all-staff email:

Harry Parkinson owes Frank Thornton $400 which, at time of writing, he has shown no inclination whatsoever to pay.

He clicked send and resumed his position on the couch.

A few minutes later he heard his computer say 'ping'. It was the one word of computer language he understood, and meant 'someone's just sent you an email'.

It came from the keyboard of Harry Parkinson.

get fucked
harry

Frank recalled where he had seen his boss's daughter on Saturday night. It occurred to him that the old patriarch might have said the same thing to her — once too often, perhaps.

As he was making his way back to the couch the phone rang — for the fourth time since he'd arrived. It was a telephone's way of saying 'someone needs to speak to you urgently' but Frank didn't trust telephones to tell the truth. This time he gave it the benefit of the doubt.

'Where are we meeting for lunch, son?' said the jovial voice of Eddie Longman.

'I thought you were on a shoot,' said Frank.

'Don't be fucking silly, Frank. It's Monday morning. I've only just got out of bed!'

'Make it the Allegra at twelve-thirty?'

'Half the office will be there! I told them I was out on a shoot. See you at Benoit's at twelve.'

'Twelve-thirty,' Frank insisted.

'You sound busy.'

'I've been working my arse off all morning and, besides, I've got an appointment with Mister Whippy shortly.'

'So I'll expect you to bring dessert,' said Eddie.

'Sandra, I don't know what I'd do without you,' said Frank as she walked through the door and handed him his money and his keycard.

He looked at his watch: twenty minutes before he had to meet Mister Whippy. He might as well get going. He'd take the paper and finish reading about the game down there. Might even get a start on the crossword.

The phone was still at it. It had accumulated God knows how many messages all morning and now it was ringing again.

Bugger the phone, he thought, and closed the door of his office, glad to be getting out of the place.

Benoit's, on the Finger Wharf at Woolloomooloo Bay, was the perfect spot for lunch on a warm, cloudless day. Frank had wasted no time in sampling young Whippy's provisions in the bathroom of the coffee shop and was relieved to find it was of better quality than the previous batch. His head was as clear as crystal when he arrived and saw Eddie perusing the wine list.

Rani, the Singhalese waitress who attracted more customers to Benoit's than the menu and the location combined, materialised as soon as he sat down, bearing two ice-cold beers on a stainless steel tray. Things were looking up.

Frank gazed out over the glittering water of the harbour and followed the progress of the Manly ferry as it glided past, towering over the yachts and pleasure craft, the fishing boats and sightseeing cruisers. Thousands of postcards of this scenic cliché were sent to Japan every day of the week and Frank loved it. At Benoit's you could watch it while doing absolutely nothing for hours on end, and that was precisely what he and Eddie had in mind.

Eddie found everything funny, particularly personal disasters, and regarded Frank's turbulent romantic life as a reliable source of amusement. He asked Frank to remove his dark glasses so he could evaluate the state of his black eye. It had escalated from comical to hilarious.

'It looks even worse than yesterday! Did she hit you again last night?'

'I've got very good news regarding Harriet. She's gone. Made a mess of the place first, though.'

'How bad?' Eddie managed between chuckles, taking off his own glasses to wipe away a tear.

'You wouldn't want to walk in without protective clothing, put it that way.'

'So you hope you've seen the last of Harriet, do you, Frank?' Eddie had refined stating the obvious into an art form and had the income to prove it.

'I met a nice one on Friday night, just quietly,' Frank said. 'She's a writer. Name's Xin-Xin Leroq. Came to Arthur's exhibition with Puss. I suppose you would have heard about the opening by now.'

'Read about it in Saturday's paper. Disaster.'

'Absolute fucking fiasco. Still, it was worth it just to meet her.'

'What did you say her name was?'

'Xin-Xin Leroq.' Frank spelled it out to a disbelieving Eddie. 'The most anagrammatically impossible name I've ever heard.'

'Asian?'

'Chinese, I'd say. Married, though, if I remember rightly.'

'That's never stopped you before.'

'Actually, it has. Question is, do I remember rightly? I'd know if I hadn't been so pissed. Which reminds me — my bag. I left it at AD's on Saturday night. As usual.'

Only after the subject of Frank's amorous adventures had been drained of all its comic potential did Eddie allow the conversation to proceed to the more serious business of footy. Yesterday's glory had been relived the night before in conversations neither of them remembered, so it was necessary to go through it all again.

Eventually, with football and sex having been covered, the subject of work became unavoidable.

'Has that tight-arsed bastard Parkinson coughed up the four hundred he owes you?' Eddie asked.

'What do you reckon? He sent me an email telling me to get fucked instead.'

Eddie wasn't surprised.

'I've just about had a gutful of Harry,' said Frank.

CHAPTER 21

Where do I start, thought Frank, as he surveyed the wreckage of his home. It was too much work for one man. Well, too much for this one.

He mused on what his father might have done if faced with a similar problem. Not much point asking old Mick for help these days; his dedication to drinking didn't allow work to impair his performance. But years ago, he would have donned gumboots and leather gloves and started by hurling the biggest bits of debris straight out the window. He'd have proceeded to the more delicate part of the operation with the help of a large shovel, and finished by tearing up the carpet with a crowbar, a claw hammer and his bare hands.

Some poor bastard must do this kind of thing for a living, Frank thought. He'd find out who that man was and ring him first thing in the morning.

One room had remained untouched: an oversight on Harriet's part and an important one. It had probably been a bedroom in a previous life, but under Frank's stewardship it served as a repository for all the things he'd accumulated over the years and couldn't find space for anywhere else. Most of his treasured possessions were there: paintings he'd bought without considering he hadn't a wall big enough to accommodate them, and two mapping cabinets full of drawings, etchings and lithographs by various artists. He'd get around to having them framed one of these days.

The one task he would perform himself was removing the broken glass from the frames of those pictures that had fallen victim to Harriet. Following the operation — involving a few hammer whacks and a good shake — each patient was transported into the storeroom and left to recover.

Frank came to his framed print of Goya's *Duel with Cudgels*. There they were behind cracked glass, those two men locked for all time in a fight to the death. His thoughts returned again to his father. A cartoonist could replace those wooden clubs with bottles of metho and that would be old Mick fighting his losing battle against himself. Half closing his eyes, Frank fancied he could recognise his dad in the bloodied man on the left. But who was the bloke on the right, trying to protect himself from the inevitable by shielding his frightened face with his arm? It wasn't the same man — he looked younger. Could it be the other's son?

They didn't call them the Black Paintings for nothing.

Harriet should have given this one first priority but the bitch had left the hardest job for him. The hammer went straight through it. Frank hurled it across the room onto the pile of the rest of the garbage of his life.

Thirsty work, this, he thought, and headed for the fridge. Another smashed bottle or two wouldn't make any difference.

He made a list of the few items of furniture that had escaped unharmed and put it in his pocket. Then he had a shower, changed clothes, threw his toothbrush, some undies and socks into an overnight bag, borrowed his neighbour's phone to ring Arthur, and arranged to meet him at a Japanese restaurant a block away from AD's.

Arthur looked even gloomier than Frank had expected, so he decided to leave reflections on Friday night's debacle till later. He started by discussing his own.

'You should see the flat, it's a write-off.'

Arthur's only concern was for the paintings, quite a few of which were his. He was relieved to hear they were safe, and stashed away in the storeroom.

'I'd get the locks changed if I were you,' he said. 'She might come back to finish the job off properly.'

Frank couldn't imagine Harriet feeling dissatisfied enough with the job she'd done to be contemplating a return to work, but he sighed, took out the list of undamaged furniture, added 'change locks', and put it back in his pocket as the sashimi entrées arrived.

'When's your twelve months up?' Arthur asked.

'Couple of weeks.'

Eleven and a half months before, Frank had bought a new Porsche. The acquisition was celebrated the same evening, and afterwards Frank had ploughed it into four parked cars on his way home. According to the record of interview, the policeman who arrived on the scene asked Frank the standard question, 'When did you have your last drink for the evening, sir?' to which Frank had replied, 'I haven't'. The word 'insolent' had been written into the margin.

His blood-alcohol reading, which the magistrate had consigned to the annals of courtroom folklore, was always going to be a problem, as was his history of similar violations. His solicitor — a mate of Arthur's — failed spectacularly to establish a case based on recent traumatic events in Frank's personal life, the stress occasioned by the nature of his work and his profound feelings of remorse. But the thing that finally reduced the proceedings to farce was the character reference provided for Frank by the 'highly respected illustrator and artist' Arthur Blackwell, who, the magistrate noted, had dabbled in violent assault both in and out of the ring in his early years and had a criminal record as long as his paintbrush.

'I was only trying to help,' said Arthur. 'You going to buy a new car?'

'I'll be buying a new fucking everything. She pinched a lot of stuff too. Telly's smashed but there's no sign of the DVD player. Stereo's gone and Christ only knows what's missing from the kitchen.'

'And your CDs?'

Frank sighed and nodded. 'And she didn't even like jazz.'

They were both in a sombre mood when they walked into AD's. So was Daryl, who complained when he handed back Frank's bag that he'd found it a bit light-on for powder. When Frank found Xin-Xin's book still inside, he was so flushed with gratitude he almost felt compelled to apologise for the lack of drugs, but melancholy prevailed. When Arthur ordered triple scotches to go with the beers, the barman realised these two regulars weren't looking for idle banter.

Neither Frank nor Arthur liked country and western music and an earnest young hippie girl with a guitar was playing both. For ten interminable minutes they squirmed in silence, trying not to listen. But they couldn't just sit there, pretending nothing had happened three nights before and Arthur wasn't in a spot of bother of his own.

If his black look is anything to go by, Frank thought, I might soon meet a similar fate to Barry O'Connor for bringing the subject up. Fingers crossed.

'That was a big hit you put on O'Connor on Friday night,' he said. 'Word has it that he actually shat himself.'

'Yeah, well, I nearly shat myself too, today, when he rang.'

This could only mean one of two things: O'Connor was going to see to it that Arthur went to jail; or sue him for every penny he was worth.

'He wants me to have another exhibition towards the end of the year. Apparently there was a write-up about it in the papers and he sold the rest of the paintings on Saturday.'

Basher Blackwell was at it again — landing knockout punches. This one had Frank reeling, but he wasn't unconscious just yet.

'So what did you say?' he managed feebly.

'I told him to go and get fucked.'

Frank could hear the referee's voice, distant but still audible: '... eight, nine, ten — he's out!'

The hotel room Frank had booked into for the night boasted every possible convenience he wouldn't need. He didn't bother to pull back the curtains and gape at the view of the Opera House, nor did he open the doors that led onto the private balcony from where you could marvel at the Harbour Bridge. Instead, he took a nightcap from the minibar, turned on the bedside lamp, piled up the cushions and lay down and started reading.

After the first few chapters, Frank was convinced Xin-Xin was deserving of even more praise than the critics had lavished on her, but puzzled as to why Puss had identified with the lead character, Lenny. At this early stage, the young fellow seemed to be rather more like Frank.

He reached over, turned off the light and was almost asleep when he remembered he had something important to do.

He turned the light back on, leapt out of bed and rummaged through his overnight bag, pulling out a camera and a tripod. He set them up: camera facing bed, remote shutter switch attached.

Returning to the bag he extracted Harry Parkinson's long-stemmed pipe, which he'd stolen from his boss's office, adopted some unusual positions, took a dozen photos from a variety of angles, packed the gear away and went back to bed.

One of those will be just perfect, he thought, chortling as he fell asleep.

CHAPTER 22

What is it about staying in a hotel that makes a man wake up with an appetite? This question and a force three were troubling Frank's head the next morning.

The hangover was a near-death experience; he couldn't remember the last time he'd had one of those. But in those dark days when they were regular events, it was only after he'd spent the night in a hotel room that he could face food in the morning. For Frank, breakfast didn't involve a call to arms to enzymes in his digestive system and didn't need chewing either. It consisted of coffee and cigarettes for the entrée; hair of the dog for the main. He could usually take solids by lunchtime, but, inexplicably, it was only when he woke up in a hotel that he salivated while he shaved.

He wiped off the last traces of shaving cream, gave himself the once-over and realised there was another peculiar thing about staying in hotels. The lights in their bathrooms always made your hair look greyer than it really was. Made you look haggard too. He couldn't get out of there quickly enough. At the prices they charged, the least they could do was provide humane lighting in the shithouse.

He climbed back into yesterday's jeans and fetid shirt and made his way down to the dining room. Looking at himself in the mirror in the lift, he was pleased to see his age had dropped by ten years in the time it had taken to cover the distance between the spotlit bathroom and this dimly lit cubicle.

The restaurant offered a panoramic view of the harbour along with a smorgasbord of delicacies, none of which looked appealing to Frank. The thought of experimenting with a bowl of fresh fruit occurred to him, but was dismissed for health reasons. Could be a shock to the system; put a man on the dunny for the rest of the day.

The man next to him seemed to know what he was doing. Frank eyed his tray: grapefruit, pineapple and watermelon on a plate; glass of orange juice; two slices of toast; and now, while dropping a couple of preserved apricots onto a cauldron-sized bowl of muesli, he was waiting for Frank to get out of the way so he could hook into the yoghurt.

He looked a normal enough bloke — about Frank's age and similar build, but nicely turned out in a suit, white shirt and silk tie, all expensively understated. Not the sort of man to be seeking refuge in a hotel because the manner of his lover's departure had rendered him homeless. Not the sort of man who would have difficulty deciding what to consume for breakfast because eating in the morning was a novelty.

A man like Frank tended to gravitate towards the first thing that struck him as even remotely familiar in a situation like this: the greasy offerings in the shiny samovars. He found a place out on the terrace, where smoking was allowed, and got to work on the fried eggs, bacon and sausages, and overdid it with the sauce.

One thing he did have in common with his sartorially superior doppelganger was a busy day ahead. Forward planning, that was what was needed. Frank rummaged through his bag and extracted his diary, turned to Tuesday, 7 April and wrote:

1. Get photos developed (Josh at Adlab).
2. Return Harry's pipe.
3. Find someone to clean up flat.

That wasn't going to be easy. Where would he start? Who would he ring? He thought of Eddie, who'd lived in apartments all over Sydney and knew a thing or two about home renovation.

He reached into his bag for his phone then thought better of it. He didn't feel like talking to anyone now; he could catch up with Eddie back in the office. What he really wanted was to finish his list so he could settle back, enjoy Xin-Xin's book and banish his force three with a heart-starter.

He scribbled, 'Yellow pages — rubbish removalists? cleaners? ask Eddie', and pressed on:

4. Call Xin-Xin (email?)

He put the diary back into the bag and pulled out his copy of *Gang-Gang*. The author's card protruded from page seventy-two, where Lenny Matthews was boarding a train at Central Station which would take him back into the bush and forth into his new life as a schoolteacher. The poor little bugger had had a terrible time living in Redfern and was a bit young to be hitting the bottle as hard as he was. Boy could finish up a drunk if he stayed there any longer.

Two cups of coffee, two Bloody Marys, eight cigarettes and a few chapters later, Frank speculated Lenny would probably be in bed with precocious Rose, his screwed-up but sympathetically portrayed student, in about ten more pages.

He had to catch a cab across the bridge to North Sydney, to drop off the photos with Josh, then get another one back to the office. He reckoned the two trips combined should give Lenny and Rose more than enough time to do the business before he arrived for work.

The narrative moved at a faster pace than the traffic and they had consummated their affair by the time Frank arrived at Adlab. But dark clouds were gathering: Rose couldn't keep her mouth shut; the pair were the talk of the town; and Lenny was about to end up in the shit.

'Josh,' Frank said, placing the book reluctantly into his bag, 'I've got a special job for you. I need a few photos developed and one good ten-by-eight print. Any chance of this afternoon?' He explained the clandestine nature of the assignment, paid cash up front and finished the chapter in a pub across the road.

On the way back to the city, the traffic was jammed solid. A motorcyclist, who had ingested something similar to what Frank usually had for breakfast, had killed himself at the turn-off onto the Cahill Expressway, thereby giving Frank the luxury of doing some further reading while his taxi remained parked in the middle of the bridge.

He paused at the end of chapter seventeen and read the last paragraph again:

Dead Roses don't make it into the papers, Lenny. He was right. No mention in the local rag of Rose, his darling Rose. What had he taken from her with his hands that had caused her to take her life with her own? *Not your fault, Lenny, you ain't seen her for a year and a half. Lotta girls end up that way when they go and live in the city.* He might have thought he was right on that one too, but Lenny knew better: she'd started dying the moment he'd held her in his arms, then finished the job alone. And it wasn't as if he hadn't warned him. *Don't point your black bone at no white sheilas round here, Lenny. Big trouble.* How they'd laughed when he'd said that.

Frank marked his place with Xin-Xin's card, closed the book and closed his eyes.

According to a quote on the back cover, an American critic had found the experience of reading *Gang-Gang* 'deeply disturbing'. Frank could only concur. There were things happening in this book that had happened to him and it was disturbing him deeply. He laid his head back and thought hard.

He must have been about twenty-three when he came out of hospital after that soldier gave him a hiding, and a year later he'd met Monique. Not much older than Lenny when he'd met Rose.

Frank remembered the day he'd woken up wondering why Monique wasn't in the bed beside him. He'd gone through the house looking for her, calling her name, had found her crouching in a corner in the kitchen, naked and terrified. He spoke to her but she didn't reply. He held her shoulders and shook her but she didn't react.

Twenty minutes later she still hadn't moved. Cursing himself for not paying his phone bill, Frank draped a blanket over her shoulders and found his keys.

'Everything's okay, Moni. I'm going out but I'll be back soon. Don't be frightened, all right? I'll only be gone for a few minutes.'

There was a doctor two blocks down the road, an affable Pakistani with about twenty-four letters in his surname. Frank ran on bare feet to his surgery and told the secretary that his girlfriend's case was an emergency and she needed immediate help. The woman didn't seem sure what to do. One of the other two patients stepped in on her behalf.

'Wait your turn or fuck off,' he said.

Frank took the former option, which seemed to take forever.

'Has she shown this kind of behaviour before?' the doctor asked as they half-walked, half-ran towards Frank's home.

'She sometimes freaks out when she smokes dope.'

'Does she smoke a lot of dope?'

'No. Did last night, though.'

Monique was gone when they arrived. The doctor recommended a consultation with the police, who treated the matter politely and efficiently, reassuring Frank every day for the next three weeks that, no, they hadn't found a corpse that matched her description. After that they told him to stop worrying and yes, they'd contact him if there was anything to report.

A corpse matching Monique's description was found eighteen months later in a bathroom in Byron Bay. Suicide by self-mutilation made for an eye-catching headline and, because she was the daughter of 'a colourful Sydney racing identity', the event was deemed newsworthy enough for a few paragraphs in a Sydney tabloid. Puss rang Frank with the news.

Later that afternoon, he found him distraught in a pub.

'It wasn't your fault, Frank. You haven't seen her for a year and a half. Anything could have happened in that time and none of it had anything to do with you.'

At first this sounded reasonable. Frank had been good to Monique. He'd cared for her, loved her. And she'd loved him. But a suspicion arose in Frank's mind that maybe that was where her trouble had begun. He'd infected her with something, some emotional condition that had worn her down for eighteen months and killed her in the end. Puss could exonerate him if he liked, but he blamed himself just the same.

The parallels between young Lenny Matthews' life and his own were a little too close for comfort, and some of the similarities seemed to go beyond coincidence. How long had Puss known Xin-Xin, he wondered, and how much had they talked?

Back in the office, Frank took a beer from the fridge and stretched himself out on the couch to resume reading. The phone promptly rang. Whoever it is can leave a message, he thought. A moment later it rang again.

'Persistent bastard,' he muttered. 'Hello?'

'Eddie here, mate. You checked your emails yet?'

'No.'

'There's one from Harry I think you'd better have a look at,' said Eddie, laughing.

'Shit!'

Frank logged on to his computer for the first time since Friday and was appalled to see how many emails had accumulated in just four days. He suspected someone — Roy, perhaps — had been spreading a rumour in cyberspace that he had a smaller-than-average-sized cock that wouldn't stand up, because a hell of a lot of ads for penis enlargements and Viagra had interpolated themselves amongst the porn sites. There were also any number of work-related messages he was in no hurry to look at, plus a couple from Roy and a few from Puss. That was strange. Roy and Puss didn't often send emails. He'd get back to them later.

Ah … there it was: an urgent all-staff alert from Harry Parkinson.

Reward: Lunch at Benoit's for information leading to the identification of the idiot who stole my pipe.

The idiot who'd stolen Harry's pipe took it from his bag, stuffed it under his belt, covered it with his shirt and headed down the corridor. The door to Harry's office was wide open, the room apparently empty, but it was better to be sure. That all-staff email might have been intended as bait. Harry was just the sort of low bastard to lie in wait behind the desk in the hope of catching his man.

Frank poked his head in the adjoining office and said hello to Brenda, Harry's personal assistant. Advertising sold products made by others, but Brenda Bischoff was a product of the industry itself. Her nerves were made of stainless steel and in place of a heart she had a mechanical device that kept her animated, efficient and immune to emotional experience of any kind. The one person she affected affection for was the rebarbative Harry, who would have sacked her if she didn't.

'Harry around?'

'He's in a meeting. Should be back in about twenty minutes.'

'I'll pop back later then.'

'Why do you need to see him?' she asked. It was an ominous sign. She might have fingered him for the pipe job already.

'Bastard owes me four hundred bucks,' Frank said. 'Just wanted to remind him.'

'Good luck,' she said, and laughed.

Frank laughed too and, as he walked past Harry's office, lobbed the pipe through the door and watched it land safely on the plump leather couch.

With that out of the way, he turned his attention to finding someone to clean out his flat. He rang Eddie, and when Eddie failed to answer was forced to take the initiative himself. He was amazed to find fourteen pages of advertisements for rubbish removers in the *Yellow Pages*, several of whom were located within a block or two of his own address in Surry Hills.

'What size skip will you need?' said Wayne from Good Riddance. 'Two, five, ten cubic metres?'

'It's a bit hard to say, Wayne. I've never done this sort of thing before.'

'How much shit do you want us to cart away?'

'About half a flat's worth of furniture for a start.'

'Carpets?'

'Carpets — the lot.'

'Seven-thirty: Wayne from Good Riddance,' he wrote in his diary for the following day. Why was it that blokes like Wayne always started work at a time when a normal person should be sound asleep?

Consulting his schedule again, Frank transferred 'call Xin-Xin' to the next day and added a question mark. There was no hurry, especially with a black eye marring whatever looks he may have possessed and requiring explanation. There'd be no curling up in bed with Xin-Xin for a while; the best he could hope for was to curl up with her book.

'Harry's been on the rampage,' Eddie said as they set off to the Allegra for lunch. 'He's got his pipe back but he's not very happy. Says he'll sack the bastard if he finds out who it was.'

'He won't find out much by offering a reward like that, will he? Who'd want to have lunch with him?'

'I don't think you're high on the list of suspects, Frank. The place is full of militant anti-smokers. They're the ones he's got his eye on.'

'When he came into your room, was he smoking the thing?'

'He lit it up before my very eyes,' Eddie said with a knowing grin. 'Feel like a drink?'

'I've got a thirst you could hit with a hammer.'

'There's a parcel here for you, Frank,' said the barman as he pulled their beers.

'Christ,' said Frank, 'that was quick.'

Josh had followed Frank's instructions to the letter. Inside the plastic package was a plain white envelope with Harry Parkinson's name typed on the front. It contained a ten-by-eight glossy photograph, the quality and the detail of which exceeded both Frank's and Eddie's expectations. They looked at it admiringly while howling with laughter.

'You're a better photographer than I thought,' said Eddie, finally. 'From a purely technical point of view, it couldn't have been easy.'

'One has to be prepared to suffer for one's art,' Frank explained as they ordered their first bottle of wine.

At roughly four o'clock, Brenda Bischoff found a white envelope on her desk with Harry's name on it. She delivered it to his office immediately.

'What's this?' Harry asked, clenching his pipe between his teeth and reaching for his letter knife.

'No idea,' Brenda replied and returned to her desk.

A moment later she heard Harry scream and, simultaneously, an almighty clang as his pipe was hurled into a metal garbage bin with terrific force.

Brenda rushed into her boss's office to find him staring into space. The blood had drained from his cheeks and he was shuddering.

On his desk lay a photograph of his newly discarded pipe poking out of a hairy anus.

He picked it up with trembling hand, forcing himself to examine it more closely.

No. This was not a rectum he could recognize.

CHAPTER 23

Frank sat in his office chuckling. He'd heard Harry's scream and was trying to picture the look on his face. He had to give Eddie a call. The operation had been a complete success and deserved to be celebrated.

'Where the fuck are you?' he hissed when Eddie failed to answer.

A flashing red light on Frank's office phone indicated messages wanted to be heard. It had been dropping its pulsating hints all day and was becoming impossible to ignore. He'd check the messages first then try Eddie again.

He had nine new messages.

The first, from Roy, was one of the calls Frank had ignored while lying on his couch during the hectic morning of the day before.

'Frank, it's Roy. I just read about what happened to Nina and Mandy. There's not a lot of detail in the paper. You're probably out visiting them right now. Give us a call when you get back and let me know how they are and if there's anything I can do to help. I'm really sorry, mate. Hear from you soon.'

'Fuck!' Frank jabbed the phone to hear the next one.

'Puss here, Frank. I just heard a news report about what's happened. I can't believe it. Nina and Mandy — are they okay? Ring me as soon as you get this message, will you?'

'Jesus Christ!'

His hand was shaking now, fingers hitting the wrong numbers to retrieve messages. Hang up and start again.

'You have seven new messages.'

'Yeah, yeah, come on, come on.'

The next one had also been recorded the previous morning, just as he'd been dashing off to meet Mister Whippy.

'Frank, it's Puss again. Where the hell are you? Ring me on my mobile and let me know if there's anything I can do. I can come and pick you up if you need a lift. Just ring me for Christ's sake.'

Next one, midday, yesterday.

'G'day, Frank. Arthur. Puss just rang me and told me what happened to your sister and her daughter. I'm very sorry, mate. Give me a call.'

Next one, and the one after that, hang-ups.

Next one, ten o'clock this morning.

'Roy here, Frank. Where the fuck are you? I've been sending fucking emails and trying to ring you since yesterday morning. I went around to your place last night but you weren't there. I just rang the journo who's been covering the story for the *Telegraph* and he told me about Nina. Thank Christ Mandy seems to be okay but listen, mate, I've got to talk —'

Shit. Roy. Gotta ring Roy.

'Roy?'

'Christ, Frank, where the hell have you been? Have you seen them yet?'

'No. I don't know what's going on. Harriet smashed up my flat and busted the phone and I was out all day yesterday. I went out on the piss with Arthur last night and crashed in a hotel. I've only just got in and heard the messages. Christ Almighty, Roy, what's fucking happened?'

'Mandy's okay but Nina's really fucked up. She's in a coma over at Westmead Hospital.'

'A coma?'

'Yeah, Frank, a coma. That arsehole husband of hers is up on two charges of attempted murder.'

'Shit! I'll ring the hospital and call you back.'

Hospital. Westmead Hospital. Ring directory assistance, get them to put me through. Few more beers in the fridge, thank Christ — come on, hurry up …

'Hello? My name's Thornton, Frank Thornton. My sister and my niece are there and I need to know what's happened to them — I need to know how they are — Her name's Nina, Nina Morrow, and my niece's name is Mandy — I've heard she's —'

'I'm sorry, Mr Thornton, but I'm not allowed to give you any information about Mrs Morrow or her daughter. I'll have to put you through to the NUM.'

'Your *Mum*?'

'The Nursing Unit Manager. Connecting you now, sir.'

'Hello? Denise Prescott speaking.'

'Are you the Nursing Unit Manager?'

'Yes, sir, how can I help you?'

'My name's Frank Thornton. My sister, Nina Morrow's there, I'm told. I've been away and only just heard the news. Is it true she's in a coma?'

'No, Mr Thornton, your sister came out of the coma last night and is now in intensive care.'

'Does that mean she's going to be okay?'

'She's been very badly injured, Mr Thornton. We're doing our best.'

'Oh Christ! What about Mandy, her daughter, is she okay? Can I speak to her?'

'Amanda left the hospital this morning. She was picked up by friends about an hour ago.'

'What friends? Where have they taken her?'

'I'm not allowed to give you that information, Mr Thornton.'

'Jesus Christ! I'll come over and see Nina. Is it all right if I come over and see her now?'

'That won't be possible. Mrs Morrow won't be able to see any visitors aside from her immediate family for quite some time.'

'But I am her immediate family. I'm her bloody brother!'

'I realise that, Mr Thornton. Her other brother is with her at the moment. He's instructed me to tell you she doesn't want to see you at all. I'm very sorry, Mr Thornton. If you'd like me to put you back to the front desk, the secretary will take your number and we'll be able to call you if your sister changes her mind.'

Frank left his number with the secretary. He unzipped the pocket inside his bag and pulled out his mobile. There were seven messages waiting to be answered. He listened to the first three.

'Frank, it's Nene here. Red still isn't home and I've decided to come over with Mandy. Please call me as soon as you get this message. Thanks, Frank. Bye.'

'Oh Frank, where *are* you? Please call me when you get the message. It's Nene.'

'Frank! Mandy and I are coming over. I'll try you at home. Oh Christ, it's him.'

Frank rang Eddie and told him they were going out for a drink. Eddie said he couldn't stay long because they had visitors coming around and Chloe needed him to pick up some things on the way home, and Frank said that didn't matter 'cause he was going out for a drink, a real big drink, and if Eddie had to piss off and leave him what the fuck did it matter — he could always drink alone.

PART III

CHAPTER 24

Why, after staggering home from a big night and locking the door behind you, would you then go to sleep on the floor? It seemed like a silly thing for the human body to do. Having gone to the effort of finding its way home, why hadn't it propelled itself just that little bit further and collapsed on the bed?

For years such questions had bothered Frank. But when life's imponderables reared their ugly heads in his mind, help was only a phone call away. Roy, who'd pondered everything, was able to explain.

'Think of your brain as a big office block,' Roy had said. 'Everyone in it's got a job to do, but the last two blokes who are allowed to leave are the one whose job it is to get you home and the one responsible for reminding you to breathe. When you get pissed, you're making the first bloke do overtime, so, as soon as you get through the door, he considers his work done and calls it a day. He couldn't give a fuck where you sleep. The bloke whose job it is to tell you to sleep in a bed has gone home hours ago and that's why you wake up on the floor.'

'What about the little bloke who tells you to keep breathing?' Frank asked. 'Does he ever get a holiday?'

'He can't afford to. His job's on the line. You're just lucky that the guy who got that job in your office block likes a drink. If he didn't, you would have been dead about twenty-five years ago.'

The little man inside his head who made the music selections often chose songs Frank hated, then played them over and over for days on end just to get on his nerves. It was probably the same bloke who recorded Nina's phone messages and had been repeating them ever since: Oh Christ it's him Oh Christ it's him Oh Christ it's him. And, like the one in charge of breathing, he must have liked a drink, because Frank had been trying to drown him with whisky all night and it hadn't worked.

When it was daylight again, the little man charged with getting Frank's body home got it as far as the door of its building, where Frank found a large stranger in a blue singlet pressing the doorbell and muttering obscenities.

'G'day, mate,' he said. 'You don't happen to know a Frank Thornton do you?'

On hearing this, the little men in Frank's office block responsible for housekeeping sprang into action, impelling him to say, 'Yeah, that's me.'

The blue singlet introduced himself as Wayne from Good Riddance. 'I was just about to give up and go home,' he added.

'Sorry, nicked out to buy the paper,' said Frank, who was not carrying a newspaper.

As he opened the door of his apartment, Frank saw a look of horror flash across Wayne's face. Frank had assumed a man in Wayne's line of business would see this sort of thing, if not on a daily basis, then certainly often enough not to consider it out of the ordinary.

'Break and enter?' he asked.

'Inside job, I'm afraid,' Frank croaked. 'More a break-up than a break-in, if you know what I mean.'

'Right,' Wayne said with a sigh. 'Where do I start?'

'You're the boss,' said Frank.

Wayne had worked up quite a sweat by the time Xin-Xin woke at nine o'clock to find herself alone in her bed for the third morning in a row, lying on the side where she always slept. She wondered why, with the whole bed to herself, she hadn't exercised her right to spread out and reclaim it as her own.

She also wondered why she felt so afraid. Was it the silence within the empty room — the empty apartment— that was immobilising her? Or was it a silence within herself; some internal blackout that had temporarily shut her down?

As Xin-Xin closed her eyes and hoped for more sleep, Frank ordered a coffee and read the article on page five of the *Daily Telegraph* for the third time. Nina Morrow's condition was serious but stable and Red Morrow's lawyer was confident his client's charges would be reduced from attempted murder to assault occasioning grievous bodily harm. Mr Morrow had been intoxicated when committing the offence and had no recollection of the event. He was cooperating with the police in their enquiries and, while he vigorously denied his actions were premeditated or homicidal in intent, was prepared to plead guilty to the lesser charges.

Frank speculated about how much time Red would get for having nearly punched and kicked his sister to death and bashed his niece to a pulp. Six years? Eight? Either way, he'd probably be out in three or four.

He made his way to the bathroom and vomited again. Politely, this time. The first two spews of the day had ended up on the grass in someone's garden, and on the footpath on his way to the coffee shop.

Back at his table, he noticed how violently his hands were shaking as he pulled out his phone. Why did they always do that after a big night on the piss and no sleep?

'You have rung Bob and Melissa Thornton. Please leave a message.'

I've rung Bob and Melissa Thornton ten times in the last two days, Frank thought, and if you won't talk to me either, Bob, you can go and get fucked.

He tried Denise Prescott at Westmead, who made it clear she was sick and tired of hearing from him and didn't want to have to tell him again.

Frank's own sentence, it seemed, had been determined by Nina and she'd decided to give him life.

The increasingly terse NUM also refused to give him a number for Mandy, who was being well looked after and was at liberty to contact him if she felt the need to do so.

'What if I feel the need to contact her?' Frank shouted into the phone. 'I don't have a number for her. I don't even know where she bloody well lives!'

'Well, that might explain why she doesn't want any help from you, Mr Thornton. Goodbye.'

Frank glanced again at the newspaper. The front page informed him of recent atrocities being carried out by Serbian police and paramilitary forces in the predominantly Albanian province of

Kosovo. A meeting of foreign ministers would be convened in London the following Monday to agree on a set of limited sanctions against the Belgrade government of Slobodan Milosevic.

If Red's parents had stayed over there, Frank thought, he'd still be Redenko Morosevic, raping and pillaging on behalf of the Serbs. He'd heard Red's diatribes about the necessity for ethnic cleansing in that part of the world and been filled with disgust. But they were occupying the same position on the moral low ground now.

Frank folded the newspaper, stuffed it into his bag and headed down Kippax Street towards the Aurora. They made a good Bloody Mary down there.

He sought distraction in *Gang-Gang* by rereading the last chapter. The amount of distraction he found was minimal; the amount of comfort, nil. Things spiralled down quickly for Lenny Matthews at the end of the book and, while Frank had seen similarities between Lenny's life and his own, he didn't fancy a similar death: in a gutter, anonymous and alone.

Frank rarely walked to work, but he found himself plodding through Hyde Park at around eleven that morning. The last time was because he'd lost his wallet; the time before that, the taxis were on strike. This time it was because he'd forgotten to hail a cab. He was too busy thinking about the blood on his hands.

He was late, even by the standards of the advertising industry, but instead of proceeding towards his office on Macquarie Street he deviated at the Archibald Fountain and turned left towards the centre of the city. He dawdled around a corner into Pitt Street and disappeared into Grosvenor's Bookstore. After buying a copy of *Lost Sheep*, the Fleetwood Award-winning novel by Xin-Xin Leroq, he climbed the stairs in the hope of finding distraction in Henry Grosvenor's office on the second floor.

Frank was not a good judge of character. Fortunately for him, the same could not be said about his friends. Men like Roy, Puss, Arthur and Eddie loved Frank for qualities he didn't know he possessed and rewarded him with a loyalty he didn't believe he deserved. But if they were the core in the apple of his life, there were also quite few blemishes on its skin. And while blemishes came and went, some lasted longer than others, became ingrained, and left an ugly scar when they were finally excised. It was thanks to Frank's lack of judgment that he'd picked up some of those, and one of them was Henry Grosvenor.

A good judge of character could have summed up Henry by visiting his office when he wasn't there. The daunting paintings by 'emerging' young art stars were there to convey the message that Henry's eclectic tastes weren't restricted by convention — and he paid art critic Victor Hollings a generous consultancy fee to ensure the message got through loud and clear. The hard-edged designer furniture proclaimed that Henry knew where to shop for a chair, but when you went into his office and saw the one he'd chosen, it didn't make you feel like sitting down. The expensive exotic rugs, and the books scattered everywhere, were intended to convey an impression of bohemianism and cover up the conservatism of the order underneath. Henry's office was putrid with ostentation, but, although he thought the paintings stank, it smelled okay to Frank.

Henry rose to his feet, a process that took longer than expected. He tended to move slowly and, starting from his stooped position behind his computer, had a fair way to go before attaining his height of six foot four. It was just as well Henry was so tall, because he liked looking down on people as much as he liked them looking up to him. When they did, he wanted them to see a man who had risen above their petty concerns such as style and fashion, so he made sure his handmade Italian suits were rumpled and his silk ties hung askew.

At fifty-three, Henry himself was still in good condition, thanks to the efforts of a personal trainer whose existence he denied. He also denied he paid through the nose for his haircuts, which were performed in his office by a freelancer from the film industry who knew the secret of how to make his silver mane look unkempt. Henry was a man who didn't grow old but matured, with a blend of charm and ruthlessness that made admirers or enemies of men, and women queue to fuck him on the side.

As they shook hands, Henry arched his eyebrows in a way that asked a question without the need for words.

'Oh, that,' Frank answered, fingering his black eye, now in full bloom after five days of unhindered development. 'You wouldn't want to know.'

'I can guess. You're a piss-wreck, Frank, you really ought to cut down.'

Henry, who drank French wine with every meal and never went to bed without a cognac beforehand, annoyed Frank with his pontificating on the subject of drinking. It was drinking that had first drawn them together ten years ago, when, after meeting at a book launch and realising they were kindred spirits when it came to their tastes in literature, they discovered they also shared similar enthusiasms for those other kindred spirits: vodka and whisky. On that occasion, it was Frank who, at three in the morning when Henry was slurring his witticisms, told him he was as blind as a welder's dog and should go home. Henry had relished the phrase, and borrowed it whenever he needed to prove he was not the overbearing snob people often took him for and could talk like one of the boys if he wanted to.

'Not just yet,' he'd said that night, before whisking Frank off to a brothel where they discovered they had similar tastes in women too, finding themselves arguing over who should spend the next hour with number six of the seven available. Henry had put paid to further discussion by producing a credit card, insisting it was his shout, and waving farewell as Frank disappeared down a corridor with number four.

Frank occasionally reminded Henry of that night, finding some amusement in the fact that serial-marrier Henry had then been with wife number two, was now with number four, and there was every chance he'd end up, one day, with another number six. It was a subject most likely to come up when Henry presumed to lecture Frank on his heavy drinking.

'Is this any good?' Frank asked, taking *Lost Sheep* from its plastic bag.

'I'll say,' Henry confirmed. 'She's done a second one that's even better.'

'I've just read it. Very impressed.'

'By the writer or the book?'

'By the book,' Frank said, proceeding with caution on the subject of women around Henry.

'She's quite beautiful.'

Now it was Frank's turn to ask a question with his eyebrow.

'By all accounts,' Henry added.

He pulled copies of the *Guardian* from one of the piles of newspapers on the floor. 'There's a photo of her in one of these, and a profile,' he said. 'Bloody good review too. Here it is.'

170

'Can I borrow it?'

'Keep it,' said Henry. 'But don't get too excited.'

'What do you mean?'

'I don't think you'd have too much in common. That's what I mean.'

Frank laughed, as he always did when excusing Henry his sarcasms. He'd arrived with the intention of luring Harry out for a drink and confiding his feelings regarding a crime that had taken place in Mitchellton over the weekend, but now he looked at his watch, lied that he had a meeting to attend, and left.

Sometimes I hate you, he thought, recalling the emphasis Henry had placed on the word 'common'. Fucking snob. He wondered what, if anything, he had 'in common' with Henry. Their senses of humour and intellectual compatibility united them across the divide of their socioeconomic histories, but never obliterated it.

While Frank was brawling his way through Mitchellton Boys' High, Henry was cutting a dash at Oxford, where, as a Rhodes scholar from Australia, he was not only considered brilliant but somewhat exotic as well. In his role as the Oxonian Errol Flynn, he cultivated a laconic style and a reputation as a Lothario.

Frank, after the trauma of school had worn off, had embarked on the process of educating himself. By the time he met Henry Grosvenor, he was an autodidact who'd graduated from a university of his own. 'It was a bloody long course too,' he would say, when reflecting on his schooling. The first seventeen years had been devoted to self-defence; the succeeding ten to self-destruction, attacking whatever brain cells he may have possessed; and the rest had been spent variously educating and drowning the survivors.

Secretly, Frank was envious of Grosvenor's erudition, attested by the letters after his name. The two rarely discussed anything seriously, preferring to outsmart each other in a class war of witticisms, like the two toughest kids from a private and a public school having it out after class. Frank went into these encounters with a handicap: a naive belief he could trust all the men he regarded as friends. Henry mightn't have been able to fight when it came to hand-to-hand combat, but he knew how to teach Frank a lesson. A patronising remark could bring him to his knees.

Emerging from the bookstore, Frank headed not to work but straight for the nearest pub. He took a beer to a table in a corner, opened the *Guardian* and found the article about Xin-Xin. He read it, ordered another beer, and read it again.

He had two papers to choose from now: this one and the *Telegraph*, with its stories of atrocities in Kosovo and Mitchellton. He left the *Telegraph* in his bag, bought another beer, and tried to concentrate on articles about books he wasn't interested in by authors he'd never heard of. It didn't work. He kept returning to the review of Xin-Xin's book and the article about her. He could concentrate on them; he was interested in her.

CHAPTER 25

A few kilometres to the east, Xin-Xin was sitting outside a coffee shop in Double Bay, doing the cryptic crossword while waiting for her mother.

With the crossword and a coffee already completed and fifteen minutes left to kill before her ever-punctual parent was due to arrive, Xin-Xin took her phone from her bag and rang Lola, who could always be relied upon for an amusing anecdote or two. When Xin-Xin mused about a man she found attractive named Frank Thornton, Lola provided one of her best ever.

'Frank Thornton!' she shrieked. 'Is he a tall skinny guy with a dragon tattooed on his arm?'

'Well, he's tall and pretty skinny. I don't know about any tattoo.'

'Does he live in Surry Hills? Works in advertising?'

'He works in advertising. I'm not sure where he lives —'

'Wait a minute, Xin-Xin, have I ever got something to tell you about him!'

The fifteen minutes went by very quickly as Lola related a tale of mayhem and hilarity that offered unsavoury insights into the man in question.

Xin-Xin's mother arrived to see her daughter laughing on the phone. 'What a hoot!' she heard her cry. Then, with a quick change of tone and demeanour, she added, 'Oh, Mum's here. I'll ring you back later, bye.'

A wolf whistle rang out as Lian Leroq took her seat and leaned across the table to kiss her daughter on the cheek. Both women frowned at the impertinence and looked sideways at a disappearing sports car, each privately wondering who was the intended recipient. The driver would have had to pass by very slowly to suspect he was ogling a mother and her daughter.

They'd finished lunch and were waiting for coffees by the time the subject they'd met to discuss actually came up. Each had been avoiding it. After a long silence, it was Lian who finally broached it by asking Xin-Xin if she'd heard from Phillip.

'Oh for God's sake, Mum,' Xin-Xin snapped. 'Of course not.'

'You mean he hasn't even rung?'

Lian was here to comfort her daughter, not upset her further, but she was her mother after all. Sooner or later, she would have to say what needed to be said.

Phillip had rung twice, in fact, leaving tearful messages on the answering machine intended to evoke pity. The first had aroused Xin-Xin's contempt, the second, fury; pity hadn't got a look-in.

'No, he hasn't called. And I don't want him to.'

It was the moment Lian had been waiting for. 'Dad and I are really rather glad, you know, dear. We always had our doubts about Phillip.'

'But I thought you adored him.'

'He was a pleasant enough young man. Devoted to you, of course, we never doubted that. It's just that ...'

Xin-Xin wasn't in the mood to tolerate pauses. 'It's just that what?'

'It's just that his prospects weren't particularly promising. It's all very well reading books about ancient history and giving lectures — all that muddling about in the university — but where does it all end? It's not a career, is it?'

'Not everyone has a "career". Some people are quite satisfied with having a "position".'

'Well that's not good enough. Phillip just doesn't seem to have what it takes. To make it in life, a man needs to have ambition — a bit of get up and go.'

Xin-Xin was not yet at the stage in life where she could forgive her mother her gaffes, particularly those so revealing of a snobbishness Xin-Xin abhorred — and which was so disturbingly similar to sentiments of her own. She looked at her watch and lied about having to get back to work.

'I'll get this,' Lian said, smiling tight-lipped.

'Thanks. Bye, Mum.'

God, you annoy me sometimes, she thought, as she marched off. Insufferable snob!

At around the same time, Frank was slinking into his office. The irate little man in charge of putting his body to bed regarded the couch as a worthy substitute and directed it there in emergencies.

When he woke it was nearly four o'clock. He'd given reality a full two hours to improve its performance but it had refused to cooperate. If things had changed in any way at all, it had been for the worse. The *Daily Telegraph* was still in his bag, the article on page five was still telling the story of a crime for which one man had been arrested and omitting any mention of the other man who was to blame. And now that man had a force four.

Foraging in a drawer, Frank found paracetamol and cocaine, which he ingested in that order, washing down the former with a beer from the fridge. The combination worked quickly. The newspaper still existed, but now he could ignore it. He'd been tried, found guilty and sentenced, but someone else was doing his time. Technically, he was a free man. And a free man had options: he could drink and obliterate his past; he could drink more and start creating his future. He was also entitled to pursue happiness, and might even find it if he knew where to look. This free man had met a woman named Xin-Xin and was allowed to make phone calls.

Should he call her? No. Send an email? No harm in that.

He read the review Henry had given him again, even though by now he could have recited it by heart. He scoured the short profile piece one more time, in case it might yet contain surprises. It didn't, but it confirmed 'listening to music, especially jazz' and 'doing cryptic crosswords' as pastimes she enjoyed. And definitely no mention of her being married. Then again, he was pretty sure she'd told him she was when they'd spoken after Arthur's exhibition.

Maybe I should send her a cryptic message, something she might find amusing. After that I'll read her other book and then, if I ever see her again, at least I'll have done my homework. Wait a minute. What about Puss?

Frank had been consulting one lousy article in the *Guardian* for information about Xin-Xin when he had a direct line to her via Puss. What had happened to the little man in charge of commonsense inside Frank's office block? Was he the only one up there who didn't like a drink? It was time to ask Puss a question or two. For example: does she have a husband? And how much background information had Puss provided for her book?

Frank lunged at the phone.

'Puss, mate, I'm in a bit of a state here.'

'I'm not surprised. How are they?'

They? Frank snapped back to reality.

'To tell you the truth, I don't know. There's this old cow, the Nursing Unit Manager, who's refusing to give me any detailed information. All I know is, Nina's in intensive care. I don't know where Mandy's been taken.'

Puss's silences were sometimes more expressive than his words. This was a long one, forcing Frank to go on.

'I don't know, Puss. You know me — don't keep in touch with the family as much as I should. Thing is, it's all my fault, see?'

'You blaming yourself again, Frank?'

'Sure am. Hang on, can you hang on for a moment?'

'Of course ...'

Frank went to the fridge and pulled a bottle of scotch from the freezer. He poured himself a large one and returned to the phone.

'Puss, we'll have to sit down and have a good talk about all this. More complicated than you'd think. You see, I knew Nina was having a rough time with Red and I knew he might have —'

'Frank, you're blaming yourself, just like you did about Monique.'

'No, mate, this is different. This time I ...'

Puss's silence was more gentle this time. He cut it short by saying, 'I'll see you down at the Allegra in half an hour, eh? Talk about it over a drink.'

Frank thanked him, hung up and looked around for a diversion to soak up half an hour. He found one in the form of work. A major new account for a car company had been picked up by the agency and he was in charge of the campaign. He liked doing ads for cars. Cars were fun. Besides, he thought, I'll need a new one soon. Might be able to swing a deal.

He stared blankly at the brief, flipped through a couple of rudimentary layouts, paused at some photographs. Bloody nice-looking cars, all right. He'd need to think about this. He wasn't in the mood, right now. Right now, he was in the mood for a drink.

He took *Lost Sheep* out of his bag, stuffed it into the pocket of his jacket and walked out.

'Be down at the Allegra,' he told Sandra, 'in case anybody's looking for me.'

When Puss found him twenty minutes later, he seemed less drunk than Puss had expected, although it was hard to tell with Frank. Puss recognised the book he was reading. It provided the perfect excuse to begin the conversation with something other than Frank's seemingly endless supply of those two corrosive commodities: guilt and shame.

'Hello, you old lost sheep you,' he said, placing a beer in front of himself and a fresh one in front of Frank as he sat down. 'It's good, isn't it?'

'Only read about fifty pages,' Frank answered, 'but there's no doubt about it — she's good all right.'

'Ah, Xin-Xin. I think you're a bit smitten by our Xin-Xin, Frank.'

'You could say that. I've been thinking of getting in touch with her but she's married, isn't she?'

'Xin-Xin? No way. She lives with a guy called Phillip. Met him a couple of times. Don't know what on earth she sees in him.'

'What's he do?'

'I don't know what he does, but I know what he could do.'

'What's that?'

'He could bore an arsehole into a wooden horse.'

Frank, who'd been starved for good news, was suddenly getting it in large amounts. Not only not married, but living with a boring deadshit. Things were looking brighter by the minute.

''Nother beer?' he said cheerily, heading for the bar.

Puss nodded, although the one he'd just started was already making him feel bloated.

'Suppose you heard about what happened to my place and how I got this bloody black eye,' Frank said on returning.

'No,' Puss lied.

Eddie had rung him with an account of Frank's most recent misadventure and Puss had assumed, as always, that Eddie had greatly exaggerated it for their mutual amusement. This time, it seemed, he'd been wrong. There were lurid details in Frank's telling of the story that Eddie hadn't touched on, and Frank's deadpan delivery only made it funnier. It was clear for Frank, however, that this was one in his encyclopaedia of life experiences that he wouldn't be able to laugh about wholeheartedly for quite some time.

'Well,' Puss said with a grin when Frank had finished, 'can't wait to get home so I can ring Xin-Xin and tell her all about it.'

'Don't you dare,' Frank said, glaring.

'Only joking, mate. As if I would.'

'Seriously, Puss, it's the sort of thing I don't want her to know. She wouldn't have anything to do with me if she knew about the sorts of things I get up to. Or the things I've got up to in the past.'

'You might be wrong there. You're already putting her up on a pedestal. It's what you always do when you think a woman is unattainable. It's that chip on your shoulder about class, but it's all in your head. Xin-Xin's not naive or stupid, Frank, and she does have a sense of humour.'

'I'm sure she does,' Frank replied, 'but I'm also sure I'll have to clean up my act a hell of a lot if she's to be interested in me.'

'Turning over a new leaf, are we?'

'Maybe,' Frank murmured. 'It was on that same night that Red bashed Nina and Mandy and I —'

'You were in Kings Cross and they were in Mitchellton,' Puss interrupted. 'And you are not responsible for what goes on in their lives.'

'No, but —'

'No, Frank, just no. We'll have to talk about that some other time. Sorry, mate, but I should have been home an hour ago. Here, you finish that.'

Puss pushed his second, untouched beer in front of Frank, shook his hand warmly while giving him a good firm hug, and left. Frank's story about the girl he'd picked up at AD's and the subsequent trashing of his apartment by Harriet had given him more than enough opportunity to wallow in guilt and shame for one evening. It was out of compassion that Puss refused to hear any more.

As Puss's taxi passed Rushcutters Bay Park, it also passed Xin-Xin who was strolling home after a long walk around the foreshore of the harbour, which had given her time to cry until she ran out of tears and revived her to the point where she felt she could at least attempt to do some work. She knew if she forced herself to sit at the keyboard, eventually she'd become absorbed in the uncertain destiny of her depressed, lonely saxophone player, who, lately, had even been abandoned by her. Maybe he could help her out of her own misery. He was in pretty bad shape at the moment but who knew what might happen in the next few pages?

Her notes for the penultimate chapter included various methods of committing suicide, but she couldn't bear the idea now. She decided to delete all of them and work out a way to help him survive. If he could do it for her, she owed the same to him.

Back at her desk, she put Oliver Nelson's *The Blues and the Abstract Truth* on the CD player, turned it down to an acceptable volume for working and composed herself in front of the computer.

She checked her emails before commencing work. Quite a few had accumulated over four days of avoidance. She double-clicked on the one at the top. It was from Frank Thornton.

Lost sheep? Sounds like it (7,3).
Frank

Xin-Xin understood immediately: Missing you.

What a hide, she thought, as Lola's story sprang to mind in all its sordid detail.

She hit reply and banged out:

Ewe'll have to do better than that.
X

With her finger poised ready to click send, she stopped, lit a cigarette and sat back. Her eyes were filling with tears again, her message starting to blur on the screen. Was that the truth? Did he really have to do better than that?

She was angry with Phillip, but was she angry with this man, and if so, why? Just because he'd almost added his name to the long list of men who'd had one-night stands with the irrepressible Lola? Had she thought about him since they'd met on Friday night? Frequently. Could that be construed as 'missing'?

Xin-Xin deleted the reply and spent a few moments formulating an alternative.

Absent second person hears second number (7,3,3).
X

She hesitated, read it again, and clicked send.

She admitted she was anxious to see how he'd reply. He was a fascinating guy, even if he was a bit on the wild side. There was no denying a certain rough-hewn attractiveness. Sometimes she envied Lola's wild times — she could do with a fling herself. Judging by what Lola had told her, Frank Thornton would be capable of providing her with that, if nothing else.

And if half of what Neil had told her about him was true, he had the required get up and go to mollify — and mortify — mean old Mum.

CHAPTER 26

The next morning Frank reflected on Roy's explanation of the mechanics of the brain when he woke on a bench in Belmore Park and realised the man responsible for getting him home had conspired with the man in charge of putting him to bed and they should both be sacked.

One of them, at least, had had the sense to instruct him to use his bag as a pillow, and Providence had ensured it was still there. All in all, a good result, Frank thought, as he wandered home. It wasn't a bed or a couch, but at least it wasn't the gutter. Still, they'd proven themselves to be unreliable employees, capable of treachery. He'd have to keep an eye on those two.

He remembered starting out at the Allegra and heading off to some pub near Eddie's place, where he'd bought a gram and lost some money on the pokies. That was when he'd bumped into Andy, who now worked in the Melbourne office but had flown up to Sydney for a couple of days. Funny bloke, Andy — one of the best joke-tellers he knew. Told him some good ones too. What was that one about the ninety-year-old bloke who went into a confessional? Couldn't remember. And where had they both gone when Eddie decided to call it a day? Couldn't remember that either. And how did he end up in Belmore Park?

All too hard, and what did it matter? He was almost home now. All he needed was a shower, a shave and a change of clothes. And a procedure to cure a force six.

You had to hand it to Wayne — he was thorough. He'd been and gone, and so had everything else.

Frank looked around his empty apartment and tried to remember the colour of the carpet he'd walked on for the past fifteen years and what the couch had looked like. Prodding the lumps on the back of his head and his black eye, he realised things would have been a lot worse if he'd stayed any longer that night. It could have been his head that had ended up inside the telly. Recalling Arthur's advice, he rang a locksmith, who said he could be there in half an hour.

An ashtray and a coffee mug had somehow escaped Harriet's attention. Frank deployed them in the service of his customary breakfast after borrowing some instant coffee, a Vegemite jar full of sugar and a kettle from Mike, his next-door neighbour. Mike had emerged from his flat in his underpants at the height of Saturday night's mêlée and quickly retreated at the thought he might be summoned to appear as a witness at some future date. He'd shown impressive judgment in doing so: Frank had taken a swing at one of the coppers and the last thing he wanted was to prevail upon a friendly neighbour to perjure himself.

He put on the kettle, showered, shaved, got changed and busied himself by making a start on a list of 'essentials'. He'd amassed a staggering eighteen items and was still going when the locksmith arrived, a tiny rotund man shaped like an egg.

'Nice shiner you've got there,' Humpty said as he went about his business. 'The missus belt you, did she?'

''Fraid so,' said Frank.

'Paying cash?'

'I doubt it.'

'There's a drink in it for you if you do.'

'How much are we talking?'

'Four hundred and twenty.'

'Christ,' said Frank. 'I haven't got that much cash on me. I'll have to give you a cheque.'

'You don't have to be dead to be stiff. You'll have to make it out for four eighty.'

Little prick, thought Frank, as he closed the door and threw his four-hundred-and-eighty-dollar keys on the table, appalled to have found a man who earned more money for doing less work than he did.

The coffee had made him feel sick. He took a beer from the fridge and returned to compiling his list. He needed to get to the office early to see if Xin-Xin had responded to his email. Now that was 'essential'.

Taking a last look around before leaving, he was struck by the range of decorative possibilities Harriet had placed at his disposal. He found himself warming to the prospect of choosing a few sticks of furniture, maybe getting some bookshelves built. He'd make a point of not allowing it to get too cluttered. Before Cyclone Harriet, the place had looked like the home of Steptoe and Son.

I'll start with the floorboards, Frank thought. Get them sanded and polished. Start from the ground up. Have it looking good before Xin-Xin comes around.

As he locked the door and made his way to the lift he wondered what feng shui was and where he could buy some.

'You're in early,' said Sandra as Frank passed by her desk at twice his normal speed. 'Busy day?'

'Busy as a long-tailed rat in a room full of rocking chairs,' she heard him say as he disappeared into his office.

He jabbed the on switch on his computer and leafed through the *Yellow Pages*, looking for F for floor-sanders, while his technological slave went through its routine of flashing one display of meaningless text after another before declaring itself ready for action.

He placed the directory face down on the floor and clicked onto his mailbox. There it was! A message from Xin-Xin Leroq.

Absent second person hears second number (7,3,3).
    X

Frank was on the second lap of a brisk walk around the perimeter of the Turkish rug on the floor of his office, rubbing his hands up and down his thighs and sucking and blowing air in and out of his cheeks like a man reviving from cardiac arrest, before even realising he wasn't sitting down. He resumed his seat, cheeks still working away like bellows, and stared at the screen as though witnessing a miracle.

He set off on a couple more laps, in the opposite direction this time, and trying out a different combination of hand movements: clicking the fingers of his left while swinging it back and forth; rubbing his forehead with the right while staring intently at the floor.

'I don't believe it,' he muttered. 'I don't fucking believe it.'

But there it was — undeniable, irrevocable — an email from Xin-Xin Leroq, and it meant 'missing you too'.

Around the carpet he sailed again, this time via the fridge, opening a beer while trying to think of an appropriate reply. He'd have to come up with something quickly. He'd have to see her tonight!

How did you encrypt a message that said 'I want to see you now; I want to hold you in my arms now; I want to rip your clothes off and fuck you to a standstill now; I want to marry you now!' and do it subtly, without the slightest hint of desperation?

The shiner! How long would it take to disappear? Five more days? Four if he was lucky. And the flat! How long before he'd knocked that back into shape?

Reality again. Cold and hard as always. It had never held much appeal for Frank, and he'd developed more techniques than most for avoiding it over the years, but there was no way of avoiding this. It was a logistical nightmare.

Xin-Xin's heroin-addicted saxophone virtuoso had been having nightmares of his own. But things were looking up: 'I've been out of detox for less than a week, Angel, and I've got a gig with …' Someone. Right now, Xin-Xin couldn't make up her mind who it should be.

She sat back with her elbows on the armrests of her chair, her hands locked in the shape of a church. Her index fingers made the spire and at the top, where the cross should be, they pressed against her bottom lip. She appeared to be gazing out the window at the view, but she wasn't seeing it. She was thinking, thinking hard, about who should ring her sax player and offer him a job. God knows, he needed it.

She sat up and lit a cigarette, and checked her emails. Only one. From Frank Thornton.

> *Syringe or sublimity? Clumsy, but truthful I'm afraid (7,3,8).*
> *Frank*
> *PS: I have to go to Melbourne for work. Be gone about six days — a week at the most. Can I call you when I get back?*
> *F*

Xin-Xin got up and did a couple of circuits of the lounge room, puffing on her cigarette and staring at the floor.

She sat down again and studied the message, wrote down the letters left after subtracting those that formed 'missing you' from 'syringe or sublimity'. After some juggling they formed 'terribly', which was, she thought, terribly obvious, terribly presumptuous and, well, terribly sweet.

Terribly frustrating too, she thought, pacing the room again. I was hoping I'd be able to see him tonight! Still, you had to hand it to him: he was a pretty cool customer. She liked that in a man. Not the desperate type, at least. A desperate type would have called off a work trip to Melbourne.

She sat down, experimented with combinations of the letters of 'please do', clicked reply and sent:

Confused, also deep (6,2).
  X x

That should keep him happy while he's down in bleak old Melbourne, she thought. And only six more sleeps to wait.

Her sax player might be living happily ever after by then.

CHAPTER 27

Henry Grosvenor was on the A-list.

He received many invitations to charity balls for good causes and studied each one carefully in order to accurately assess exactly how good the cause was. Henry could glean more information from studying the words on these documents than a gambler could from the form guide. Obviously, the venue itself was important, as was the price of the tickets. But it was from the fine detail that Henry picked up his clues: the quality of the paper; the wording of the message; the style and sophistication of the presentation; which company was organising the event. These factors enabled him to predict the quality of the thoroughbreds he could expect to find there, the proportion of fillies amongst them, and how many in that subgroup were unattached. He'd then make a few discreet phone calls to fellow tipsters who provided details of the recent track records of the nags he was interested in. If he fancied his chances of backing a winner, he'd decide it was a charity he was only too happy to support.

Wife Number Four was rarely seen at such events, all of which Henry deemed strictly work-related and therefore too tedious for her to waste time attending, but she served as a glamorous accessory on more sedate occasions, when networking was his sole objective.

Henry scrutinised the fine print on the back of an austere but seductive request for the pleasure of his company at a function at the State Library the following Saturday night. The purpose of the evening was to raise funds for the acquisition of a portfolio of original watercolours, complete with handwritten notes, by Sir Joseph Banks, for the Library's collection. But the highlight would be the awarding of the Fleetwood Prize, to be presented by last year's winner, Ms Xin-Xin Leroq.

He recalled a recent conversation over lunch with his close friend and fellow yachtsman, Michael Halliday QC, during which the subject of Ms Leroq was dealt with at length, and decided the works by Sir Joseph Banks were of such significance it was incumbent upon him to do his utmost to ensure they found their way into the Library's collection.

How remiss of me, he thought, checking the RSVP notice and seeing it had been required on or before the previous Friday. This would make it a little more difficult to ensure satisfactory seating arrangements, but there was nothing that couldn't be organised, provided you knew the right people.

He made four phone calls.

The first was to his secretary, Melanie, who located the sumptuously illustrated book on the life and work of Sir Joseph Banks in the Australian History section on the third floor of Grosvenor's Bookstore, and delivered it to him within minutes.

The second was to his good friend Morty Carmody, whose company, EmCee Promotions, was organising the evening's festivities. On Morty's suggestion, Henry agreed to meet him for a game of golf the following Wednesday. Morty played off a handicap of four, while Henry's languished in the twenties. Despite never having beaten Morty, Henry agreed to wager a case of Veuve Clicquot on the outcome. Seating arrangements for the State Library function were also discussed and Morty could see no reason why he couldn't secure a spot for Henry next to Ms Leroq, given his status as a doyen of the literary scene, not to mention his generous contributions to the Library in the past.

The third call was to Wife Number Four, who didn't sound at all disappointed when he told her, due to the long waiting list for seats, it wouldn't be possible for her to attend. Besides, the function promised to be a boring affair of long speeches in dull company.

It occurred to Henry that Wife Number Four had, in fact, sounded utterly indifferent, which was why his fourth call was to a private investigator currently in his employ and compiling a dossier on Number Four, instructing him to keep a close watch this coming Saturday night.

Having been taken to the cleaners by all three of her predecessors, Henry had no intention of being escorted there again.

Arriving on time is a male compulsion; arriving late is a woman's prerogative. Xin-Xin mused on this irreconcilable genetic divergence as she soaped herself down in the shower, and wondered how many divorces it had contributed to.

The invitation said seven for seven-thirty and, for once favouring the male position, she was determined to be amongst the first through the door. Even under the shower her hands felt cold and clammy, refusing to respond to either soap or hot water. She didn't need reminding she was nervous, so what the hell were her hands playing at? What she did need was a drink or two before taking her place at some prominent table where people would be staring at her: last year's winner, Xin-Xin Leroq, the pretty Asian girl with her hands under the table, wiping them dry on her damp serviette. That was why she needed to be there at seven, because it was during that crucial half-hour that a squadron of waiters would be urging champagne on the guests.

Why, why did Frank Thornton have to go to Melbourne this week of all weeks?

She shuddered at the prospect of being seated next to some dreary socialite or boorish lech with roaming hands in a roomful of people who would expect her to say something memorable during her ten-minute ordeal at the microphone.

She dried herself, daubed on some lip gloss, threw open the doors of her wardrobe and grabbed the first dress that came to hand. It happened to be a simple garment made of a silver-grey synthetic material that took on a metallic lustre under strong light. The designer had saved on the cost of the fabric by wasting almost none on the back, using as little as possible to construct the delicate shoulder straps and saving a fair amount at the neckline.

Shoes. She selected a pair of Prada stilettos and emerged into the kitchen a considerably taller woman who looked as though she'd spent all day being fussed over and was now ready for the photographer from *Vogue*.

One last look at the speech, she thought, lighting a cigarette and glancing at her watch. Good. Only twenty to seven. Plenty of time to make some minor changes.

Shaved and aftershaved, Henry Grosvenor made his way down the aisle of his wardrobe to the formal wear section and lit on a recent acquisition, yet to make its Sydney debut.

He approached the mirror, swung his right arm over the back of his head so his hand dangled in front of his face and reefed open his left nostril with the tip of the forefinger. No, no unsightly bristles poking out. He repeated the contortion with his left arm and right nostril, stood back, took one more look at the man in full and was pleased with what he saw.

'Cab's waiting, darling,' said Number Four, whom he deigned to kiss lightly, bestowing upon her a whiff of cologne to dwell on after he'd gone.

Henry arrived on the dot of seven, condescended to a glass of local champagne and kept his eye on the door. Thirty minutes, two more glasses and much mingling later, the call was made for guests to kindly proceed to their tables. To Henry's chagrin, Ms Leroq still wasn't one of them.

Ten minutes later, with four hundred guests seated and the entrées about to arrive, Xin-Xin entered, turning every head in the room as she picked her way to her table. If beauty is in the eye of the beholder, there were plenty of beholders at the State Library that night. Chief amongst them was Henry Grosvenor. Ever the gentleman, he stood when she arrived, introduced himself and the other diners at Table One, and took a good look down her cleavage as she sat down on the chair next to his.

'Sorry,' she said, 'I forgot I needed a speech for tonight. Had to make a few notes at the last minute.'

'Would you care for a drink?' asked Henry, midway through filling her glass with champagne.

Yes, she would indeed care for one.

Like genius, beauty has its drawbacks. Those blessed with preposterous good looks are perceived by those without them as alien creatures upon whom higher expectations can justifiably be placed. If they don't look like normal people, it's reasonable to assume they don't feel like them either. The seven normal-looking people Xin-Xin had just been introduced to would never have suspected that a millimetre or so behind her assured demeanour and impossibly beautiful face lay a skinful of nerves and confusion.

Xin-Xin knew that Ted Everingham, bursting at the seams of a tuxedo he'd bought some ten kilos earlier, was important. He was the chief executive or owner of some company that had shown its support for the Library by donating a collection of someone's manuscripts or paintings or the funds to purchase whatever it was the Library wanted to purchase, and Xin-Xin thought his name was Fred.

His wife was important too. She was a member of the Friends of the Library or was on the board of directors, or maybe that was the woman on her right with the sharp profile and severe haircut who looked like a man and whose name might have been Edna or Emily. Then again, the ruddy-faced, cheeky little bloke with the bald head and goatee next to her had a name like Edgar or Emile so maybe it wasn't Edna or Emily after all.

Seated to her left were the Premier and his wife. At least Xin-Xin knew their names — everybody did.

She pretended to wipe the corner of her mouth with her serviette, then slipped it below the table where she could wipe the sweat off her hands unnoticed. Around her, the conversation continued much as one would expect in such a situation, oscillating between the stilted and the gushing, and all of it becoming increasingly incomprehensible.

She understood what the bloke on her right, Henry Someone, was saying though, and every time he did she answered, 'Yes, please, but just a little top-up, thanks.'

By the time she found herself walking towards the podium, Henry Whatever-His-Name-Was had obliged a few too many times.

Ten minutes later she was back in her seat, he was congratulating her effusively, the audience was still clapping, and she couldn't remember what she'd said to deserve it. The Premier shook her hand warmly. He'd given her a flattering introduction after delivering an excellent speech, and she couldn't remember a word he'd said either.

'Yes, please,' she said on hearing Old Silvertop's familiar proposal. 'I can sit back and enjoy myself now.'

'And so you shall, my dear,' said the silver-haired someone. 'So you shall.'

Gallant Henry wasn't about to let the belle of the ball go home unassisted, not in the state she was in by twelve o'clock. Escorting her to a taxi was the least he could do, he assured the few guests still lingering at the table as he placed Xin-Xin's jacket over her shoulders, helped her to her feet and guided her out.

Xin-Xin was almost asleep when the taxi pulled up outside her apartment block and Henry insisted on walking her to her door. He handed the cab driver some money through the window and informed him his services were no longer required.

'Thank you, I'll be fine now,' said Xin-Xin, fumbling about for her keys. She dropped her bag, spilling its contents onto the footpath.

'Come on,' said Henry, chivalrous to the last, 'you'd better let me help you get inside.'

Once inside, Henry proceeded to take chivalry a few steps further by helping Xin-Xin totter all the way to her bedroom and kindly offering to assist her out of her clothes.

'Thank you,' she said, like a semi-conscious accident victim being dragged from the wreckage of a car, and pulled her bedclothes around her shoulders.

She was on the verge of sleep when she realised she wasn't alone. Chivalrous Henry, it seemed, was in for the long haul.

'No, please,' she murmured as she felt his hands on her breasts, on her behind, her thighs, between her legs. 'No, please, no ...'

But there was no stopping the Errol Flynn of Oxford now, as he turned her over, pressed his mouth against hers as she writhed and squirmed, misinterpreting her flailing as a sign she was yielding to his legendary ardour. There wasn't a woman alive who could resist old Casanova Grosvenor.

Xin-Xin was suddenly sufficiently sober to find the strength to thrust him away. His face became a caricature of embarrassment and alarm at the realisation that the only one who was going to do any thrusting tonight was her.

'S-sorry,' he stammered. 'A terrible misunderstanding.'

'Get the fuck out of my house,' she screamed, 'before I call the police.'

Dignified, sophisticated Henry Grosvenor's repellent arse was the last thing Xin-Xin saw as he scampered out of her room.

A few seconds later, she heard the front door close. She rushed into the bathroom, fell to her knees, held her arms around the toilet and threw the stinking stew of the whole miserable evening down the bowl.

Henry blamed Wife Number Four as he stared out the taxi window, watching the night flash by in a stream of neon. If that bitch hadn't been giving him so much grief this would never have happened. Christ, what a fiasco, he thought, as he reached into his pocket for his phone.

He punched in Number Four's number and heard it ring and ring until it gave up. He tried again. Still no answer.

I'll call that fucking detective and find out what she's been up to.

Now it was the detective's phone's turn to ring and ring. Henry had had enough. He instructed the driver to head straight for the bludger's home in Darlinghurst.

I'm paying this prick to work, he thought. If she's out on the prowl, he should be tailing her, not knocking off when he pleases and going home to bloody bed.

'Left here, driver,' he said as they approached the corner of Womerah Avenue. 'About three hundred metres down on the right.'

About two hundred metres down, he asked the driver to pull up when he spotted a car usually found in the driveway of his own home.

He checked the numberplate. It was hers.

'What a bitch!' he wailed. 'And what a fucking bastard!'

Mr Investigator was keeping a closer watch on Number Four than they'd agreed to.

Henry headed home, rubbing his hands together, kneading his thighs and gyrating about in his seat.

Private eyes? he thought. They can't keep their private parts to themselves. No wonder they call them dicks!

CHAPTER 28

The maturation of a black eye can take up to four or five days. A good example can leave the lid permanently closed for most of this time while colour progresses from a combination of deep crimson and chartreuse to puce, climaxing in indigo. Surprisingly, it's not always a blow to the eye itself that produces the best result. A solid whack above the brow can be equally effective. The forehead, when assaulted, often refuses to accept responsibility for the aftermath and leaves the eye to take the blame.

Such was the case with Frank's shiner.

Harriet had struck him a good inch above the left brow, but hadn't broken the skin. The only evidence at the point of impact was a lump that had almost disappeared by Wednesday, when the black eye was at its most grotesque.

Appraising it in the mirror on Thursday night, Frank knew the worst was over. By the time Xin-Xin was struggling to resist Henry's attempt at seduction on Saturday night, it had reduced itself to a crescent of violet.

Two more days at the most.

In the meantime he still had a lot to do. The flat had been turned into a construction site where transformations were taking place at a breathtaking rate and cost.

'Leave it to me,' Eddie had insisted, before embarking on a flurry of phone calls to an assortment of tradesmen, salesmen and someone whose delicately textured business card alerted its recipients to the fact he regarded himself as an interior designer. When Frank heard his fees, he regarded him as a conman.

'Trust me,' Eddie said, deflecting Frank's protestations with the ease of a man who knows someone else is paying. 'Louis is the best in the business.'

By Tuesday morning, Frank was beginning to concede Eddie might be right.

There was no disputing the new bookshelves were worth every cent the carpenter had overcharged for them, the floorboards looked great, he couldn't get over the difference the shutters made, and those track lights — with dimmers! — worked wonders when directed at the paintings. Why hadn't he thought of that before?

Eddie arrived on Monday evening for a final inspection, along with a six-pack and a bottle of Krug. He went from room to room, approving craftsmanship and subtleties, while Frank connected the speaker wires.

He'd been to Birdland that day and picked up the CDs he considered essential to any respectable jazz collection, plus a few new ones he'd been intending to buy anyway, and then gone on to Michael's for the classical must-haves. There he'd prevailed on the salesman to help him carry the boxes out to the street, where he caught a cab home with barely enough cash in his wallet to pay for the fare and a credit card now worth its own weight in plastic.

Frank rifled through the piles of discs until he found something worthy of the honour of christening his new sound system. Eddie opened the bubbly to the strains of Bach's Double Violin Concerto in D Minor.

'Here's to Harriet,' said Eddie. 'You have much to thank her for. I think you might be ready to tell this Chinny-Chin-Chin you've finally arrived back from Melbourne.'

The doorbell rang. Frank heard Roy's voice booming through the intercom. 'Open the door, you silly bastard. And the lift had better be working 'cause we're not dragging this thing up the fucking stairs.'

He and Arthur appeared a few moments later, struggling under the weight of an enormous painting in a heavy frame. Arthur had dredged up some drawings and studies he'd painted during a trip along the once-mighty Murray River and commenced on a series of powerful images in keeping with the mood he'd been in since having made an exhibition of himself. This one was as black as any Goya; a eulogy to a spent life force, atrophied through salination and decay.

'This is to remind you of what your place looked like before you started,' the artist said. 'Give us a hand to get it up on the wall. It'll look pretty good under one of those track lights.'

194

It looked more than good after Frank, Roy and Arthur had secured it into place while Eddie controlled the operation by shouting instructions from the couch; it looked majestic. Frank's portrait, which had been taken away for Arthur's exhibition, would come home in a few days to find itself usurped by a landscape. Might be better, Frank thought, if it didn't come home at all.

Frank had to touch, smell and get intimate with his new painting before tearing himself away to take in its tragic grandeur from a distance.

'It's the best painting you've ever done, Arthur,' he said, using up the only words he could find.

'Well, I wouldn't give you a crook one, would I? Not after all the work you did helping me with the show.'

Arthur divulged the news that his exhibition had been a commercial, if not critical, success and that another was planned for the same time next year. Roy opened more champagne. They had a lot of celebrating to do.

Next morning, sipping coffee and nursing a force four, Frank roamed his new surrounds like a visitor to a luxury resort on the first day of his holiday. So much space! Such elegance! Eddie was right: he had Harriet to thank for this. He stopped in front of his new painting. Perhaps he'd found love at last. He could live with this picture for the rest of his life.

In the lift, he pressed B for basement for the second day in a row, and paused to admire his new car before unlocking it by pressing the button on the key. No doubt about it, he thought, it's a good-looking car. Lucky the agency picked up the account.

When Frank arrived at the office, Sandra's absence from her secretarial post unsettled him, as did the absence of all his other colleagues. Everything was so quiet in this interval between the departure of the contract cleaners and the arrival of the early birds who curried favour with Harry by commencing, on schedule, at nine. And the place was so dark, with little slivers of sunlight creeping through the venetians and making patterns on the walls. On reaching his office, he was surprised the light worked when he switched it on; even more so when his computer did the same.

Right, he thought, as he sat at his keyboard, I'm back from Melbourne and it's time to get in touch. Should I, perhaps, have arrived a couple of days ago but haven't had time until now to email? Don't want her thinking I'm so desperate I've come in straight from the airport. Better to play it cool. Not too cool, though. I'll say I got back yesterday and was as busy as buggery.

Next problem. Should he invite her to dinner or check to see if a good concert's coming up soon? Rick Manning was playing tonight down at AD's, but AD's might be a bit downmarket for her. Dinner was probably the go. Benoit's if the weather was good.

Frank clicked onto his mailbox. There was only one message and it was from Xin-Xin. Under the title of 'Welcome Home' it said:

Are you back yet? Your week's up and I'm sick and tired of lost sheep (7,3).
X x
PS: Rick Manning's playing down at AD's tonight. Just a thought.
X

Frank checked the time on the email. It had been sent five minutes before: 8:40 am.

Christ! I need a ciggie. Can't smoke in here. What was he going to say? He needed a Bloody Mary too. He could get one at the Intercontinental while he thought about how to reply. It might look desperate if he sent one straightaway.

A vacant table, half-hidden by a rainforest in a ceramic pot, beckoned in a corner of the lounge area of the Intercontinental Hotel. Frank made a beeline towards it and collided with a waiter. The mishap cost the hotel three cups, a saucer and a sugar bowl.

'Sorry, mate. Heading for that table over there. Could you bring us a Bloody Mary? Ta.'

Frank threw his bag onto the table, pulled out a notepad and a pen, lit up a cigarette and started to think. Okay. What did her email say? She mentioned lost sheep. Said she's been missing me and wants to see me at AD's tonight. Tonight! Rick Manning's playing. She must like Rick Manning's band. I can't believe it. How long's it take for this bloke to make a Bloody Mary?

He brushed the foliage aside roughly. The waiter showed great skill as he danced around the unexpectedly animated pot plant while balancing his tray, saving the hotel the cost of a Bloody Mary and a tall glass.

'Thanks, mate. Oh, hang on! Could you bring me a copy of the *Herald*? Ta.'

'Dear Xin-Xin,' he scribbled.

Now what? Come on, Frank, you're a copywriter for fuck's sake. Let's see. The band doesn't start playing till about nine-thirty so maybe she'd like to catch up for dinner somewhere first. We could go to the Japanese down near AD's and then hear the show.

'Your newspaper, sir.'

'Ta. Oh — another Bloody Mary, thanks.'

Frank scanned the front page of the newspaper. Red was old news by now. Outclassed by a bloke who shot a copper in Hurstville and a woman up in Gosford who drowned her baby in the bath.

'Dear Xin-Xin,' he wrote again on a fresh page, and lit another cigarette.

Maybe he should do the cryptic. It'd take his mind off what to say. He could think about that when he got back to the office.

One across. Always good to get off to a flying start with one across.

AFALLOAM (3,2,1,6).

Shit. He hated these clues that were all capital letters and made no sense at all. Afalloam. A-F-A-L-L-O-A-M.

Fuck this. No sense in getting myself in a lather over it. I'll ring Puss and ask him when I get back. And answer Xin-Xin's email after that.

'Waiter! Bill, please. Ta.'

Puss, as usual, had finished the cryptic. It embarrassed Frank to confess he was stuck on one across.

'Thought you would have twigged to that one pretty quickly,' joked Puss. 'It sums you up rather nicely.'

'Come again?'

'You're all in a lather.'

'So?'

'That's the answer: "all in a lather". "All" in "a foam" — get it?'

Frank groaned as he filled in the spaces.

'I'd better tell you the truth, Frank. I couldn't work it out either so I rang Xin-Xin and she told me.'

'What?'

'I often ring her when I'm having trouble with a clue. How was the trip to Melbourne?'

'What?'

'Xin-Xin told me you've been in Melbourne for a week.'

'Oh, right. Look, mate, the truth is —'

'Yeah, I know. Eddie told me the whole story. Can't wait to see Chez Thornton. Eddie tells me you got Louis Grieco to do it. Smart move, that. Louis's made a bit of a specialty of feng shui. Trying to impress Xin-Xin, are we?'

'Puss, I don't even know what feng shui is.'

'Don't worry, Xin-Xin does.'

'Listen, I hope you haven't said anything. Not only about me not being in Melbourne, but about that other story I told you.'

'I haven't. And I can tell you one thing, she's waiting for you to contact her again. She told me this morning you're due back from Melbourne today.'

'You're making it sound like she's pretty keen,' said Frank, starting to enjoy the conversation.

'Of course she's keen. Trust me, I'm a girl. We know these things. We also worry a lot. Are you okay, Frank?'

'Of course I'm okay. What do you mean?'

'I was thinking of Nina and her daughter — what's her name?'

'Mandy,' said Frank, no longer enjoying the conversation. 'I dunno. I'm still being kept in the dark. I don't know how to get in touch with Mandy and I'm not allowed to visit Nina while she's in hospital.'

'But you're her brother, for God's sake!'

'Yeah, well, I told you I was feeling guilty. Nina doesn't want to see me, so maybe she thinks I'm guilty too. And maybe this time I fucking well am!'

'Okay, okay. Calm down, mate. I only wanted to know how they're getting along.'

'Sorry, but like I said, I don't fucking know, all right? Now look, I gotta go.'

Bloody hell. Why the sudden interest? Puss had never met Mandy in his life. Hardly knew Nina for that matter. And who was it that helped her out the last time she was in trouble? Me! Stayed at my place for a month. Brought Mandy with her. I didn't let her down that time, did I? Oh fuck, what have I done? No, what am *I doing*? What am I going to write? Bugger it, I'll suggest the Japanese and AD's tonight and see how we go.

Dear Xin-Xin,
    Thanks for your message.
    Just got back this morning. Was hearing lost sheep (7,3) in Melbourne.
    RE: just a thought — I like the way you're thinking. Would love to go down to AD's tonight and hear RM's band.
    Frank
    PS: You like Japanese food? There's a good one a block away from AD's. Just a thought.
    F

Yep. That looked okay. Click and send.

Shit! He'd forgotten to put an x after Frank. She'd sent him one. Fuck the fresh-air fascists — he was going to have a smoke. And a beer.

'Ping.'

Subject: Re: Welcome Home
    Dear Frank,
    I like the way you're thinking.
    I love Japanese food.
    X x (!)

Subject: Re: Welcome Home
    Dear Xin-Xin,
    Now I'm thinking I could pick you up at about 7:30 if I knew where you lived.
    Fxx(!)

'Ping.'

Subject: Re: Welcome Home
    19/184 Burrawong Ave, Woollahra
    See you at 7:30.
    X xxx(!)

'Ping.'

> *Subject: Strictly Confidential*
> *Frank,*
> *Someone pinched my long-stemmed pipe last week. You heard anything about it? I'll sack the bastard when I find out who it was.*
> *Harry*

Oh, Jesus!

> *Subject: Re: Strictly Confidential*
> *Harry,*
> *Stick your pipe up your arse.*
> *Frank*

Frank rang the intercom at 19/184 Burrawong Ave, Woollahra, at seven-thirty exactly, after overestimating the time needed for the trip from his home in Surry Hills by a factor of twenty-seven minutes, which he'd made bearable by finishing off the cryptic in the pub down the road.

Bloody hell, he thought, I've got sweaty palms. Better not wipe them on these clean trousers.

'Hi, Frank.'

'Hello, Xin-Xin.'

'You've surprised me already, Frank. I wouldn't have picked you for the roses type.'

Frank had bought a dozen red roses and was handing them to her. He shrugged and felt his face turning a similar colour. He'd handed dozens of roses to dozens of women and not once felt ridiculous. Until now. Was she turning a little red too? This was getting awkward.

Nevertheless, Frank found it surprisingly easy to lean over and kiss Xin-Xin as she took receipt of the flowers, arching her neck towards him as if a kiss was the least he should be entitled to expect. Steering her away from the door with his hand on her waist came pretty naturally too. So much so that he didn't realise he'd made this first milestone of intimate contact until after the event, when they were walking down the front steps towards the gate.

'Where's your car?'

'Just around the corner,' he said, thinking: wait till she cops a load of this.

'A Z3,' she said as he pressed his key button and opened the door for her. 'Same as mine, only black.'

Neither Frank nor Xin-Xin could later remember the details of the conversation that rattled along in fits and starts as they drove to the restaurant on that warm, still evening in early autumn. Xin-Xin knew for certain it was *Ruby Vroom* by Soul Coughing in the CD player and not, as Frank insisted, a Cassandra Wilson album that hadn't even come out then. She remembered quite clearly asking him who the band was and saying she'd never heard of them before. And it didn't sound like jazz to her. They were able to agree that they'd laughed a lot, and found a parking space in front of the restaurant when a car pulled out, as if commanded to do so, at the moment they arrived.

Frank remained adamant they'd talked about her books over dinner but the subject of Puss hadn't come up till much later, when they were listening to Rick Manning's band at AD's. Xin-Xin always maintained the subject of Puss had come up over dinner, arguing it was discussion of *Gang-Gang* that had led to Neil's name being mentioned: Frank had said he'd found it difficult to understand why Puss would have identified so strongly with Lenny when Lenny was straight and Aboriginal and Puss was neither.

One conversation they both clearly remembered for a long time afterwards took place at AD's, when they were drinking red wine and getting to the stage where close contact was becoming the norm. Frank was taking full advantage of the loud music to speak closely into Xin-Xin's ear, ostensibly so he could be heard without disturbing other patrons' listening enjoyment, but, more accurately, to get close enough to drink in the smell of her skin, which was far more intoxicating than the wine.

'They're a great band, aren't they?' Frank said. 'I couldn't believe it when I realised you liked them too.'

'To be honest, I've never heard them before.'

'So how come you knew they were playing down here tonight?' Frank breathed, turning his head and offering his own ear as he waited for her reply.

Instead, he heard applause and an announcement from the stage. The band was going to take a short break.

'A friend of mine told me about them. She came to see them a couple of weeks ago and met some guy she quite fancied.'

'Go on,' said Frank.

'She's a bit of a wild one. Loves a drink. I think she takes those party drugs too, sometimes.'

'So what happened?' Frank asked, wiping his sweaty hands on his thighs and thinking: bugger the trousers.

'She went home drunk to this guy's place and when they both tumbled into his bed, his girlfriend was in it — asleep! Can you believe it?'

'No,' said Frank truthfully. He couldn't.

He laughed as best he could, excused himself and went to the toilet, where he threw up, then genuflected and prayed to a line of cocaine.

He washed his face and hands in cold water at the sink, looked himself in the eye at the mirror and made a vow to walk straight out now and fess up. Otherwise he was going to be in one almighty load of shit when she found out from another source that it was him molesting Lola that night.

Tell her, Frank. Just do it!

Tomorrow.

It was Xin-Xin who insisted they catch a cab, although Frank always denied he'd even suggested he was still okay to drive.

They both recalled how Xin-Xin had said something about feng shui when they arrived at his flat. For some reason, Frank found it hilarious and they both cracked up laughing.

And they never forgot how they broke into each other's body that night, like two burglars cracking a safe in an unguarded bank, free to take whatever they wanted.

CHAPTER 29

Few women had found the going easy after moving into Frank's place. Animal magnetism, while attractive, remained so only if the animal was domesticated. And Frank was far from that.

Frank ate out. Always. Grocery shopping was accomplished weekly at the local liquor store. During his twelve driver's licence-free months, it had been made even easier thanks to their home-delivery service, reducing the process to a phone call and a necessity to be at home at around eleven o'clock on a Saturday morning, ready to open the front door. His fridge had rarely accommodated food but was always well stocked with beer, white wine and champagne, and there was never any shortage of ice cubes, scotch, and freshly ground coffee in the freezer.

Natalie, who had persevered longest, never understood why Frank failed to conform to the chauvinistic archetype she thought he typified. He showed no enthusiasm for the prospect of coming home to a hot dinner, followed by extended mutual preening and massaging sessions in front of the telly as precursors to bubble baths and sex at bedtime.

For his own part, Frank was confused by Natalie's refusal to concede that in him she'd found the perfect man. He *didn't* demand dinner on the table the moment he arrived home, *didn't* require being fussed over for hours on end, and *didn't* pine for her company when she decided to go out for a night with the girls.

'The only time we're close is when we're having sex,' she'd complain.

This bewildered Frank, who thought, given the amount of sex they were having, she could hardly grumble about shortage of closeness. Besides, they sat close to each other when they went to hear jazz, sat close to each other when they met in the pub and sat close to each other when they went out to restaurants. If you added it all up that came to quite a lot of closeness. So what the hell was she talking about?

'Intimacy,' she said. 'The only time we're intimate is when we're having sex.'

Frank had no comeback for this. How could any two people be 'intimate' when they weren't having sex? That's what sex was for, and he and Natalie were having it day and night. The woman was just plain greedy. Or mad.

When, after fourteen months, three weeks and two days of living together, Natalie told him she felt she'd spent the entire time alone, the sad truth dawned on Frank: she was both.

After Natalie walked out, he found he was capable of pining after all. So much so that, after several months of torment, he confided all to Roy over a few beers, including her perplexing reflections on intimacy. Wise Roy might be able to explain what Frank had failed to comprehend in much the same way as he'd been able to explain why, on a roulette table, after five reds had come up, black wasn't necessarily a certainty: and why, in a jar of nuts, the big ones migrate to the top.

Even Roy, who knew everything, didn't know the answer to this.

'Frank,' he said, 'you're trying to come to grips with the female mind and you're wasting your time. We're talking about a separate universe here, and it's one with which simple, straightforward blokes like us are utterly unacquainted.'

Well, Frank thought, if Roy can't understand it, what hope have I got? From then on, Frank applied the coffee test.

If he spent the night with a woman, made her a cup of coffee in the morning and then wanted her to leave, and she wanted to as well, this was a 'good result' and would go down in the books as a 'one-night stand'.

If, after the coffee, he wanted her to leave but she showed no inclination to do so, it was a sure sign she was hanging around waiting for 'intimacy' and he was out of his depth. This was a 'fail' and would be marked down as a 'problem'.

A 'pass' was when, after coffee, he didn't want her to leave and she didn't want to either. A 'pass' would evolve into an 'affair', the duration of which was dependent on the quality of the pass and would begin to disintegrate when the first fail occurred.

A 'pass with flying colours' was rare and would result in a 'relationship' involving threats of 'commitment' and 'marriage', about which the less said the better.

A 'high distinction' was only ever registered once, when, after Frank and Xin-Xin's first night together, they drank their first crucial cups of coffee and raced back to bed before attempting the second cups, which were consumed in the bedroom, as were several subsequent ones and a couple of pots of tea.

Intimacy, like happiness, is not something we recognise when it's happening; it's something we remember later, when it's not. Frank subsequently recalled experiencing both that day.

The confluence occurred in the afternoon, after the delivery man had arrived with the seafood banquet. Frank opened a bottle of champagne, Xin-Xin talked about problems she was having writing a novel about a saxophone player, and he realised he could help.

'I've been working on this for years,' he said, opening a manila folder to reveal some handwritten notes and a couple of hundred printed pages. The front page had the words 'Spotted Dog by Frank Thornton' typed in the middle.

'It's a biography. Or it will be if I ever finish it. It's about Mark Simmonds, the tenor player.'

'Why "Spotted Dog"?'

'He only ever recorded one album and "The Spotted Dog" was the first piece on it. I'll put the CD on. See what you think of it.'

Accompanied by the inspirational music of Mark Simmonds and the Freeboppers, Frank and Xin-Xin trawled through the rather less accomplished notes of Frank's homage to it. They eventually came to the conclusion that what lay before them was a collection of anecdotes, facts and literary meanderings which, while interesting enough as a source of information, bore no resemblance whatsoever to a book.

'It's a bit of a mess,' Frank conceded, flushing with embarrassment in the presence of a real author, clearly capable of committing an act of extreme verbal cruelty if she so wished. He was grateful when it didn't happen; elated when she suggested collaboration instead.

'Why don't you pick out any bits you can use,' he said, 'and chuck the rest in the bin?'

'Better still, why don't we do it together? I could use your Mark Simmonds as the model for the main character in my book and rewrite the whole thing from start to finish.'

Implicit in this suggestion was an acceptance on Xin-Xin's part that Frank had established himself as an integral part of her future. More than that: being together meant doing things together — things neither of them had been able to accomplish alone.

Louis Grieco had blown Frank's renovation budget so far out of the water that Frank had even agreed to dimmer controls on his bedside lamps. They work a treat too, he thought, as he lay beside Xin-Xin after that evening of mutual preening and massaging while listening to music — the perfect precursor to a bubble bath and sex at bedtime.

He wasn't sure what it was about her he loved most. It could have been her smell, which, even after the bath, emanated from her as though her soul itself was made of vanilla orchids. Then again, it could have been her eyes: the shape of them, and the way they sparkled. If eyes were windows to the soul, then hers wasn't only comprised of vanilla orchids; there was intelligence, humour, kindness and honesty in the mix as well. It could have been her body, but that was too obvious. At certain times during the day he'd thought it could have been her voice, or her laugh, that attracted him most. It could have been any number of things, but right now it was her skin. The smoothness of it. Not a rogue hair to be found. He'd read somewhere there were about twenty types of hair that grew on different parts of any given human body: on the head; in the earholes and nostrils (already requiring occasional lopping in his own); on the chest and the belly; pubes; whiskers on the chin, and so on. But not on Xin-Xin's body. As nearly as he could tell she had just two types: the straight, jet black hair on her head and the decorative little triangle of wispy ones, the final touches to an evolutionary masterpiece that had been a million years in the making.

Xin-Xin, Frank concluded, was a million years of evolution well spent.

He was pretty well spent too. They both were. Frank turned out the light and held her in the darkness.

'I love you, Frank,' she said.

'I love you too, Xin-Xin,' he heard himself say, and realised the voice was coming from a part of him that rarely spoke at all.

Frank's claim to being the happiest man in the world would have lasted until he'd fallen asleep, and probably remained intact after that, if only he hadn't thought of Lola and what had happened that night in his home. And in a fibro home in Mitchellton.

The wicks on the two bombs had been lit and Frank had no way of knowing how long they were. The only thing he did know was that, if he didn't defuse them, they were going to explode.

There was no way round it. He'd have to come clean. Be honest. Get it over with.

Tomorrow.

CHAPTER 30

The next day Frank was exhibiting signs of odd behaviour. Why had he been heard singing alone in his office all day, his colleagues wondered, and why had he left work early and not gone to the pub?

They were reasonable questions, but neither arose in Frank's mind as he drove home. Instead, he was asking himself: if we've done it after one day of eating lobster and drinking champagne, why do other people buggerise about for years before deciding to live together?

The answer came to him as he steered into the basement car park. It was like great art: we did it without thinking.

He was pleased with himself for having solved such a profound mystery without having to resort to phoning Roy. As he sauntered towards his apartment another question posed itself. If a man buys an enormous bunch of flowers to give to the woman who's just moved into his own home, shouldn't he have first bought a vase big enough to put them in? The answer was clearly yes, but there was nothing he could do about it now.

A few metres before reaching his front door, two more questions popped up: what the hell's that smell and is it coming from my place? As he opened the door he realised the answers, respectively, were 'food' and 'definitely'.

'Hmm, smells like feng shui,' he said. 'My favourite.'

Old habits die hard but new ones are born easy. Something funny happened on the way to the fridge. It happened on the dining-room table, took about twenty-five minutes, and resulted in the flowers getting crushed and falling to the floor. Twenty-five minutes wasn't enough. Back to the ankles I go, thought Frank, and he did.

'Now you can have a drink,' said Xin-Xin, who'd had enough, and showed it by refusing him access to the ankles.

'Oh, that's nice,' he said, opening the fridge and finding himself confronted with groceries, 'you've left a few in there. What's all this stuff?'

'It's called food, Frank.'

'The beer, where's the beer?'

'It's in the spare room. There's still a six-pack so don't panic. And a bottle of champagne.'

'Let's start with that then, shall we?'

Having transformed his home in advance of Xin-Xin's arrival, Frank soon noticed that changes were continuing now she was there. The meal he was eating, for example, had been prepared in a wok he'd never seen before and the chopsticks he was eating it with were also strangers in his home. There were vegetables in his bowl that he didn't know the names of and flavours had been used in their preparation that must have originated in one or more of the mysterious bottles that had appeared on his kitchen shelves.

An array of feminine potions on the vanity in the bathroom caught his eye when he went in for a pee. He sneaked a look into the right-hand side of the built-ins in the bedroom and saw that what had previously been a space to rent was now a fashion store. A quick peek at the bed indicated Xin-Xin must have had a poor regard for his taste in sheets because he was sure he'd never seen those ones before.

Frank felt like an immigrant who had just arrived in a foreign country and realised how much he preferred it to the one he'd left behind.

Returning from his round of sightseeing, the newcomer found the local custom was not to stop at one course, but to enjoy dessert as well. Baked cheesecake, ice-cream, whipped cream and two elegant glasses of dessert wine were arrayed on the table, just asking for trouble.

As Frank and Xin-Xin gave them what they were after, and then some, their conversation centred on comparative social history, with particular reference to individual experience in the periods of 1956–98 and 1969–98 in the disparate environments of the western and eastern suburbs of Sydney, culminating in lively discussion about the significance of a character known to them both as Lenny Matthews.

Books need to be researched, and Frank was quietly proud of having been appointed, on the basis of his superior knowledge and experience of the world of jazz, as 'research assistant' on Xin-Xin's novel about a saxophone player. But in *Gang-Gang*, Xin-Xin had written the story of a young man whose life had evolved out of the same primeval swamp as his own. Lenny was from his side of the socioeconomic divide, not hers, but she'd managed to write about it with the authority of one who'd lived there. Who, he wanted to know, had been her research assistant? Number one on his list of suspects was Puss.

'No one,' she said. 'I decided where I wanted the story to be set and I visited the place. The people I met made me feel like an intruder, a rich girl from the city coming to take something from them. I suppose they thought they'd had enough taken from them already. I got a bit of a feel for it, but that was all. When I got back home, I started writing and found I couldn't stop. Once I'd invented Lenny, he just told his story to me as I went along.'

Frank was still plagued by the increasingly paranoid-seeming notion that the book had been written about him.

'Puss told me a couple of times that he recognised himself in Lenny,' he ventured.

'I can understand that.'

'Well, I can't. Puss's family were pretty well-off. What would he know about —'

'Estrangement? Probably quite a lot if you think about it. And I know what you're getting at: you think the book's based on you. Poor little boy from the wrong side of the tracks. Poor little misunderstood Frank.'

'No need to be sarcastic. Surely you can understand why I felt a certain empathy with Lenny's character.'

'Of course. But you think that having people make the wrong assumptions about you based on where you come from is part and parcel of being "underprivileged". You think it's the exclusive domain of poor little urchins like you and Lenny Matthews.'

Christ, thought Frank, she makes a better bad cop than Arthur. If I'm under interrogation, I have the right to remain silent.

'Am I right, Frank?' she asked.

He was relieved by the gentle tone. And accompanying the question by reaching across the table to stroke his hands helped enormously.

'There were quite a few things in your book I thought went a bit beyond coincidence. That story about Rose, for example.'

'You had a girlfriend called Monique who killed herself.'

'How did you know that?'

'Neil told me about her — after he'd read the book. But it didn't go beyond coincidence. I went to a posh private school and I had a friend there who did the same thing. Rich girls commit suicide too. You see?'

Frank was beginning to. But even immigrants were allowed to bring their most cherished possessions to their new land and he wasn't about to leave his victimhood behind that easily.

'I know what you're thinking, Frank. Your circumstances might have been a bit like Lenny's and mine weren't. But you're not black, and you're certainly not Chinese. Look at me.'

Frank did as he was told.

'I hope we have misunderstood each other now, Mr Thornton.'

'We've misunderstood each other perfectly, Ms Leroq.'

CHAPTER 31

As an ad man, Frank was paid a lot of money by various people to come up with ideas for them. His best ideas were the ones he came up with for himself — and they were also the most expensive. He had one a week later.

Driving home, he hoped Xin-Xin's passport was up to date because the tickets for this idea were not refundable and he'd had to pull a few strings to organise visas.

He found her selecting ingredients and planning dinner. Frank had other plans, the first of which involved champagne and an hour or so in the bedroom. The second included dinner in a restaurant at Bondi overlooking the sea. The third was presented, over dessert, in the form of a printed itinerary.

'But we can't just up and leave on Saturday!'

'Yes, we can,' said Frank. 'It gives us a whole day to pack.'

Xin-Xin knew Frank was impulsive, but it wasn't a word she'd ever used to describe herself. She would have to, from now on, if she agreed to this.

'Why Madrid? No, don't tell me — the Goyas.'

'Amongst other things,' he said, trying to give the impression he had another ace up his sleeve.

'Bullfights, perhaps?'

'Lots of other things,' he insisted. 'El Greco, Picasso, Velásquez. *Las Meninas* is there!'

'All your favourites, Frank,' she laughed.

It was starting to feel as if he'd picked the wrong present again. As if he'd chosen a book for her that only he wanted to read.

'My favourite is the one of the little dog,' she said. 'I've always wanted to see that painting.'

It wasn't his favourite but it showed she knew her Goyas all right. He wanted to reach over the table and kiss her on the spot.

'So you're happy to go there?'

'Happy? I'm ecstatic.'

'Me too,' he said. 'Two more sleeps!'

'God, we're impulsive, aren't we?' she said, reaching for his hands and drawing him close for an across-the-table kiss, revelling in her new description of herself.

Frank travelled light. He always spent more time packing pharmaceuticals than clothes, and even the toiletries bag took less than five minutes to prepare: toothbrush, toothpaste, shaving gear, paracetamol, Valium for emergencies and sleeping pills for the plane. The process might have taken a moment longer, but, for reasons he'd never been able to understand, cocaine was considered a dangerous substance and had to be left at home.

Xin-Xin, who knew nothing about drugs, considered it a dangerous substance too. While preparing her own toiletries she discovered a sachet in the drawer of Frank's bedside table.

'What's this?' she demanded, tossing it onto the bed.

Frank, who had such little treats hidden away like Easter eggs in every nook and cranny, had forgotten about the existence of this one.

'Looks like a little bit of cocaine.'

'I didn't know you used cocaine.'

'I don't,' he lied. 'Used to now and again but haven't touched it for years.'

'In that case it's probably passed its use-by date,' she said sternly, while heading towards the bathroom where she flushed it down the toilet.

At best it was a flagrant waste of a precious resource. Frank considered mounting a protest along the lines of, 'There are starving children in poor countries like America who'd kill for that cocaine.' He realised there were bullet holes in his argument, however, so decided not to put it, thereby preventing it from becoming their first.

They didn't manage to avoid opportunity number two. It erupted somewhere between Sydney and Singapore and took Frank by surprise.

'We're travelling first-class so we can order whatever we like,' he said.

'But you've had so much to drink already,' she complained. 'If you want another glass of wine, fine — you didn't have to order a whole bottle.'

'It'll help us get to sleep.'

'If I'd had as much to drink as you have, I'd have been asleep hours ago.'

'But it's French,' he tried, 'and it's free!'

'Well, I won't be having any more. You can do what you like.'

Frank thanked the steward for the fresh bottle of wine and felt resentment at having to celebrate alone. It was intended to be a party for two.

He decided against telling her about the Mogadons he'd taken in the bathroom and offering a couple to her. He drifted off to sleep after the third glass, thinking, bugger it, I'm on holidays and, yes, I can do what I like.

Xin-Xin and Frank never had their third argument. They might have, if Xin-Xin didn't enjoy shopping and an agreement hadn't been struck in the airport in Singapore that saw her punishing her credit card while Frank sat in a bar doing the cryptic crossword in the *Guardian*.

Towards the end of the flight between Frankfurt and Madrid, champagne caused Frank to burp.

'Honestly,' Xin-Xin said, 'you're turning from a handsome prince into a frog and I've hardly kissed you.'

They both laughed as he poured himself another glass and offered to refill hers.

'No more for me, thanks,' she said, clinking her near-empty glass against his full. 'We're almost there.'

She gazed out the window and watched the sun setting over Madrid as the plane approached. She was glad the trip was over, and glad she'd resisted the temptation to make a remark that would have resulted in argument number four.

Frank had booked into the Hotel Suecia on the advice of Sandra, the creative department's secretary, who had found it for him on the internet, assured him it had a reputation as one of Madrid's best and was within easy walking distance of the Prado, the Museo de Arte Thyssen-Bornemisza and the Museo Nacional Centro de Arte Reina Sofia.

'She didn't tell me that "Suecia" meant "Swedish",' Frank lamented as he perused the menu. They decided to go for a walk before, rather than after, dinner.

Their stroll took them, arm in arm, to Puerto del Sol, where they stopped chattering like excited children, stopped walking, and stood for a while kissing each other instead.

'You know what we're doing?' Frank asked.

'Kissing, I would have thought.'

'Yes — but where?'

'On the lips?'

'Right in the middle of Goya's *The Second of May*. That's where we're kissing.'

The next time they stopped to kiss was in the middle of Plaza Mayor, and the time after that in a restaurant they found nearby called Las Cuevas de Luis Candelas. It was one of those long, lingering kisses, which might have gone on forever if the waiter hadn't curtailed it by arriving with servings of the house specialty: suckling pig.

Frank recalled the night they'd met, how they'd eaten a similar meal, been served a bottle of Spanish red wine in a similar bottle, and what its unusual packaging had reminded him of. He'd thought better of commenting on it then, for fear of offending Xin-Xin, but felt free to remark on it now. So did she, and she got in first.

'This wine is delicious,' she said, inspecting the bottle, 'and I like the way they wrap it up like a leg in a gold-mesh stocking. Very sexy. Let's have another one.'

'I like the way you're thinking,' said Frank, waving to attract the waiter's attention.

CHAPTER 32

In Frank's view, the walk to the Prado was disappointingly short. For such a majestic opera, he would have preferred a longer overture. Xin-Xin was more pragmatic.

'Thank God we're here,' she said, 'and out of that heat.'

On the way, they'd passed an enormous digital clock that gave equal importance to the time and the temperature, informing them that it was 11:09 am and thirty-nine degrees. By the time Xin-Xin had pointed it out to Frank, the time had moved on to 11:10 and the temperature to forty.

'At this rate it will be fifty degrees by the time we get there,' she'd moaned.

Many visitors to the Prado Museum turn up intending to spend most of their time concentrating on the work of one painter, only to find themselves seduced by other offerings. They lose all sense of time and purpose as they dawdle from one masterpiece to another. Often their legs give out before carrying them to the work of the artist they've come to see, or they happen upon it just as they place is closing.

Frank and Xin-Xin weren't about to let that happen to them and studied the floor plan as they waited in the queue. El Greco, Velasquez, everyone else would have to wait till tomorrow at least. Once through the starting gates, they hurried towards the Goya rooms like blinkered racehorses, each as determined as the other to be first past the post.

It was a dead heat. The winners celebrated by pausing for a moment to embrace and kiss. Then, in another dead heat, they said 'I love you' and started their tour in front of an unremarkable picture called *The Quail Shoot*, painted in 1775.

'He must have been twenty-nine,' said Xin-Xin, before Frank, who knew Goya was born in 1746, had had time to work it out.

'It's so much smaller than I expected,' he said, in front of the idyllic *Meadow of San Isidro*. This time his maths was up to speed. 'He was thirty-two when he painted this,' he added.

Assuming the roles of guide and authority, he was about to provide the novice with some information to prepare her for *The Pilgrimage of San Isidro* — a variation on the same subject painted after another thirty-two years had transformed the artist's vision into something less forgettable — when Xin-Xin said, 'It doesn't look like a nightmare to me.'

'Should it?'

'I thought it was one of the Black Paintings. From the description I read, I was expecting it to look like a scene from a horror film.'

'You're thinking of *The Pilgrimage of San Isidro*. Bear this one in mind when we're looking at that later.'

The self-appointed professor had hit the front. He was surprised his student had done so much homework, but relieved she hadn't learned everything.

Pausing in front of *Blind Man's Buff*, painted in 1788, she said, 'This one's interesting' and Frank agreed. He was about to say it had been painted five years before Goya succumbed to an illness that left him stone deaf, when she said, 'It was painted four years before he went deaf in 1792.' Frank was sure it had happened in 1793, but said nothing, thus averting what could have been argument number five.

'And look, Frank,' she added, 'what does it remind you of?'

If this was an exam, the professor feared he might fail. It didn't remind him of anything.

'Matisse's *The Dance*. That figure down on his knee on the right — I'm sure the figure in the same position in Matisse's painting is crouching down too.'

Frank struggled to conjure an image of *The Dance*. It was a painting he knew well, but trying to recall it now was like trying to remember the tune of 'Take the A Train' while listening to Beethoven's Fifth.

'I think you're right,' he said, and moved on.

'Puss!' he exclaimed in front of a portrait of Ferdinand VII. It had been painted when Ferdinand was made King of Spain in 1814, but the effeminate pose, extravagant costume and his tight grip on a phallic object suggested he might just as easily have been crowned Queen of the Sydney Mardi Gras.

'Doesn't look a thing like Neil. And Neil doesn't advertise his homosexuality by dressing up in outfits like that.'

'That's not what I meant.'

Xin-Xin laughed loudly and covered her mouth, aware she'd attracted the attention of other onlookers. 'No more than a caricature,' she said.

'Vulgar enough to have taken out the Packers' Award if he'd put it into the Archibald Prize,' said Frank, who couldn't care less if people felt compelled to stare at two lovers enjoying themselves in front of the Goyas. He was going to remember this as the happiest day of his life, whether they liked it or not.

'I've always wanted to see this room,' he said, as they stood at the door of the small salon where two paintings, *The Second of May* and *The Executions of the Third of May*, hung on opposite walls.

Frank's well-rehearsed dissertation on the significance of being in that unique space, the defining moment between 'old' and 'new' art, seemed superfluous now. Xin-Xin was no student in need of instruction. He knew when she gestured towards the blood seeping into the canvas under the bodies on the ground in *The Third of May* that this was not a time for words. It was a time for recognising something deep inside that they both shared; a time for comforting each other against the troubles of the past and the uncertainties of the future. And a time for lunch — their rumbling tummies told them that. But he wasn't expecting it to be a time for tears.

Where did they come from, he asked himself, these tears born of happiness?

The answer was obvious: from the same place all this beauty came when it was born of sadness.

Both Frank and Xin-Xin had a sceptical view of marriage. Frank's family paradigm could hardly be expected to engender faith in the concept. Xin-Xin's believed her parents' blissful union represented an aberration, a daunting example for anyone else to try and emulate. She was too wilful, too restless, to aspire to a marriage like theirs.

But although neither of them said it, each suspected they'd been married by accident when they shared that moment between Goya's Second and Third of May, in June. If marriage was about uniting two people to form one, it must have happened to them, because, emerging from the restaurant after lunch, they'd forgotten what it felt like to be alone.

And if the wedding had taken place in the Room of Life and Death, the reception was about to follow, downstairs in the Hall of Horrors.

Just as Frank was a bloke who'd had sex a lot but was only now learning what it meant to be intimate, he was also a man who'd laughed a lot and was now learning how to be happy. He'd mastered the art of dismissing his disasters as jokes and making anecdotes out of his tragedies, but he felt he'd survived enough of both over the years to be able to relate to Goya's Black Paintings on something of an equal footing. As for Xin-Xin? Well, he still had his doubts. Her twenty-nine years had been sheltered ones. As they stepped onto the roller-coaster, he felt ready for the thrill but expected her to scream and close her eyes.

The first painting they confronted was *The Pilgrimage*, all four and a half metres of it: a nightmare vision showing an endless procession of haunted figures lost in a void that spoke only of despair.

This'll test her, thought Frank. 'What's it saying to you?' he whispered.

'Hello from Hell,' she replied, 'because in Hell, you're always alone. No matter how many others are gathered around you.'

Nothing more to add, he thought.

'You were right about this place. The whole world's here and we haven't seen it all yet.' Glancing around, Xin-Xin's gaze lighted on something familiar, and she added, 'Let's go over there and have a look at that painting of the dog.'

It was a good idea: it took them straight past *Duel With Cudgels*, any discussion of which Frank wanted to limit to man's inhumanity to man, avoiding any mention of a more personal interpretation involving his drunken father. And him.

Besides, he'd never understood what all the fuss was about when it came to Goya's painting of that dog. From reproductions, it had always struck him as looking like a Turner: all sky and space and bugger-all else. The only difference as far as he could see was that where Turner would have lobbed a marker buoy, Goya had chosen to stick in a dog.

But the dog was saying something to Xin-Xin that he couldn't hear. She said nothing, but drew Frank closer. When he glanced at her face, he noticed the tears were starting again.

'Now that's loneliness,' she said. 'That's despair.'

Frank looked back at *The Pilgrimage*, dumbfounded that she'd survived it tearless but was weeping over this. He showed his confusion with a shake of his head.

'He's in quicksand,' she explained. 'He's lost his friend, his home and all hope.'

Frank felt tears of happiness coming on again but didn't need to ask himself what was causing them this time. He had found all three.

CHAPTER 33

That night they sat sipping red wine on their balcony in the hot night air. From an adjoining apartment, they heard the sounds of two people fucking noisily on a squeaky bed.

Xin-Xin feigned disgust. 'These Spaniards,' she whispered, 'they don't even have the courtesy to close the door.'

'They might know their art but they know no shame,' Frank added, with a stern look of disapproval.

'Nor guilt, I'm told.'

'And who told you that?' he murmured.

'A Spanish girlfriend of mine in Sydney. She says that when she's having sex, she couldn't care less who hears it. Some people would pay good money to hear that sort of thing, so others shouldn't complain if they get it for free.'

'Healthy attitude.'

'Healthy girl.'

Spanish, eh? And I thought South American.

Frank knew this was his chance. He could tell Xin-Xin now about what had happened on the night he'd met Lola. He could confide, rather than confess; he knew she'd understand. But could he go on to tell her what had happened in Mitchellton on the same night, and why he felt responsible? Was there any way she could understand that? Blood on his head was one thing, but blood on his hands was another. He could tell her another time. Madrid was half the world away from his home in Surry Hills, and his home was another world away from Mitchellton. No, no more shirking, he thought. This is the right time and I'll do it now.

He reached to pour Xin-Xin another glass of wine but his hand was trembling and, in the process, he knocked her glass onto the tiled floor. It smashed and the wine spilled, spattering Xin-Xin's bare feet, ankles and shins with red.

Frank grabbed a serviette and somehow managed to stop himself from adding vomit to the mix as he wiped away the blood of his sister and his niece from her skin. His hands were shaking, Christ, it was hot.

'Don't move, you might cut your feet. I'll clean this up.'

She was standing over him now.

'Don't worry about it, we can clean it up in the morning. Besides, I'm sure the hotel's prepared for emergencies such as this.'

Frank rubbing his hands through his hair, Xin-Xin noticing how he was sweating and trembling.

'So where will we go tomorrow?' she asked. 'Back to the Prado?'

'We might be in need of some light relief,' Frank suggested. 'Why don't we go to the Reina Sofia and see Picasso's *Guernica*?'

They laughed and laughed, went to bed, and loved and loved each other.

On their last day in Madrid, Frank ordered champagne for breakfast. Xin-Xin took her glass reluctantly and topped it up with orange juice.

'Are you trying to turn me into an alcoholic?' she said. 'I worry that you drink so much.'

I've been happily married up until this point, Frank thought. Don't tell me the nagging's about to start.

'Don't be silly,' he said. 'We're on holiday.'

Xin-Xin thought it was hard to tell the difference between how much Frank drank on holiday and the amount he put away daily when he was at work. But she said nothing, thereby avoiding argument number six.

When their plane touched down in Sydney, the process of bringing Frank back to earth began. At home, he cleared out his mailbox and found a letter from Nina amongst the bills. Under the pretext of making coffee while Xin-Xin picked necessities from her suitcase in the bedroom, he read it in the kitchen. After that, the process was complete.

Frank,

It causes me a lot of pain to write this message to you. You probably think I mean emotional pain but I don't. I'm just talking about pain — pure and simple. Everything I do seems to hurt me now.

You might also think that I set out to cause you pain when I refused to see or talk to you after I was brought into the hospital but that's not all I was trying to do. I was trying very hard to find ways of relieving my own as well.

The only good thing to have come out of what has happened to me is that here in the hospital I've had a lot of time to think about things I've never thought about before and to see things in a new light.

I always thought that when you found your career and left the rest of us behind that you had somehow risen above us all. I thought you had managed to get away from all the problems that Dad and Red have and that my boy Matthew had but now I realise I was wrong. You like to THINK you're a cut above them but you're not.

For you life is just one long party. You've never been able to see that you're the only one you've invited along. No one else is at the party with you, Frank, and from the outside I can tell you that blokes look pretty silly when they're drinking and dancing alone. If you want to see what it looks like, have a look at Dad. If you want to see what happens when it takes the coppers to break the party up, go out to Long Bay and have a look at Red. And if you want to see what happens to the people you don't make welcome, have a bloody good look at me and Mandy.

You're a bastard, Frank. You and Dad have kicked me in the teeth just as hard as Red did. If you ever decide the party's over for you because the damage bill is getting too high, then give me a call. We'll be able to speak then but I can't talk to you now because I've finally realised I'm better off without Red and I'm better off without Dad and I'm better off without you.

Nene.

Frank folded the letter and put it into the breast pocket of his shirt. It wasn't a good place for it. As Xin-Xin came into the kitchen asking how long it could possibly take him to make a cup of coffee, he realised it could stab him in the heart from there.

He didn't want to read it again, but he couldn't let it go. It moved a lot over the succeeding days, from one pocket to another, but no matter where he put it he could feel it burning into his skin. It reminded him of getting his tattoo in Darwin, realising it was there for life. Even though it didn't hurt, he could feel it on his arm when he lay down every night, thinking: what have I done? what have I done?

CHAPTER 34

A week after arriving home, Frank resumed work and two regulars turned up for lunch at Benoit's.

'Come on, Frank, lighten up,' said Eddie. 'Here comes Rani with the beers.'

Rani with the beers, the harbour with the sunshine, Benoit's with the award-winning menu, Eddie with the wine list and Frank with the shits.

'Don't know when I'm going to tell her. Have to do it soon.'

'Frank, you just have to get it over with. Do it and be done with it.'

'It's not just about Lola. As if that isn't bad enough, I have to tell her what happened to Nina and Mandy.'

'You've got to stop blaming yourself. You're driving yourself mad. And me.'

Eddie's right, Frank thought, it wasn't my fault. Then again, Eddie didn't have Nina's letter sitting in his back pocket, burning a cheek of his arse.

'Let's have another bottle,' he proposed by way of resolving the problem.

Frank was doing his best but he wasn't good company. Eddie would have had more fun if he'd gone to lunch with Harry Parkinson. He ordered cognac and another couple of beers and decided to try it one more time.

'You've got to stop beating yourself up over what happened to your sister. If you're so worried about Xin-Xin's reaction, don't tell her. Not yet anyway.'

'I still have to tell her about Lola.'

'Wait till the honeymoon's over and tell her then.'

'I don't want the honeymoon to be over. That's the whole fucking point. It will be when I tell her.'

'Stop worrying. She'll see the funny side.'

That was the trouble with Eddie. He saw the funny side of everything.

Another week later, Frank bought a copy of Miles Davis's autobiography at Grosvenor's Bookstore and climbed the stairs for a chat with the owner.

Frank had news he was bursting to pass on to Henry, but their conversations always started with banter. Besides, a casual mention that he was living with Xin-Xin Leroq would be a far more impressive way of imparting the good tidings than setting them off like fireworks on his arrival.

'I've got a bit of bad news, I'm afraid,' said Henry, choosing to skip the banter with an important announcement of his own. 'The shit's hit the fan with Number Four.'

Frank managed a look of concern and waited for Henry to elaborate.

'You wouldn't believe what the bitch did.'

Oh yes he would, and he was dying to hear.

'I thought she was playing up so I put a detective onto her.'

'Did he get anything on her?'

'Never mind what he got on her; it's what he got up her that concerns me!'

Henry was at his funniest when not trying to be. The effort involved in not laughing was becoming painful.

'So what are you going to do?'

'Divorce the bitch, of course. And she won't get a cent out of me. Not this one.'

Frank made commiserative noises and considered withholding his own information for a more appropriate occasion. Henry probably wanted to hear another black-eye story from him. Bad news of one's own becomes more bearable when a friend's news is worse. And it wasn't as if he didn't have something worse in reserve. His jacket was draped over a chair on the other side of the room with Nina's letter in its inside pocket. Regardless of how he turned his head he could see it out of the corner of his eye. But he didn't intend to mention it — Henry didn't need cheering up that badly.

'Anyway,' said Henry, 'how are things with you?'

Frank couldn't resist. He had to tell him.

'Things are quite the opposite for me, to tell you the truth.'

'We're not in love, are we?'

'Afraid so.'

'Anyone I know?'

'I don't think so. Remember that copy of the *Guardian* you gave me?'

'Not Xin-Xin Leroq!'

'We met, fell in love, and we're living together. End of story.'

Oh no, it's not, thought Henry. Frank's responsibility was to make him feel better with talk of failure and he'd let him down badly. He'd fix him.

'I do know her, as a matter of fact. Hasn't she told you about the night we went to the Fleetwood Award presentation together?'

'No.'

'I shouldn't have said anything. If she hasn't told you, perhaps it's because she doesn't want you to know what happened.'

'What did happen?'

'Nothing.'

'Henry, you just said that you went with her to the Fleetwood Award night and something happened. What was it?'

'No, I only said we went there together. I didn't say that anything happened. You'll just have to trust me.'

That was the trouble with Henry, thought Frank. You couldn't trust him. He wouldn't have to tell you to if you could.

Later that afternoon, two women met for coffee in Elizabeth Bay.

'I can't believe you moved in together so quickly. That's not like you, Xin-Xin,' said Lola.

'I can't believe it either.'

'Has he cleaned up his act?'

'He's cleaned up his apartment. I'm working on his act. I've made him my new research assistant. Frank's been writing a biography of a saxophone player. Someone called Mark Simmonds.'

'Great player. He had a band called the Freeboppers. One of the best bands ever. They put out a CD called *Fire* with this piece on it called "The Spotted Dog"—'

'That's the name of Frank's so-called biography, *Spotted Dog*. As a book it's all over the shop. But there are some great stories in amongst it all.'

'I'm jealous. I thought you were getting your inside information exclusively from me.'

'The more info the better.'

'Only kidding. It's wonderful — and it's also very funny. Has he told you about that night when we met?'

'Not yet.'

'I knew it.'

'He will, though. I've sensed he almost has a couple of times. Almost felt sorry for him and wanted to say something myself. But I want it to come from him. There's more to him than you'd probably think. He's basically a decent, very honest bloke, but terribly insecure. Must be agonising over it. Waiting for an appropriate moment. I'm sure he's working up the courage to tell me about it right now.'

'You might have to drop a hint.'

'I'll tell him tonight that we met up today. That might do the trick.'

'Whatever. Let's go up to the Brasserie and have a drink to celebrate.'

Lola liked a drink, especially on happy occasions like this one, and was disappointed when Xin-Xin said she'd had enough. Any more and she wouldn't be able to drive. Besides, it was getting late. Frank would be home soon. She loved to cook dinner and wanted it ready before he arrived.

It would have been too, if she hadn't ploughed her car into another one that was waiting for the lights to change at Taylor Square. She wasn't hurt, but she was breathalysed. Given the result — and the amount of the damage — it wasn't surprising the constable insisted she accompany him to the station.

Frank had made up his mind. He'd tell Xin-Xin about Lola the moment he arrived home. Get it over with. His best hope lay in stressing it was in the past and using it as a point of comparison when trying to persuade her how much he'd cleaned up his act.

As for the story about Nina and Mandy, Eddie was right — that would just have to wait. Frank had made the mistake of reading

Nina's letter again. Where had he put it? Ah yes, there it was in the left-hand pocket of his jeans. He didn't need to touch it to confirm its location. It was getting crumpled, but the ink hadn't faded and would never disappear.

He pressed the button to open the doors of the security garage, wondering what Henry had been going on about earlier. Fuck Henry, he was all bullshit. Xin-Xin would tell him if anything had happened. If Henry had laid a finger on her, he'd kill him.

He needed a drink. The afternoon with Eddie at Benoit's wasn't enough to fortify him for this. He'd head for the fridge first and confess all while they shared some champagne.

There was no smell of feng shui on the landing and Xin-Xin wasn't in the flat. But there was a message on the notepad next to the phone that said she was going off to meet Lola at four.

Frank shuddered and groaned as his thoughts ran wild.

She hasn't come back because Lola's told her and now she's gone. You should have told her in Madrid. You should have told her last night. You could have told her any fucking time and now she's not answering her phone. Please answer your phone, Xin-Xin, why won't you answer your phone?

Because she doesn't want to talk to you, Frank. You've done it again, you stupid gutless piece of shit. She's gone and she won't be coming back.

PART IV

CHAPTER 35

'Is your name Frank, mate?' asked a young man Frank didn't know. He was holding a pen in one hand and a clipboard in the other. Nurse by the looks of him, Frank thought. Must be in hospital.

'Yeah.'

'Frank Thornton? Nine stroke thirty-nine Downey Street, Surry Hills?'

'How'd you know?'

'The ambos found it on a letter in your pocket.'

'Why didn't they look in my wallet?'

'You haven't got a wallet.'

Frank could move his head a bit to one side. One eye was open enough to make out people walking past, some being helped, the odd one on a trolley. He was on a trolley too, in a corridor. There was a lot going on. He could hear it now.

'Been here before?'

'Dunno. Where am I?'

'St Vincent's.'

'A bucket, quick a bucket —'

He was able to move his head far enough to aim most of it onto the floor. He tried to wipe his mouth but his arm hurt.

'Sorry, mate.'

Frank closed his eye again, tried to take stock. Something wrong with the right arm. Hell of a lot wrong with the ribs. Someone must have given him a fucking good kicking. Must have belted him over the head with something too, lot of pain up there somewhere, oh shit —

'That bloke down there is spewing again,' said one of the interns. 'When did he arrive?'

'About four this morning.'

'Was he conscious when he came in?'

'No. Ambos brought him in. Just a drunk. Found him in the Cross somewhere. Taken a hell of a beating by the looks of him. Right arm could be broken. Face is an awful mess.'

'Clean him up a bit, will you, Max?'

Max cleaned Frank up a bit by wiping his face with a sponge and told him the doctor would have a look at him within an hour or so.

'What's the time?' Frank asked.

'Nearly nine.'

'How long have I been here?'

'About five hours. Just lie still.'

Frank saw his right arm was in a sling and moved his head slowly into a position that didn't hurt much. He became aware of noises: someone screaming somewhere; a couple arguing about something. I'll be arguing with this bloke shortly if he doesn't leave me alone. What's he trying to do to my ear?

'That hurts.'

'Sorry. Taking you in to see the doctor now. Here we go.'

'Frank, is it? What happened to you, Frank?'

'Dunno.'

Woman doctor. Where the hell were his clothes? They'd wrapped him in one of those idiot aprons with strings down the back. What was she doing looking in his eyes with that torch?

'You're going to need a few stitches in this face of yours, Frank. Now, let's check your ribs. Does that hurt?'

'Yeah.'

'And that?'

'Yeah.'

'Now your arm. What about when we bend it this way, does that hurt, Frank?'

'That hurts too.'

'Hmm.'

Now what was she up to? Checking him over like a panelbeater.

'We'd better have a look at this ear of yours. Can you turn your head to the left for me? That looks nasty. Did someone attack you with a knife, Frank?'

'I dunno.'

'I'm just going to give you a little needle — there you go — just lie back now and we'll take you off to have some X-rays.'

234

'I'll need some details, Frank. You got a job?'

Who was this bloke? Didn't look like a nurse. Where was he now — back in the corridor?

'Yeah.'

'Where do you work?'

'Parkinson's Advertising Agency, Macquarie Street.'

'Do they know where you are?'

'I don't even know where I am.'

'We'll give them a ring then. Do you know someone we could call who might be able to pop in and bring you some clothes?'

'Yeah, call Xin-Xin.'

'How do you spell that?'

'No, don't call Xin-Xin, call Eddie.'

'Eddie?'

'Eddie Longman — his number's … wait on … it's 04 … Call the switch at Parkinson's, they'll put you through. Bring me a bucket.'

'There's one right here. I'll give Eddie a call.'

'Thanks. Oh shit —'

Spewing really hurt the ribs. He needed another shot of that stuff the doctor gave him …

'Frank. Frank. Can you hear me?'

Someone was shaking him.

'G'day, Eddie. Christ, good to see you.'

'What the fuck happened to you, mate?'

'Somebody must have rolled me.'

'Jesus, Frank, you've been gone for a fucking week!'

'You got some clothes?'

'Yeah.'

'Tell 'em I want my letter back.'

'What are you talking about?'

'They took a letter out of my pocket. Tell 'em I want it back.'

'Okay.'

'You got your car?'

'Yeah.'

'Mind giving me a lift home?'

'I'm not giving you a lift home, Frank. I had a chat to the doctor. She said you should stay here for a couple of days but they can't put you up right now. A social worker's coming to see you and she'll take you to Mission House.'

'Fuck that.'

'No, Frank. You're going to have to do as you're told.'

'I'm going home, Eddie. Just give us a fucking lift, will you?'

'Now you listen to me, Frank. You're all fucked up. These people want to help you and you need help. So I'm not going to drive you home. And that's that.'

'Mission fucking House! I'm not going there. It's full of fucking derros — metho-drinkers and junkies.'

'It's just for a couple of days. Oh Christ, mate ...'

Eddie didn't know Frank could cry. Didn't know where to look.

'Xin-Xin's been ringing me, Frank.'

'What did you tell her for, Christ's sake?'

'What could I tell her? I didn't have a clue what had happened to you. You want me to ring her now?'

'I couldn't talk to her now. Don't tell her they're putting me into Mission House.'

'Okay, I won't. Come on, sit up. I'll help you put on some clothes. Can you sit up?'

'Yeah. Thanks. Careful — ribs. Someone's kicked the shit out of me.'

'Jesus. What happened to your ear?'

'I dunno. Doctor said it looked like someone's tried to cut it off with a knife.'

'Shit, what a mess. Can't remember. Now, you wait for this social worker and do as she says. Okay?'

'Don't tell Xin-Xin they're putting me into Mission House ...'

'What do I tell her?'

'Tell her you don't know where I am, or tell her I'm sorry, but don't tell her they're putting me into Mission House.'

'I'll talk to her, okay? And I'll tell her you're sorry.'

Eddie hated leaving Frank there, battered, shattered and desolate. But he couldn't take him home. Not after what the doctor had said.

CHAPTER 36

Ron had worked at Mission House for years. He was used to obstreperous bastards like this Frank.

'Of course it bloody hurts. Just try and stand still and we'll get it over with.'

'Do you have to make that water so fucking hot?'

'Nearly finished. Don't move that cap, mate. Got to keep that ear dry.'

'Do you have to do that?'

'You've lost a lot of bark off these legs. Just trying to clean them up for you. Righto, you can step out of the shower now.'

Ron dried Frank and presented him with a pair of pyjamas. 'Put 'em on. You're going to bed.'

'Not in these I'm not. They stink. Where did you get 'em, Long Bay?'

'They're clean. Just put 'em on and shut up.'

Ron escorted Frank down a short hallway and opened a door. He directed the beam of his torch at the empty bed of four in the room.

'There you go,' he whispered.

'There I go what!'

'Keep your voice down. Get in there and go to sleep.'

'Fuck you. I'm going home. How do I get out of here?'

'Don't try and cut up rough with me.'

'Well, take me to the bloody Führer then.'

'Who?'

'The fucking Nazi running this place. Got my ear hanging by a thread, a sore arm, busted ribs and Christ knows what else and all she's given me is a lousy Valium.'

'You've had two. And she's Polish.'

'I'm shaking like a bloody leaf. Can't she give a man a Mogadon or something?'

'You're not here to take drugs, you're here to give them away. Now get in there and shut the fuck up.'

'Jesus Christ,' hissed Frank, as he went in there and shut the fuck up.

Frank writhed about on the little bed, unsure if it was a hot night or a cold one. Every time he pulled the blanket up to stop the shivering, he'd be throwing it off again within minutes, unable to bear the heat. Spasms, starting in the cheeks of his arse, raced up his back, climbed over his head and ended by rattling his teeth; or downwards to his icy feet, making his legs vibrate as they coursed through his veins like slow electricity. One of his room-mates was a virtuoso snorer, another a frequent farter and a few of the loonies were screaming and ranting in rooms not far enough away. And to think — there was a pub just around the corner! All he needed was a drink and this would all be over. It was only the pain that stopped him. That and knowing he had no money. Everything hurt. If a man had to stop drinking and suffer withdrawal, at least he should be in a fit state to endure it, not fresh from a good beating with stitches and lumps on all his moving parts.

He eventually fell asleep, and woke soon after when someone tapped him on the shoulder. Everything hurt worse as he rose from his bed. A severe-looking woman with her hair pulled back in a bun handed him two Valium and a plastic cup of water.

'What's this? Breakfast?'

Nurse Mayhew had been at Mission House for years too, and had struck far bigger clowns in her time.

'Come on,' she said and led him down the hallway to a door, which she opened and closed behind him without saying another word.

The room looked like it had been painted and furnished in the thirties when paint jobs and furniture were meant to last, and was proof they did. A doctor sat at the desk: a raw-boned, hard-looking bloke with black-framed glasses and closely shaved hair around the sides of his otherwise bald head. He was reading something and hadn't looked at Frank yet.

'Sit down,' he said and gestured towards the chair.

Frank did. Slowly, and painfully. After taking Frank's blood pressure and making a note of the result, the doctor picked up a sheet of paper. Frank caught a glimpse: lines of type on the left, little empty squares on the right. Here we go, he thought, time for the questionnaire. The doctor turned towards him.

'I'm Jack Hayes,' he said. 'Dr Jack Hayes, but you can call me Jack.'

'Righto.'

'Do you know where you are?'

'Yeah. The Hilton in St Tropez.'

'Did you see any little green creatures running around the walls during the night?'

'Must have missed 'em. Lights were off. How am I going so far?'

Jack Hayes placed the piece of paper face down on his desk and peered over his glasses straight into Frank's eye.

'You're a real chip off the old block, aren't you, Frank?'

'Meaning what?'

'You know what I mean. You're just like your father.'

'How do you know my father?'

'I work at Selwyn Lodge, where he lives. I'm one of the people whose job it is to keep metho-drinkers like old Mick alive.'

'Well, I don't live at Selwyn Lodge and I don't drink fucking metho.'

'We all live within our means, Frank.'

Jack Hayes waited for a response. When he didn't get one, he continued.

'So what do you drink, Frank?'

'Depends what time of day it is.'

'Righto. Let's start in the mornings, shall we? Do you start in the mornings?'

'Only on days that have a "y" in them.'

'You have a lot of blackouts?'

'About average.'

'What's the longest you've gone without a drink?'

'Six weeks.'

'How long ago was that?'

'About twenty years. Bloke put me in hospital.'

'So why are you here?'

'Some other bastard put me in hospital a couple of nights ago. They didn't have room for me so they sent me here. And I'm fucked if I'll be staying another night.'

'You'll be fucked if you don't. Now you listen to me. You're here because you're an alcoholic. You might as well get that into your head for a start.'

'Oh, for Christ's sake — I went out on a bender and got pissed. That doesn't make me an alcoholic.'

'All right. Let me put it this way: if you're not an alcoholic, who is?'

It was a tricky one. All of Frank's mates were heavy drinkers. He tried to decide who was the heaviest drinker out of all of them. It was him.

'How about Mick, your father? Would you rate him as an alcoholic?'

'How would I know? Don't see much of the old man these days.'

'Well, I do. I see him a few times every week and you can take it from me.'

Frank said nothing. But he didn't move. Jack made himself look busy, shuffling through some notes while he waited. He glanced at Frank who was biting his lip, jaws clenched, and glaring out the window. Tough bastard, Jack thought, but he's starting to crack.

'You've got a choice, Frank. You can stay here until I tell you you can leave or you can piss off now. If you piss off, I can guarantee I'll see you again in about a year or so, and then, if you like, you can move back in with your dad. Might even be able to take his bed by then, the way he's going. Call it a family tradition.'

Jack Hayes turned back to his desk and started writing something on a small sheet of paper. Frank could hear his biro scratching. Then he put the paper into a folder and turned again to look at Frank.

'Right. Go out and see Nurse Pawlowska and tell her to call me. I'll see you again tomorrow morning.'

Class systems evolve in all societies and that of drunks and junkies is no exception.

Frank spent the morning listening to the alcos slagging off the junkies in the adjacent building, and his afternoon in the adjacent building listening to the junkies banging on about what lowlifes the piss-heads were. He couldn't decide whose side he was on. Boozers or users — who gave a fuck? They all seemed like losers to him.

The only inmates of Mission House who seemed to be having a good time were the madmen. Some had idiot grins on their faces and one, who was walking around talking to himself, must have had at least a few jokes up his sleeve because every now and again he'd burst into hysterical laughter.

Frank considered asking one of the nurses if he could be upgraded from alcoholic to lunatic on the grounds it might make his stay more enjoyable.

His piddling allowance of five milligrams of Valium every four hours prevented him experiencing a full-blown fit but didn't do much to stop the muscular spasms in his back and limbs. Every time he felt one coming on he braced himself for the pain it caused in his ribs. Coming down from the grog was one thing, but doing it with a bagful of busted ribs was too much. His arguments, when he put them to all three nurses individually, fell on deaf ears. It was a conspiracy, that's what it was.

The hot and cold sweats weren't exactly pleasant either. You'd think they'd allow a man a couple of Panadol or something, but no, not this lot. Grin and bear it seemed to be the accepted practice around here.

The next morning started off in much the same way, the only difference being that the nurse who woke him up and escorted him to Dr Hayes' room wasn't one he'd seen before. She didn't bother to introduce herself.

Jack Hayes looked exactly the same as he had the day before. One of those blokes who had a wardrobe full of identical white shirts, identical grey suits and one daggy-looking tie.

'How are you feeling?' he asked.

Hmm, thought Frank, a bit friendlier today.

'Fucking crook.'

'Sweat much during the night?'

'Yeah — still am.'

'Getting many muscular spasms?'

'Yeah. They hurt like buggery too. I don't see why they can't take a few broken ribs into account when they're handing out the tablets.'

'Your ribs aren't broken. They're bruised.'

'Doesn't make any difference. They hurt just as much.'

'Well, that's stiff shit, isn't it?'

Jack Hayes took a small white card from a pile on a shelf and placed it on his desk.

'I'm going to ask you a few personal questions.'

'Like what?'

'Like are you married?'

'No.'

'Any kids?'

'No.'

'Do you have a girlfriend or a de facto?'

'No.'

Jack Hayes waited patiently. He knew Frank would say something more soon.

'I did have a girlfriend until recently.'

'How recently?'

'Until I went out and got on the piss.'

'Have you called her?'

'No.'

'Heard from her?'

'No.'

'You expecting to?'

'No.'

'Maybe you should give her a call. She might be wondering where you are. Might even be missing you. Did that thought occur to you?'

'That's not a thought, it's a hope. She won't be ... not by now.'

'You seem pretty sure of that.'

'I am.'

'Okay. In that case,' said Jack, leaning forward and resting his elbows on his knees, 'I want you to be very honest with me. I want you to tell me why you think she's not missing you.'

They were all the same, these deadshits. Jack knew what he was going to hear and was only surprised by Frank's way of putting it.

'You're the doctor so you tell me,' Frank began. 'If a cancer patient gets cured, does she lie awake at night missing the tumour?'

'No, I don't suppose she does.'

'Doesn't take her long to realise she's better off without it.'

'So, that's what you are in this woman's life, eh? A tumour. What if she loves you, Frank? That would mean she's developed a pretty serious condition because of you. Cancer. Cancer of the heart, perhaps.'

'Maybe.'

242

'Well, like you said, I'm the doctor. And I'm telling you: she's not the one who's sick, you are. You're the one with heart cancer — you and all these other drunks and junkies in this place. You and your old man and his mates at Selwyn Lodge. You're sick, all right, so you take a lot of medicine and you think it helps because it makes you feel better — makes you forget you're the worthless piece of shit you think you are.'

'I've just about had a gutful of you.'

'I'll bet you have,' said Jack, 'and I might have had a gutful of you too, but that wouldn't matter, would it, Frank? You're the only one that matters. Not your wife, not your kids — just you.'

'I already bloody told you, I've got no wife and no kids,' Frank snapped. 'And I don't have a girlfriend.'

'That's right. I forgot. She's the one who's better off without you. And maybe she is. But your father's got kids — one of them's you. And one of them's your sister. She's got a kid too, hasn't she? Your niece. How are they travelling, Frank?'

'You've done your fucking homework, haven't you?' Frank retorted. 'What happened to them had nothing to do with me.'

'Of course not.' Jack Hayes was up and pacing now. 'And it wouldn't have had anything to do with Mick either. He's like you. He knows they're better off without him. Poor old Mick. His heart cancer's been playing up a bit lately.'

'What do you mean by that?'

'He's upped his dosage since he heard what happened to them. Been taking an awful lot of medicine. He's very dark on the bloke responsible for what happened to your sister. Thinks he deserves a death sentence.'

'So do I.'

'Well, why don't you just go out and jump off the bridge?'

Questions like that didn't need to be answered, but they needed some time to sink in. Jack Hayes waited a moment, before sinking the boot in and getting the job over and done.

'I'll tell you why. Because you think that would be letting yourself off lightly. And that would be too good for you, wouldn't it? Too good for *this* bastard,' he said, pointing at Frank. 'You want him to get what he deserves.'

Jack, who'd done it a thousand times, hated this part of the job. He didn't enjoy breaking men and he didn't like to see them cry. It was dirty work, the demolition. But if you wanted to build a new house, you had to knock down the old one, so you might as well start with the bulldozer. Laying foundations required heavy equipment too. The building itself was a complex structure; it couldn't be thrown up overnight. It took a long time to get to the stage where you'd be shopping around for interior decorators, asking for advice on furnishings and feng shui.

'Now you listen to me, son,' he said. 'I'm going to go very easy on you. I've spoken to your girlfriend quite a lot over the past twenty-four hours and she doesn't think she's better off without you at all. She'll be here at nine o'clock and I'm going to let you go home with her. I've written out a couple of prescriptions and told her exactly what you're allowed to take. I want to see you three times a week from now on. Talk to Nurse Pawlowska and make the appointments. And don't fuck up, Frank. Your girlfriend will tell me if you do, and I won't be happy, because I don't want to finish up with another Mick Thornton on my hands.'

What a job, thought Jack, as he helped Frank to his feet, put an arm around his shoulders and guided him to the door. What a bastard of a job.

CHAPTER 37

'I'm sorry,' said Frank, as Xin-Xin drove them away from Mission House.

'No, I'm sorry,' said Xin-Xin.

'What have you got to be sorry about?' said Frank, who might have been stripped of everything else but still had his culpability.

'It was all my fault. That's why I'm sorry.'

'Everything is my fucking fault, okay?' Frank shouted. 'I was the bloke who took your friend Lola out that night and tried to fuck her and it was my girlfriend we landed on in my bed. And I never had the guts to tell you about it.'

'I knew what had happened between you and Lola before we went out together and I never told you. I was waiting for you to tell me. That's why it's my fault.'

That shut Frank up for a bit, but not for long. 'Okay, but what you don't know is that on the same night, my sister and my niece nearly got bashed to death and it was my fault because they were depending on me for help and I was too busy trying to fuck your friend to bother to answer my own fucking phone. I suppose now you're going to tell me that was your fault too?'

'I didn't know anything about that.'

'Well, you do now.'

'I'm here, Frank, and I'm driving you home. That's my fault, my decision, and I take full responsibility.'

Frank squirmed around in his seat, trying to adopt a position less painful for his ribs. 'By the way, how come you're driving my car?' he asked.

'Because I had too much to drink that afternoon when I met up with Lola and pranged mine on the way home. That's why I wasn't there when you came back to the flat. My fault, Frank.'

They stopped at a light. One more block to go. Frank couldn't wait to get home. Home! His new place with all the space and Arthur's new painting and the new furniture and bookshelves and a new sound system and shutters on the windows and polished floorboards and dimmer switches on the lights and the feng shui and Xin-Xin and Xin-Xin and Xin-Xin …

… and sobriety.

Considering his fondness for cocaine, Frank had responded with admirable equanimity when Xin-Xin had flushed a gram of it down the toilet. But the shock on that occasion was as nothing to the one in store as he headed, robotically, for the fridge when the two of them arrived home. Where handsome rows of wine and champagne had formed a colourful display alongside six-packs of beer in the past, fruit juices, soft drinks and bottles of mineral water had become the order of the day.

'What have you done?' he whimpered.

'Dr Hayes said you'd have to give it away so I did it for you.'

'He's a hard man, that Jack Hayes. Bloody hard.'

'He's trying to help you, Frank. So am I.'

'Still think it's a bit brutal, doing it like that. If a man's best friend dies he should at least be allowed to go to the funeral.'

He stared at the plastic bottles and cardboard containers and cried, 'I mean, what the fuck am I going to drink?'

'I'll make you a cup of tea.'

Frank sighed, reached into his pocket for a packet of pills and said, 'I'll have one of these with that. Even Jack Hayes wouldn't begrudge a man a Valium under these circumstances.'

'It depends on how many you've already had today.'

Frank looked into her eyes and pulled his most pathetic face, the black eyes adding a frightening realism to his basset-hound impersonation. When Xin-Xin remained unmoved, it was clear she was working in tandem with Jack Hayes.

'It's a conspiracy then, is it?'

'No, it's love.'

Love, eh? Frank caressed her from behind while she made his cup of tea.

The workers in the office block of Frank's brain were in revolt. He'd closed down the staff bar, where they spent their many leisure hours, and it wasn't a privilege they were about to concede without a fight. And fight they did. On this, their third day of being refused entry, they were at their most militant: staging lightning strikes and walk-outs, issuing threats, and holding demonstrations that could escalate into riots at any minute.

They scoffed when, after lunch, Xin-Xin allowed Frank to mount an ineffectual offensive against them with another Valium.

But what Valium couldn't do, sex could. As well as being drunks, his brain staff were satyrs and, even though they were about to disport themselves sober for the first time in living memory, they still expected the experience to be enjoyable enough to call a ceasefire and allow Frank to get on with it when they heard him say, 'Be gentle now, won't you?'

'I was going to say the same thing to you,' said Xin-Xin.

Black-eyed Frank, who still had a bandage on his arm, another holding his ear in place, was covered in stitches and bruises and whose ribs made him frightened to cough, was mystified.

'A lot of girls might fantasise about going to bed with Frankenstein's monster,' she explained, 'but I'm not one of them.'

Frank accepted his new role gladly when he realised Frankenstein's monster felt no pain, not even in his ribs. It seemed Xin-Xin had no intention of being gentle so he didn't feel compelled to be either. They made love as ferociously as ever, both secretly delighted to discover Frank's virility was not related to his drinking in the way Samson's strength was to his hair.

'My God,' said Xin-Xin when they'd finished, 'I'm sweating almost as much as you. Feel like a ciggie?'

It was a rhetorical question, so she wasn't surprised when he didn't answer.

'Oh Frank, I'm exhausted,' she groaned, still staring at the ceiling. It was her customary prompt to Frank to head off in search of cigarettes. This time he didn't respond. Xin-Xin rolled on her side to look at him, and saw that he was fast asleep.

God, he looked a mess: all grey skin, black eyes and stitches. He stank, too. Jack Hayes had warned her about the hot and cold sweats. He'd explained that drunks went through withdrawal just like junkies did; warned her it wouldn't be easy keeping this bloke off the drink; told her it was really a job for experts and she should leave him at Mission House for another week at least. But Xin-Xin wanted to bring him home. She wiped Frank's forehead, nurse-like, with the sheet and held his beaten head in her arms.

Why, she thought, why has the world of men narrowed itself down to this one?

Unlike the last time she'd asked herself this question, this time she came up with an answer: because this one needs me.

'I need a drink,' Frank moaned after they'd finished dinner and the prospect of another dry evening loomed. Three in a fucking row.

'Try to ignore him if he becomes irritable or obnoxious,' Jack Hayes had advised. 'He'll try anything. Best thing is to take his mind off it by keeping him busy. Don't let him sit around watching TV or doing nothing. If you do he'll reach out in no time.'

'I have a suggestion,' Xin-Xin said.

Frank had heard this phrase often enough by now to know what it meant. It meant, 'Frank, this is what we're going to do.'

'And what's that?' he replied without enthusiasm.

'I have to work on my book tonight, so why don't you drag out those notes you've made for your biography of Arthur Blackwell and get to work?'

Arthur. It seemed ages since Frank had seen Arthur. There was a dividing line in his life now and Arthur existed on the other side of it. How could he relate to him, let alone write about him, without a drink in his hand? Frank grunted as he stared at his empty plate, fiddled with his knife, remained in his chair.

'Ignore him if he becomes irritable,' Jack had said.

'I've thought of a title for my book,' Xin-Xin offered, heading for the coffee-maker. '*High Notes*. Do you like it?'

'Yeah,' said Frank. Half a smile appeared on his face as he ran the title over a couple of times in his mind. 'Yeah, I like it.'

'That's good. I've been making steady progress. I really love my sax player but he's such a hopeless case.'

'Like me?'

'No, not like you. Not like you at all.'

The phone rang. Xin-Xin showed no inclination to pick it up and Frank was grateful for the opportunity to break away. When he answered it, Arthur's voice crossed the dividing line. It was reassuring to know you could hear it from this side.

'Yeah, Arthur, three days so far,' Frank mumbled as he drifted from the dining room into the lounge and sat on the couch opposite his beloved painting.

Xin-Xin strained to hear what he was saying, but soon gave up and went back to coffee-making. A few minutes later she was surprised to hear Frank laughing. After he hung up the phone, she thought she heard him crying.

He made for the bathroom. She didn't hear the toilet flush but she could hear water running. What was he doing in there? Jack Hayes had told her he might be sick. No retching noises, though. Maybe he had been crying and had gone in there to wash away the tears.

She listened to the bathroom door open and close, and Frank going from one room to another.

'Coffee?' she asked, as he breezed past the kitchen en route to the spare room. In it was his new computer and Xin-Xin's former desk, along with his jumbled art collection. A major work was still missing: Arthur's portrait, now hidden away in a corner of the painter's studio. The Frank who had never returned.

The room next door — previously Frank's ironically named workspace — was now Xin-Xin's, and work was being done in there for the first time ever.

'Love one,' he called.

'You okay?' she asked as she brought him his drink. 'I thought you might have been sick.'

'I am. But I'm going to get well.'

Xin-Xin placed the mug of coffee on the desk. Beside it lay Frank's folder of notes on Arthur and it was open. She placed her arm around his shoulder. Frank rose to his feet, turned and embraced her. Xin-Xin had never seen Frank cry before. She held him close and felt him trembling while she stroked his hair.

'You know what Arthur said?' he managed with a faltering voice. 'He said he was proud of me.'

Xin-Xin tightened her arms around him. She could feel his wet face pressing against the nape of her neck, her shoulders becoming slippery from tears of guilt and shame. 'I'm proud of you too, Frank,' she said, and the shuddering started again.

'Why, Xin-Xin, why?'

'Because you're trying, Frank. And it's hard.'

It was hard to sit in front of a blank screen and start working without a drink. Frank, for whom writing had always come easily, felt as helpless as a child being ordered to build the Harbour Bridge. Hearing Xin-Xin's fingers gliding over her keyboard at fifty words a minute in the next room only made things harder. But, soon after midnight, Xin-Xin finally heard Frank's fingers tapping away too. They didn't tap for long but he'd made a start.

She peered into the room. 'How's it going?'

'Great. Really great,' he said. 'Come and have a look.'

There on the screen, under the title, *The Art of Arthur Blackwell*, were the first words of Frank's introduction:

Like all great art, the paintings of Arthur Blackwell appear to have happened by accident. Each is the product of a series of fluid gestures, held together more by rhythm than design. Something has danced across the canvas and left the painting behind.

What a good boy, Xin-Xin thought, as she rewarded him with a Valium and packed him off to bed.

CHAPTER 38

'Christ, I haven't touched a drop for nine days. Give me a break!'

'You're going great but it would be a lot easier if you went to a few meetings,' said Jack.

'I went to two.'

'In the first couple of weeks you should go every day. A lot of blokes go to a couple of meetings every bloody day for the first three months.'

'In that case there are a lot of blokes out there with fuck-all else to do.'

'There are a lot of blokes out there with the brains to know what's good for them. And when I send them along to AA, they do as they're fucking well told.'

'Well, if you tell me to go to AA again, I'll tell you what I'm going to do: I'll stop at the pub on the way and go there instead.'

At moments like this, Hayes had a habit of getting out of his chair, rolling up his sleeves, washing his hands at the basin in the corner and then turning to stare at Frank while he dried them on a towel.

Frank was onto him. He'd worked out that this was a ploy intended to intimidate, to make him look as though he had something more important to do than sit there listening to bullshit artists like Frank.

'What are you doing that for?'

'Doing what?'

'Washing your hands. You going to stick your finger up my arse and take my temperature or something?'

'Now you listen here, Frank —'

'No. Bugger it, Jack. I'm not going to AA. It's bad enough going to a dinner party and meeting people who bore you talking about the things they do. You want me to spend every night of the week listening to people boring my arse off talking about what they don't do. And how long it's been since they did!'

'Have it your way.'

'Anyway, Xin-Xin's looking after me. You're looking after me. And I reckon, as long as I keep busy, I'll be looking after me the rest of the time.'

'We'll see how you go.'

'I'm going okay now. Woke up this morning feeling on top of the world. Reckon I might have it beaten.'

'It's a cycle. You were as sick as buggery for the first four days, a bit better for the next four, and you've woken up this morning feeling great. That's pretty normal. Don't be surprised to wake up in the morning feeling worse than you did on day one.'

'I hope not. I start back at work today and I told my mate Eddie I'd have lunch with him tomorrow. Was looking forward to it. Won't be much fun if I've got the shakes and sweats again.'

'You won't. But you might wake up feeling inclined to go out and kill yourself. Where are you supposed to be meeting your mate — in a pub?'

'We'll go to a pub first and then go on to lunch.'

'Don't go to a pub.'

'But all my mates meet in the pub.'

'Look, Frank, if you spend all your time hanging around in a barber shop, sooner or later some bastard's going to give you a haircut.'

Frank couldn't dispute the logic of that.

'You might be all right in the morning and you might not be,' Jack went on. 'Different in every case. But you'll be up and down like a yo-yo for a long time so you might as well get used to it. Try to avoid social situations, especially on days when you don't feel you can cope. If you do have to go out, make sure you take a Valium in advance.'

'Righto.'

Jack resumed his seat, put his elbows on his knees and looked Frank in the eyes. It was another sign Frank had learned the meaning of: question time again.

'Now. When your old man used to give you hidings when you were a kid, how did you react?'

Frank bowed his head and started to remember.

Everyone at Parkinson's knew Frank was bullshitting when he told them about his accident. No one doubted he'd had his face smashed up, but his injuries didn't appear consistent with what you'd expect for a man who had airbags in his car. And why had he lost so much weight? Frank was looking leaner and hungrier than ever.

'Welcome back, Frank,' said Sandra, looking him up and down. 'How are you travelling?'

'Good as gold. Ribs still hurt a bit so I'll be keeping the laughing down to a minimum.'

He caught the doubting look in Sandra's eye, and added, 'I hit 'em pretty hard against the steering wheel,' before bolting towards his office to make sure the interrogation went no further.

He spent the morning deleting emails and returning phone calls. At twelve-thirty he received one from Eddie, asking him to join him for lunch.

'Can't today, Eddie. I'll duck out and get a sandwich.'

'A sandwich?' cried Eddie, who'd eaten his last sandwich at primary school and regarded a grown man eating one as a sign of failure. 'Well, don't forget we're having lunch tomorrow. Andy's up from Melbourne. We're meeting him at The Australian in The Rocks and I've booked a table at The Wharf.'

'I'm not sure I'll be able to make it.'

'For Christ's sake, just because you're off the grog it doesn't mean you can't go out and enjoy yourself.'

'I'm not sure if watching you blokes get pissed is my idea of enjoying myself.'

'Don't be silly. We're on for tomorrow and don't forget it. I'll shout you a pineapple cordial.'

There were many inquisitive glances into Frank's office that first day, but, for once, he seemed too preoccupied to look up from his terminal. Everyone assumed he had work to catch up on.

Frank did have work to catch up on. By four o'clock he'd finished the introduction to his book on Arthur Blackwell, and by five he'd run the spellcheck over it, cleaned up the punctuation and despatched a copy to Xin-Xin's email address. It wasn't a bad week's work in his assessment. Well, not bad for a man who didn't drink.

When Frank's introduction landed in her mailbox, Xin-Xin was on the phone to Arthur, who'd called to find out how Frank was and, forty-five minutes later, was still being told. He was becoming confused too. It was one of those conversations that involved a fair degree of role-swapping: one minute Arthur would be reassuring Xin-Xin and telling her to stop worrying; the next minute it would be the other way around. Arthur, who didn't know Xin-Xin well but knew how to comfort neurotic women, decided to end the conversation on a definitive note.

'Look, love,' he said, 'if he's not home in an hour, ring me. If he's gone to the pub, I'll find him, thump him and bring him home.'

It was his way of helping and Xin-Xin appreciated the offer, but the memory of seeing Arthur thump Barry O'Connor was one she was still trying to erase. Besides, Frank was recovering from being thumped by someone else and, as his nurse, she didn't want to see him have a relapse.

'Thanks, Arthur,' she said hesitatingly. 'I'd rather you didn't do that, but I'll call you if he doesn't come home.'

As she hung up the phone, he did. The oriental lilies in his hand provided a momentary distraction, but she still made sure to breathalyse him with a test disguised as a kiss. When his reading came up as 0.00 she decided to take him back to the surgery for some further tests. She led him towards the bedroom, smiling, and thinking: okay, it might be like making love to Robert De Niro in *Raging Bull*, but it's an improvement on Frankenstein's monster.

Frank and Xin-Xin had developed an evening routine that involved sharing the cleaning duties after their meal before heading for their respective workplaces and seeing who could get the most done. Xin-Xin won hands down every night, but Frank's lucidity was coming back at such a rate she suspected he'd be giving her a run for her money if he sustained it for a year. He was bashing out words at a speed that exceeded his previous personal best when Xin-Xin interrupted him with the phone in her hand.

'It's Dad,' she said. 'He's inviting us over for dinner tomorrow night. What do you say?'

Xin-Xin covered the mouthpiece and adopted an expression that said she had doubts of her own.

'Try to avoid social occasions, especially on days when you can't cope,' Jack had counselled. But right now, productive Frank could cope with anything. He was in as good shape as he'd ever be for taking on the challenge of meeting his girlfriend's parents.

'No worries,' he said with such confidence that Xin-Xin's doubts evaporated.

'We'll be there,' she told her father.

Their evening routine concluded with a cup of tea before bedtime while perusing each other's efforts. Perusing Frank's was not time-consuming and consisted, largely, of Xin-Xin making encouraging remarks while avoiding condescension; perusing hers took longer, and resulted in agreeable discussion of the progress she had made.

When they went to bed, dimmed the lights and held each other, Frank thought how wonderful life could be as long as you didn't have a drink. 'You'll have your ups and downs', he recalled Jack saying. This must be one of the ups.

He woke the next morning feeling inclined to kill himself.

CHAPTER 39

By the evening he was glad he hadn't, but it hadn't been an easy day.

Jack was right when he'd said Frank shouldn't meet his mates in the pub, and Frank had been right himself, the previous day, when he'd told Eddie that watching him and Andy drinking might not be his idea of fun.

In the end, he'd caught a cab back to work and left them, laughing their silly fucking heads off at jokes about blokes who didn't drink. The effort he'd been making to laugh along with them had drained him to the point where he couldn't keep it up. On the short trip back to the office he tried to pinpoint the moment in his life when he'd been at his most drunk, and concluded there were certain things a man would never know. The only thing he did know was that this was the most sober he'd ever felt and it didn't feel good at all.

Things became even more depressing when he realised Harry Parkinson had no intention of subsidising his production of Arthur Blackwell's biography and had left work for him to do. Who, Frank thought, really gives a fuck whether this brand of razor blade cuts whiskers off closer to the skin?

And who, he thought, as he listened to the news in the car on the way home, really gives a fuck whether some pop star's marriage has finally broken up? And who would be stupid enough to go out to meet his girlfriend's parents on a night when he was feeling like this — even if the stitches in his forehead, chin and right ear had been removed, the wounds had been covered with neat white adhesive plasters, the black eyes had retreated to small crescents of violet, and a story involving a freakish car accident had been invented and rehearsed?

'You see that place over there on the left,' said Frank as they drove along Bligh Avenue in Darling Point. 'My dad worked on it. He took me over there one day and I helped him pinch a load of bricks. We used them to build a barbecue.'

'You never talk about your parents. Are they still together?'

'Mum died about ten years ago. Lung cancer.'

'God,' said Xin-Xin. This wasn't a good start to the evening and they were almost at her parents' home. 'I'm sorry. What about your dad?'

'He's still around.'

Xin-Xin steered into the driveway of the house at the end of the street.

'I've known you a lot longer than you think,' Frank said.

'What do you mean?'

'When you were born, your parents had a silver Mercedes, right?'

Xin-Xin looked at Frank suspiciously, and nodded.

'It was you,' he said, shaking his head and laughing. 'It was you.'

'What are you talking about?'

'That day I was telling you about, the day I came over with my dad to knock off those bricks — I saw you. I saw your parents take you out of the car in a little bassinet. I knew it was a baby girl because you were all wrapped up in pink.'

'I can't believe it.'

'Neither can I.'

As Frank approached the front door of the perfectly positioned, with sweeping harbour views, ideal family home, he wondered what sort of people could afford a house like this. Even if he put together all the money he'd drunk and snorted, he still wouldn't have enough for the deposit.

He knew Xin-Xin's mother was called Lian and had practised the pronunciation of her name to her daughter's satisfaction. He also knew her father's name was Benny. Although the question of how a Chinese name could, through the process of anglicisation, result in Benny Leroq had confounded him, he'd resisted the temptation to probe out of fear reciprocal questions about his own father might be difficult to answer. All he knew about Benny and Lian was they'd arrived rich in Australia from Hong Kong and had become richer through selling boatloads of authentic oriental antiques, most of which originated in a factory in Bali, where they could be made to measure and delivered within three months.

On the basis of this fragmentary description, Frank had constructed images in his mind. Benny would be a Buddha lookalike in an expensive suit, and too much plastic surgery would have reduced Lian to a spindly Christmas tree with diamond and gold decorations hanging off every branch.

Who then, he wondered, was this handsome man embracing Xin-Xin? Who was the serenely beautiful woman now doing likewise, and where were her parents?

'And you must be Frank,' said Benny, shaking Frank's hand and placing an arm around his shoulder while introducing him to his wife. As Lian took his extended hand in both of hers and planted a little peck on his patched-up face, it occurred to Frank how lucky he'd been to meet Lola that night at AD's and not her. Things could have been a lot worse.

'Feng shui to burn in here,' he whispered as they made their way into the mansion's inner sanctum. Xin-Xin responded with an encouraging squeeze of his arm.

Frank thought Benny seemed like a lovely bloke. Generous. The first thing he did was pop open a bottle and offer him a glass of French champagne.

'I won't thanks, Benny. Don't drink.'

'Not at all?'

'Not at all.'

'What can we get you then, Frank?' Lian asked.

'A cup of tea would be lovely. Black, thanks. No sugar.'

'You'll have one, won't you, dear?' said Benny, passing to his daughter the first glass of champagne ever offered to Frank Thornton and refused.

'If I must,' said Xin-Xin, casting a sideways look at Frank.

'Do you like Lapsang Souchong, Frank?' Lian asked.

'Love it,' said Frank, assuming it was some sort of tea.

'Tell us about the accident,' said Lian. 'From what Xini said, it must have been awful.'

'I can't remember it all that clearly, to tell you the truth. It happened so quickly —'

He was saved by the bell.

'That must be Lawrence,' said Benny, putting down his champagne. 'Have you met Xin-Xin's brother yet, Frank?'

Tradition, it seemed, required that a doorbell be answered by all present in the Leroq household. Frank followed the other three dolefully, still clinging to his cup of foul-tasting liquid and pondering a future in which such things as Lapsang Souchong would be what he had to look forward to at parties and special occasions.

With so much familial greeting, embracing and introducing going on, confused, sober Frank didn't recognise Evie until Benny said, 'And this is Lawrence's girlfriend, Evie,' and Evie said, 'Of course I know Frank. He works for my father.'

'That wasn't so hard, was it?' said Xin-Xin, in the passenger seat by mutual agreement. 'They like you, Frank. I knew they would. You were wonderful. And I'm so proud of you not having a drink all night.'

'Your parents took me by surprise. No offence, but I wasn't expecting them to be quite such nice, easygoing people. Thought they might frighten me a bit.'

'I was more worried you might frighten them.'

The parents are okay, thought Frank, but the brother's a bit of a worry. Apparently, Xin-Xin thought so too.

'I'm sorry about Lawrence,' she said. 'He doesn't say much. He never used to be like that. I don't know what's wrong with him these days.'

'I would have thought that was pretty obvious.'

'What do you mean?'

'Darling, your brother's a junkie. Blind Freddy could see that.'

Xin-Xin blinked and stared. 'How do you know?'

'You don't wear long sleeves on a hot night unless you've got something to hide.'

'Lawrence always wears long-sleeved T-shirts. He's got dozens of them.'

'I'll bet he has.'

They drove down Bourke Street in silence as Xin-Xin struggled with the idea that the money she'd been lending her brother had been supporting his habit instead of his business.

Frank felt like Jack Hayes: brutal work, but someone has to do it. 'So's his girlfriend.'

'But Evie wasn't wearing long sleeves.'

Women in her line of work had to be more careful. If you were looking for track marks, you'd start by checking between her toes.

'You can just tell,' he said.

He noticed Xin-Xin's tears when they kissed while waiting in the basement for the lift. Inside, with the doors closed, she put her head on his shoulder and cried properly.

'He'll be okay,' he said, stroking her hair, her beautiful straight black hair. 'Your little brother will be okay. He's sick but he takes the wrong medicine, that's all.'

CHAPTER 40

Frank found it hard to sympathise with Lawrence who, it seemed to him, was a fuck wasted. A drug habit picked up along the way by a socially deprived man was a sad thing, but it was hard to pity a bloke who got one as the result of being spoilt.

Roy disagreed but didn't argue. He'd been just as irascible after a month off smack as Frank was now after a month off the grog, and knew what his friend was up against. It had been a decade since he'd used heroin and he still felt grateful it wasn't advertised on billboards or available behind the bar. Temptation was easier to resist if you had to go out of your way to find it.

'It can happen to anybody, Frank,' he said, and left it at that.

He reached for his wine and caught Frank's glance in the glass's direction. He hadn't wanted to bring wine on this first visit to Frank's home since his friend had stopped drinking, but Frank had insisted. After Roy had been subjected to the Thornton method for heroin withdrawal, parting company with fellow junkies had been an essential part of the process when it came to staying clean. Keeping company with supportive friends was just as important. During that time, the loneliest and hardest period of his life, the most supportive friend he'd had was Frank, and drinking in front of him now didn't feel like an appropriate way to return the favour. Then again, it was something Frank would have to get used to, because, unlike heroin, booze was advertised on every other billboard, it was available at the bar, and all his friends were drinkers, who, while they wanted to see him stay on the wagon, didn't have his reasons for climbing aboard. Keeping his head while all those about him were losing theirs was just one of those things Frank would have to get used to.

Frank jumped from his chair and headed to the kitchen for yet another cup of tea.

Over the years, Roy had crashed at Frank's place so often he'd regarded it almost as a second home. But there was little about it now that struck him as familiar. He recognised some of the drawings despite their new frames, and those Goya etchings were still there in the hallway. Roy, whose musical tastes enabled him to appreciate the subtleties of swing, Dixieland and any pop song that comprised three chords or less, were more sophisticated than his taste in art, which, according to Frank, was nonexistent.

Roy's appreciation of visual art derived from watching Puss slapping on paint in the art room at school. He'd been duly impressed but, aside from Puss's pornographic caricatures of the teachers, the other stuff just looked like colours smeared on flat surfaces for no good reason. He'd spent any number of evenings listening to Frank and Arthur discussing this or that painter's work, but he found their conversations as impenetrable as the works they were referring to. The painting he was gazing at now — this alleged masterpiece Arthur had painted of the Murray River — what was it but a frenzied attack on a piece of canvas by a bloke who hadn't even taken the trouble to pick some decent colours? Perhaps, because of the chemicals needed for their production, the brighter-coloured paints were more expensive, so Arthur had done this one on the cheap. Looking closer, Roy considered the possibility that Arthur's technique was so minimalist, so 'economical', that he'd abandoned the use of paint altogether and dipped his brushes directly into the mud and slime available at the site. And as for the site? Roy had seen as many views of the Murray as the next man, and damn fine they were. Surely an artist with an eye for the visually seductive could have driven a few miles further down the road until he'd found something more picturesque.

'I mean, what the fuck is it?' he demanded when Frank returned, cup of tea in one hand, freshly opened bottle of red in the other. 'You've gone to all this trouble, sprucing up your flat, turning it from a shithole into a five-star hotel, and then you've let Arthur slap this … this *thing* in the middle of it. It's as if everything else is coming to life around here — flowers in bloody vases, fruit bowls, food in the kitchen — but you've given pride of place to this desolate bloody eyesore. It's dead!'

'It's a painting of something that's dead but that doesn't mean it's a dead painting. Anyway, getting back to Lawrence —'

'Who's Lawrence?'

'Xin-Xin's brother.'

While Roy and Frank discussed Lawrence's heroin addiction, Xin-Xin was trying to extract an admission to it from Lawrence, and hearing some of the most elaborate lies her brother had ever concocted. And while Frank was telling Roy that Harry Parkinson's daughter, the woman he had by chance seen working in The Favourite, was Lawrence's girlfriend, Lawrence was explaining Evie's absence by telling Xin-Xin she was doing a gallery management course at evening college, to develop the skills she'd need for joining him as a partner in his business. And when Xin-Xin was putting questions to her brother about what he'd done with the money she'd loaned him, and he was being evasive, Frank and Roy were discussing a way of dealing with the expensive problem Lawrence was being evasive about.

'When you did that to me, Frank,' Roy said, 'you saved my life. But at the time I hated you for it — I thought you were trying to kill me. He'll hate you for it too, you know.'

'I couldn't care less whether the bastard hates me or not. I'm doing this for Xin-Xin, not him.'

'Well, then, it'll be easier if I give you a hand.'

Frank's friends attributed his legendary impulsiveness to his equally legendary fondness for drink. The two went hand in hand: he made up his mind to do things before thinking them through because he was never in a fit state to think them through.

He proved his friends wrong when, after two months without a drink, the idea occurred to him to commission Arthur to paint Xin-Xin. A minute later, before having thought it through, he was on the phone to Arthur, determined to set a date for the first sitting and determined to establish a price in keeping with those Barry O'Connor was now charging for Arthur's landscapes, not one in the order of a few beers and a plate of fish and chips.

Arthur's friends attributed his legendary aversion to selling his paintings to his love for them, and they were right. For Arthur, exchanging his paintings for money was akin to a man prostituting his own daughter, and he still lost sleep over the fact that, these days, he routinely allowed his own to bide their time in Barry O'Connor's brothel, waiting to catch the eye of some salivating brute with a hard-on for landscapes.

If Frank had thought it through, he would have realised his plan constituted both an honour and an insult. Arthur would not know how to respond. When Arthur didn't know how to respond he'd end by getting confused, and when Arthur got confused he got angry.

Also, if Frank had thought it through, he might have considered that, as a man separated from his last drink by a matter of two months, he was also disposed towards getting angry, and the shitfight he had on the phone with Arthur that day might have been avoided. But he didn't, and it wasn't, and they both told each other to go and get fucked.

The next morning, when Arthur made the first move by phoning Frank, their conversation started as a race to see who could apologise first, a date was set for the first sitting — assuming Xin-Xin would make herself available — and an agreement was struck to discuss the price later.

Xin-Xin and Frank had long since given up counting arguments. Minor ones occurred every day, so it was only the major ones that mattered. Both sensed they were about to have a major one, which wasn't surprising given that Lawrence was Xin-Xin's brother, forty thousand of the dollars he'd shot up his arm were hers, she didn't want to believe Frank's diagnosis of his condition — after all, he'd only met him once — and the jargon of armchair psychologists, including the expression 'in denial', infuriated her as much as it infuriated Frank. Retrospectively, he regretted saying it, but at the time he hadn't been able to think of another way of phrasing it.

The argument happened the day after Frank had met her family, and Xin-Xin wasn't 'in denial'; Frank was 'out of order'. What's more, if Lawrence did have a 'little problem', there was no need for Frank to belittle it by calling it 'little'. And if she decided to talk first to her mother about it, what the hell was wrong with that?

When Frank said, 'Because if he's ended up with this problem as a result of being a mummy's boy, I hardly think mummy's the person to solve it,' they both knew they had a major one on their hands.

It got worse when Xin-Xin accused Frank of being a reverse snob and, because he'd never heard of a 'reverse snob' before, let alone been accused of being one, naturally he'd become offended and defensive. Xin-Xin had prosecuted her case very effectively, however, and it wasn't an argument he wanted to lose again.

Consequently, for almost three months, the subject of Lawrence was rarely mentioned. The therapeutic procedure Frank had in mind couldn't be put in place until Xin-Xin became convinced that Lawrence really needed it, and even then it was something he wanted to discuss with her after the event and not before.

Another person Frank took care not to mention was his sister, Nina. He was even more careful to avoid the subject of Lola. Although she and Xin-Xin remained good friends, Frank preferred their relationship to exclude him and always managed to come up with a believable excuse whenever Xin-Xin suggested the three of them get together.

One evening, after a meeting with Lola in their favourite brasserie in Kings Cross, to which Frank hadn't been invited, Xin-Xin rang home in tears. Half an hour later, Frank met her there, relieved to find Lola had left. They ate together and Xin-Xin conceded she was no longer in denial. Lola, who had her own drug connections and knew some of the people Lawrence regarded as friends, had been doing some investigative work on Xin-Xin's behalf and had told her that yes, her brother was a junkie, it was widely known in certain circles, and he had been one for quite some time.

Frank did a good job of comforting. He was holding Xin-Xin tightly and walking her towards the car when she managed, between sniffles, to say, 'I'm dreading the thought of telling Mum and Dad about it tomorrow.'

'I wouldn't tell them about it if I were you,' Frank said, in a tone he'd hoped sounded soothing.

'And why not?' Xin-Xin retorted.

Memories of the repercussions of 'mummy's boy' came back to Frank, as did the expression 'reverse snob', and he remained in consoling mode.

'Sorry,' he said, 'I just don't think you should tell them yet. Let's see if we can do something about it first.'

'Don't be ridiculous,' Xin-Xin snapped. 'He belongs in hospital.'

'The only way he'll wind up there is if he's peeled up from the footpath unconscious. He stands a much better chance of going to jail.'

'What about a clinic? There are special clinics for people like him.'

'You think he's going to go to the door of one of those and beg to be let in?'

Xin-Xin's look of despair unearthed reserves of sympathy in Frank he hadn't known existed. He held her even tighter and opened the door for her.

'Wait until I've had a talk to Jack about him tomorrow,' he said as she got into the car. 'There might be something I can do.'

CHAPTER 41

'Congratulations,' said Jack Hayes, standing to shake Frank's hand when he entered his surgery the next morning. 'Ninety days is a good effort and you should be bloody proud. Let's get out of this place and have a cuppa down the road.'

As they walked around the block to the café, Frank had his first opportunity to see Jack outside his natural environment. The harsh sunlight accentuated the lines in his face and did nothing to diminish the severity of his gaze or the grimness of his lips. If you didn't know him and someone told you he was a hitman, you wouldn't be surprised. It occurred to Frank that this probably wasn't the only block Jack Hayes had been around.

'Can I ask you a question?' said Frank as they settled at a table on the footpath.

'What do you want to know?'

'Have you ever had a drink?'

'Not for thirty-one years, four months and three days. Not that I'm counting.'

'Do you still feel like one?'

'No, Frank, I don't. I know the harm it did me and I see it doing worse to other blokes every day of the week. Novelty wears off after a while.'

'I wish to Christ it would for me. How long does it take?'

'All depends on how you go about it. You're refusing to do AA and I've told you often enough you're making it harder on yourself. But I think you'll get through because you can see what your choices are. You can count yourself lucky that Mick's your old man. If you feel like reaching out, just take a look at him.'

Nina's words 'have a look at Dad' came back to Frank, as they often did. 'If you ever decide the party's over then give me a call' were Nina's words too. Maybe it was time to give her a call.

Jack, who'd been shown Nina's letter, interpreted Frank's silence as a sign he'd gone too far.

'I'll put it like this,' he said. 'If you're legless, you end up in a wheelchair. If you're lucky enough to get new legs, you're free to move around. Who'd want to go back to living in a wheelchair — do you?'

Looking at Jack, Frank thought for the first time that he was probably about the same age as his father. This led to speculation as to how much misery might have been avoided if his dad had done the same thing Jack had done, thirty-one years, four months and three days ago. So much pain and so much regret. And what good had it done anyone, least of all old Mick? You couldn't sit here and talk to him, and you couldn't admire him either. You simply couldn't love him like a son could love Jack Hayes.

'There's something I've got to talk to you about,' Frank said.

'You'd better hurry up.' Jack looked at his watch. 'I haven't got much time.'

'It's about Xin-Xin's brother.'

'What's his problem?'

Frank explained Lawrence's problem and what he intended to do about it. He also told him about his girlfriend Evie's problem and what he intended to do about hers. He was pleased when Jack gave his plans the thumbs up.

'You've got to get them apart and you've got to get them away from the scene. They're the main things when it comes to junkies. Sounds like your idea fulfils both requirements. Don't think the young bloke's going to like it very much. Do you think he'll be up to it?'

Frank enjoyed seeing Jack's thin lips stretch into a grin. Like Xin-Xin, Frank was working in tandem with him now, and it was good to have a man like him on side.

'I've got a mate called Roy and I did the same thing with him. He's been clean for ten years now.'

'Well, you said you need to keep yourself busy so you'd better get cracking. See you again Wednesday. And good luck, Frank.'

Frank got cracking.

By now he was used to being the first person to arrive at the office on Mondays, Wednesdays and Fridays after his sessions with Jack. He'd developed the habit of throwing his bag on the couch and sitting at his desk like an efficient senior executive with a busy schedule and not enough hours in the day. A few minutes later it would dawn on him that he wasn't an efficient senior executive, he didn't have a busy schedule and there were too many hours in the day, a few of which would have to be killed off in some place other than a pub. The first two could be despatched with the help of the newspaper, the cryptic crossword and lots of coffee and smokes at the café down the road. After that it was back to the office, where the really gruelling part began as lunchtime approached and, with it, the exhortations to join his colleagues for a drink.

Today was different. He mightn't have a schedule but he did have something to do. He'd already had a coffee with Jack and bought a couple more to keep him going. They stood at the ready on his desk in their polystyrene cups.

What time is it in Darwin? he wondered. What did it matter — those blokes were up and working by 4 am anyway.

'Is that you, Harvey?'

'Who's that?'

'It's me, Frank.'

'Frank who?'

Fair enough. It had been a couple of years.

'Frank Thornton.'

'Oh. G'day, Frank.'

'You out at sea at the moment?'

'I'm flat out right now putting a new motor in the boat. Coming up for a visit?'

'Got a bit of a problem. Wondering if you might be able to help.'

'What's up?'

'I've got this mate. He's in a pretty bad way.'

'Oh no, Frank, not another one of your fucking junkies.'

'Afraid so.'

'I'm running a prawn trawler, mate, not a floating detox.'

'I know, Harvey, I know. I wouldn't ask you if I didn't have to.'

'How bad is he?'

'Pretty bad. No point in bullshitting you. He won't be very useful for a while. I don't think the bastard's ever worked a day in his life.'

'You're making it hard, Frank.'

'Roy hadn't worked a day in his life when I sent him up to you. He turned out pretty handy.'

'Yeah. How is Roy? Behaving himself?'

'Hasn't touched it since. Drinks like a fish, though. Listen, Harvey, I know it's a big ask. Tell you the truth, I don't know this bloke very well. He's my girlfriend's brother.'

'Go on.'

Frank went on. And on and on and on. He could talk forever on the subject of Xin-Xin, with Lawrence scarcely rating a mention. After a few minutes Harvey had heard enough.

'Righto, Frank. Send the prick up here.'

'Thanks, mate. I appreciate this. How much do you reckon it's worth?'

Frank grunted as he hung up the phone. He was a good bloke, Harvey, but hard as nails when it came to money. If the amount Frank had given him for helping Roy had set the standard, Harvey's rate wasn't keeping up with inflation, it was leaving it well behind. He seemed to forget what a bastard of a trip it had been for Frank when, as a twenty-year-old, he was the one doing the work while Captain Harvey was in the fo'c'sle hitting up smack.

Now he had to find out where Lawrence was and work out when would be a good time to nab him. Sooner the better, but first things first. Better find out how often planes flew to Darwin. He rang a travel agent. After that, he rang Roy, who told him he was sitting at home marking essays all day and would be grateful for an excuse to get away.

'Okay, mate, I'll call you when I need you,' said Frank.

Xin-Xin next. She had a set of keys to Lawrence's place but getting them off her would be the tricky bit.

'Darling, have you got your keys to Lawrence's flat?'

'Yeah. Why?'

'I need to go around there.'

'He wouldn't be home now. He'd be at work.'

'That doesn't matter. I need to pick up a few of his things.'

'What are you talking about?'

'I talked about him to Jack Hayes this morning. It's all a bit complicated — I'll explain it to you later. By the way, do you know where he hangs out at night?'

'I wouldn't have the faintest idea.'

'See if you can find out. Ask Lola. Anyway, main thing is, I have to get over to his place now. I'll see you in about fifteen minutes.'

'Okay, if you must.'

Frank made his home visit as brief as he could, trying to imitate a busy executive with too much to do and too little time. Back behind the wheel of the car, with the address and the keys for Lawrence's apartment in his pocket, he recalled that galleries — including Vacant Space Fine Art — were always closed on Mondays. Today was a Monday. Good thing, that. Could save him a lot of time.

He rang Roy, gave him Lawrence's address and agreed to meet him there in half an hour. Then he rang the travel agent and made a booking.

Roy took forty-five minutes.

'Where the fuck have you been?' said Frank, agitated.

'Traffic,' said Roy. 'Okay, where does the silly cunt live?'

'This must be it.'

Frank proceeded to the front door of Lawrence's apartment block with Roy close behind, unlocked it, then marched onward to the lift. 'Come on, come on,' he grumbled while they waited.

'Settle down,' said Roy, and the lift doors opened.

Frank pressed P for penthouse. When the doors opened again, they made their way across a marble hallway and Frank unlocked Lawrence's door.

'Anybody home?' he called. Apparently not.

Where had Xin-Xin said his bedroom was? Down the hallway on the right. There they both were, sleeping like babies.

Lawrence stirred when he heard Frank opening cupboards and drawers, throwing things into an overnight bag. Roy stood impassively in the doorway. If Lawrence woke up thinking he'd gone to sleep in a nightclub and wanted to make a run for the door, he'd think twice after taking a look at the bouncer.

'What the fuck are you doing here?' he slurred.

'Packing up some of your clothes. Where do you keep your undies?'

'Frank, what are you fucking doing?' Lawrence was waking up properly, and he wasn't happy.

'I just told you. Where are your undies? Ah.' He threw four pairs into the bag.

'And who's this?'

'Roy,' said Frank, still rummaging in drawers. 'Roy, this is Lawrence. Lawrence, Roy. Now where are your socks?'

Evie was semi-conscious now, blinking and wondering what was happening. Lawrence was sitting up. Getting ready for action, perhaps. Get in first, Frank …

Frank lunged at him and held him down on the bed with one hand around his throat and the other clenched in a fist.

'Listen to me, Lawrence. I don't want to have to belt you so you'd better just do as you're told.'

'Fuck off!'

All right, thought Frank, one punch.

Evie started screaming, leapt from the bed and groped about on the floor for clothes. Roy remembered Frank saying he'd rather be in her than the Boy Scouts, and could see why, but he was a disciplined man. He was there to do a job, which, at this stage at least, involved standing in the doorway looking menacing, and he was doing it very well.

Frank's punch might have been a bit hard, judging by the amount of blood. Might even have broken his nose. But it seemed to have done the trick — Lawrence didn't want another one.

'Come on, get up and put some fucking clothes on,' Frank shouted. 'And you piss off, Evie. Go into the bathroom and get his toothbrush.'

'What are you doing, Frank? What's happening?' she blubbered.

'Lawrence is going on a holiday — that's what's happening.'

Lawrence didn't like being manhandled while he dressed and Evie was becoming hysterical. Frank decided to make up a story, quickly.

'Right!' he roared. 'I might as well tell you the truth. Roy here is a fucking copper. I've talked him into giving you a chance and it cost me a lot of money. Now do as I fucking well say or I'll ask for my money back. Then he'll do a search of the place and the pair of you can go back to the station with him and spend the rest of the day answering questions. And you won't be able to bullshit Roy and his mates the way you bullshit your sister, Lawrence.'

Roy moved aside to allow Evie to go to the bathroom and get Lawrence's toothbrush.

Frank and Roy bundled Lawrence out to the car and made sure his door was locked.

'Well done,' Roy said, slapping Frank on the back as they shook hands. 'That was a great idea, telling him I was a narc.'

'You know me, Roy,' said Frank. 'I'm in advertising — I bullshit best under pressure. Now get back upstairs and make sure Evie behaves herself.'

In the departure lounge Frank maintained his silence and a brooding demeanour while sitting next to Lawrence. It seemed to take forever until the flight to Darwin was ready for boarding.

'There's a man picking you up when you get there,' said Frank. 'He's a great big guy with a beard. Name's Harvey. He's a good bloke and he's there to help but he won't take any shit from you. And I'm sorry about smacking you in the head, Lawrence, I really am.'

Lawrence wasn't talking, he was sulking. But it didn't matter because a couple of minutes later Lawrence was gone.

When he got back to the agency Frank went straight into Harry's office and slammed the door.

Brenda Bischoff could hear voices being raised in there. Frank's was being raised a lot higher than Harry's and that wasn't something Harry would tolerate for long, she thought. That Frank Thornton had been a big enough pain in the neck when he turned up drunk every day, but he was insufferable sober. And he'd been sober ever since he'd gone missing a few months ago and come back after having that so-called accident, which didn't damage his car. Harry should have sacked him then and there.

'And by the way,' she heard Frank shout as he opened the door, 'it was me who took your fucking pipe out for its big night on the town.'

'What am I going to tell my mum and dad?'

'Just tell them he's gone for a holiday. Be gone for a couple of months.'

'A holiday!'

'All right, why don't you tell them the truth? Tell 'em it's a world gone mad: you've been writing a book about a junkie and only now realised your own brother is one, and you've written a book about

273

an alcoholic and now you're living with one. Tell 'em your alco boyfriend's abducted your junkie brother and condemned him to cold turkey on a hot boat. Tell 'em you're dealing with reality now and it's starting to lose its appeal.'

Oh, Christ. Now she was going to water.

'Darling, I'll tell you what,' said Frank, pushing his untouched meal aside and reaching across the table to hold her clammy hands. 'Tomorrow I'll go and see your parents and tell them what's happened. I'll tell them the truth. They'll just have to cop it. Don't have much choice. I'll keep in touch with Harvey and, as soon as Lawrence is over the worst of it, your mum and dad will be able to give him a ring. Stay in touch. It'll be okay.'

'What's happening with Evie?'

'Don't worry, she's not going to Mission House. I had a talk to her old man today. Had no idea. Seems he wants to take on the role of responsible caring father now he's left his run too late. Wouldn't want it getting out, I suppose. It might tarnish his image if people knew his daughter worked in a brothel.'

'She what?'

'Heroin costs a lot of money, Xin-Xin. More than Lawrence was earning. You know that.'

Xin-Xin put her elbows on the table, her hands to her forehead. 'So what's this father of hers going to do with Evie?' she asked.

As she raised her face and looked at him, Frank noticed again that tears never reddened Xin-Xin's eyes. Sadness only made them sparkle.

'Don't worry about her. She's agreed to let him put her into a nice expensive place for nice expensive junkies and he'll be giving her a job when she gets back. Then it'll be my job to keep an eye on her.'

'But my father could have sent Lawrence off to a place like that! Why didn't you let me talk to my parents first?'

'Your father couldn't send him if he doesn't want to go. And even if he did, your parents couldn't stop him getting out. Especially if he wants to go and cheer up his girlfriend 'cause she's in detox too.'

'So what? They could find him and have him put back in again,' Xin-Xin pleaded. 'Evie's parents could find her and they could —'

'Xin-Xin,' said Frank, holding her wet hands tighter, 'junkies only know one way to cheer each other up. And then they're back to square one.'

Xin-Xin ripped another tissue from its container, mopped up another sniffle, dried a few more tears and said, 'What's going to happen to Lawrence when he gets back?'

'He'll be seeing a lot of Jack Hayes, just like I do. And he couldn't be in better hands. He's a good bloke, that Jack Hayes, a real good bloke. He'll look after your brother. He'll look after anyone, even no-hopers like my —'

Xin-Xin could see it was Frank who was going to water this time.

'I love you, Frank.'

'Oh, Xin-Xin,' he wept. 'Christ, I could do with a drink.'

CHAPTER 42

Running through the streets, I think I hear him playing. No one else can make the saxophone sound like my Johnny: the screeching high notes — *wailing baby* music he called it — cutting jagged laser beams through the night and my heart; the rumbling low notes — *crazy voices music* — getting louder, more menacing as I run and run. I can hear him blasting out those honking noises — *traffic chaos music, Angel* — these cars, swerving to avoid me; this percussion — my footsteps — beating rhythms, cross rhythms, *Kings Cross Rhythms, MAN!* High, piercing notes again — *cop car sirens music* — flashing lights flashing past; an ambulance beside the fountain; people everywhere, gawking at his body as the medicos wrap it in a shroud; a policeman stepping forward, holding me and saying stop lady, stop lady, stop crying lady.

Xin-Xin's saxophone player's song had ended on a mournful note. She sat at her computer and read the last paragraph of her novel one more time, thinking: still not sure. I didn't want it to finish like that. I didn't want him to self-destruct like Lenny Matthews. But I was as helpless as his lover, watching him go down as she tried to save this loser. Still not sure if I should have named her Angel. Not sure why she failed either. I'll wait till Frank comes home and run the ending past him, see what he thinks. And *stop crying, lady*!

She had stopped when she heard the phone ringing, and was able to say hello without an accompanying sniffle by the time she answered it.

'Xin-Xin? It's me, Jack. Any chance you could duck out and meet me? There's something I want to show you.'

'Right now?'

'Yeah, right now, if you can get away. I'll meet you in the usual place.'

'Okay, Dr Hayes. I can be there in ten minutes.'

'The usual place' was a coffee shop where they met every few weeks to discuss Frank's progress and plan strategies. It was a block from Selwyn Lodge, where Jack went every morning after he'd finished his duties at Mission House. At Mission House he offered hope to men like Frank. At Selwyn, he offered help to men like Frank's father, for whom hope was no longer an option.

Jack was waiting in front of the café when Xin-Xin arrived. He advanced towards her, shook her hand and said, 'Sorry, Xin-Xin, we'll have to make this quick. We can pop back here for a coffee in a minute. Just come with me down to the end of the block.'

A minute later they were standing in front of a small park. With a nod, Jack directed Xin-Xin's attention to three men sitting on one of the benches. Two had taken their shirts off, the other was wearing a dirty white singlet. The one in the singlet was sitting forward with his neck outstretched and a woman was giving him a shave. Another woman, a towel slung over her shoulder, was kneeling in front of him holding a bowl filled with water under his chin. The other two men were lathered up and ready to go.

'Have a good look at the one getting a shave right now,' said Jack.

From twenty or thirty metres away, Xin-Xin watched while the old man's personal beautician finished her treatment and the other woman wiped his face. Our Lady of the Razor looked closely at the old man's skin, checking for nicks and scratches, and said, 'There you go, Mick, pretty as a picture. Come on, love, your turn now.'

Mick Thornton reached under the seat for a dark-coloured shirt that might once have been deep red or purple. He put it on as he got slowly to his feet, and stumbled off around the corner without saying a word.

'Come on, we'll go and have that cup of coffee,' said Jack.

'So that's Frank's father?' Xin-Xin asked.

'That's him.'

'Who are those women?'

'The Brown Sisters — used to wear brown habits. Dress in civvies these days but the name still sticks. Good people.'

Back at the café, they sat at a table on the footpath.

'Nice of him to get cleaned up for you,' said Jack. 'Must've known you were coming.'

'Do you think I should tell Frank about this?'

'Can't see why not. It might prompt him to come and see his dad himself. He'll have to do it sooner or later, and he'd better not leave it too late. Old Mick's not long for this world.'

'Really?'

'Xin-Xin, you've just seen a man in the terminal phase of heart cancer.'

'What's that?'

'Frank hasn't told you?'

Xin-Xin shook her head.

'I've been specialising in the condition for thirty years but it was Frank who helped me find a name for it. It's an illness some people pick up at an early age and it affects them for the rest of their life. You ask Frank about it. You're the one who's curing him of it so you have a right to know. How's your book going?'

'I've finished the first draft. More importantly, Frank and I started on our little project last night.'

Jack's face was all lines and furrows as it broke into an unaccustomed smile. He'd been waiting for this.

'And? How did he go?'

'Great. He was a bit slow to start but after a few minutes I couldn't shut him up.'

'I have the same problem myself,' he said, and they both laughed.

'There's been another significant development since I saw you last,' said Xin-Xin. 'He showed me Nina's letter.'

'That's good. When it comes to Frank's wounds, that was one of the deeper ones.'

'He must have decided to have it stitched. He's going to visit her on Sunday. His niece will be there too.'

'I know. He told me this morning. Nina used to come and see me to talk about her dad. It was terrible, what happened to her. Still, she's a pretty strong woman and she's pulling through. Our patient's doing well too. Very well indeed.' Jack looked at his watch. 'Sorry, I have to get back. Have to see a couple of blokes in the PP.'

'What's the PP?'

'Proclaimed place. Better known as drunk tanks. There's a few of them around here, down in the basements of places like Selwyn Lodge. Keep up the good work and keep an eye on that boy. If he looks like playing up, tell him Jack doesn't want to see him in the PP. That'll put the fear of God into him.'

He laughed, shook Xin-Xin's hand and told her to keep in touch.

It was a hot day. The hottest September day for twelve years, according to the weather report. Only ten o'clock and already nudging the mid-thirties. Arthur Blackwell, stripped down to a pair of shorts, was lumbering about in his studio, looking for the freshly stretched canvas he'd prepared a few days before by applying a ground of rabbit glue. He was concerned it might be too big; Xin-Xin wasn't a big woman and he didn't want to magnify her to prevent the painting from being more about its background than its subject.

Arthur was concerned about the heat too. His studio had a tin roof and it was years since the air-conditioner — a rusty piece of junk metal set in a high window — had worked. He was the kind of man who treated weather in all its forms with equal indifference: in summer you worked in a pair of shorts; in winter you wore a jumper. It was only when he painted portraits that the climatic conditions in his ramshackle workplace became a matter for concern. On these rare occasions, Arthur would be reminded that not everyone was as impervious to temperature as he was.

On finding the canvas, he placed it on his easel and felt immediately reassured. It was big enough to cause Frank a problem when it came to mounting it on a wall, but not too big for what he had in mind. He could already visualise Xin-Xin's slender body finding itself quite comfortable in all that empty space. If not, if she felt a little lost, he could fill it up with something.

He experienced the familiar thrill of not yet knowing what that would be. It would be air; air of a certain warmth and humidity. It would be space; space of a yet-to-be-determined density and depth. At this stage he had no idea what the weather would be like in his painting; that depended on the mood and demeanour of his subject, and the way he responded to them. Arthur mightn't notice the difference between a hot day and a cold one, but he was a qualified meteorologist when it came to gauging the atmospheric conditions in his paintings.

He checked the time: almost ten-thirty. Good; she wouldn't be there till two. Heaps of time to dig out one of those fans he knew was in here somewhere. If the worst came to the worst, he could always pop down to Bing Lee and buy a couple.

Xin-Xin didn't share Arthur's insensitivity to the weather. By the time she arrived home after seeing Jack Hayes and glimpsing Frank's father, she was sweltering.

Under the shower, she wondered what to wear to her portrait sitting. It wasn't every day you were immortalised in oils — she'd have to choose something timeless; something that would still look good a hundred years from now. It wasn't going to be easy; the weather ruled out most of her favourites for a start. She'd often wondered why so many of the great painters chose to paint nudes. On days like this, she concluded, it was probably on the model's insistence.

While she'd been in the shower, someone had rung and left a message. It was Frank, bubbling over like a boy on his birthday.

'Xin-Xin,' he said, 'I've been jotting down notes — all sorts of things I've remembered that we'll have to put into the OB. Give us a ring back when you get this message. Bye.'

The first words of their collaborative project were yet to be written but Frank was already referring to it as the OB: 'Our Book'.

Xin-Xin smiled and shook her head as she dialled his number. He was nothing if not enthusiastic, this man of hers.

'Have you started?'

'Not yet, but I will soon. I had to go out unexpectedly and haven't had a chance. Only just got home.'

'Where did you go?'

'I'll tell you all about it tonight. What do you think I should wear for my portrait sitting?'

'I don't know, I'll leave that to you. Bloody hot in Arthur's studio, though. Don't let the old bastard talk you into modelling in the nude.'

'I'm a bit nervous about the whole idea, you know.'

'So you should be,' said Frank, laughing. 'He did one of me once and wouldn't let me see until it was finished. Took about twenty sittings.'

'Why haven't I seen it?'

'I made damned sure that you didn't.'

'You're a funny man, Frank. Anyway, must go. I want to put a coffee on and try to get a start on this book. I mightn't be able to paint but I feel sure I'll be able to write a reasonable portrait of you. Could even have a page or two sketched in by the time you get home.'

'Can't wait. And good luck for this afternoon. If Arthur can't make a beautiful painting out of you, he might as well throw his brushes away.'

Xin-Xin made her cup of coffee, sat down at her computer and set up a new document with the title of 'OB'. She placed the tape recorder on the desk. It was time to listen to the first interview she'd recorded the previous evening with Frank, and make some notes.

She'd started by reminding him of the night when they'd driven to her parents' place for the first time, and Frank had said something about his father having taken him to a house in the same street when he was a kid and they'd stolen some bricks.

She'd made a mistake — clicked the wrong button — and only clicked the right one after Frank had begun answering her first question.

'... was forever getting me to help him do shit jobs on the weekends. That day — it was a Saturday, I think — Mum and Dad were having a terrible row. "You get out and wait in the car," the old man said.

'"What for?" I asked.

'"Just do as you're fucking well told," he shouted.

'I didn't know what they were fighting about but it sounded pretty serious. I could hear them screaming and shouting. Smashing things.'

'Where were you?' Xin-Xin's voice.

'I was sitting in the car, waiting for the old man.'

She clicked off the tape. She'd seen 'the old man' today for the first time. What was that condition Dr Hayes said he suffered from, the one Frank suffered from too? Heart cancer. She wrote it down. Must remember to ask Frank what that's all about.

She rewound the tape, listened again and heard a stranger ask, 'Where were you?'

Her own voice was unfamiliar. Maybe it belonged to that child she used to glimpse in the mirror and fail to recognise. She'd grown up, that girl; you could hear it in her voice. A woman now; older, more mature. But Xin-Xin still wasn't quite sure who that woman was. Maybe Arthur's portrait would provide her with the answer.